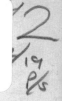

Tim Pears was born in 1956. He is a graduate of the National Film and Television School. His first novel, *In the Place of Fallen Leaves*, won the Hawthornden Prize for Literature and the Ruth Hadden Memorial Award. His second novel, *In a Land of Plenty*, was a major BBC television series in early 2001.

Critical acclaim for *In the Place of Fallen Leaves*:

'Long in abeyance, the English rural novel flourishes again in Tim Pears' story of a 13-year-old Devon farmgirl's confrontation with sex, death and the weather ... an unusually well-made novel which, through being less English than one would expect, produces a very English kind of magic'
Giles Foden, *Independent on Sunday*

'What excited me was that feeling one rarely gets as a reader, a kind of prickling excitement: "This is it. This is the real thing. This is whatever I mean by the work of a born writer" ... The novel is comic, and wry, and elegiac, and shrewd and thoughtful all at once. Please read it'
A.S. Byatt, *Daily Telegraph*

'Last year Adam Thorpe's brilliant *Ulverton* appeared; now here is Tim Pears' remarkable first novel, also evoking a southern English village's history and individuality ... a gorgeous tapestry of country life as it was and, perhaps, in a few places, still is. And it is tough and trenchant enough to be enjoyed by people who are not otherwise interested in rural idylls'
Jessica Mann, *Sunday Telegraph*

'There is a trace of Gabriel Garcia Marquez in Tim Pears' first novel. While quietly detailing everyday lives, Pears' invests transitory moments with an aura of enigma or the significance of universalities . . . An unusually strong début'
Kate Bassett, *Independent*

'An engaging, well-written and original novel. Pears could write about doing the washing up and make it interesting'
Philip Hensher, *Guardian*

'By turns elegiac, moving and extremely funny, Pears is also unafraid to muscle up his formidable powers of Proustian evocation. An extraordinarily promising début'
Andrew Yale, *Time Out*

'Highly atmospheric . . . It had an intoxicating, magical quality which completely beguiled me'
Jeremy Paxman, *Independent*

Critical acclaim for *In a Land of Plenty:*

'A big book with a big heart . . . Tim Pears is an unashamedly moving writer, and this marvellous book will reduce many to tears long before the end'
Henry Sutton, *Punch*

'The story of our own lives . . . The individual dramas . . . are set against a brilliant backdrop of British history . . . that lends the narrative a tidal flow that is impossible to resist. Pears has a God-given gift for characterisation . . . a superb sense of place, a mysterious knack of describing ineffable emotion and a generosity of spirit that is genuinely uplifting. I could go on and on about how wonderful it is but read it for yourself. I bet right now it wins the Booker'
Leo Colston, *Time Out*

'The painstaking, episodic build-up of detail and history grew on me . . . a memorable record of a family and its times'
Jessica Mann, *Sunday Telegraph*

'A state-of-the-nation novel'
Patrick Gale, *Independent*

Also by Tim Pears

IN THE PLACE OF FALLEN LEAVES
IN A LAND OF PLENTY

and published by Black Swan

A REVOLUTION OF THE SUN

Tim Pears

BLACK SWAN

A REVOLUTION OF THE SUN
A BLACK SWAN BOOK : 0 552 99862 1

Originally published in Great Britain by Doubleday,
a division of Transworld Publishers

PRINTING HISTORY
Doubleday edition published 2000
Black Swan edition published 2001

1 3 5 7 9 10 8 6 4 2

Copyright © Tim Pears 2000

Extract from 'Queen Victoria', p.31: words and music by
Leonard Cohen © 1973 Sony/ATV Music Publishing Acquisition
Inc. All rights for British Commonwealth (ex. Canada), Eire,
South Africa and Zimbawe administered by Chrysalis Songs Ltd.
Definition of 'organology', p.47, reprinted from *The
New Oxford English Dictionary* (1993) © Oxford University
Press 1973, 1993, by permission of Oxford University Press.

Set in 11/13pt Melior by
Falcon Oast Graphic Art.

Black Swan Books are published by Transworld Publishers,
61–63 Uxbridge Road, London W5 5SA,
a division of The Random House Group Ltd,
in Australia by Random House Australia (Pty) Ltd,
20 Alfred Street, Milsons Point, Sydney, NSW 2061, Australia,
in New Zealand by Random House New Zealand Ltd,
18 Poland Road, Glenfield, Auckland 10, New Zealand
and in South Africa by Random House (Pty) Ltd,
Endulini, 5a Jubilee Road, Parktown 2193, South Africa.

Printed and bound in Great Britain by
Clays Ltd, St Ives plc.

For those dancing
when they should be sleeping.

ACKNOWLEDGEMENTS

The author is indebted to Hawthornden Castle International Retreat for Writers, for a precious month.

Special thanks to my editor, Alexandra Pringle, and to my other editor, Bill Scott-Kerr – from a writer who knows how lucky he is. Not to mention Victoria Hobbs, the kind of agent other writers hate you for.

The author consulted countless libraries, oracles and idiots in the writing of this novel, some of whom may be responsible for its errors and flaws and so should not be named. But greetings to Phillip Smith, for the oldest pizza joke, and apologies to Doug Lucie for an observation stolen and Andrei Voznesensky for a poem corrupted. And thanks to Dr Deborah Waller and Nick Porucznik for technical support.

Salute Roger, Mariella, Gary conducting the crowd, Charlie, Karen, Hania beloved belly dancer, Phil, Greta, Geoff, Denise, Craig on English and Welsh summer nights. Especially Richard, who began the search, which ends and begins again.

All characters in this novel are fictitious, except for Gemma, who is a real cat.

CONTENTS

Floating (1)

It's New Year's Eve and we're far away from anywhere.

Five days ago Jack drove me and the dying woman in his lorry through the rain to this old stone cottage. We bedded down beneath heavy layers of musty blankets, as if their weight might induce warmth. Our churlish breath condensed in the air. Mice scrabbled along the loft above us as we slept and the rain fell on the slate tiles.

The next morning Jack saw to the animals we'd brought and the old woman was upstairs, silent, alone, when I was seized by a compulsion to clean.

I had some joss-sticks and lit them and let them fumigate the dank rooms. Smoke of sandalwood and musk settling in my nostrils. Patchouli. There was no central heating. Jack had lit the woodburning stove in the living-room: a reassuring muted roar came from behind its glass doors; hot orange flames. I ignited Calor gas heaters and in the kitchen lit all the hobs on the gas cooker. The air melted above them.

I wheeled the heaters from one room to another, oblivious of my distended belly in this eruption of

13

energy. Your birth looming incontestable before me.

With their own wax I glued small plantations of candles in stone alcoves, which may partly explain why we whispered so much in the days to come, and I lit hurricane lamps. The smell of paraffin was both unpleasant and comforting. An unplaceable nostalgia.

You had been kicking for weeks, increasingly vigorous, and then began to shift position, to settle and engage. Your kicks gave way to prods and pokes from knees, elbows. Rehearsal contractions gripped me like brief bouts of indigestion; memoranda from my womb, *I am almost ready*. Slowing down as labour approached, of course, reining in your energy, gathering your minuscule strength. Slyly reminding me you were there, nudging my memory with your elbows and knees.

You were still, though, as I worked, see-sawing a decrepit sweeper across the bumpy carpets. Surely sleeping. I hunted mouse droppings with a dustpan and brush. Swiped cobwebs from the corners of wall and ceiling. Calm inside me as I moved.

The old cottage's wooden beams creaked and groaned like an old woman's bones and the thick stone walls began to unfreeze. Out of hibernation, insects stirred. A spider scurried drunkenly across kitchen surfaces as I scoured them. I heard a fly buzzing half-heartedly, with barely charged batteries, before I saw it flying blindly, as if searching out a safe place to crash-land. A daddy-long-legs lolloped across a wall lifting its legs, loath to set any of them down on too cold a spot. And then as I was polishing a window, a butterfly with black and red and orange wings appeared, and battered at the glass.

It was a scene from a science fiction film. Insects waking on an inhospitable planet, where they were doomed soon to die. Horror, on a miniature scale.

'What are you doing, love?' Jack's voice quailed. 'You shouldn't be lifting and stretching like that.' Panic can ripple across his fat face like a child's. His concern, too. 'Let me help. I'll do it.'

'It's OK,' I said. I probably looked wild. 'I'm fine.'

On dead Saturdays back in Brixton when Juice and Davey were out of the flat, I sometimes had a spring-cleaning blast. Open all the sash windows, put on music loud and scour bathroom scrub kitchen scrape grime; hoover, dust; wipe, polish, shine with chemical fresh aromas; pile black plastic refuse bags in and on the dustbins, haul others with surplus possessions to the Barnardo's on Brixton Road.

I'd collapse in the evening, bathe slowly, then sit with solitary glasses of dry Riesling, Golden Virginia rollies, peck at olives and Pringles, and contemplate my uncluttered space; my home. Moments of rare self-sufficiency.

So this cleaning spree now was not entirely out of character. Nor was the occasion, three days later, when Jack and the others who'd arrived at the cottage by now came down the squeaking stairs in the seven a.m. dark. I'd enticed them out of sleep with smells from a baking oven; they found me in the kitchen with loaves of bread and a tray of raspberry jam tarts. I figured I was pulling my weight, that was all. I played the hostess, served up mugs of tea, with honey and melting butter on hot bread in the winter darkness. Then I retreated to my room.

You know it's going to happen and you want it to but you're terrified and you hope it never will. At the same hour the next morning I sat on the toilet, my waters broken, amniotic fluid and urine confused on old linoleum. I thought how much I'd like a cigarette, staring at the bathroom floor, snivelling. There was nothing for it, they'd just have to help me, these people. It was absurd, after all, how I came to be here, now, with them. Strangers. Where were those I used to know? My life had turned upside down, inside out. Everything – not just my body – altered.

How did we get here? Through some karma of chaos; cause and effect without meaning. Didn't we? An inconsequential chain of moments that had brought us to this, the unalterable present. Or, if you like, the fragile architecture of our insignificant, interweaving narratives, during . . . what? The last twelve months? A year ago I knew none of them. And if it wasn't for you, my unborn son, it wouldn't matter.

But it does. Because then the first contraction came.

1

E IS FOR EVERYTHING

12 midnight.

DONG
Big Ben strikes
DONG
on the radio.
TEN!
People shout
NINE
hands in a circle
EIGHT
Mr Bone
SEVEN
skull glazed with
SIX
sweat. Lights out
FIVE
the barman shouts:
FOUR!
A private party
THREE!

in a public bar
TWO!
feet stamping
ONE
shout it out:
DONG!

Party poppers, finger whistles. Clapping, cheering. Shrill blow-outs and fag-burst balloons.

Then 'Auld Lang Syne'. Blissful intoxicated camaraderie, in a swaying circle, singing that song of nostalgic redemption.

But. But-but. Only two people present know all the words and 'Auld Lang Syne' stutters, stumbles, peters out and there's a moment of silence in which resides a terrifying anticlimax. Because an abyss has opened up which is the whole enormous year empty ahead. Chill-sobering seconds. Then, with a tremendous, communal surge of will everyone fights back, with sounds to fill in forgotten words, giving it all they've got, yelling to the moon, dancing ridiculously, prodding and poking, ugly laughter, sweet smiles, have another, gizzakiss, and the night becomes a caricature of New Year's Eve, it becomes itself.

In a pub between Cowley and Iffley roads in Oxford, many people friends from work with partners if they have them.

'Tell me, Mishter Bone, have you New Year's resholutions?' Joe Snow asks.

Mr Bone, straight-backed and handsome Administrator of the Department of Organology, turns to his swaying assistant. 'I resolve here and now,' he whines, with a grin that bares his gleaming teeth, 'to be nice to lab technicians and furry animals.'

Joe tries to focus but gives up. 'Can't shay fairer than

that.' He burps, swallows another throatful of beer and pushes himself off the wall towards the toilets on the other side of the throng.

Throng of limbs jerking without space out of time with the music, beat of odd familiar medleys hectoring from the speakers. Intimate suggestions yelled above the uproar. Virgins' anxious prayers unanswered. A cold-nosed latecomer enters; his eyes disappear behind steaming-up glasses. Glitter and tinsel, streamers and mistletoe. The ropy gropings of past-it Romeos. Fairy lights, bright bursting battery of pinball and fruit machines, flashbulbs of cheap cameras. Joe struggles through conversations that coagulate in his ear; is blocked beside a man's incoherent confession of some long-suppressed, inconsequential failure, sodden-eyed, to an addled listener. Pushes, towards:

The pent-up heat of Mrs Smoyle from Accounts, statuesque matron, triumphant beside her belittled husband, her unmanned man. She sees Joe coming. Makes a beery leering lurch, he tries to sidestep neatly but ricochets off unhelpful bodies, only wedges himself between cigarette machine and wall.

She whispers hoarsely in his shy ear: 'I'm a big bad-mannered woman,' her lipstick tacky on his lobe, her breath warming the caverns of his ear, her tongue inviting itself in. He feels his hand taken by fingers stubbier and stronger than his own and placed on Mrs Smoyle's thigh, skirt riding up roiling flesh contained miraculously in tights like the sheaths of plump sausages.

'I'm all woman,' she breathes and Joe begins to tremble and he won't stop, his bladder is full and the year yawns before him full of promise or not.

In a corner Mr Bone slumps and paws another man's whisky, thinks I should be with the nobs not gobshite proles like these, me, I'm a man of consequence. He sinks the whisky, sour at his throat, burning down his gullet. Mr Bone smiles.

1 a.m.

While on a motorway not far from Oxford at that moment, in his cab Jack Knighton weeps. Another scientist of sorts: full-time lorry driver, spare-time astronomer. The north-driving rain ushers Jack's rig north through a carwash world. Wipers keep time across the windscreen; they mock the minutes home. Home. Jack lets a last sob break and pulls himself together.

He wanted so much to be home before midnight, Miranda my angel awaiting. He'd towed a refrigerated tanker of cool milk sloshing behind him from one milk marketing depot in Scotland to another in Cornwall. Wondered whether it'd turn to clotted cream by the time he reached the West Country. Why he was carrying milk from one end of the country to the other, however, was the kind of question Jack no longer asked himself. He had some excuse; his mind was busy with others.

Jack thought, for example, of European bureaucrats, those modern day Olympians on their mountains of meat and butter, their Elysian Fields of rape and clover, their narcissistic reservoirs of milk and wine. And then:

Miranda, my Aphrodite, she should bathe in milk, I should have taken this home and siphoned off a bathful for her luxurious ablutions. Miranda, though, had told him to take the job. Phil Scritt, haulage contractor, phoned on Christmas Day.

'Do a load on the thirty-first, Jack. I need a fleet on the road,' he said.

Jack had never not seen the New Year in without Miranda in the eighteen years of their marriage. Can't, he told Scritt. Do it, Miranda encouraged him. It'll be good money. We need it. We want it.

'What's the rate?' Jack enquired.

'Usual,' Scritt told him.

'But it's New—'

'I've got a queue of drivers, Jack. Keep you on 'cos you're a friend, but let me down and you're yesterday. You up for it or down and out, mate?'

Christmas had been a triumph. Jack got home Christmas Eve with his cab full of shopping. They made love and he was sure she enjoyed it, was in a good mood all evening making jokes with her wicked sense of humour. Christmas Day he'd given her her presents after the lunch he spent the morning cooking and she gave him his: a pot plant from the conservatory she'd been tending for months, and a lovely smelly bar of soap wrapped in paper he'd wrapped something for her in. The lout, she gave gifts and saved trees both.

'Last minute nothings,' Miranda said. 'You deserve no more,' and Jack laughed, with his eyes closed, and she did too.

He'd wanted so much to extend the holiday, to celebrate the season in full with his beloved, but wouldn't make it now; that Cornish supervisor took his time on purpose, enjoyed holding us up in our line of lorries.

And now although it's long gone twelve Jack in his very own unshackled cab scuttles home along near-deserted motorways, and his mind too casts its load. Miranda sinks into her milk-imaginary bath. The windscreen wipers mesmerize, a pair of ragged claws; crab skedaddles over wet tarmac ocean floor.

Another unloaded rig passes on the other side of the

central reservation, heading south. Jack flashes his headlights, the other replies and fades away. We have come and gone from each other, Jack muses, like particles in symmetrical, or perhaps parallel, universes. One north, one south; or maybe one forward, one back. Perhaps I have just in fact passed myself: at the tiniest unimaginable size, on an immeasurably miniature scale, a scale so small that atoms look like galaxies, some physicists maintain that time is flipping back and forth like a coin tumbling through the air.

Jack's mind is unhitched. I may flip for ever between Christmas and New Year. Or perhaps we just crossed the halfway point in the life of the universe – a few billion years earlier than scientists expected, it's true – and time has started rewinding: it wound out from the Big Bang and a moment ago began to go home to the Big Crunch, its mirror image. I just passed myself, and now? I'll go walking back to happiness with my one true love, back to dreaming days, courtship, our first kiss, the first time ever I saw her face. But then we'll be parted but it won't matter, back to school, again a boy in shorts, Daddy running in the park, my dog skitters with me, Mummy please don't go, blue sky, I'm a baby once more and I'm going home to the womb.

The world reverts too, to ice, mammoths breathe briefly, tundra, stone, fire and soup unstewing. Stars leap into black holes, planets disappear in swirling clouds of primordial dust, the mass of our universe beginning to squeeze, sucked in, collapses into a single point. Then peace.

3 a.m.

An hour or two later, while Jack tiptoed to his front door, turned a key and let himself in, so without one

22

did Martha Polkinghorne. In the East Anglian heartland, between the Fens and the Broads, at three in the morning on New Year's Day. A house surrounded by vast fields. The air saturated with fog that clings like doubt to the flat damp earth. Pyramids of swede loom, ghostly eggs, as if some giant reptile of the North Sea had crawled inland and laid them there. Mounds of tuberous sugar beet, gnarled hearts torn from the mud. In an irrigation trench a swan folds its neck inside its wings. There are no forests here, though in one of many copses where pheasants are bred and sportingly slaughtered, a mouse scurries across dead leaves and a barn owl watching drops from its branch.

Martha parked her van a mile away down an empty lane. She tilted the rear-view mirror to reflect her split eyebrow, her cool blue irises, her pinprick pupils, and stared herself down. Waiting with the window open for the silence to prove itself to her, Martha stepped out, placed car keys behind tyre and set off. It's cold, she knows her breath condenses unseen, but she's warm in black layers of Lycra, nylon, elastane, Spandex, polyester, and she walks brisk through the trees, at home in the dark. Invisible.

From the copse an irritating fifty yards across cloying mud to the outer corner of a field; a further three hundred yards skirting the hedge till she reached the edge of the property. As she walked, Martha felt a familiar process taking place: it was both a loosening of her springy limbs – ligaments relaxing, tendons untensing – and a growing compactness to her body. She felt herself despite the cold becoming lupine, like a werewolf woman from the movies, metamorphosing, her blood runs hotter, muscles elasticate, sight smell hearing touch and taste keener. And yet her mind is ice.

Martha climbed carefully over a gate into a paddock,

prowled along a fence, through a smaller gate to the garden, slowly pulled it to behind her and felt it latch shut noiselessly. Methodical, performed actions rehearsed in her mind along a path reconnoitred in daylight. Martha unzipped her waist belt, pulled a balaclava down over her blond bouncy hair and hunched over approached the house: she loped across the lawn crouching low, thermal fingers skimming the grass.

At the house Martha heeled off her outer shoes – as if out of politeness slipping off muddy galoshes – and started to climb. She knew she had to with dogs on the ground floor inside but preferred to anyhow, especially with this house one of those that, looking the day before through bogus ornithologist's binoculars, made her smirk with gratitude to the architects whose irregular bricks invite climbers. Reaching the window of an uninhabited guest room Martha cut glass, pressed back a fastening, slid up sash-cord window, eased herself in over the sill and closed the window behind her slow, slow, slowly.

The owners of the house still slumbered deep and drunkenly dreamless in their king-size bed. A few feet from them Martha calmly ransacked the drawers of the woman's dressing-table by the light of a pencil torch, slipping worthwhile jewellery into her belt.

Satisfied with what she had, Martha switched off the torch and crept across the carpet and out of the room. Nothing stirred in the dark silent mansion but she, and she made not a ripple in the air. No man or animal could see hear or smell her: Martha always burgled clean, as she had once wrestled in the palaestra, after bathing with odourless soap. She wore no perfume; and she generated none of her own, for the fact was she had no fear.

4 a.m.

While a young wiry scrag of a man could be filled with dread, and reek of it, and no-one might know, so common was the smell. Not that Solo's fear was for himself: it was all for his son. As Martha slunk back to her van so, far away from the flat lands, in the north country beyond the Pennine chain, on a mid-rise estate in the urban wastes of Manchester, the bent hunchback figure of Solo O'Brien scurried home from his three friends' party. One of his trainers was holey and though it wasn't raining there was water on the tarmac and his foot was wet and cold. His mouth had a hunger, he paused to light a fag, but had forgotten that his hands weren't free. Solo pressed on.

He wanted his son to sleep, it was four in the morning and there was bedlam abroad: windows were bright, doors were open and the estate was full of people, slurring, stumbling, yelling. No-one asleep anywhere it seemed and no-one old either, as if at this turn of the year the old had in a flash become young again. Magic.

What lovely skunk it was. Robbie surpassed himself, saving it up for New Year's Eve. He unveiled a new bong, too. Solo's son fell asleep on the settee as Robbie Stiles, engineer extraordinaire, lifted a dirty tea towel like a lordy dordy mayor and extolled the merits of his own invention in one long riff.

'Make it from clay,' Robbie said. 'Wood's good for grass, glass is OK, don't let plastic anywhere near. Charas may be better in a chillum, true, but when you've got good ganja, smell this, Solo, there's nothing like a water-cooling bong.' Robbie passed a bag over, Solo sniffed. 'People say it gives them water vapour on the chest, believe me, they're right. But look, the mouthpiece fits my lips.' Robbie closed his red eyes.

'Play it like an instrument it rewards you, bubbles like farts in the bath; like a straw at the bottom of a bottle. Of free milk at primary school.'

Robbie, Solo's mate, seeking the perfect bong. A Marconi of marijuana, an Edison of dope. Our very own Thelonius. Oh me oh me oh me oh my. That skunk was good.

This load is heavy. Don't be a fool. There's no magic. The old are indoors wishing they could sleep, and everyone else? It's a reckless amnesty; let's party and we'll pay the price.

'Oi!'

Solo O'Brien flinches. Slips in and out of concrete shadows. He's Quasimodo. Jounces up a stairwell and along walkways. Inside the shadows are suggestions of human form, potential confrontations of hopeless bonhomie. There's no-one Solo wants to see, no-one can do anything but take from him what he has, apart from his three friends whom he just left: Robbie, Wick hovering over his turntables like an insane insect, Luke and his tongue-gun, his cartridges of jokes. Here Solo acknowledges no-one, heads home head down across the estate and wonders why, when I'm still high, am I a party pooper? And remembers it's because of the boy. My little prince. His lovely quiet breath. At least he's asleep.

This year it's going to change, man, Solo can feel it in his blood, there's a job to be had that's mine, there's money minted and printed already that's due to flow through my fingers. There are places to go and sights to see, a life for us both that's better than mine. Hail Mary, mother of God, let it be so. Solo O'Brien pads his cold feet along the concrete, takes a lungful of piercing air, leans forward, almost home, his son is sleeping, his son is sleeping, he carries his son on his back.

6 a.m.

Rebecca Menotti, meanwhile, woke up about then, and she found herself a queen of the morning. An empty bed in a strange house in Exeter her throne, her subjects entering the house in intermittent ones and twos and coming by her room to pay court.

She hadn't even made it to midnight before she'd begun to feel her heart go skipping then trippysick, paranoid in a club by the river filled with a crush of hundreds and thousands. Whatever was in her disco biscuit – ketamine or ephedrine? speed or paracetamol? – had ruined New Year's Eve. A succession of people in her extended group had helped her and as each cure failed – from rest to water to fresh air – she was virtually carried to someone's house nearby and tucked up in bed with a hot-water bottle by strangers who then abandoned her to return to the party.

Rebecca dozed and mused and wept, and hid beneath the duvet, and dozed in molten sleep some more, body sluggish, mind torpid, until around six the first clubbers came home. At which point Rebecca began to recover: they brought her sweet tea and she sat up in bed and maybe what was bad had gone and now the residue of some good MDMA came up from below. The room glowed. People lounged on the bed and sat on the floor skinning up, drinking beer or vodka, snogging in the corner, crushing halves and snorting them. Davey and Juice came in and beamed at her like proud parents. Music was on the stereo downstairs and whoever was there must have been many and the small house trembled with pleasure. Then the decks came upstairs: the mock opera of one anthem cascaded into another. Tired and loaded bodies began to move, they couldn't help themselves. Rebecca remained still but floating in bed and she knew her smile was beatific and she bestowed it upon those around her. New Year's Eve was resurrected just as Rebecca was and towed her into the Year of our Lord nineteen ninety-seven. It will be bountiful, she was sure, though she knew nothing of what bounty and what pain would be hers in the year ahead. Rebecca was queen of the morning, at the epicentre of everything.

2

THE DIARY

At seven thirteen on the third of January, according to a luminous alarm clock, a man woke up in a dim room. As his eyes became accustomed to the light, though, confusion, not clarity, poached his brain. The wardrobe was wrong. The ceiling too low. Had the door jumped to a different wall? Objects startled him, nothing was as it should be. The opposite of *déjà vu*, but the same uncanny sense. But wait. What is this lurching movement? Blistering barnacles. He was on board ship. The man looked out of a porthole: atop the ocean outside lay a street, criss-crossed by cars and people; beyond it buildings.

Yet the room was floating, the slap of water almost audible. Impossible. Unless? A waterbed. Of course. He'd woken on a waterbed.

Except that the bed was firm. No: this queasiness was nothing more, he now admitted, than the shoddy remnants of dissolution. Of which he could remember nothing. A sickly swilling pool in his guts and a humdinger of a skull-squeezing hangover, bone contracting, constricting his dried-out brain. And with the dehydration he suffered an incredible thirst for a certain drink, a universal nectar from the juice of a delicious fruit. That doesn't exist.

The man groaned as he rose, agony inevitable, only to discern as he did so that his diagnosis was wrong. His self-pity splintered. Actually he felt fine, brisk, light-headed even. Now that was worrying: it was his mind that floated. He took a deep breath, closed his eyes and remembered: I am an insomniac. No, that's not right. I am an amnesiac, that's the word. It takes me a while to orientate myself in the morning. I don't know where I am. Who am I?

The man lay and no-one came and after a while he was disturbed by hunger. So he pulled on clothes he assumed were his and ventured forth in search of food, making his discreet way down through the floors of an impressive film set of some epic medical drama, actors without scripts rehearsing their lines, untold extras waiting patiently for lights and cameras.

Not far from the hospital the man found himself immersed in metropolitan hullabaloo. Eight lanes of cars buses taxis vans on heat: growling, then sultry beacons winked and horny vehicles leapt forward only to stop inches from ramming each other up the rear and prowl again at bay, in their urban choreography, their auto-erotic ritual.

'The city is turning itself on,' the man said to himself and blinked. Beyond the traffic KING'S CROSS STATION ⇌ sprawled. He crossed the road through the snarling traffic. Tannoy, sirens, horns pierced the general roar of noise, human exclamation further complicated his ears: '*Big Issue*! Spare a quid, mate. Fancy a quicky, darlin'? Hand job for a tenner? Jesus loves you. Twenty pence for a cup of coffee, mister. Taxi? *Big Issue*!'

The man's mind was blank but his stomach pro-pelled his footsteps on and he found a dingy café, its windows steamed. He opened the door and damp warmth drew him in. He sat at the one vacant table. Men read newspapers or stared, said nothing, vacantly ate, two women delivering plates to their tables and cleaning up around them. One wiped the Formica surface in front of the man with a damp dishcloth: a sprinkling of white sugar granules remained; he pressed them one by one on the pad of his forefinger and licked them off. Then a male voice he sensed directed at him.

'What's it to be then, sir?' He turned. The proprietor, Mediterranean, in a tight grey linen coat. 'Waitress service and that, sir? Course we do for gents, innit? Full breakfast?'

The man nodded.

'Tea coffee?'

'A cappuccino, please. No sugar. Thank you.'

A mug came promptly; the man sipped it – beneath a hot mouthful of froth, insipid instant coffee – and then felt through his pockets and found nothing at all except for a black spiral-bound notebook. He opened and began to read.

My name is Sam Caine. It says so on my wristband. I am in the middle of my life. I have forgotten who I am.

New Year's Resolutions: 1) to search for evidence of myself; 2) to keep a diary of this search (of which this is the beginning).

I should write a little about my condition and me; the little I know. A scrap of autobiography. I left a doctor's office a short while ago and she explained that I was recently found wandering and was brought by police to this hospital. The clothes I wore were undistinguished and their pockets were empty. My photographic likeness and description were spread around but no-one has yet come forward to claim me. I am one of a small, statistically insignificant number of people in the same predicament. Most are traced eventually. But I may be a little different.

The doctor explained that it seems I forget when I sleep. I retain all that happens to me until I sleep, and then forget. I have a sense when I wake of having been asleep a century. The doctor is pleasingly intrigued: she suspects that I suffered either a violent accident or else contracted a form of herpes that has caused damage to the cerebral cortex where new memories are stored. Except that what's curious is that I have a gaping hole in my long-term memory. 'It's extremely odd,' she said excitedly. 'For the hole is you.'

Life. I have this sense that just as I'm beginning to get an idea of what it's all about, so it's slipping away. I know what you mean, the doctor smiled.

We soon deduced that I'm not ill educated. I know other people's history, just not my own. I remember many things – perhaps everything I have ever known – except for my own personal experience. I told her of the political leaders, issues, battles of our time, but did so without opinion. I had no idea for whom I'd voted. The doctor had her secretary ring around the wards and obtain a copy of the board game Trivial Pursuit, which the two of us then played. The doctor was enormously gratified by my narrow victory. Every question I got right seemed to confirm or deny – neither of us quite sure which – a great theory; as if verifying details of a past life, proving the case for some neurological form of reincarnation.

'But you remember nothing of your parents?'

'No.'

'A childhood home? An image of a house that is . . . sensually familiar, perhaps.'

'No.'

'A wife? Children?'

I shook my head. 'I feel myself drawn to recall something, only to find my memory in tatters. Like desiccated material that crumples to the touch.'

The doctor told me what she thought had happened. Memories themselves, she said, are stored among the neurons of the cerebral cortex as physical traces. Other regions of the brain, though, have responsibilities for memory. The medial thalamus, which lies within the temporal lobe, relays incoming sensory information to the cerebral cortex. This region can be reached via the nostril, something we know, she said, since certain unfortunate participants in her own sport, fencing, have had their opponent's foil jammed up there, damaging this medial temporal lobe: until it recovered, they suffered amnesia of all events that occurred during the crisis.

Beneath the cerebral cortex lies the hippocampus, responsible for the laying down of memories. The doctor conjectured that I, however, may have sustained damage to my prefrontal cortex. This region, working in conjunction with both the medial thalamus and the hippocampus, plays a particular and as yet not fully defined role in making our memories personal. What it seems able to do is to give our individual memories a space and time reference. This doesn't have much impact on facts, but rather on events: without this mechanism for placing experience in context events remain undifferentiated, and may not register or be felt as personal.

'I believe it is this', she said, 'that makes us truly human.'

33

Without a fully functioning prefrontal cortex a person may experience memories of events more as we believe an animal does – as generic rather than particularized, unique. Instead of recalling driving a certain car on a specific sunny day on this road with that person beside me, I may have simply a general recall of driving. The doctor said that this form of malfunction is called sauce amnesia. Perhaps this meant there was a lack of a certain juice or enzyme in the brain, I wondered, but was too timid to ask.

Now that I have written it down I realize I misunderstood. Sauce, indeed. Perhaps I was never very bright.

As the doctor brought the session to a close she added, in a light-hearted manner, one or two other possible explanations for my condition.

'Many men approaching forty', she said, 'do develop mysterious symptoms – erratic pulse, breathlessness, lack of mental acuity. These usually disappear. But a person who fears he is losing part of his memory may respond by shutting out all of it; in this drastic way denying the pain of his decline. Self-imposed,' she explained. 'Elective dementia. Psychosomatic.'

'You think this might apply to me?' I asked.

She shrugged. 'It can happen to those with highly developed egos.'

I left her office, and was directed to this room.

Why write this diary? Several reasons.

1) The act of recording experience may help to fix it in my brain; habitual activity may encourage physiological habit.

2) At least my experience will be recorded on paper. I can refer to it; if necessary by reading the diary each day I will remind myself of who I am (a task which would of course take up more and more of each day; it will become a burden, the paper and the weight

34

*of the ink on the paper bending my neck, stooping my
shoulders).*

*3) It's done for others. The doctor said I was a
fascinating case, my diary may constitute useful
research. It might help other people.*

*4) I write this to an unknown reader, who is you.
(Which may be me.) I understand that people change.
They see a picture of themselves when much younger
and it is – they feel – of another person. Yet I shall read
this diary later to establish what is* unchanging *in me.*

*What else? A few disconnected thoughts should be
committed to paper. My name. Sam Caine, in case it
hadn't already crossed your mind, is an anagram. I
thought of it myself. The name came to me and seems
apt, suggestive of: a forties private eye by Chandler or
Hammett – and that is what I must be, a detective; a
drug (which I may need, the doctor says); a poet – Hart
Crane, Thom Gunn – and here I write; and finally
a simple cane for I am long and thin, stiff-jointed, a
beanpole of a body I walk around in. Sam Caine. An
anagram.*

*I believe I am unhappy, and have been for a long
time.*

*It occurs to me that life is a path laid out through
time's landscape. We are walking. We resent the fact
that some other force or entity has laid this path and
decreed that we must follow it. The path is not visible
before us until each footstep (with whatever freedom of
choice one thought one had) reveals its shape and con-
firms our course upon it.*

*Or is each breath a gurk at God, a defiant yawn in
the face of extinction?*

*Perhaps it is simply true that life is a labyrinth in
which we search for the way out, except that we dare
not find it.*

Sam Caine reached the end of what was written in the notebook. He finished off the breakfast that had been brought to him – 'sausage egg bacon tomato beans two toast' – and ordered a cup of tea. He pondered the mystery of his circumstances. Those resolutions are sensible, he considered; I shall search and write, write and search. The proprietor appeared at his table and handed him a pencil with a wink. 'Go ahead, mister, write. I don't mind – it's not rush hour no more, innit?'

The café was less full than it had been, had moved on to another, slower shift, workers' din replaced by pensioners and slow cups of coffee, chewable food. Smells of dry skin powder, pipe tobacco, incontinence; the atmosphere yet more warm and moist. Replete, Sam closed his sleepy eyelids and composed the first words of the next entry he would contribute to the diary – *My life as an amnesiac. I remember it well* – and dozed off.

Meanwhile, on this day after the day after E, Rebecca Menotti allowed Great Western to carry her body home. Her mind was elsewhere. A depression was forecast, awaiting her slide into it, but she knew by now the important thing was not to dwell on what was wrong with her life. The train, with the sound of an orchestra tuning up, scraped out of Exeter St David's station.

Rebecca sleepwalked to the buffet car and lurched back with a coffee. The train was crowded in the open cars. Loud with beercan boys, babies, fractious families; a loquacious conductor, the PA system his spoken karaoke; the seething insects of Walkmans. Rebecca retrieved with relief her quiet carriage at the back of the train.

Davey and Juice had returned to London on New

Year's Day but Rebecca stayed on: when the party in her commandeered room had wound down, the last one to leave had slithered under the duvet. Already on the verge of sleep Rebecca let her eyes stay closed, succumbing to sensation without attempting to decipher it. Smooth hands roamed the surface of her skin, slender fingers probed her, a tongue explored with clumsy hunger. She only knew for sure he/she was male when he entered her, and she opened her eyes upon an eyes-shut, mouth-open face of a child; no more than thirteen or fourteen. She closed her eyes again and though the boy was as big as her she retained an after-image on the inside of her eyelids of a Lilliputian figure earnestly clambering across her – she a giantess – and pleasuring her heroically.

Rebecca had been home for Christmas. She disliked London at that time of year. The bustling overcrowded capital, suddenly emptied – streets still, houses blank – took on an unsettling, archaeological feel. Now, though, she was returning. At twenty-eight years old, without a family of her own, it still wasn't clear where home was: a flat shared with friends in Brixton or the terraced house in Exeter in which she'd grown up, and where her father remained.

Her younger brothers and Rebecca all went home and their father Sandro had bucketed a tree, attached fairy lights, made mince pies, bought crackers, cooked nut cutlets deluxe with bread sauce, roast potatoes and parsnips, peas and gravy, followed by Christmas pudding with brandy sauce. He'd even prepared stockings – thick rustling socks stretched and misshapen with wrapped gifts – which he deposited at the ends of their beds without waking them, children again in the house of their father.

Rebecca's brothers had left the day after Boxing Day and she'd stayed on till New Year's Eve when her flatmates, her tenants, Davey and Juice came down, which gave Rebecca three clear days of quiet companionship with her father.

After breakfast one morning Sandro Menotti had shown his daughter his television's poor reception of the new terrestrial channel. 'We're too far away down here.' Lunky actors attempted to project their Antipodean lines through a scratchy veil of interference.

'Look at that,' said Sandro. 'It's like the old days. Before your time.'

'I remember, Daddy.'

'We didn't mind then. Now, it's not watchable, is it?'

Rebecca fetched a stepladder from the garage and clambered into the attic. She unscrewed the aerial from a ceiling joist and stepped carefully, yelling towards the hatch, 'Now?'

Her father's voice rose into the roof. 'Terrible.'

'Now?'

'No.'

She crawled on her haunches from one joist to the next under the sloping roof, resisting the temptation to tread on fibre-glass insulation.

'How's that?'

'Forget it, Rebecca.'

Rebecca heard her father climb the rickety ladder. He poked his head through the hatch. 'There's nothing decent on that channel anyway,' he said. 'I'm putting the kettle on.'

The other side of the attic had floorboards, and was loaded with abandoned possessions. Rebecca stayed up there all morning, rummaging through boxes of objects she'd left behind at successive stages of her childhood and not seen since. Phases, eras, girlish epochs grown out of, parcelled and stored up here. Archaeologists of the future, she decided, will not only peck at the earth but also look up, will sift through the ossified attics of abandoned suburbs.

Rebecca shuddered. Mousetrap, Pik-a-stik, Coppit. A school photograph: her crooked nose, eyes crossed, so slightly other children had to stare to verify their intimation; black lustrous hair, skin brown even, as now, in the gloomy days of winter. Felt ballerinas on a hessian background. Mastermind, its stock of tiny pegs depleted. A plastic-faced doll with one eye missing and cropped blond hair Rebecca remembered cutting progressively shorter. A larger doll, with black hair and red cheeks, grown slackly swivel-eyed and somehow more lifelike. One rubbery vertebra pulled a string that activated the doll's voice. The battery was long dead but Rebecca heard, 'My name is Rosebud,' intact in her mind as the string retracted.

While residing here, these inert totems of immaturity had been altering their nature. Over years, they had acquired occult significance, and now embodied, contained within themselves, the secret meaning of that most profound territory, Rebecca understood, her past. Sensation welled up within her.

Seashells stuck to squares of coloured card marked Exmouth, Shaldon, Dawlish. School exercise books in handwriting of developing familiarity and sophistication, and text books Rebecca would swear she'd never seen before, except that her younger self betrayed her with her possessive name in ink on the inside covers. Objects retrieved from oblivion with jolts of recognition. The chipped remnants – or beginnings? – of a teaset. Half a scrapbook of sweet wrappers: from musty paper the real or construed smell, taste of Blackjacks, Sherbet Fizz, Sweet Cigarettes. No single thing completed.

Only her father's voice, carrying as if through water, announcing lunch downstairs, brought Rebecca out of a hypnosis of the emotions, a warm soupy anaesthesia. Besides nostalgia, what struck her about the contents of the boxes in the attic was the evidence, incontrovertibly displayed, of a profligacy of unfinished interests. The family tree she drew as far back as grandparents could provide, and then extended speculatively, attaching a few half-hearted roots to Eleanor of Aquitaine, Bonnie Prince Charlie. Or cups, rosettes, for activities – tennis, public speaking – she couldn't remember taking part in, never mind being good at. Or a stack of diaries each begun with resolution, kept assiduously, then faltering in March. Petering out by May.

Even given childish fad and whim Rebecca's range was extravagant. And the point was, the same pattern was still being repeated: she hadn't grown out of impatience. Waitress at Pizza Piazza, artists' model, belly dancer at restaurants and private parties at seventy-five pounds a time, researcher for her old Modern History lecturer in the archives of the British Museum, summertime swimming pool attendant, occasional piano teacher to small children. Holder of this dazzling portfolio of a career, Jill of all trades, Rebecca Menotti closed her eyes. Here it was all around her in the cold dry loft. Unfinished projects, incomplete collections, half-filled books. An appetite that was never satisfied because she moved on before it could be. Because something new enthused her.

Cradled in the railway carriage, Rebecca's mellow body cruised forwards while her mind rocked back.

She'd climbed down from the attic, slid shut the hatch lid, folded the stepladder, resolved to investigate the mechanism of incompletion. She always moved on because she was aware of no drive within herself to master something, only enthusiasm for the taste of something else. It was her problem and her nature both. Unfulfilled appetite.

In the kitchen her father poured two glasses of cider. 'Vegetarian Cornish pasties,' he announced. 'For you, girl, I break the basic laws of regional cuisine. With frozen peas, and carrots from the garden, on the side.'

'Looks great, Daddy,' Rebecca said, letting slip another opportunity to admit she'd been a vegan only during her final year at university – her degree being one thing she had completed. It was the smell of bacon for breakfast in greasy spoons that had seduced her back into the company of carnivores. Organic chicken. Roast lamb. But Sandro took such pride in the dishes with which he filled the freezer before his daughter's visits that she omitted to disabuse him. Each year that passed made the fraud more problematic, though Rebecca wasn't sure whether it was the existence of however benign a deception between them that bothered her, or that she was not the moral paragon her father took her for.

Aside from some white hairs degrading his jet black crop, and a shading under his eyes even darker than the rest of his olive hue that suggested mild insomnia rather than the weariness of fifty-three years on this earth, Sandro Menotti still looked remarkably like the father of Rebecca's childhood: a glance in his direction could give her an uncanny temporal lurch. A small, compact man, he was two inches shorter than his daughter. When they hugged, the reassuring smell of Brylcreem. And he spoke with the hint in certain syllables of an Italian accent in his West Country burr, even though he'd been born in Devon. His birth Rebecca and her brothers' favourite story.

41

Sandro's parents had come to England, economic migrants from Calabria, in 1936, only to be interned in 1940 in a camp near Newton Abbot. Their son's conception three years later was unplanned but afterwards they saw it as an invocation and symbol of resistance: their child's foetus grew in his mother's womb as the Allies struggled to gain territory in the south of their homeland. While she suffered morning sickness, sore breasts, water retention, her husband sat and listened to the wireless and followed the battles for Salerno, Napoli, Anzio and Monte Cassino. Finally, overcome by the mood of anticipation and excitement, although not due for a fortnight Sandro disobeyed orders and made an abrupt, surprise appearance in the world, exiting from his mother as Clark's American troops entered Rome, on 4 June 1944, the newborn baby wailing a rapture of liberation.

Sandro Menotti left school at fifteen, following in his father's unskilled footsteps, too early to benefit from the rising expectations of the welfare state. Marrying in his early twenties a village girl in the same Exeter food-canning factory, Jean Westcott, he had three children before he was thirty, and present and future were settled. Rebecca's father was an intelligent, unqualified working-class man who pushed the same levers every day on a machine in a line with other men who laughed when they called him wop dago spic; he remained aloof, never one of the boys, getting into scrapes two, three times a year; at lunch he sat in a corner of the canteen eating cheese and pickle sandwich, packet of crisps, apple, a smart alec eyetie doing the crossword in the *Guardian*, reading the political columns.

The train carries Rebecca home and her heart could break when she allows herself to ruminate on her father's wasted life. When she tries to recall her mother what Rebecca remembers is her father's love, his adoration. Jean was a plump, unprepossessing woman he called Princess. Rebecca and her brothers used to watch them dancing in the front room to scratchy records, ballroom dancing but to the soundtrack of their honeymoon: late Beatles, Stones and the Summer of Love. Waltzing to 'California Dreaming'. The children wrote numbers on squares of card and held them up like judges for marks out of ten. But it wasn't always easy, for sometimes Sandro and Jean became mutually absorbed, wrapped up in each other, and forgot their own children. 'Are you Going to San Francisco?' Rebecca and her brothers, transfixed, felt as if they had interrupted their parents – as children do, she understood, to couples that are happy.

She remembers how her father used to look at her mother when they had guests in. Jean liked to tell funny stories but did so badly; even as a five-year-old child Rebecca saw that her mother's jokes were agonizing, punchlines premature, and guests sweated in their seats with plastic smiles, pained eyes. But her father gazed at his wife with pride, pleasure, surprise even, at stories he must have heard countless times before. As if he was simple, yet he wasn't; he really was as bright as anyone she knew. He watched nature programmes on TV, listened to discussions on Radio 4, devoured history books from the central library in Queen Street where he took the children each Saturday morning; certain evenings of the week there were quiz programmes they watched together – *University Challenge, Mastermind* – to witness their father taking on the world, invariably winning. Though he did so with so little braggadocio, smiling off his wife and children's exhortations to become a bona fide contestant himself, that they never ventured to mention let alone boast about it outside the home; his modest erudition a closely held family secret.

Subtle legacies of immigration, or just her own, individual paternity?

Rebecca's gaze focuses on the country easing past. Wintry England rolling by. The copper-red soil of east Devon; lush Somerset pastures; the Mendip hills; across Salisbury Plain; along the vale of Kennet; Reading; and on to London. You could cut a huge square of south-east England, she recalled – west of London as far as Bristol, north to Birmingham – that with the exception of an Oxford ward was a Labour desert: the political map royal blue with some orange Liberal-Democrat shading. And yet the train passed close to where civil disobedience sprouted like some benign tumour in the Tory heartland of her country: strident protest for a radical status quo at Fairmile, Newbury, Twyford Down, sites of road protest; not far north of Shoreham, a coastal town where demonstrations against veal calves' export were being made by elderly women; past timber yards occupied by environmental campaigners against the importation of Brazilian mahogany. Save our holy trees, our precious earth; end cruelty to animals.

Rebecca glided remotely through the towns along the line. Seen from a car, at street level, urban life is in urgent flow, uncertain flux. Observed from a train, however, cities become objectified, changeless, totemic. The world slipped by.

Jean Menotti contracted cancer when her children were six, five and three and it ravaged her. She was in and out of hospital and the children watched their father sitting at the bed holding her hand, in love with a decomposing woman. Surgeons cut off one breast,

44

gouged out part of her stomach, extracted a lung, only to find themselves each time one step behind the disease that was eating her up. The children spent days with their maternal grandparents in Christow or paternal Italians in Newton, travelling back to Exeter to visit their zombified father and a mother fading to a skeletal stranger. Jean lost her hair, her liver was invaded, bewigged she turned yellow and still he called her Princess, my angel, holding her hand then weeping when she slept, oblivious of his children behind him; his adoring gaze unwavering as if he couldn't see the cruel disaster flaunting itself in front of his eyes, as if he was simple. Even at the end when she was raving.

Sandro mourned Jean with his children, though, and then he let his grief reside in some private space beside him, and he resumed bringing them up, alone, without fuss. His mother and mother-in-law came in one day a week each and cleaned, washed, cooked food for several meals – the family's diet alternated thus bi-weekly between southern Italian cuisine and English country fare, pasta and pasties, passata and pickles, rice and spuds. The children were latch-key kids who learned to look after themselves during their father's shifts – Rebecca the eldest with most responsibility – and it seems to her now that they gave him no trouble, were early single-parent successes, because he earned their respect; that even very young children could, perhaps subconsciously, take the measure of a man and recognize his stature. For so it was. The four of them compressed together, a tight unit, impervious. The children came home, cleaned up, made tea, did home-work, studied their music; were polite, made friends, did well at school; inherited their father's self-sufficient dignity.

The sound of the train, almost rhythmic, brought back piano lessons, and then a recent boyfriend who'd accompanied her to concerts because, he said, he liked to daydream.

'You mean the music is a soundtrack to your reverie?' she'd asked.

'No,' he had said. 'It's more like silence. Where else can you find silence in the city?'

He disengaged his mobile phone, watch alarm, bleeper, over pre-concert drinks in the yawning foyers. Royal Festival Hall, Queen Elizabeth, the Barbican.

'Music seals off the noise, and I can let my mind drift. Can't move, of course. It's gorgeous. I love classical music.'

But Rebecca was baulked of disdain by her own unadmitted thrall to those moments *before* the concert begins, when orchestral musicians warm up. She couldn't help herself listening and hearing limitless, voluptuous possibilities. It brought to mind Schumann, driven crazy in the first stages of his syphilis by non-stop, beautiful music in his head.

And it's a paradox Rebecca's long been aware of: she loves men because of her father's example; and he's the only man she's truly loved, maybe ever will. She even knows that she loves him much more than he loves her. Too mature – or simple – to transfer his feelings for Jean to their daughter, his is an undemanding love. He's not inquisitive about Rebecca's life, wishing only to be reassured that she's not ill, broke or miserable; beyond that concern he appears incurious. He's not judgemental but it's easy to believe he's not interested either. Or that she's disappointed, even bewildered him, has wasted her life with her dead-end jobs, unused degree, boyfriends none of whom she's ever brought home, her wasted talent. She's never stuck to any damn thing, music meant so much but she gave up, looks back at the meagre scales of her achievement and shudders; so much research for other people's books, never her own; she could have done anything, has done nothing at all. Stop this, don't dwell, it's only the E comedown; the dreaminess and introspection, Daddy, that's all. And no, it's not disinterest, it's detachment, which is very different, and that she loves him more than he loves her is how it is and should be.

They're coming through London suburbs now – do all the cities of Britain look the same from a train, with their back yards, washing on lines, allotments? Or is it that they are all imitative satellites of the capital? – and Rebecca feels a familiar mixture of anxiety and relief: life in the metropolis must be wound into action again. Rebecca gathered her stuff and herself as the train approached Paddington.

Sam Caine meanwhile dozed in the café in King's Cross and was woken by an old man bumping his table as he wardled past. Sam had been asleep no more than a minute, and came to consciousness with the comical jolt of a ham actor recalling something vital, causing a haggish bag lady opposite to titter. In fact, ironically, Sam remembered precisely nothing, the brief lapse from consciousness enough to erase all sense of self from him.

The clumsy man's contribution was significant. Not because he woke Sam then – whenever Sam awoke it would have been with the same wretched taste of loss and bewilderment – but because he nudged Sam's notebook off the edge of the table to land unheard unnoticed upon the floor of cigarette butts, chewing gum, grit and greasy linoleum.

A bone-chilling panic kept Sam rooted to the spot:

utter stillness might keep him inconspicuous, surrounded as he was by people-like beings not quite human, eerie archetypes, in this café he suspected was a waiting-room between worlds. It was only the bile rising that made him rise, and to keep ahead of it climbing his throat he floated like a clone of himself out of the dank café and into cold grey petrol air and off along the pavement; leaving Mediterranean proprietor and waitress astonished at the space from which a full-grown man had vanished.

'He left his bloody book though, innit?' the owner beamed, holding it aloft.

'He won't be back to pay for nothing,' the waitress advised. 'His type never do.'

'I reckon I'll chuck it out on the rubbish and that,' the proprietor announced, ripping the small black book satisfactorily apart, his shoulder blades like the stumps of wings shuddering with the exquisite pleasure of however small an iconoclasm. The torn pages of Sam's scrawl and hymenal ones unwritten in fluttered towards a plastic bin.

Sam, however, was strolling carelessly into the concourse of King's Cross Station, chemicals of curiosity replacing those of anxiety inside his volatile nervous system. Enticed by bodies flipping down stairs, he descended and watched people feeding tickets to barriers that clapped open. He picked up a half-spent ticket a generous passenger had left on a turnstile and used it; followed a woman who strode with beguiling purpose to a platform, thence onto an Underground train that carried him around the Circle Line.

The tube reached Paddington and Sam alighted, for he knew that from here trains left London, where he didn't belong. Another escalator carried him back up to the surface and into another, less raucous, concourse. He joined a queue for TICKETS and when his turn came said: 'I'd like a single please.'

'Yes?'

Sam smiled. 'Yes,' he affirmed.

'Where to, sir?' the clerk queried irritably.

'Oh, anywhere,' Sam volunteered.

The clerk stared dully. 'Move along. Go on. These people have got trains to catch.'

Sam stumbled away. A spasm of irritation was succeeded by confusion as he put his hands in his pockets and shambled across the smooth floor, but hard on its heels came a flush of embarrassment: he had no money. If the clerk had given him a ticket he wouldn't have been able to pay for it.

Possessed of a sudden surge of assertiveness, Sam assailed a stubby man in uniform standing before a train to Wales.

'Excuse me,' he said. 'I've had my wallet stolen.'

The man cut Sam off shaking his head: 'Lost property.'

'No. I was wondering whether you could let me onto the train without a ticket.'

The official gazed up at Sam with what appeared to be admiration. 'I could lose my job for less than that,' he twinkled. 'Inspector'd have my guts for garters. Give me a break, mate.'

As he retreated from Wales Sam became aware that his bladder was full, and walked across to the TOILETS from which he found himself barred by a turnstile that coveted not tickets but coins. By good fortune a lavatory attendant passed by with a mop beyond.

'Excuse me,' Sam hailed him. 'I don't have change but I need to pee. Can you possibly let me through?'

The attendant's black skin made the white tiles bounce light. He beheld Sam with sullen suspicion.

'You mess wid me?' he asked, and made it plain by the challenging shape of his body there was no way Sam was going to outwit him.

'Do you want me to do it out here?' Sam pleaded.

The attendant's eyes narrowed even as he shrugged. 'Why yer asking me? That's not my business. That's Security.'

Sam lurched away. The fact that he couldn't pee made him need to all the more. He trotted out of Paddington Station and down a side road where all the buildings were stitched together. Speeding up, his bladder swelling, he carried on into another street, saw green through railings and stumbled towards it fumbling with his flies. He thrust his pelvis forward between two stanchions, aimed his prick towards trees weeds shrubs, felt urine flow through urethra, along penis, closed his eyes, blessed relief . . . at which moment a barking dog hurled itself out of the undergrowth towards him, teeth bared savagely growling.

Sam leapt backwards, the dog pressed itself against the iron railings snarling hideously. Piss sprayed on trousers, splashed on dog's enraged snout. Managing to stop peeing, Sam then felt sharp pain as the price of thwarted micturition, just as bushes parted and an elderly lady, burbling 'Come here, petal, what's the matter, diddikins?', peered at Sam, who had gathered his wits and now let piss stream onto the pavement between them with an idiot smile, apologizing, 'Sorry. Sorry,' as he did so.

He returned towards the station. He needed a cup of coffee with which to analyse his predicament. He summoned up the shameless courage of a beggar as a man approached. At ten paces Sam raised his arm just as the other man did likewise. Sam opened his mouth to speak but his opposite number issued sound first:

'Spare fifty pence for a sandwich, mister?'

As they reached each other Sam drew out the linings of his trouser pockets in a parody of poverty, two white triangles like the ears of an animal. It occurred to Sam to whip out his prick again and have the man guess which animal. But the man was looking in that direction anyway.

'Have an accident, did yer?'

'I was robbed,' Sam told him.

'Weren't we all? I could tell you some stories. Ain't you got nuffink?'

Sam shook his head. 'I just want a cup of coffee.'

One for sorrow. The man's pupils dilated as he saw Sam's watch. 'You need money, friend, I'll help you out. Buy your watch off yer even though, see, I've one of me own. I'll give you a quid 'cos I'm kind of a fool, and you get yourself fed up and watered, friend.'

Back in Paddington Sam gratefully ordered a cup of coffee from a stall. As the woman poured it Sam leaned back and smiled, content with the self-vacant world, grateful to his good Samaritan. People rushed to and fro. The tannoy announced one train's imminent departure for Reading and another soon arriving from Exeter St David's. Pigeons clustered in the dirty cavernous roof. *I feel like an empty cast-iron exhibition. I want ornaments on everything.*

'That's one pound twenty.'

'Excuse me?'

'Coffee. One pound twenty.'

'I'm short,' Sam said.

'Nah,' said a man with a razor cut and suit beside him, 'you're six foot for sure, mate,' and chuckled in a cordial way.

'I'm short of twenty pence,' Sam explained. 'Could you help me out?'

The man made a face that questioned Sam Caine's sanity. 'Fuck off,' he said and turned away.

Sam looked at the stall server. She shook her head disapprovingly, tut-tutted and picked up the styrofoam cup of coffee she'd just poured, and began to tip it. Sam mumbled, 'Can I have a pound's worth then?' but could only watch as, still shaking her head, she emptied the contents into the sink. Then she turned to Sam with a pout and flicked her head away just to make sure she had adequately conveyed her annoyance at how much trouble he'd put her to, as she let the cup fall into a bin.

Sam scavenged for food or drink in litter bins and searched for coins on the ground. Bending over to inspect a rounded shape in a shadow he was struck from and on the behind.

''Ere,' a voice rasped. A man dressed in orange equipped with brush and shovel. 'Go on. Clear out. 'Op it.' Poking the brush in Sam's direction and nodding vigorously towards the exits. 'Bugger off. Go on. Out of it.'

Sam stood uncertainly outside Paddington Station, moving from one foot to the other. Hungry thirsty dirty friendless, he was loath to leave the comforting familiarity of the station concourse for the vast metropolis behind him. Those who passed Sam saw him only for a split second, assessed his worth or threat (harmless, insane asylum evacuee, trembling with what appeared to be servile agitation; low on the visibility scale in this city of beggars), then shut him out of sight and cut him off from memory.

Just another man reduced to destitution, powerlessness, imbecility. Sam didn't understand that he had only to sleep for this misery to be washed away for ever; for the restoration of his innocence. To go back to square one and start again. He stepped from one foot to the other, as if the rhythmic movement might whisk resolve and stiffen his prevaricating body.

Rebecca came off the train with a small shoulder bag, a cloudiness in her head and throat and a knotted elasticity in her legs that made her want to walk. So rather than catch the Circle Line to Victoria she set off from Paddington Station to stretch out across Hyde Park and take the Victoria Line from Green Park tube station.

On such whims, at such odds, are destinies enacted. Did a guardian angel plead with her, unheard, to change direction? Did a cupid hover, or a handmaiden whisper, *Blessed art thou among women, and blessed is the fruit of thy womb*? *Hail Mary, Mother of God, pray for us sinners now and at the hour of our death*?

Rebecca strolled out of the concourse in an unusual state of mind. She was, or had had to become, a hard-hearted city woman. Had engaged in versions of the same conversation ever since she came to the capital: do you give to them? There but for the grace of God but they'll spend it on drink. Where does compassion become irresponsibility? It's the government's job, anyway, homelessness a political issue. Except charity begins where? What's best? By general consent: buy the *Big Issue*, reward a busker. But now without doubt Rebecca was vulnerable to emotional appeal. She still felt the melancholy that stayed with her a day or two after leaving her father. A residue of empathogens lingered in her neurochemistry. Perhaps emerging into the blue but freezing cold made her likely to sympathize with anyone forced to stay outside. Whatever. She stepped towards a fumbling beggar.

Sam Caine, abject, raised his eyes to the next person

53

coming his way, his blue eyes, and as she met his gaze said to her, 'Help me.'

Rebecca Menotti looked at the man as she approached him, her gaze locked into his. Tall, rangy. Brown hair, and was there auburn mixed in as well? Not young, not quite middle-aged. There was something strange about him: he was less wizened than a wino; too well dressed for a beggar; soft. No reek of alcohol as she reached him.

'Help me,' Sam said quietly, and Rebecca's chest was flooded by a surge of compassion such as she had never known. Or indeed could know, for as her grandmother might have told her, it was not compassion.

'I will', she whispered, 'help you.' She took his hand. 'Come with me. You are safe.' And Rebecca led the man with her, unaware that she had just been struck by *il colpo di fulmine*. The thunderbolt of love.

3

THE LABORATORY

'Love,' said Mr Bone, 'is a simple chemical reaction. We proved it', he told Joe Snow with dismissive modesty, 'in one of our first experiments here. Before you joined us, Mr Snow. Testing potential anti-depressants. We gave baboons a drug that mimicked endorphin transmitters in a localized part of the brainstem, and they fell in love with whatever appeared in front of them.'

'Did you get to try it on volunteers?' Joe wondered.

Mr Bone shook his head. 'Too risky.'

'I suppose so,' Joe nodded.

'No. It was bad enough with baboons,' Mr Bone grimaced. 'The last thing I wanted was human beings overcome with lust for us.'

Which, in Joe's opinion, was not impossible to imagine. For in the slovenly milieu of Oxford academia Mr Bone glowed. A man able to stave off the bloodshot, paunchy dishevelment of middle age may grow into a handsomeness, a glamour even, he'd not previously known. Mr Bone owned, in addition, a rangy frame, which enabled style on a budget. He bought concrete-coloured suits off the rack that seemed to alter their very tailoring as he put them on, flattering him as he did them. Underneath, against white cotton shirts he wore bright ties in electric reds, neon blues, glaring yellows. Splashes of dazzling abstraction.

When Mr Bone returned from a spot of wet lab work to his administrator's desk in the Department of Organology, scrubbing hands and discarding apron, it was with the charisma of a surgeon. That a faint chemical odour clung to Mr Bone seemed only to enhance his clinical aura.

His image was completed with a pair of white socks and tennis shoes, creating a sartorial mismatch he carried off triumphantly. Striding down the corridors of the department or along the Broad and into Blackwells Mr Bone had the look of an executive man of action, an elegantly restless maverick.

The Department of Organology was a great squat concrete cube set adjacent to the rest of the Science Area in one corner of a playing field. Wayward under-graduate strikers ballooned a football over the bar and it bounced back with a dull thud. The blank façade was broken only by faint indentations of decoration that less described than merely hinted at gables, tympana and buttresses, and that slight, almost mocking archi-tectural fancy, allied to tall frosted bullet-proof windows, only conferred upon the building an Albigensian grimness. It was an academic fortress, and perhaps that medieval allusion was made with gritted teeth in order to obtain planning permission. Certainly visitors during the ten years since its construction were amazed that this concrete square had ever been allowed to materialize so close to the ancient heart of the city. It didn't look quite man-made, somehow; rather, like an ancient bunker that had been vomited out of the rejecting ground, or a concrete wart that had appeared overnight in some awful architectural disease, a new and more virulent strain of modernism attacking an immune-deficient earth.

But no, a moment's further consideration would confirm that it was man-made. The Department of Organology had the forbidding and paradoxically obtrusive presence of all secret places: like a nuclear power station or a military base, it both hid and at the same time proclaimed the fact that diabolical deeds were done there, in the name of greater good that need not be questioned; a monument at once ashamed and shameless.

Mr Bone aimed to be the first in to work each morning. Spurning the lift, he liked to climb his sinewy way floor by unoccupied floor to his office at the top. Surveying his unpeopled domain stimulated in Mr Bone a strategic, martial appetite with which to begin each day. The occasional obsessive student he discovered already hunched over computer or dissecting mat irked him, however gratifying it might be to find someone whose appointment he'd approved so committed to the department.

Overall responsibility for both research fellows and ancillary staff was a burden Mr Bone carried lightly. The key to recruitment, he believed, was to nurture a vision of their joint enterprise the simplest employee could embrace and be inspired by. 'Through knowledge to truth,' he confided. 'Through truth to happiness.'

It was surprising what people could give if you let them. Take his assistant up ahead already, chatting to the night porter. Joe Snow, once a loyal, bewildered misfit, now a notable protégé. A sterling example.

Joseph Snow had been, fifteen years earlier, the cleverest young man in Oxford. As an undergraduate

57

scholar, up from a Hackney comprehensive at the age of sixteen, he gained a double first . . . or was it a first class honours? Well, one degree or the other; Mr Bone forgot which. He embarked upon a D.Phil. in Languages, received a research fellowship, was given dining rights by one college and punting privileges by another.

Two years into his thesis Joe was persuaded to deliver a lecture to fellow graduates, a dissertation from his work in progress followed by questions. That seminar, conducted in an underground room in All Souls College, at which Joe spoke without notes at breathless length on various manifestations in Arabic languages of the glottal stop, had entered academic legend. It was said the sound effects alone were worth the price of admission. And he responded to questions with a sigh; a long, unnerving gaze at his Socratic interrogator; and a concise yet elusive answer.

'He's the most brilliant mind of his generation,' said dons and professors alike. 'He can speak thirteen languages, four of them dead ones.' Joe was more than just a disembodied brain, though: he possessed a distinctive body, too. He had the blubbery flesh and the moony face of a Mongol, with piggy browless eyes squinting through pebble specs, beneath a singular hairstyle; close-cut back and sides but neglected on top, his wiry brown hair grew high, wild and untended, a bird's nest built by a slapdash starling.

Joe's academic career continued along customary lines: he spent six more inconclusive years in the Bodleian Library, his head filling up with arid facts and dreams of love – neglected by his supervisor, signing on the dole after his grant ran out – and had a nervous breakdown. For some months Joe was incarcerated in a secure unit at Littlemore Hospital, where he liked to sit in a corner whistling to himself like a preoccupied bird. It was a stroke of extraordinary luck that someone else's visitor who'd been on holiday to the Canaries, gone island-hopping and been entertained by the whistling waiters of Agulo, recognized the sound of *el silbo*: she pointed out to one of the nurses that the scarecrow over by the wall wasn't crazy at all, he was merely conducting a private conversation with Wittgenstein in the whistling language of Gomera.

For a while after that Joe lived in a halfway house in Headington, venturing outside to watch the traffic in suits too small, and attended the Warneford Hospital as an outpatient. Psychologists analysed him, hoping to unearth the sexual origins of his psychosis, psychiatrists juggled cocktails of drugs to balance his nervous system and therapists toyed with his body. Between them they alleviated the immense loneliness of his schizophrenia, and his widowed mother moved to Oxford from London and with him into a council flat in Jericho. It was difficult to find Joe a job, however, since he had first to get through an interview: he was incapable of conducting a straightforward conversation on account of the fact that he was so clever he could see where it would lead. Like a chess player, no sooner had Joe started to say something than he predicted the sixteen most likely responses of his interlocutor, then his own subsequent delivery, and so on, so that his every sentence started, stuttered, and trailed away.

'No previous . . . employment, not the other, ha . . . not been inside . . . not prison anyway . . . is that a diffic . . . I can see . . . on the other hand . . . no, I suppose . . . yes . . . really?'

It was a mode of conversation incomprehensible outside Senior Common Rooms, and a series of prospective employers in petrol stations, factories and shops gaped at the idiot with an IQ of a hundred and ninety, until Joe applied for a position as a junior porter at the Department of Organology. Mr Bone interviewed him and offered Mr Snow a job on the spot.

Joe became a familiar sight making his way to work each morning. He strolled out of Jericho up Cardigan Street, which echoed with the twang of the Buddhist chanting group, sniffing the bitter smell of hops in the air carried from Morrell's brewery, and bought a copy of the *Independent* from the newsagent opposite Gluttons. He ambled past the Observatory built by James Pears, across Woodstock and Banbury roads, along the railings of the Parks where painters sell their wares, past Keble College whose ugliness Ruskin had altered his daily constitutional to avoid, past the oldest pizza in the world on permanent display outside the Pitt Rivers Museum, and into the Science Area. While remnants of that morning's breakfast congealed upon his skewed tie and his schoolboy's satchel bumped against a buttock, Joe scanned the newspaper as he progressed, discarding finished pages into litter bins and bicycle baskets. He walked with splayed feet and in such an indecisive manner that it looked as if with every step he might change direction: what he actually did was to veer all over the pavement like an inebriated crab. Joe stumbled into people without noticing, and bumped into lamp-posts to whom he mumbled an apology.

'That's the cleverest man in Oxford,' local residents told visitors proudly. 'He can translate fourteen languages – in both directions!'

After a probationary period Mr Bone put Joe on nights, clocking on at twelve and off at eight. He often wandered to work by circuitous routes, around the centre of town, watching and watched by fierce

60

emperors' heads, mooning nudes, rotting gargoyles, their stone skin blistered by acid rain and corrupted by carbon monoxide, his mind as unencumbered as the endless vacant niches on the outside of buildings emptied by Henry VIII and the visual apathy of a nation bent beneath a lowering sky.

Joe's duties at work then were straightforward and habitual: having relieved the evening porter he checked a list of students permitted to work in the labs that night, locked certain doors in the building in sequence, sorted late mail into pigeon-holes. After this flurry of activity it was chiefly a question of filling in time until the morning porter's shift began. Once per hour Joe stirred to patrol the five floors of the building: at two points on each storey there was a clock into which he had to insert a metal card that registered the time and proved his scrutiny. In practice that was all he or any of the other porters did – trudge up the stairs and amble along each floor's central corridor punching the clock at either end; the proof of his patrol became its purpose.

Joe mastered his tasks and carried them out per-functorily, and his curiosity got the better of him. It was a measure of Mr Bone's capacity for intuiting people's potential that when he came across Joe sat cross-legged talking to an off-limits room full of rabbits who hopped around and nuzzled him, far from sacking Joe for ruining a delicate experiment he promoted him to the post of junior assistant laboratory technician.

By this academic year – an *annus criticus* in the funding of Higher Education – Joe had been in the Department of Organology five years, and left his dysfunctional days behind him. Senior academics sometimes waylaid him and asked him to translate a fax from a foreign colleague, while female staff occasionally found themselves stirred by an un-accountable desire to ruffle his startled thatch of hair.

Ever hoping to arrive before Mr Bone, Joe scurried in one early January morning. He dashed into the video box to give his Employees Drug Abuse test sample, and emerged still securing himself. 'Here's today's *Independent*, Monty. Part of it, anyway,' he said to his successor in the night porter's snug at the back of the ground floor. In a corner of the little office three shrivelled Christmas balloons still hung, perishing rubber scrotums. Monty was another academic casualty rescued by Mr Bone. He was said to have read everything contained in the Bodleian on the subject of pre-Babylonian jurisprudence, and was now content to muse over cryptic crosswords that kindly employees and students cut out of their newspapers.

'Thank you, Joe. Hope it's not as easy as yesterd-d-day's.'

'Are you harassing the security staff, Mr Snow?' came a nasal voice. Mr Bone approached the porter's cubicle. 'He doesn't want to bother with riffraff like you. He's an educated man, aren't you, Mr Montagu?' Mr Bone addressed Monty with the formality he accorded one and all. 'A quiet night, I trust.'

'Everything under c-c-control. Cleaners been and gone. Only the animals in the library are b-b-b-barking.'

'Whereas you'll be late for work, Mr Snow,' Mr Bone smiled, 'and I'll be able to dock your wages.'

Joe sighed and scurried towards the SECURITY LIFT, and Mr Bone nodded to Monty and followed after. Without increasing pace he requested: 'Hold those doors open, please,' in his uniquely annoying voice. It sounded as if Mr Bone could set a note playing in the roof of his mouth, an adenoidal drone, which he then twanged with his tongue and by reshaping his thin lips. It seemed in addition to reverberate even more maddeningly in the confined lift.

'We don't want any problems today, Joseph,' he whined. His skin smelled of vinegar; his electric sunset tie flashed in the elevator's mirrored metal. 'There's a board meeting downstairs and the Al-Shalir brothers may want to tour the directors around.'

'Right, Mr Bone.'

'Keep an eye on those research students this time. We don't want another bloody mess. You know how squeamish some of these nobs are.'

'Yes, Mr Bone.'

The lift doors opened, and Mr Bone entered his realm, the smell of formaldehyde sweet in his nostrils, the sound of moaning, mewling animals music to his ears.

The building in which the Department of Organology was housed was of ostensibly simple but inherently complex interior arrangement: it was in fact an architectural maze, whose confusion was exemplified by the lifts system.

The six floors of the building were separated into two sides, east and west, by a wide corridor, at each end of four of which stood a lift. One, public, lift was for general use, and went neither down to the basement nor up to the highest floor. Inside this lift were buttons designating storeys in the customary manner: Ground, 1st and so on.

The other, security, lift was for use by authorized personnel who needed a special key to gain access, and the day Joe was given his own personal copy by Mr Bone he felt the pride of a free man. The security lift's buttons were marked 1st for the ground floor, 2nd for the first floor, 3rd for the second, and 4th for the third. However, instead of being marked 5th, the animal laboratories floor simply said Top, and was always and only ever referred to likewise. Officially, there *was* no fifth floor.

PUBLIC LIFT			SECURITY LIFT
	VETERINARY STUDIES	ANIMAL WELFARE	Top
3	HUMAN BEHAVIOUR	ANTHROPOLOGY	4
2	PLANT SCIENCES	MUSICAL STUDIES	3
1	LIBRARY	LECTURE HALL	2
Ground	RECEPTION / ADMIN	ACCOUNTS / CANTEEN	1
	CAR PARK / LOADING / STORES		Basement

It was a mess of a system that was easily justified as a modern tradition worthy of the university of which it was a part – whose cathedral church's daily six o'clock Evensong commenced at precisely five minutes past; whose senior members were allowed to vote on important matters for up to three years after their deaths. But it still confused new researchers, particularly Americans. They thought they'd mastered the dumb British method of designating storeys, only to gain a pass key to the security lift whose buttons in fact corresponded to their own system. Up and down they yo-yoed in hiccuping confusion, which was exacerbated whenever one of them made the mistake of seeking clarification from the haybale-haired lab technician.

'Where on earth's the fifth frickin floor, mate?'

'There is no fifth floor,' Joe explained. 'Perhaps you want the fourth?'

'I was working in Human Behaviour on the third floor last term.'

'Possibly you're using the wrong lift?'

'I want the animal labs. So I get a key off Mr Bone, I try the goddamn fourth floor, and come out in Human Behaviour, which was on the third floor last term.'

'You're coming out on the wrong floor.'

'I know I'm coming out on the wrong damn floor. I can't find the right floor.'

'You need the top floor. It's simple.'

'Hell, why didn't you say so in the first place? What I need now is a damn fine cup of coffee.'

'That'll be the canteen. Ground floor.'

'Hey, you don't fool me, mate. There is no ground floor. The ground floor's the first floor.'

'Very true. The ground floor is the first floor.'

'And the first floor is the ground floor.'

'That depends on which lift you're in.'

'So which frickin lift do you recommend?'

'Neither,' Joe said quietly. 'We're standing on the ground floor. The canteen's just along there.'

The American snarled. 'I blame that Alice guy,' he muttered as he strode away.

Each floor was further complicated by its own intricate layout of corridors and hallways, of wet labs and dry labs, of offices and store rooms. The building's interior Byzantinism was all the more off-putting after the brute simplicity of its exterior.

Joe Snow's chief function in the labs was animal maintenance, which entailed daily feeding and cleaning and administration of certain substances by certain methods, according to instructions. In addition, when he had time he assisted the post-grad students more or less as he wanted.

At ten a.m. Willem van der Bierstoonk, a stout, tanned, rugged, blond South African behavioural psychologist, strode in, and Joe swooned. Willem was involved in ground-breaking research that according to Mr Bone was bringing the department its best publicity in years. This consisted of benign experiments designed to examine the effect of positive social interactions on the development of coronary heart disease and other such pathologies. His partner in the project was a Bulgarian biologist of such beauty only reckless fools approached her. Magenta Hroichkova came to work wearing clothes which resembled charity shop rejects from the mid-seventies, jewellery hanging from her earlobes like flashing mobiles, enough make-up for a gaudy circus act, and perfume of such cheap pungency Mr Bone pleaded with her not to wear it because it interfered with other experiments. Men trembled and monkeys chattered at her arrival. Magenta put on a starched white lab coat, gaining dull uniformity, and succeeded only in exacerbating her sexual allure.

Only a man of steel could have worked with Magenta. Depending upon their preference most people sighed at either her or Willem and accepted that such specimens were destined for each other. Willem always arrived first, allowing Joe a few minutes in which to hope that Magenta would miss that day and he could provide Willem with close assistance, only to hear the sound of high heels click-clacking across the floor towards them.

'Sounds like that bleddy Balkan gypsy's on her way at last,' Willem announced loudly.

'I heard that, you African Polar bear gorilla,' Magenta said, flouncing in. 'You are so unamusing, I laugh.'

'Will you hurry up and get sorted out? We've got a 'eap of work to do.'

'If you had the smallest idea in your pea-sized brain about the proper scientific working methods it wouldn't take so long.'

'Ah, get out those bleddy syringes, woman,' Willem scowled.

Magenta pursed her lips and pouted. 'Look. Here's one. Why don't you sit on it?'

Owing to the significance of their research Willem and Magenta had been allocated three adjacent carrels in the Animal Welfare section: on that side of the central corridor on the top floor (Veterinary Studies on the other) was a kind of open-plan office subdivided by movable walls and doors into an ever-changing maze of smaller corridors and rooms whose size depended upon the scale of the experiment within. These carrels (or cages, as Mr Bone gleefully called them) could be sound-proofed and windowless if desired; and owing to the cutthroat and paranoid nature of academic research all but the most unambitious made just such a request, so that the section had the spooky atmosphere of a catacomb.

In their first carrel Willem and Magenta were repeating an experiment for the fourth time, on Magenta's insistence, to verify identical results already thrice achieved, showing what Mr Bone regarded as admirable rigour. In fact they pretty much let Joe get on with this exercise alone, a small measure of responsibility he enjoyed in an anxious way, and he left Magenta and Willem to their bickering. Two groups of ten rabbits had been housed in identical conditions, and fed identical diets rich in cholesterol, which could be expected to predispose them to hardening of the arteries.

The first group was left alone, but Joe visited the second group several times a day and stroked, spoke to and played with them. They'd soon come to recognize him and eagerly sought his attention, hopping towards him and brushing against him like cats, proffering their heads to be scratched behind the ears. Joe developed a real affection for those bunnies.

After six weeks all the rabbits were humanely killed and their aortas examined: the second group had on average 60 per cent less damage. This remarkable figure (and proof of it) had been repeated each time. After the third similar result Willem and Magenta had published their research to great acclaim and envy, and were now repeating it yet again only because, as Magenta pointed out, it was being copied universally by competitors hoping to find it flawed. The pair were meanwhile receiving invitations to conferences around the world at which they would present the findings of this and their next two experiments, which if as good as the first might land them the prize each was separately hoping for: a permanent research fellowship at Stanford or MIT in the States. Unfortunately, it was also beginning to dawn on each of them simultaneously that the more successful they were together the more they would be seen as a team, future renown dependent upon continuing their fractious partnership.

While Joe stroked rabbits' ears, Magenta fumed in the next carrel at the prospect of being stuck with Willem for the rest of her career in a kind of hideous experiment herself. But she kept part of her mind clear and her fingers steady as she worked in the midst of dogs with adoring eyes. She turned knobs that measured on precise dials electric shocks administered via electrodes attached to the dogs' ears. The first group was left alone, the second Magenta petted and soothed, as the current jolted through them all, calming these ones' grimaced twitching and agitated yelping. So far (it was the third run through this experiment) prospects looked promising: in post-mortems the second group's blood vessels were half as hardened as the first.

From next door, meanwhile, Magenta could hear through the sound-proofed partitions that oafish South African conducting his investigation; which, thank God, required less precision than hers. Willem was studying for the second time domestic chickens which had been separated into three groups within a day of hatching. Over a four-week period, while being fed the same food, one group was ignored, the second group was socialized – spoken to, hand-fed, treated gently – and the third group (which Magenta could hear Willem attending to now) was hassled. Which meant being shouted at and subjected to other loud noises, being surprised and upset. Magenta could hear herself already telling people over coffee in the vestibules of conference halls what he'd done, the manifestly junior partner in their research: while she was amassing painstaking evidence he was making faces at chickens, creeping up on hens, ha, jumping out at them from behind filing cabinets. Really.

After a month all three groups of chickens were to be inoculated, first with pathogenic bacteria and then with foreign blood cells, to test the effectiveness of their immune responses. In the first test the tamed, befriended birds had showed significantly more pronounced immunity to both substances.

Mr Bone was in no doubt that he was a man coming into his own. He'd been patiently dreaming, planning and building ever since the Al-Shalir brothers offered him the post of Director of the Animal Welfare Section at the department's founding ten years earlier. Having risen through the technical and administrative ranks, he well understood that some people had failed to appreciate his ascent. They saw him as little more than a glorified lab technician, those arrogant Oxbridge prodigies, haughty blue-stockings and snooty boffins that trooped through his laboratories. Who guarded their experiments as if they were state secrets, then published the results — always last minute panics — in a bound volume read by three examiners before being consigned to the slush pile at Oxford University Press and oblivion in the bowels of the Bodleian Library.

But Mr Bone (it was generally agreed that his Christian name had withered through lack of use) had retained his dignity, and in secret meetings with the Al-Shalir brothers had communicated his vision of happiness; had in return seen himself reflected in the twinkle in Ben Ali's eye and felt his heart flip at a wink from Mohammed.

'We'll make your dreams come true,' Ben Ali said as he enveloped Mr Bone in an eau de colognial embrace.

'We have the power to do so,' Mohammed nodded gravely. Mr Bone knew that it was so and his time had come. It all came down, after all, to money.

Ben Ali kissed acquaintances and manhandled friends, with a volatile abandon that was at once ingratiating and bullying. Mr Bone was never quite sure whether he was supposed to acquiesce passively or hug back with equal enthusiasm. At that moment, though, he had few options, as Ben Ali grasped his head by the ears and bent it down towards him. 'For you, our friend, shall make our dreams come true too,' he said, before planting a smacker on Mr Bone's forehead.

Ben Ali Al-Shalir and his twin brother Mohammed had a great passion in common: each had been smitten by England. They'd come up to Oxford as students and been seduced by its smoky institutions, its musty customs, its intellectual transcendence. Upon coming into a modest inheritance when they graduated, aged twenty-one, the brothers made London their base. They cultivated friendships with every ruler and royal family member in the Middle East and beyond, and over the next decade became indispensable agents in Britain's most vital export trade.

Not that either of the brothers knew the slightest thing about weapons. When some Iranian general, Saudi warrior prince or British Aerospace salesman mentioned this transport plane or that leisure helicopter both Ben Ali and Mohammed had the identical habit of closing eyes raising chin wrinkling nose to show how distasteful a subject this was to them, far far beneath, please. They merely effected introductions between interested parties for the good of free enterprise, east–west friendship and defence of the free world.

The brothers' ambition was to enter the House of Lords in tandem and to that end they had worked assiduously. The income tax their accountants saved by diverting it to offshore investments they generously brought back to Britain in donations to the Conservative Party. They challenged members of the House of Windsor to polo matches at their mansion near Marlow. And they'd capped it all with a massive gift to Oxford University for the establishment of an entirely new department: organology. And there was no doubt that, even if no-one could honestly say they knew what organology meant, exactly,[1] the department had been a great success: a number of new laboratories had provided work for professors, junior fellows, equipment manufacturers, animal suppliers and post-graduate students engaged in pure research which had seen literally thousands of experiments that had thrown up profound knowledge of no use to anyone. It was the one prize above all for which the brothers would surely be granted citizenship.

For it was all about to change, as Mr Bone knew. His years of complaining about dirty needles, blocked sinks and discarded body parts were coming to an end because his private conversations with the brothers over the years were about to be formalized; because his vision and their ambition were being finally wed; and because in the voluminous contracts which the chancellor of the university and his hebdomadal council had signed when taking the brothers' money had been small print no-one had had the stamina to reach let alone read. Small print inserted after long negotiations between the future Lord Ben Ali Al-Shalir and senior civil servants in the Treasury and Department of Education. Small print which decreed that in ten years' time the Department of Organology would while remaining within the university be re-constituted as a limited company; and also that the department would then be legally forbidden from applying for public money. It would have thenceforth

---

[1]**organology** n. <f. ORGANO- + -LOGY.> **1** The branch of knowledge that deals with the supposed organs of the mental faculties etc. indicated by regions of the cranium; phrenology. **2** The branch of anatomy and physiology that deals with the organs of animals and plants. **3** The study of anything as an organ or means of doing something. **4** The branch of knowledge that deals with the history of musical instruments. *The New Shorter Oxford English Dictionary*

to be entirely self-funding, by whatever means the board of governors deemed necessary.

And while Willem van der Bierstoonk was clapping his hands and yelling at chickens on the top floor, Mr Bone made his way down in the security lift to the boardroom on the ground floor for a secret extra-ordinary general meeting, exactly ten years to the day after the foundation of the department.

Glancing in the mirror in the lift Mr Bone licked a finger and stuck down an errant eyebrow or two, ran his fingers through his wavy hair and smiled at himself through shining teeth. He adjusted that day's garish tie, then impulsively threw it over his shoulder, giving himself the air of a man with flair who'd rushed here from slightly more important business elsewhere. He was on his way, Mr Bone, a martinet maybe who'd risen slow but inexorable, a once small man about to enter the big time.

Minutes of the first board meeting of The Laboratory Limited.

Those present: Mr Ben Ali Al-Shalir (Chair); Mr Mohammed Al-Shalir (President); The Right Honourable Roderick Pastille, Minister of State for Defence; Dr Helen Horlock GP DBE JP, councillor, governor and judge; Dr Theodore Cologne, emeritus professor of philosophy; and Mr Bone; amounting to six persons, a quorum as required by the Articles.

Apologies received: none.

Minutes of last meeting: not applicable.

Mr Ben Ali Al-Shalir welcomed those present to the first board meeting on this day of the establish-ment of The Laboratory Ltd, a quasi-charitable private limited company within, superseding and separate from the Department of Organology, having

73

this morning received from the Registrar of Companies the Certificate of Incorporation.

Mr Ben Ali Al-Shalir thanked those present for kindly accepting his and his brother's invitation to join the board of the new company in addition to their doubtless countless other responsibilities and giving of their time and energy to a largely charitable venture in return for a pittance and no thanks from anyone.

Mr Pastille said he was sure he spoke for his colleagues in saying they were glad to do what little they could in the pursuit of scholarly wisdom for the good of all and the provision of higher education for young people in a land of opportunity irrespective of their background and circumstances. This sentiment was seconded by Dr Horlock.

Mr Bone, Administrator of the Department of Organology, was then presented to the members of the board as Company Secretary, with an additional and separate salary. Mr Bone explained that his first duty had been completed this day before dawn, namely: attaching a plate engraved with THE LABORATORY LTD *to the wall outside the front entrance of the Department of Organology.*

Mr Bone then read out the principal Objects Clause of the company:

Sub-clause 1. Beginning with the Animal Welfare section, by procuration and submission of quotations to undertake specific research for other companies; and to undertake pure research with a view to selling intellectual property so gained to the highest bidder.

Sub-clause 2. To pay undergraduate and postgraduate students basic salaries to be determined, plus negotiable percentage points on profits

74

accruing from their particular projects, which shall remain the intellectual property of the company.

Sub-clause 3. To turn the department round from loss-making educational charity to profit-making educational institution with quasi-charitable status within one calendar year.

Mr Ben Ali Al-Shalir then enumerated the principal Articles of Association of the company, i.e. those relating to shareholding, as follows:

1) The members of the board shall be also the principal shareholders in the company.

2) The non-executive directors (namely Mr Pastille, Dr Horlock and Dr Cologne) shall receive one ordinary share each to the value of £1.

3) The Company Secretary (namely Mr Bone) shall receive two ordinary shares to the total value of £2.

4) Mr Ben Ali Al-Shalir and Mr Mohammed Al-Shalir shall receive all other shares, which shall be preferential shares, in exactly equal measure, up to an unspecified amount.

Mr Bone explained that a bank account in the company name has been opened and the signatories shall be any two of the Chairman, President or Company Secretary. And that these minutes are to be kept in a Minute Book that shall not be available for inspection by any persons other than executive board members, and non-executive directors at board meetings. It shall be kept in safe keeping by the Company Secretary.

Any Other Business

Mr Ben Ali Al-Shalir proposed that on second thoughts the company nameplate be removed from the front entrance and a smaller version attached to a back or side entrance. This motion was seconded by Mr Pastille who recommended the plate be *placed beside whichever entrance was least frequently used. Everyone laughed. Mr Ben Ali Al-Shalir hugged Mr Pastille and they wrestled. Dr Cologne requested permission to smoke his pipe which was granted.*

Dr Horlock then asked what about biogenetics. Mr Ben Ali Al-Shalir asked what she meant by what about biogenetics. Dr Horlock stated that she had served on two government committees on the subject which was one about which the public had justifiable concern, and she wanted to know whether the company proposed research in the sensitive area of biogenetics at this time. Mr Mohammed Al-Shalir looked out of the window, Mr Pastille coughed and Dr Cologne woke up and said, 'Hear, hear.' Mr Bone gave his opinion that for pure scientists to close off any avenue of research was to fail to meet their responsibilities and to betray the public. Then Mr Ben Ali Al-Shalir put his fist on the table and said of course the company would promote research into the vital field of biogenetics for the good of mankind, and Dr Horlock said what a relief that was.

Mr Ben Ali Al-Shalir then thanked those present for coming and invited them to the bloody Randolph for lunch, and so concluded the meeting.

Roderick Pastille had his driver called and so his car was waiting in Beaumont Street when he strode out of the Randolph Hotel. A doorman opened the car door, Roderick got in, said: 'To the House, Peter,' burped, said: 'I'm having a nap,' and closed his eyes.

He was woken some minutes later by his driver's, 'Excuse me, sir.'

Roderick bumped awake bad-temperedly. 'What is it?'

'I'm sorry, but which house did you mean, sir? It's just that we're coming to the ring road. Your town house, your wife's country house, or the Commons, sir?'

Roderick shook his head. It didn't seem to matter what he did or where he went, he always seemed to be saddled with imbeciles. 'You're the driver, Peter, you tell me,' he said. 'What do you think? Mmmm? Highgate I call home. Herefordshire I call her place. So where do you think I mean by the House?'

'It's just that you've a meeting at the Ministry at three thirty, sir.'

Roderick rolled his eyes. Smart-arse imbeciles. 'OK, Peter. Thank you. I'm going to have a nap now. Please be so good as to drive me to the Ministry.'

Roderigo Pastile had been born and brought up in South London by his Spanish parents. At the age of eleven he featured in the local newspaper, the *Croydon Gazette*, when he first attempted to change his name by deed poll to Roderick for the simple reason that he wasn't a flipping dago, he was British through and through. Come to think of it, the boy bullishly proclaimed, he was going to change his surname, too: no longer was the L silent. In fact, he would *add* another L, just to make sure people understood it wasn't to be pronounced the way the English pronounced Castile, but rather Pastille like the sweet, the lozenge; like that footballer Jeff Astille. Under the headline OUR PINT-SIZED PATRIOT stood Roderick Pastille, a rather cross-looking schoolboy with a cap sitting atop a generous clump of black hair.

A couple of years later Roderick joined the local Conservative Party and at fourteen he gave a speech to the Party Conference in which he inveighed against flower power and the permissive society. Under the headline OUR TINY TORY the *Gazette* reported the views of the precocious lad who wanted to make heard the voice of the silent majority of God-fearing, law-abiding, loyal, ambitious young people.

In the middle of the meeting he'd forgotten at his Ministry, Secretary of State for Defence Roderick Pastille was troubled by a physical sensation as some brigadier general or other droned on about the effects of proposed cuts in the military budget, dire consequences, British Army's capacity to respond, crises, stretched, breaking point . . . Gulf Northern Ireland Balkans . . . blah blah blah.

These military people were worse whingers than the health servers. It was so much easier to deal with executives of the companies manufacturing defence equipment – whether in his role as Minister purchasing for our forces or, with the brothers Al-Shalir's help, procuring sales abroad: you discussed money and that was that, with the odd postscript for the press about jobs, to keep Labour quiet. You were on the same side. Whereas these chiefs of staff admiral of the fleet air vice marshals saw one, a politician, as their peacetime enemy. The sooner we can privatize them the better, that'll shut them up.

The old bellyacher was blathering on and Roderick's mind began to drift: its destination was what caused the disturbing sensation, for the table beneath which his legs were bent was rather low, or else the chair upon which his arse was parked was too high. Whichever, his mind kept returning to the memory of an Indonesian transvestite he'd met on a recent trip to Singapore, and his hard-on was pressing urgently against the underside of the table, in a comparatively pleasant and potentially embarrassing manner.

He liked transvestites but what Roderick figured he'd really prefer was a girl who looked like a boy, not a dyke, obviously, but a prettily gorgeous young man to all intents and purposes except that he had female rather than male pudenda – a Viola, a Rosalind. What a sad historical quirk that Elizabethan theatre was acted solely by men, not women, was it not? The world is full of youths who look like whatever you want them to, but not young women and he didn't mean girls, pubescently boyish, that was no good, child prostitution forget it, that wasn't his bag.

The agenda moved on painfully slowly: Roderick on one side of the table flanked by his junior ministers, opposite the military, with supposedly neutral civil servants in the middle (who without his yet knowing it referred to their boss amongst themselves as Fruit Pastille), and each group despised the others.

Next item on the agenda: gays in the military. Marvellous. Rile the old buggers a bit. Because Pastille had the results of a survey the MoD had commissioned, which the top brass hadn't yet seen.

'Homosexuals in the armed forces', declared General Watt, 'would have a catastrophic impact on the men's morale.'

'Gays are claiming equal rights, just like women, gentlemen,' said Roderick. He relished articulating the word gay and seeing them squirm.

'We don't allow women in the front line,' said Admiral Bow.

'Not yet, Ben,' Roderick agreed.

'If men are fighting beside someone they love, whether man woman or child, they'll become less efficient fighters,' said Air Vice Marshal Hampshire. 'Only the Platonic love of comrades enhances warriors' ability.'

'Spartan,' corrected Watt.

'Gentlemen,' Roderick said, 'does it never strike you that it's only a recent notion that homosexuality is emasculating? It used to be thought that hetero-sexuality, consorting with women, was.'

'Quite,' Watt gruffed, while others shuffled their feet.

'O sweet Juliet,' Roderick continued, 'Thy beauty hath made me effeminate, And in my temper softened valour's steel!'

The room was silent. Roderick let it remain so long enough to bring blood to the ears of his adversaries. Then: 'No, no.' He shook his head. 'I agree with you.' Roderick spoke with a mobile mouth, supple lips, exaggerated. He loved the sound of his voice but there was more to it than that; it was as if he was snogging the words as they came off his own tongue, a kind of oral narcissism. 'And I want you to rest assured that as long as I'm Minister not only will the ban on queers remain' – he saw them preen at the word queer; they were so easy to play – 'there will be no – read my lips, gentlemen – no compromise between front line troops and support services. As you may know I com-missioned a survey of servicemen's views. We now have the results.' He brandished a folder. 'We asked them whether male homosexuality were as abhorrent as women shagging each other, and if not, would lift-ing the ban on them be bad for discipline and morale. The overwhelming majority said male homosexuality was *especially* repellent, and voted nine to one to keep the ban in force.' He could sense the relief spread amongst the medal-bedecked men before him. 'These so-called gay rights activists, the Stonewall lot and so on, will of course be appealing. Well, they can appeal to the House of Lords, the European Court of Human Rights, and to King bloody Solomon for all I care. We had another survey carried out, a straw poll really, and found public opinion, i.e. tabloid editors, ha ha, to be massively behind whatever our servicemen wished. Our upstanding boys. So, there you have it, gentlemen.'

Roderick leaned back and accepted the uncommon plaudits that followed, and then let his junior minister lead the next item on the agenda: the formation of policy in response to the recent dismissal in the High Court of the case against four women who'd entered a British Aerospace factory and disabled a Hawk jet with hammers, and how this absurd miscarriage of justice might encourage other lunatics to take matters into their own hands. The implications for security were vast. The implications for this meeting were even worse. How Roderick wished he were somewhere else. Like on the hustings. When, oh when, was that apology for a Prime Minister, dithering in the shadows, our leader hovering in the background like a diffident schoolboy, going to call the bloody election?

4

CORNISH WRESTLING

A grey transporter van was parked in the shadows of urban trees. Inside, seated in the lotus position, Martha Polkinghorne breathed deeply. First through her left nostril, then through her right. Pooraka, inhalation, brought vitality into the body. Rechaka, exhalation, eliminated impurity. As time went by she retained each breath deeper, longer, until Martha felt herself filling up with warm light. And she began to imagine herself invisible.

Three a.m. in a winter night and the Midlands town was sleeping. From the dark windows of Victorian, Edwardian houses in prosperous suburbia red digital cyclops stared. Alert videos, computers, faxes. Telephone answering machines. On the floors above, families hibernated in four, five bedrooms.

Outside, an almost rural silence. Snow accepted the woman's footsteps in the deep gardens. An urban fox eyed her warily. Occasional shivering tomcats, too, mistrustful of this human intruder in their nocturnal domain.

Martha Polkinghorne's rosy cheeks felt pinched by

the cold, and pink, she reckoned; her nose glowed, probably. She pulled her balaclava tight down over springy blond hair, and continued in the murky light from distant streetlamps and a greasy moon; climbed over a fence, veered between shrubs, squeezed through a laurel hedge.

The snow moulded her footprints. It amused Martha to mark the trail towards, later away from, her objective. Saying to subsequent investigators, 'Here, this way, let me show you.' Teasing them, because the path would peter out back on the road where snow turned to slush. Then they'd measure her footsteps, and learn nothing from the overshoes she wore, two sizes larger than her own.

Not that detectives would investigate this case. But if they did they'd find no self-incriminating evidence left by Martha Polkinghorne, unlike inept criminals whose exploits made Martha laugh in empty hotel rooms: bank robbers addressing each other by name, captured on closed circuit television. A car thief on a prime-time programme giving the Vs to his pursuers as he slips into a labyrinth of alleyways, unaware of the helicopter with its infra-red camera above him, omniscient, inescapable.

Martha's favourite was one she read of recently. An aggressive villain, cocaine and alcohol fuelled, was carrying out a robbery on a betting shop in London's Whitechapel. He pretended to be armed with a gun and demanded cash from the terrified staff. His accomplice became increasingly unhappy with his violent be-haviour: eventually wrestled him to the ground, and held him in a headlock until bemused police arrived.

Such a fate would never befall Martha. She had no accomplice. Martha worked alone, and always would. Her father, James, had taught her that lesson, in his own unique way.

As a toddler James Polkinghorne antagonized the farm-yard cats and sheepdogs, grabbed their legs, bundled them over onto their backs and pinned them down. The boy did so less with the speculative cruelty of a child than as a fellow animal and was undeterred by the scratches of infuriated claws or a collie's petulant nips, the taste of his own blood bringing forth only a wide grin on the infant's freckled face. When James flipped a tomcat or pinned down a dog it seemed to be only to gain a legitimate fall or exact a submission – which the more intelligent of the sheepdogs learned to acknowledge by tapping the floor with her paw.

'I can't take my eye off him for a moment he's up to mischief,' said his mother of her only child.

'No, woman,' her husband mused. 'It's just us have another wrestler in the family. Do have his ancestor's genes as well as his name.'

James's father, Simon Polkinghorne, tall and gaunt, a laconic, morose farmer, accepted society as a conspiracy against the yeomen of the world, of Cornwall in particular, and himself above all. He was a martyr to banks and butchers, prey to unfavourable weather and animal disease. His only friends were other farmers, except that they were enemies. The men met on market days in Bodmin where they shared common grudges, beer and mutual suspicion.

As he grew up and out of the house young James terrorized the other farm animals, graduating in accordance with his weight from chickens and geese to lambs and piglets. The animals ran away as soon as they saw the grinning boy approach – whole flocks of sheep scattered across fields – but he'd corner one and tussle and tumble with it. His mother grew used to seeing a ram scampering along with her small son hanging on its back, clutching its greasy fleece, giggling.

As with animals, so it was with other children. Outgoing, gregarious, James liked to make friends normally enough: through sharing jokes and metaphysical speculations; it was just that he preferred to wrestle. When he liked someone he fixed his gaze upon them and a mischievous grin creased his face.

'Uh-oh,' said anyone who saw it, for there'd be no escape for the recipient until James had cornered them in the playground and proved his affection by holding them down with his legs wrapped around their body.

James's teachers feared the boy was simple. He took little interest in the subjects he was taught, sitting instead at the back of the class smiling patiently, waiting for playtime. As he entered double figures, however, the academically slothful child's brain was ignited by a mentor: Abraham Cann ran Bodmin wrestling club, and he explained to James that wrestling was not merely his own most instinctive behaviour but a sport with a proud history; one, moreover, with its own once thriving branch in Cornwall.

Through a combination of connoisseurs met at local tournaments, the tentacular reach of the public library service and the multiplying mind of a pubescent child, James Polkinghorne found the world open out around him. History, hitherto meaningless lists of names and dates, made sudden sense when he found out that wrestling was common to all the first great empires of civilization around the Mediterranean, along the valleys of the Nile and the Euphrates, in India and China. Geography, too, began to attain meaning. Wall paintings found in the village of Beni-Hasan, in Middle Egypt, were three or four thousand years old, yet they showed two combatants in virtually every hold of modern freestyle wrestling. Art had a purpose as well, it seemed. At twelve James discovered the Babylonian *Epic of Gilgamesh* – and so the worth of literature – in which the gods created a wild man, Enkidu, to punish the arrogant, bullying shepherd Gilgamesh. The two wrestled for hours but were perfect equals; the gods removed their enmity, they became friends and set off on adventures together.

'That's what unarmed combat's for, it do bring men together,' Abraham Cann concluded, when James related the story to his teacher.

Inheriting the hunger for learning of a Celt, along with the appetite for meaningless statistics of an English schoolboy, James memorized the thousand and one holds in classical Indian wrestling, many named after heroes mentioned in the *Mahabharata*. He understood that the population of the world is made up of different races: there were the Japanese, enormously fat men whose form of wrestling, Sumo, involved bellying each other backwards; Turks, who covered their bodies in oil and wrestled en masse, one village writhing against another; tribes of Africa where wrestling between men and women was part of the strict codes of courtship; the Mongols of Central Asia, who could wrestle on horseback, as they did in the days of Genghis Khan.

And all this before he discovered the Greeks.

Notwithstanding his burgeoning academic achievements, kindled by wrestling, James, an only child, was always going to take over the farm. And it was clear that he was growing into the opposite kind of farmer from his father: the animals were his companions and allies; the mud in which he grappled with bullocks, as they had in ancient Egypt, was the stuff from which he came; rain, sun and snow showed up as equally welcome surprises in the cycle of seasons; and he was always glad to catch up with fellow isolated farmers at market, with the hiccuping auctioneer, the lugubrious shopkeepers of Bodmin, even Mr Horne, his bank manager. James was one of those people who embraced the world, even if he liked to do so in a half nelson and a Butcher's Grip.

James grew into a sturdily built young man with dark, tightly curled hair and a rosy-cheeked vitality. He spent his spare time at the wrestling club and took part in summer tournaments all over the south-west, where he won most of his bouts but few ultimate prizes, beaten by more ruthless champions. For James Polkinghorne, whilst having all the enthusiasm of his famous namesake, lacked only the final degree of aggression necessary for dominance.

Far from satisfying his martial urges, James's training and bouts only made him eager to try out new grips and meet new opponents. His ever-present grin struck many as self-satisfied and provoked the beerily belligerent in the pubs of Bodmin on a Saturday night.

'Are you laughing at someone, you village idiot?' thugs demanded.

James was unaware he'd been smiling at all, but now his grin widened.

'Uh-oh,' said a witness.

'Yes, mate!' James declared. 'You!'

'I'll see you outside, sheep-shagger. I'll wipe that frigging grin off of your face.'

James got into countless fights away from the mat in his youth, and in some he was badly beaten, for the simple reason that he forswore the use of fists and feet as underhand methods deployed by the cloggers of Devon, never mind biting or butting. James withstood whatever punishment came his way and confined his own self-defence to the strict rules of Cornish

87

wrestling, soaking it up until he'd either achieved a legitimate submission or else been battered unconscious.

With the young women of the district James became renowned for his farmer's sunny vigour, and if his manner of seduction had more in common with the customs of the Latuko tribe than with English etiquette of the 1950s he rarely found it a problem. In barn dance or ballroom he'd fix some girl with an amorous grin ('uh-oh') and chase her out of the hall.

James tumbled in the hay with many a maiden who found his forceful embrace more persuasive than others' stumbling conversations and diffident kisses. They submitted willingly – their moans only faking pain – and offered him the victor's spoils.

He met his match in Ruth Tremain, the daughter of a Bodmin greengrocer. No sooner had he seen her at a Young Farmers' dance than James approached her with a wide-eyed grin and put her in an affectionate headlock. Ruth winded him with a sharp elbow to his midriff, twisted free, clapped his ears – which made James's head ring like a church belfry – tweaked his nose out of joint with a twist of two fingers, turned on her heel and flounced off with the full dignity of insulted honour. As he sank to his knees, the taste of blood seeping into his mouth, it occurred to James Polkinghorne that he was falling, not only to the floor but also in love.

James set out to overcome Ruth's resistance with a perseverance worthy of Jacob when he wrestled with the angel. For the first time he utilized conventional forms of courtship: subtle messages via mutual acquaintances, carefully contrived chance meetings, deliveries of sweaty flowers and bad poetry, awkward conversations on the chapel steps, chaperoned Sunday afternoon walks on Cardinham Moor. His persistence paid off and Ruth allowed him their first kiss in the back row of the St Austell Odeon watching *Vertigo* early in 1959.

Once they were going steady, however, James slyly introduced an arm-wrestling element to their lovers' embraces, at first as an ironic reminder of that first meeting, which Ruth found as funny as he did only to realize too late that the joke had somehow been extended to a brief contest – one fall or one submission – that took the place of a normal greeting each time they met. Her suitor was irrepressible. And the trouble was, by then she had fallen for him too.

Simon Polkinghorne died too young, anxiety-ridden, worn down and out. James took over and the small farm thrived. His dairy cows gave rich and plentiful milk because he believed in massaging them when they were in melancholy moods and his bullocks grew powerful flanks and sides of beef. The pigs were veritable porkers, since they were generally intelligent enough to see the funny side of wrestling with a human being, and snuffled and snorted their way through their brief lives. Only sheep abhorred their playful shepherd's attentions; James Polkinghorne's sparse flocks were even more highly strung than is usual for their species, and dashed away terrified at the sight of him.

Ruth Tremain consented to become a farmer's wife after confirming that she was pregnant, and shortly thereafter followed her soon-to-be-born son down the aisle of the tin tabernacle, the Methodist chapel of Bodmin, to join her bridegroom James Polkinghorne in marriage.

The Polkinghornes' first child was a boy whom they

christened Jacob for obvious reasons, and James was disappointed in him from the beginning.

'Look at all that dimply-dumply fat on him,' he complained. 'It be no shape for a wrestler,' James reckoned, as Jake remained a placid overweight bovine child, moony and ruminative, who seemed content to follow his mother around or else stare out of the window, chewing the cud of his cheeks.

After the rumbustious, rough and tumble days of their courtship Ruth decreed that it was undignified to fight with a wedding ring on, and pregnancy solidified her resistance. James accepted this state of affairs and awaited his Jacob's growth until he could teach him to wrestle. Whenever his father dropped down on the floor to play with him, however, Jacob burst into tears. As soon as he learned to walk he staggered away from his father into a corner of the kitchen like a frightened lamb. His first recognizable sentence was: 'I submit.'

The next birth was more propitious. It had been a wretched pregnancy for Ruth because the child inside her was hyperactive, jumping and kicking from the moment it sprouted limbs.

'It's like having hiccups all the time,' Ruth complained. 'Like sneezes in my belly.'

When the twins were born James rubbed his hands with happiness, as he did before a bout.

'That do explain it,' he told Ruth. 'They were wrestling in the womb.'

The twins were called Charles and Paul, which was as close as James could reasonably get to what he'd rather have called them: Castor and Pollux, after the Gemini twins, the Greek deities of wrestling. As the boys grew, they'd beseech their father to tell them the story of their namesakes: of their valour in the

Calydonian hunt, and of how they came to represent a sign of the Zodiac.

'One of the twins was a mortal,' James began, sitting on the porch one summer night.

'That's me!' said Charles.

'Castor was slain by the sons of Aphareus,' James continued, 'and his brother Pollux—'

'—that's me!' said Paul.

'Pollux was immortal, and he implored Zeus to allow him to die as well, so that he would not be parted from his brother. This proof of fraternal affection so touched the father of the gods that he permitted Castor to return to life.'

The boys gazed at each other, their mutual love as great as the mythical twins'.

'Later on, Zeus transferred them both to the skies, where they do form a bright constellation we can still see to this day.'

From the beginning the identical twins were as boisterous as Jake was docile. They threw themselves onto the mat under their father's instruction.

''Tis like watching a man wrestling with himself,' James enthused, as what made them easy to train was that, being the same height and weight, they were a perfect match for each other. James declared: 'You're giving me double vision, boys.'

They were soon able to beat their ponderous older brother, whose only useful role was a prototype Sumo: Jacob hadn't an ounce of martial menace in him but he had a good few stone of fat which, with the help of gravity, was hard to shift, and James had his younger boys develop their strength by locking antlers with the reluctant Jake on the floor of the barn.

'Strength. Agility. Courage. Those be what a wrestler needs,' James explained. 'And nerve.'

That last quality was nurtured in what was James's innovation for his sons' improvement: a chamber, dug into the side of the hill behind the house, whose entrance was padded in such a way that, once sealed, the chamber was pitch black.

'This', James told his sons, 'be our own palaestra. You'll learn to wrestle in the dark. Once you can do that you'll be able to beat any of the other lads. With your eyes closed. When you're out on the mat there's no-one can help you. You're all alone out there. Be a Cornish boy afeared of no-one, like Corineus.'

He told them of the great Cornish hero's fight with Gogmagog. 'The daughters of the Roman Emperor Diocletian', he recounted, 'murdered their husbands, and were set adrift in a ship that eventually reached the shores of Albion. The offspring of those perfidious women were the English giants, and the last of these was Gogmagog. Twelve feet tall he was, and so strong he could give an oak tree a shake and pull it up as though it were a hazel wand. He fought and beat every strong man in England.'

The boys hissed and booed.

'Now Gogmagog heard of Corineus, and he came down to Cornwall to wrestle with him. They met on a cliff top. Each twined his arms about the other, the air vibrated with their panting breath. Gogmagog roared like a lion, gripped Corineus with all his might and cracked three of his ribs. Well of course Corineus was infuriated. He heaved Gogmagog up onto his shoulders and hurled the giant off the cliff: he plummeted to the rocks below and was dashed into a thousand pieces, staining the waters red with his blood.

'Gogmagog's Leap,' James told his cheering sons. 'As it be known to this day.'

James was preparing the twins for competition,

although he knew the sad truth was that by this time Cornish wrestling had long since dwindled to a parochial activity. Men of Cornwall had marched behind Henry V at Agincourt under a banner depicting two wrestlers in a hold. Cornishmen made up the entire team of English wrestlers who beat the elite of France before Henry VIII at the meeting at the Field of the Cloth of Gold. For hundreds of years Cornish wrestlers fought men of Brittany as a means of settling fishing disputes.

In the nineteenth century, however, the sport began to decline with the exodus of young men seeking work elsewhere, and the hostility of Methodists – whose foolhardy ministers entered the ring in the middle of tournaments and commenced singing and praying.

Revivals took place periodically, through energetic men like James's own coach, Abraham Cann. Now, with his identical twins, James reckoned it was his turn; he fancied he might even introduce an innovation, tag-team wrestling, into the Cornish tradition with his mighty midgets.

Barely noticed by her father, the boys had been joined by a new sibling: one to whom James paid scant attention, for she was a girl.

'She can keep that mollycoddled milksop Jacob company,' he told Ruth.

'Leave my Jake alone,' Ruth replied. 'Anyway, look at her. She looks just like you.'

This was true. Martha was a bouncy bundle of fizz and vip, with tightly curled hair – though blond rather than black – and the rosy-cheeked complexion of a Cox's orange pippin. Martha, however, was the apple of no-one's eye. Jacob, startled by her abrupt gestures and excited exclamations, hid behind his mother's skirts, and Ruth told her to go outside. Which she did, only for her disconcerted father to order her to stop distracting the twins from their training and get back indoors. Charles and Paul, when their father's back was turned, let their sister play with them, because it helped develop their strength and co-ordination to play catch with her, and, unlike a medicine ball, when they dropped her she rarely rolled away.

All Martha wanted was to join in. She scrutinized the twins' practice and lay in wait, tripping them as they passed through doorways, charging them without warning with bowed head aimed at their midriffs, and climbing on top of furniture for a vantage point from which to drop like a monkey onto their backs.

Her perplexed father retreated once more into his library in a corner of the front room and discovered to his surprise something that had hitherto entirely escaped his attention.

'I be gone back to the Greeks,' James explained to Ruth upon his re-emergence, 'and would you believe? There were many fighting women. Artemis, goddess of the moon but also of the hunt, twin sister of Apollo and his equal in beauty, intelligence and power.'

The children gathered round their father by the back porch.

'Artemis fell in love but once, with the youthful hunter Orion, whom she met in the forest and whom she hunted with and loved. But her brother was seized with jealousy. One day Apollo did summon her to his side and began to talk of archery. Under the pretext of testing her skill as a markswoman, he challenged her to shoot at a dark speck rising and falling far out at sea.

'Artemis seized her bow, feathered an arrow, and sent it with perfect force and accurate aim, and saw the speck vanish beneath the waves, little suspecting that .

the dark head of Orion, bathing in the sea, had been given her as a target.'

Jacob wiped away a tear, Martha sat transfixed, the twins enthralled.

'When she discovered her error, Artemis mourned Orion's death with loud lamentations, vowed never to forget him, and placed him and his faithful dog Sirius as constellations in the sky.'

'Just like us!' said Charles.

'Castor and Pollux!' said Paul.

'Yes, there they are, very close to each other,' James pointed. 'Then of course,' he continued, 'there be the Amazons, a whole nation of warrior women, who cut off their right breasts the better to use bow and arrow. They fought in a kind of early chain mail, tight-fitting garments with chequered and zig-zagged patterns which were meant to intimidate their enemies.'

James frowned. 'But I do believe that the best example', he said, 'is Atalanta. Her father was so disappointed that she was not a boy that he took the newborn babe and left her in the forest. What a dreadful thing to do, is it not?'

The wide-eyed children nodded dumbly.

'But instead of dying of starvation or being eaten by wild animals, the baby was suckled and nursed by a bear, until one day some huntsmen found her and brought her up as one of their own. And so the girl grew up hunting amid the hills and valleys of Arkadia.

'Atalanta was as chaste and as beautiful as she was fleet of foot, and skilled in the arts of war. With her bow and arrows she slew three centaurs who tried to ravage her. At the funeral games of Pelias she entered the wrestling arena and threw Peleus, father of Achilles. In the Calydonian hunt – yes, boys, where Castor and Pollux too did prove their honour – she was

95

the first to wound the great boar. She joined the heroes in the voyage of the Argo, and was wounded in battle. And later, many men died as the penalty of losing races with her, in the attempt to become her husband, until Melanion sought the help of Aphrodite, goddess of love. She gave him three golden apples, with which Melanion distracted Atalanta, who kept stopping to pick them up. Melanion won the race, and Atalanta married him.

'Plutarch advocated that girls as well as boys should wrestle in the palaestra,' James concluded. 'And so, children, do I.'

Martha reached the wall of the garden she'd been plotting a course towards. This garden was larger than any of the ones she'd traversed, with a small orchard, a vegetable patch and a shrubbery to negotiate before she reached the lawn. Martha crouched and listened. In the distance a car passed, just within the perimeter of her hearing, in cinematic slow motion, an aural glide. When it had gone the silence settled deeper. Martha stood up and walked straight across the middle of the wide lawn. She was sure there was no-one to see her. She was invisible.

A few yards from the four-storey house rose an ash tree, from whose highest branches Martha reckoned she could reach a dormer window. That calculation had been made through binoculars from a playing field a quarter of a mile away. From the base of the tree the real task looked more formidable: still, its feasibility could only be ascertained in the attempt.

The lowest branches began twenty feet up from the ground. Martha had to climb the unbroken trunk to reach them. She uncoiled two lengths of strong nylon sash each wrapped half a dozen times round her waist, and passed them both around the tree trunk. She bound the ends of one to the ends of the other, looped them behind her and, with her feet planted against the trunk, pushed her posterior back against the ties. Martha began to climb, flicking one of the belts a few inches higher, leaning back to let it take her weight, then easing the lower cord up and transferring her weight to that one.

Martha hugged her way up the tree trunk to the lowest branches. She slipped out of her cradle and lowered it to the ground on a thin string which she tied to a branch by a knot that she could pull free from below with one yank.

Ash: leafless now but saplessly brittle. Its rough bark gave reasonable grip and its main arterial branches were strong, but smaller ones could snap like wafers. Martha climbed rapidly right by the trunk until she reached a height parallel with the roof. The ground had receded dramatically; a great urban vista spread out below. Here, the trunk separated into three divergent branches, one of which veered towards the roof, up and over the dormer window. Martha eased her way along it, and it began to bend. She had only a few yards to gain, but how strong was the branch? If it broke, Martha knew, it wouldn't groan and slowly tear: there'd be a sudden crack, releasing her to plunge towards gravity's ever-hungry pull.

Martha inched higher than the flat dormer roof but was still six feet or so away from it. She had to keep climbing the branch that dangled over the roof and hope her weight would bring it drooping down. She decided to hang from the branch by her hands: leaned on it as if on the top rung of a gate and slowly rolled her body down off it, trying not to jerk and snap the wood.

Martha muscled her hanging body along the branch. With every inch she gained so the branch bent and lowered her towards the flat roof of the window. The ash tree twisted and creaked in the cold moonlight. Martha tried to focus on a crack of the branch breaking, to anticipate it, to be ready to scrabble for safety if she were to plummet, as she swung along.

The Polkinghorne farm nestled in a fold within a crooked valley. It was shaded by a mulchy, mossy wood where mushrooms and fungi grew out of black soil, with a brackish marsh at its heart; in front, a stream piddled in summer, or gushed brown-watered in spate; behind, small hedged pastures rose up towards the moor.

'We live in the lap of the earth,' Ruth told her daughter. 'We're hidden here and protected from the world.'

Martha assisted Ruth and Jacob in the moist and steamy kitchen where something was always roasting, stewing, simmering. She helped her twin brothers with the movement of grazing animals to and fro, to and fro, between sloping fields and farmyard: the parody of or perhaps homage to nomadism in domesticated husbandry. Martha liked to help her father at birthing times; an unsqueamish, clear-headed girl, she pulled reluctant lambs slithering in yellow placenta from their failing mothers or comforted anxious cows whose wild eyes revealed the sudden threat of birth-stopped extinction.

Martha appreciated the way her father treated his livestock. He patted and stroked and hugged the calves; nudged and cajoled his sheep. The milking cows he spoke to, constantly, in a one-sided inconsequential conversation, and it was easy to imagine they understood every word, they simply ignored him like ancient spouses who'd heard it all before; they couldn't be bothered to reply, but still, it was comforting to them, their master's burbling monologue.

The twins could be cruel to udder-swaying cows ambling too slow to milking, or fretful ram butting itself against pen, and struck callously. But their father never did. James was indulgent: the animals didn't take his time, they made it. On this farm time, as far as he was concerned, was aligned less to lunar chronometry than the to and fro procession of animal movement.

There was time, however, for play. As well as the blacked-out pit – the Polkinghornes' palaestra – James cleared a space for a wrestling room in the middle of the hay loft in the big barn, with a mat of heavy duty plastic tacked tight down over a filling of straw. There the fighting members of the family – James, the twins and Martha – mounted, many evenings and weekends; close, musty, chaff-prickly, sweltering in summer, beneath a single lamp's white cone of light they strove and strained and grunted.

Each session however short began with exercises: skipping, counting press- and sit-ups, stretching and, most importantly, bridging: all four of them put their hands behind their backs and rested their foreheads on the mat, with legs apart and backsides in the air; they then rocked backwards and forwards on their heads. They looked to Jacob like thwarted, ridiculous philosophers, grappling with some insurmountable conundrum. In fact they were strengthening the muscles of the neck; preparing to grapple with each other.

'You want a bull neck like me, boys,' James enthused. 'You too, girl, I suppose.'

As the boys grew towards competing age James accepted that Cornish wrestling was a viable sport no more, its rules antique, and so he taught them freestyle that they could partake in tournaments once they reached the age of twelve.

'You can win with one fall, keeping both your opponent's shoulders in contact with the mat for the count of one-two, the referee hitting the mat with his hand two times.'

'That's just like Cornish almost, Dad,' said Martha.

'Yes, and we'll work on that, always. But the fact is most bouts have no falls: they're actually decided on points. You accumulate points for achieving correct throws and holds, for dominating your opponent in brief snatches. Build up your score-card: that be the secret of success in freestyle. But I'll teach you to achieve falls, because that's our tradition. And you know why else?'

'Why else, Father?'

'Because there be nothing like it,' James laughed, 'it's the best feeling in the world, bringing an opponent over your shoulder, you've just jerked your body and he be flying, and then he's down winded and you're atop and pinning him. Ah, I love it so. And so will you, my beauties.'

Charles and Paul, the identical twins, fought each other under James's guidance, over and over (literally: a series of rolling falls and bridges, for five seconds continuously, earned three points), but they also let their little sister be a sparring partner. Out of fraternal indulgence they had her put them in the first grip of a ground throw and tried to struggle free of it. The nelsons, the cradle hold, ground Lancashire turn: time after time, on dark winter evenings in a pool of cold white light or on hot, sticky summer days Martha pinned one or other of her brothers down on the straw-filled mat. She'd trap his head and neck, wrap her arms through armpit groin knee, join hands in a Butcher's Grip and strain to press his shoulders hard against the mat for a count of one-two, while he struggled to find avenues of escape between her torso and limbs.

Martha learned alongside the twins to take the wrestling stance: feet well apart, knees bent and loose, body leaning forward from the hips, elbows well in at the sides, hands up.

'Be loose, be ready,' James exhorted them. 'Stiffness be the enemy of movement, agility and speed. And in wrestling, speed is of the essence: speed of mind and body.'

Martha mastered the initial hold: like a rugby player engaging in a scrum, she placed her right hand behind a brother's neck, her left forearm in the crook of his right arm, forehead against his right shoulder. From this stance two combatants feel each other out, probing for openings with nudge of shoulder, twist of hip, flick of foot; preparing to rebut or evade the other's aggression. The mind assessing, conjecturing, calculating. Tremendous endeavour, with little to show.

Martha took to the sport. It felt as if the rules were being less dictated to than invented for her. Like her endomorphic father she had more flesh on her muscle than the ectomorphic twins, who were wiry and fast as whips, with a supple sinewy strength, and she learned at the receiving end the cross-buttock throw, the leg pick-up and back heel, the double thigh pick-up, the cross ankle take-down. The flying mare: a standing throw in which from innocent hold the lamp hanging from the ceiling suddenly swung into orbit, the roof of the barn spun and then her body thudded on the hard knobbly mat. She couldn't expect to exact revenge on her older, taller twin brothers but she relished enough the avoidance of such a throw: tucking tight into them, counteracting their every move within the moment they made it, so that as long as it lasted the bout became a dance, two synchronized minds two bodies tangoing in intimate combat, until the inevitable, lurching disjunction of a fall. Martha loved it, not masochistically the conclusion but the wrestling itself, her mind taut in concentration and her body rubbing over sweat, skin, hair; measuring muscle, tendon, bone of your opponent; almost as if grappling was a medium as much as air or water, and one she felt at home in.

James was both coach and referee, like the football one they saw on a rare visit to the cinema in St Austell, a schoolteacher who thought he was Bobby Charlton and took the penalty he'd awarded himself – played by a Yorkshire actor James recognized scornfully, a professional wrestler who called himself Erik Tanberg, the Swedish Blond Bomber. 'They fight in a ring, like boxers,' James derided.

Like the referee in the film, though, James could not restrain himself from joining in, and ended each training session with three against one, the children attacking their father and trying to bring the man-bull down.

Martha saw why James needed to be a referee as well as a coach, though: the penalty system of fouls and cautions by which points were docked was as complex as that for scoring points positively. A bewildering number of acts and manoeuvres were prohibited in freestyle wrestling, from head-butting, kicking and pulling an opponent's private parts to clinging to the mat; from seizing the sole of your rival's foot to touching his face between eyebrows and mouth; from scissor grips to the head, neck or body to speaking to one's adversary. James proved to be an eagle-eyed stickler for the rules. No child of his could claim it wasn't fair; the twins became as a result soon renowned for their sportsmanship when, aged twelve, they began entering at junior grade tournaments organized by the British Amateur Wrestling Association.

Martha accompanied her father and brothers to tournaments across the southern counties. In their first season success outweighed failure. The boys both had their father's exuberance in equal measure as well as a secret weapon: his version of the Cornish hug, an embrace of the opponent as apparently unthreatening as and remarkably similar to a ballroom clinch, as if asking one's partner to dance, only to turn with a sudden bump of the waist and roll of the hip into a dramatic standing throw. Many a boy found himself spun unexpectedly from vertical to horizontal by one of the Cornish twins. Twins who, moreover, possessed by being identical another advantage: lads who came up against them a second or third time could not recall with certainty the subtle strengths and weaknesses perhaps once encountered, that can make the difference between well-matched combatants.

At the tournaments whose spectators were mostly friends and family Martha was just another little sister along for the ride, bored girls who made contact with each other in the corridors of sports halls. Martha, however, disdained female company: this odd girl scrutinized her brothers' bouts, and all the others too. She knew the rules as well as they, the holds and throws. Curious, outgoing, she chatted easily with people; it was just that instead of scurrying off to skip or catch ball with other female siblings she preferred to discuss tactics with a cauliflower-eared old timer, or some competing boy's chances with his father. She

103

identified with the combatants, except that there was something missing, and the time came when she could no longer deny what that was: there were no girls wrestling, no women; at junior, intermediate or even senior level. At first she'd thought it was just this tournament, then that one. She said nothing and neither did James, until driving westward home from Dorset one evening the boys fell asleep on the back seat, and Martha sobbed in the front.

'Why not, Daddy?' she pleaded. 'You always said I had a right to fight like Paul and Charlie. You know I work as hard as they do and I bet I'm just as good as they were when they were my size.'

'You are, darling,' James assured her.

'I don't understand,' she complained. 'You told me how it was. You said that women took part in the bull vaulting at Cretan festivals.'

'They did.'

'You said that girls did the same training as boys in Sparta, wrestling naked, their bodies oiled.'

'True, my dearest; and running, and discus and javelin throwing.'

'That women wrestled in the Etruscan games.'

'Yes, and there were female gladiators in imperial Rome. I know. I'm afraid times changed for the worse, child. I don't know when it happened.'

'It's not fair, Daddy,' Martha moaned.

'Well, perhaps things will improve. Women be doing all sorts of things their mothers didn't used to. I'll do what I can, girl. I'll put a word in here and there. You keep training, and we'll cross our fingers.'

'Is it worth it, Daddy?'

'Of course it be. You know what we say: walk in hope or you walks backwards.'

And so Martha continued training with her

trophy-hunting brothers, to pin them down in winning grips from which they muscled their way free. Occasionally they let her take them on on equal terms and felled her in withering seconds; the brothers competed with their sister mercilessly. Just once in front of their father Martha pinned Paul down for a winning fall. From grappling in front of each other on the ground, Paul made the arrogant mistake of lying over Martha with both his hands around her body. She reached back and seized his arms, trapped them above the elbow; then pushed up and turned to the side, twisting Paul over with his chest to her back and his back to the mat, his arms securely locked all the while. Both Paul's shoulders remained in contact with the mat for the count of one-two: James hit the mat with his hand two times.

As Martha, her face split with a grin, relaxed her victorious grip, Paul flailed free in an explosion of vindictive fury. Martha was thrown off the mat and cartwheeled headfirst into one of the barn's timber posts. The blood would eventually stop flowing, the pain lessen. The swollen bruise would after many days subside, its infernal colours fade. But the vertical cut above the middle of Martha's right eye would leave for ever a narrow ridge of scar tissue, dissecting her eyebrow in half.

In the pitch-black pit, Martha was less overawed than on the mat. Physically, she couldn't match her brothers but, as James had said, nerve was the most important quality in his palaestra, and Martha proved to have plenty of that. Considering her bumptiousness outside, stealth came surprisingly easily, her breathing inaudible, her footsteps silent; no chattering teeth, sweating glands, trembling muscles. Perhaps fear did not occur to her.

Once she was inside the pit with an opponent and James had sealed the door, Martha closed her blind eyes and her remaining senses quickened. She could smell the other person's anxiety to her left or hear his singlet rustle to her right or feel his breath on the back of her neck. Martha moved silently, assessing her opponent's position, biding her time, calmly choosing the moment to strike; sometimes pinning her brother and gaining the fall she never could in the open. In a bout there was no such thing as a submission: to even attempt one was a stipulated offence and brought a caution. But in the pit James allowed for it because that chamber was not designed to learn wrestling techniques but rather the psychological warfare between two human beings that's intrinsic to every martial art.

'You can have the quickest brain and swiftest feet in the world,' James told his children. 'But if you be scared of your opponent, he'll beat you.'

Martha gained occasional victories in the pit, from her brothers – for which she paid later – but more often from their friends. They came to play with the twins, were introduced to the Polkinghornes' palaestra, and challenged to step inside by the boys' kid sister. There, they flailed about, grabbed at shadows, began to panic in the darkness, to lash out – Martha avoiding their blind blows, having barely to touch them herself; would soon enough submit gratefully if someone anyone would just open that door.

James released them, grinning proudly.

'That's a torture chamber, not a wrestling room,' they'd blubber, clambering onto their bikes and wobbling away.

The branch of the ash tree held, drooped obligingly, lowered Martha onto the flat roof of the dormer window. When she let it go, the branch swung back up into the air in a leisurely arc.

Lying on the dormer roof Martha leaned over and cut a hole in a central pane of glass. With a suction pad she pulled it out, reached in and opened the casement window. Then she pulled herself back up, rotated her body, and curved feet first inside.

The room Martha entered had the wet chalky smell of recently applied emulsion paint. In the thin beam of Martha's torch cream walls, a corn-coloured carpet. A single table and chair the only furniture as yet. Large boxes waiting to be unpacked: electrical appliances. Fujitsu, Sony, Hansoi.

Martha descended the stairs, thick carpet cushioning her footsteps. She paused on the first floor landing. The silence of a house in which people are sleeping has a texture, she'd discovered, a certain density, due possibly to the faint, subconsciously audible sound of their breathing. But now suddenly Martha thought she could hear another sound, coming from inside a closed room. This one to her left, maybe. Rooted to the spot, she attempted rapidly to identify the sound: snoring? Talking? Or was it walking? A dramatic click. The door was opening. Martha backed precipitately through an open door behind her, scanned the room: of course, a bathroom. Why else would the door be open? Her mind racing; her pulse calm. The footsteps outside, approaching. Where to hide? She saw a shower cubicle.

Groggy feet on the wooden floorboards. The blink of a pull cord switch and light splashed the room. A male groan, and the room blacked out again. The man stumbled diagonally across the spacious bathroom. A shuffling, groping pause, then he slumped heavily on the toilet seat. Another, milder groan, another pause. Dribbling piss, on porcelain then on water.

The toilet was almost opposite the shower cubicle. If he let his reluctant eyes open, might the man discern her dark form through frosted glass? No, he was surely parked there with eyes closed; sleepy head on hands in the darkness. Unless he was insomniac and wide awake. She didn't want to hurt an old man. Martha listened. The man's stream guttered, dried up. Then he broke wind with a brief exclamation mark of a fart. He stood up with a sigh, fumbled with pyjamas, and pottered back to the bedroom, whose door he closed thoughtfully, Martha reckoned. So as not to wake a partner. Who'd none the less have woken already, she figured. She stepped out of the shower cubicle and bathroom and slipped downstairs.

The Polkinghornes were an irrepressible family. James in his mid-forties enjoyed ruddy health, as did his farm, not to mention his wife, Ruth, who'd put on more weight than he had, in sympathy perhaps with the son who was nearest to her. After a childhood in her kitchen Jacob left school and attended a catering course at the local college of further education. The Gemini twins at fourteen were as close as their name-sakes in the firmament: they achieved identical grades at school, and occasionally they faced one another in the finals of wrestling tournaments – along with a third opponent, because the final is fought between three contestants – when they took it in turns to beat each other. But neither Charles nor Paul won many trophies.

Martha, James reflected ruefully, probably would; if she could only find an opponent, she'd beat her. Blond Martha was shorter and more solid than her brothers, with a lower centre of gravity, which women tend to have anyway. If competitors didn't have to attend their weigh-in naked, it had occurred to James more than once, with a little packing of her singlet with chicken giblets she could masquerade as a boy. He sympathized with her.

Martha hoped against hope that come her twelfth birthday – the age at which boys can take part in organized competition – things might change. And they did, though not as she had prayed for. She stopped speaking, for one thing. Not absolutely; she didn't become mute; but she altered from bouncy girl to sullen adolescent. And the reason was apparent enough, Ruth surmised. Tight curls of hair spreading on her thighs; twin mounds rising powerful as soft dough at her chest; sweating armpits; brown bloodstains on her knickers.

'Our girl's growing up, poor thing,' Ruth told her husband.

Just as with her first pregnancy Ruth Polkinghorne née Tremain had forsaken playful tussling with her husband, so after her last had she decided to desist from sex, refusing James's advances.

'We've enough children and surely you'll agree as a good Methodist that the act of procreation is for nothing else.'

'I certainly do not agree,' James averred. 'What of my conjugal rights?' he demanded. 'And yours?'

'You know what the twins' birth did to me down there, James. And Martha's finished me off. None of them were as easy as Jake. I've been torn and stitched and wounded and I'm sorry. It's uncomfortable and unpleasant.'

James's carnal appetite pressed upon him and he besieged his expanding wife with seductive overtures and plaintive appeals. She relented on odd anniversaries, only to lie like a torpid cow on their marital bed and martyrishly tolerate his thrashing about. She

109

took no pleasure and gave James none; he preferred to console himself.

James had had to wait some years for his sons to grow large enough to begin to satisfy his martial desires – making do with bullocks and occasional Saturday night fights outside the pubs of Bodmin. He waited twelve years for his last-born to appease his carnal needs. James came to his daughter one evening, late, when the house slept with that earned content-ment of a farm. Martha woke and assumed with sudden clarity that he had come to help her face the inevitable, and offer sympathy.

'It's not going to happen, is it, Daddy?' Martha asked.

'No, it's not, sweetheart,' he had to agree, sitting on the bed, holding her hand. 'Women do not wrestle. Maybe one day they will again, maybe your daughters will, but it be not for you. You should give up now. In Sparta, in Greece, even when girls did attend the palaestra they stopped sporting activities once they became women. So should you, Martha.'

'What, even with the twins?' she exclaimed.

'With them certainly. There are other pleasures for a woman,' James assured her.

James's hand quivered across his daughter's body; he took her hand and led it on a similar journey. Who knows what went through his mind? Perhaps the way he saw it, Martha's birth had robbed James of sex, so she was obliged to recompense him; perhaps he convinced himself that Martha would gain pleasure as other young women once had – as Ruth once had – from him.

That first night James guided Martha's mouth to his groin bursting with the pent-up need of twelve years. Martha took her father's unbearable burden and felt bitter slithering seed spurt into her mouth. She became quiet from that moment on.

It would be a Saturday night routine. Some time after everyone had gone to bed James Polkinghorne rose again and drifted along the corridor to his daughter's room. Martha never screamed. She lay praying he would stay away, while hoping her prayers would absolve her and he would come and give her the heat they made. She begged her father to leave, she pushed him off but he pressed himself upon her and her resistance subsided.

So it went on. Martha became a shy loner, reclusive, the gregarious child withdrew inside. She no longer watched her brothers compete on the wrestling mat or joined them in the dark chamber. She envied and resented them, and would try to work out whether or not it was possible that they didn't know what befell her every Saturday night.

Just once, when she was fourteen, she confronted her mother, in the kitchen one Monday afternoon when they were alone in the house. Mouth dry, blood pounding in her ears, Martha stated quietly: 'You know what he's doing, Mum.'

'How dare you suggest such a thing,' Ruth admonished her daughter. 'You've a filthy mind just like him.'

'Mum, he does. He comes into my room, into my bed. You must know he does,' Martha cried.

'I shan't listen to this wickedness,' Ruth shrieked. 'Get out of my kitchen. Wash yourself clean, you little slattern. Be gone.'

From nestling in the bosom of her family Martha was marooned in its empty heart. After homework and the chores of a farmer's daughter she went out whenever she could, off on her own, walking to Cardinham Moor or bicycling to Bodmin Moor where with increasing frequency she made her way to the tors: Garrow, Kilmar, Rough. She climbed them and sat hunched into herself on top, gazing vacantly across the empty moorland. Gradually, though, she spent more time on the climb itself. Rather than scuttling up the quickest path she scanned the rocks for trickier routes. Climbing alone, unroped, untutored, Martha lost herself in concentration on the granite faces of the Cornish tors; she found herself in the methodical assessment of toe- and finger-holds, in the slow ascent alone, in the controlled exhilaration of danger. She was barred from martial exercise, from grappling with an opponent, but she found a solitary sport for which she now exercised as rigorously as she once had with the twins. At home, while they trained in the barn, Martha slipped into the chamber and closed the door behind her.

In order to prepare for her practice Martha initiated research: just as James had amassed his history books and his arcane wrestling manuals, so Martha took books from the library on human anatomy and studied the muscles of the body, in order to stretch and strengthen her own. In doing so she discovered in herself the same hunger for learning that her father possessed. Poring over the books in her bedroom she read that the function of muscles is to produce or control the movement of joints; she understood that the human body is fundamentally a skeleton, and the purpose of muscles is to serve it.

While Martha read, she kneaded plastic balls in her hand to fortify her fingers and, barefoot, exercised her toes. Then, in the comforting darkness of the pit Martha walked on and off tiptoes to strengthen her calves; sat and lifted, flexed, rotated her legs to build up her quadriceps; lay on her front and bent knees up behind her for the hamstrings; lay on her back, pressed its small into the floor, tilted pelvis backwards and pulled stomach in for the strengthening of her abdomen; flattened herself against the wall, sliding arms up and down against it, for the trapezius and rhomboid. As she extended each exercise, in number and difficulty, the pain that informed her of the transformation in each muscle changed in character, from unwelcome to pleasing sensation. Out on the rock face Martha hauled herself by clinical, extended degrees upward against gravity's pull, while back in the inky nothingness of the pit she methodically stretched herself for hour after silent hour, controlling the inhalations and exhalations of her lungs, sweating profusely. James would come with the twins to use his palaestra hours afterwards and find it rank and moist with condensation, and wasted days of digging trying to find out where the rising damp had come from.

The climbing and training made Martha stronger than wrestling would have. But not yet strong enough. She put on weight, little of it fat, until at fifteen she looked more than ever like a younger version of her father but with blond hair. When he came to her room on his weekly visits it must have been a little like meeting a female version of himself, Narcissus spilling his seed upon the water, distressing his own reflection. Martha retreated into her adolescence, behind plain, unprepossessing features, hair cropped without care, diffident, awkward. She withdrew into an inconspicuous youth (would only begin to re-emerge, a handsome woman, in her twenties).

Still every week Martha pleaded with her father, resisted, relented. But though she didn't struggle overmuch she measured each time her father's strength against her own, growing. And the day came, when she was sixteen, that she sensed he'd become heavier yet but infinitesimally weaker.

The following week James came to Martha's room

and for the first time found it empty. He was stunned with anger then panic, till he saw a note on the counterpane: 'Come to the pit.' Unsuspecting and addicted, James obeyed the instruction, and crept out of the house to where Martha awaited him.

'Close the door, Daddy,' she murmured, and he sealed off the moonlight.

'Come and find me, Daddy,' Martha whispered, and he tried. Only she wasn't there. He looked for her everywhere, groping blindly, but she'd melted into the darkness, except that every now and then she repeated: 'Daddy, come and find me,' from behind him. He turned and clutched at her body only to find she'd disappeared. She'd bathed without soap and gave off no body odour; moved with feline stealth and made no sound. The first time she struck him James thought it was a joke, that his daughter was teasing him. Before terror crept into his heart, and succeeding blows convinced him.

Wrestling: despite her four years' suspension from the sport Martha remembered all she'd been taught. James had drilled it into her. She recalled every foul, prohibited move and used them all. She stamped on her father's foot, elbowed and kneed him in the abdomen, squeezed his ears, gripped his throat, twisted his fingers. While James tried to defend himself from shadows Martha brawled, kicked and throttled. She applied holds liable to endanger life and fracture or dislocate limbs; she bent her opponent's arm more than ninety degrees. She scissor-gripped his head and followed a full nelson with a punishing head-lock.

And Martha spoke to her opponent, another serious offence worthy of a caution: 'Daddy, Daddy, you're the only one I love and I want to kill you, but I won't. Put it in me now, why don't you. Where is it, Daddy? But it's soft and small now, make it big for me, let me take it inside me and I'll squeeze the life from your body.'

In the darkness Martha beat her father. The twins found him in the morning, drawn to the pit by the smell of blood. And Martha gone. She'd bicycled away, left home once and for ever, and they knew to let her go. She would never see any of her family again, and took with her only cash, clothes and a question she'd never be able to ask her mother: why had Ruth sacrificed her; why had her mother abandoned her?

Downstairs, Martha looked through a dining-room, a sitting-room, the hall, scanning walls with the thin beam of her torch, with increasing dismay. Her fence had told her that the owner of this house was some great-nephew-in-law once removed of William Blake who'd inherited a single specimen of his ancestor's works. He'd added a taste of his own for cheap eighteenth- and nineteenth-century British paintings, which Martha was to ignore in favour of the genuine heirloom. The legendary lost engraving, Blake's frontispiece for the one, almost but in fact not quite complete copy of the original edition of *Jerusalem*. No, not the dreary endless epic poem of that name, her man said: 'And did those feet' comes from the preface to his other masterpiece, *Milton*.

The story Martha was told was that the present owner's branch of the family had kept their possession of this engraving secret from the rest of the family, let alone the world at large, ever since Blake's death. An ancestral duplicity, handed down from one generation to the next. An inherited guile and deceit. The beauty of which was that they'd be unable to complain of its theft.

A buyer was lined up, a collector who'd accepted that Blake's original copperplate had been lost but maintained the existence of a solitary engraving Blake had taken from it himself. He'd already commissioned articles and inquiries in order to flush the engraving out, had paid investigative writers to interview known descendants of the artist. He was a man who believed rumours even when he was most responsible for circulating them. The prospect of a lucrative sale, even a secret one, had, however, proved less appealing to the present owner than keeping it in, and from, the family. There's an aristocratic tradition, Phil said, of feuds between cousins.

The buyer, it turned out, appeared to be right about the work's existence. An ex-art student who worked as a cleaner had seen it in this house, she claimed. The buyer had not only the money ready but a time and a place in which to unveil the engraving. It was a find of millennial significance, he proclaimed; its popularity would be immeasurable, this illustration for the greatest work by a people's painter of his time and our time. A find for the new Jerusalem.

Martha passed ornate frames enclosing lurid scenes of naval mayhem. Portraits of unwell nobility. Landscapes of bucolic England and of mythical Greece that had in common the presence of similar ruins in the background. Animals: bulls, rams, sheep of exaggerated, wondrous shape and size. Patrons flattered by kowtowing itinerant painters? Outlandish blueprints for a farming society drunk on the lucrative possibilities of animal breeding? Far from her father's farm.

There were so many paintings, Martha began to doubt she'd recognize what she was looking for, from her memory of a sketch by the art student cleaner.

Then she came to a small study, whose walls bore not paintings but qualifications: thick black penstrokes on vellum, framed in plain ramin. Martha's torchlight didn't hover long enough to determine in which profession these scrolls had been awarded in its sweep across the uncluttered walls. Then she found it: in the middle of the wall behind the desk. Martha moved up close. Approaching her across a rolling English landscape, out of a red horizon, comes Man; Milton, Shakespeare; a prophet. Naked, proud, somehow sexless yet virile, with a bow of burning gold in a chariot of fire. Here it was. So small – less than six inches by four – and worth so much.

The frame was hung by nylon wire. Martha took the toolkit from her belt, dismantled the backing from the frame and withdrew the engraving. She slid it into a bag with a strap which she slung over her shoulder.

Martha slunk out of a ground floor window close to the ash tree, retrieved her climbing belts and overshoes, and retraced her footsteps across the snow-covered lawns to her van.

5

BRIXTON

In London snow rarely settles. The heat of the city.
And the capital as it sprawls seems to create its own
microclimate, an urban enclave untouched by the
weather in the provinces where – having come from
one of them – Rebecca Menotti believed the reality of
English life was located. Even though she'd moved
here ten years ago, her metropolitan days were still
flavoured with the taste of a getaway; of youthful
escape.

Rebecca said nothing to Sam Caine on the
Underground, other than to indicate where they had to
change to the Victoria Line. Their carriages were fitfully occupied and they sat next to each other on seats
in the long rows. Sam closed his eyes and Rebecca
gazed at his reflection, bemused by what she took to be
his trust.

They climbed out of Brixton tube station. Greeted by
the winter sun, Sam sneezed. Rebecca led him through
the laid-back bustle by the hand, releasing it when on
Effra Road they had to part to make way for a lime

green man sat on a machine that seemed to be fly-mowing the pavement. Sam didn't offer to carry Rebecca's bag but halfway home she passed it to him and he took it. They didn't speak until they'd turned into her road of Victorian two-storeyed houses and were crossing it: a silent bicycle wove around them and they watched it wobble away.

'Poor boy,' Sam sympathized as the cyclist's Picasso saddle pummelled his nether regions.

'This road should win a booby prize', Rebecca informed Sam as they walked, 'for the most lumpy and bumpy in London. Potholes have appeared and been filled in, see there, and there, new trenches are dug by different people every week for gas, electric, phones, cable TV, water. And then they're always being repaired. Plus there's odd ridges and ruts and pock-marks that just erupt like some skin condition, a dermatitis of tarmac. An acne of asphalt.' They reached Rebecca's place. 'Our road's like a human body, whose cells replace each other: there's probably not one stretch of tarmac over seven years old. Yet it's the same road. Come on in.'

Rebecca jiggled her keys in front of a proudly detached house one free-standing storey higher than those on either side; their chimney pots and aerials fawned before it. The front door gave onto a drab communal hallway, its one shelf stacked with junk mail and letters to long-gone residents, at the end of which stood a blank cluster of doors: one to the left was for the ground-floor flat, to the right for the basement. Rebecca took two more keys to unlock the one in the middle, a reinforced door which opened on stairs up to her top two floors.

'This is home,' she said. 'Come upstairs for coffee.'

* * *

119

Rebecca had bought her flat at the end of the eighties, she told Sam, at the worst possible moment in the history of private property, with an astronomical mortgage whose monthly repayments almost but not quite paid off the interest on the huge sum borrowed. Hardly had the ink dried on her contract than house prices began free-falling; Rebecca was parachuting towards negative equity before she'd moved in. She had a proper job then, junior manager in an artificially lit, air-conditioned, open-plan office in the city canyons: surrounded by hypnotized typists and dashing suits, a fidget of background noise, the hot ink smell and flashes of duplicating, duplicating, duplicating machines. She realized within weeks of securing a mortgage that the career whose regular salary had persuaded the building society to provide her with it was going to drive her out of the office window and onto the pavement eleven storeys below.

Rebecca handed in her notice, opting to face bankruptcy and homelessness instead. Once she understood, however, that she would never be able to sell the flat without incurring a massive debt, and that it would be a burden not only for the rest of her life but probably for any offspring she might have too, the unpayable mortgage a late capitalist inheritance of indenture, then she relaxed.

'I accepted I'd live here for ever, that's all,' she explained to Sam. 'Don't want children anyway. I just had to make it mine.'

Her first floor had had a kitchen, large dining-room and small study. The top floor had bathroom and three bedrooms. Over the next few years, doing everything she could herself, employing occasional friendly brawn, Rebecca reversed the entire layout: she turned the downstairs into a big bedroom for herself, a smaller one for Davey and Juice, and a bathroom. Upstairs she put two RSJs and skylight windows in the roof and knocked out all the interior walls, to make one enormous kitchen/dining/sitting/dancing/chilling loft space.

Davey had refused to assist in this insane enterprise on the grounds that as Rebecca was his landlady it would be exploitation, technically, while Juice found the whole idea of handling brush or roller distasteful. 'Suburbia's full of DIYers,' she sniffed. 'Decorating their own tombs.'

Climbing up the stairs and emerging in the surprising space of the opened-out floor made Sam Caine's brain light-headed, like surmounting a hill.

'Put the kettle on,' Rebecca requested, moving away from Sam across bare waxed boards towards a distant bay window, where a four-piece suite of unmatched sofa and armchairs sat like museum exhibits in the loft space. On the red sofa was a white cushion, which slowly uncurled itself.

'Miaow,' it said, standing up gradually, as if testing out its paws one by one, looking pointedly away from Rebecca while pulling her attention towards it. 'Miiiaaaoow,' it repeated, stretching out the syllables with such subtle expressiveness that it managed to convey to Rebecca its pleasure at seeing her, an acknowledgement of her understandable joy at seeing it, and the enormous distress and resentment it had suffered by being abandoned by her for a week.

Rebecca scooped the white cat up. 'You poor neglected mog. Has Juice been feeding you? This is Gemma,' she introduced her. 'Gemma, this is Sam Caine.'

The cat, having made its point, appeared to forgive and forget, and purred sonorously. Its eyes took in Sam lazily, unconcerned at the entry of a rival in her kingdom. She'd seen off numerous ones before.

Sam found implements for tea, according to Rebecca's instructions. 'Bring it over here,' she said, indicating a chair. 'We better have a chat.'

Davey came home hypnotically preoccupied. Attaining the top floor he made straight for the fridge, saying, 'This town is killing me,' to anyone there whom he otherwise ignored: he extracted a bottle of Budvar, scrunched off the top with his plastic lighter and, leaning a hand on the opened fridge door, downed it in one long throat-rasping glug-a-lug draw. He then placed the empty on the sideboard, burped, took and opened another, lit a cigarette and drifted towards the sitting area. The son of two East Enders – Pakistani Muslim mother and ex-Mod white father – Davey had a bony, square-jawed, flat-nosed face and a taut frame over which stretched sports gear he less wore than modelled, making it look as if designed expressly for his body at this precise moment in his life. His sheeny black hair was cropped tight to his skull the better to disguise, he was loath to admit, both anterior recession and a median bald-spot. Rebecca effected introductions. Davey frowned at Sam, attempting to locate him in the neuronal maze of his memory.

'Are you Richard's friend?' he enquired. 'A mate of Charlie's?'

'I don't think so.'

'One of Geoff's cronies?'

'I don't know who I am,' Sam replied.

'Know what you mean, mate,' Davey nodded, then turned abruptly to Rebecca and launched into an exposition of the trials and tribulations with which he'd been afflicted since last seeing her two days earlier. He spoke with both vehemence and an elusiveness, emphasizing the beginning of a sentence but retreating from its end.

'And Juice has really been getting on my nerves, man,' he concluded, stubbing out his cigarette and lighting another.

Sam watched Rebecca and Davey. 'Are you two married?' he asked. They laughed with derision at both the question and each other.

'She's a bird, I'm not saying she ain't,' Davey responded. 'A bit of a bangle. But she's not my type. Wish she was.'

At that moment Juice made her unobtrusive entrance, having mounted the stairs unheard, until she walked over and the floorboards protested.

'This is Sam Caine,' Rebecca introduced him. 'He's an amnesiac. I found him at Paddington and brought him home. He can't remember who he is.'

'How do you know what his name is?' Davey demanded, a smart question to cover the foolishness he momentarily felt at not having elicited such information as Sam's amnesia already.

'It's written on his wristband,' Rebecca explained, which item conveniently revealed itself from under his jacket cuff when he stretched up to shake Juice's proffered hand.

'From a hospital,' Davey observed.

'No shit, Sherlock,' said Juice, bumping onto the sofa against him with perceptibly more aggression than friendliness. Davey winced and rose at once, trampolined to his feet by Juice's arrival.

'What's this then? Care in the community?' he demanded. 'What are you, Rebecca, a social worker? The things I've been putting up with, last thing I need's, no disrespect, mate, a loony tune in the flat

123

while I'm sleeping. I've already got one in the same bed.'

Davey took a drag on his fag. As he spoke he flourished his hands in the air, three fingers fisted but thumb and forefinger each jutting out like lobster claws. In his left hand the middle and ring finger pincered a cigarette, with glowing tip and smoke trail. Davey wreathed himself in smoke but it wasn't a smokescreen; the cloud in which he was enwrapped was a prop he created for himself as an ethereal being, a will-o'-the-wisp artful dodger. This theatrical effect was unfortunately balanced by a detrimental one on his complexion, giving his Anglo-Asian skin a dull, lifeless pallor. Davey was a throwback to an earlier smoking age when men stained the tips of their thumb and forefinger with nicotine, metastatic indicators of the self-inflicted ruin within.

'Am I right or am I wrong?' he demanded from Juice. 'She's brought some wackos home before and I never objected, but in this day and age we've all got responsibilities, ain't we, babe?'

'Don't call me babe,' Juice told him.

'Why don't you make a pot of tea while you're up?' Rebecca suggested.

'My name is Sam Caine,' Sam said wanly.

'He takes one sugar,' Rebecca added.

'Don't call me lady. Don't call me darling, don't call me dear. I'm a woman,' Juice declared.

Davey saw he wasn't being taken seriously and said, turning away, 'Dave Imran Golightly tries to warn the women, but is ignored. Still, he doesn't run but stands by them, providing them with tea and toast, showing that modesty his admirers so respect.'

'He's one of those unfortunates', Juice explained to Sam, while Davey made tea, 'who only got written a bit

124

part in the script of his own life. He really does think of himself in the third person. By speaking it out loud he thinks he'll convince everyone – and maybe even himself – that he's the bloody hero.' She shook her bleach-blond head contemptuously.

'Sam doesn't know where he comes from, Juice,' Rebecca resumed. 'The name of the hospital on the tag's come off. He's got no other identification, no money, nothing. Pockets empty. He's in trouble, Juice. We'll let him stay here a while, see if he remembers anything.'

'I think we should take a vote on it,' Juice pronounced. She and Davey were Rebecca's lodgers, but only in name; only in the eyes of the law; not theirs. They behaved as if still equal tenants in their old shared house. For Juice it was a question of class resentment – the product of generations of almost aristocrats only recently, and comparatively, impoverished, she objected to the offspring of working-class immigrants taking her rent. While for Davey it had more of a philosophical basis: property was theft, so Rebecca had taken over from their old landlord the job of stealing his rent cheque.

'I vote he goes back to the booby-hatch,' Davey called over.

'Then I vote he stays,' said Juice. 'That settles it.'

'D. I. Golightly suffers once more the tyranny of democracy.'

'I am not a lunatic,' Sam pointed out. 'I'm an amnesiac, that's all. It may even be that I chose to be. What do you do?' he asked Juice.

'Apart from bicker?' Rebecca interjected, disconcerted by the way Sam was looking at Juice and the too interested tone of his voice.

'You mean real job or real thing?'

125

'Both, I s'pose.'

As he carried a tea tray over, Davey murmured, 'This city is full of wannabes who won't be, ever.'

'I work as a receptionist in a sound studio in Soho,' Juice explained. 'I can use the equipment in down time. I'm composing a symphony out of found sounds.'

Sam stared at her: whether he was waiting for her to finish what sounded to him like a sentence half-baked or -completed, or was offering his unfeasibly blue eyes to her for losing herself in, was hard to tell.

'I sample sounds,' Juice elucidated. 'All sorts of noises, voices, off the street, machines, anything. With this,' she said, pulling a small DAT recorder from her bag.

Davey had meanwhile been alerted too by a note of enthusiasm in Juice's voice and – upon visual inspection – the locked together proximity of the pair's interaction.

'It's a collage,' Juice continued, 'only an aural one. There'll be no quote music unquote in it as such, only the overall effect will be music. It's called "Today Volume 1".'

In the silence that followed could be heard a slightly agitated purring that emanated from Gemma who was undergoing a vigorous massage on Rebecca's lap.

'I already recorded like six different varieties of Gemma purring,' Juice explained.

'Really?' Sam asked.

'She's got many more, once you listen. You become attuned to the finer nuances of sound.'

'You must be remarkably sensitive,' Sam told her.

Davey scowled as he poured; Gemma's purrs became a plea for release.

'I am, yes. But people in general used to be. We've lost our sensitivity to sound. Like it was understood

126

once that sounds which can traverse long distances, or resound with abnormal volume, possess a special mystique. Certain bells used to be rung to subdue storms at sea; others to purify the air in times of plague.'

'Really?'

'Actually, Sam, I'd like to record you, if you don't mind. Just speak into this microphone, in your normal voice. Say: "My name is Sam Caine."'

Juice adjusted levels on the DAT.

'Your hand's trembling,' Sam said, and he clasped Juice's well-nourished fingers around the mike. This physical contact was too much for Davey.

'Right. That's it. You find this guy in a Joe Orton play, Rebecca? Look, mate, you want her? Good. You can have her. She's yours. Only I warn you it's like fucking a corpse.'

Juice was unfazed. 'He used to say thank you every time he came,' she told Sam.

'She used to *move*,' Davey claimed. 'There was something to be grateful *for*.'

'Now he doesn't even say thank you,' Juice said piteously.

Davey and Juice bickered constantly, though from quite different temperaments. Davey was a hyperactive flyweight who fidgeted and feinted as if anticipating blows and his words were jabs, while Juice was blonde and blobby already, placid on the sofa with fleshy white limbs, and the verbal blows she traded with Davey were sluggish sullen swipes. The trouble was they both suffered from logosultimania, Rebecca called it; a mixed-up kind of condition: the compulsion to have the last word. Juice came from a civilized background and had had an expensive education of a kind denied to Davey, who was brought up amongst East

127

End entrepreneurs and barrow boys and so had an unfair advantage.

Like all argumentative lovers, they appreciated an audience.

'Of course,' Davey confided in Sam, 'I'd be off like a shot if she let me, poor cow,' shaking his head with melancholic finality.

Sam turned to Juice, anticipating her. 'If I only had a gun, a shot is how I'd despatch him,' she managed, conclusively.

'Don't encourage them,' Rebecca told Sam.

'I'd draw a bull's-eye on my heart if it meant I didn't have to look at you every day,' Davey delivered the coup de grâce.

Juice's face trembled like a window pane in the wind and then cracked, not into tears but fury. 'And you couldn't do any more damage to anyone six feet under,' she spluttered. 'Only knowing you, you probably would. You'd manage to turn tables on the worms; you'd mess around the moles.'

Sam's attention swung from one to the other at their inexhaustible rally.

'Least I've never had worms inside me when I'm alive,' Davey sneered, in brutal culmination.

Juice stood up. 'That's because you've never *gone* anywhere,' she yelled, marching across the room and off down the stairs, ignoring Davey's ensuing response, some final word he had to get in, leaving each of them vaguely triumphant and yet dissatisfied.

'For God's sake, guys,' Rebecca lamented. 'I'm going to the 7-11. Come and help carry,' she told Sam, who obediently complied.

The following morning Sam was woken by a faint scrooping sound and an odd sensation on the skin of his cheek, to find a white cat licking the salt of his nocturnal tears. He lay in a flat spin while the white cat nuzzled his nose then curled up on top of him, and tried to work out what he was doing under a maroon duvet on a sofa bed in a semi-warehouse living-room he'd never seen before. Presently an Asian man sprang up the stairs into the space, said, 'Hey, mate,' without veering off his path towards the kitchen corner where he twitched impatiently waiting for kettle to boil and bread to toast. He put two tea bags in a mug and heaped butter and jam together on the blade of a knife held in readiness. He then drank munched sat at the breakfast bar on a stool on whose seat he wriggled like an infant, as if this were an aid to digestion. Upon importing the final mouthful of toast he instantly arose: as the cursorily masticated glob of food was swallowed and sank down his gullet so his body was already rising, his gut coming to meet that portion halfway. He then left.

Sam gazed out of the window at a world that looked vaguely familiar but a particular street that he'd never seen before, walked cycled driven along by total strangers. He wondered how long he'd lived in this city. Shortly a blonde woman entered the room sleepily. Sam watched her. She peered back in his direction with the idiotic expression of someone who hasn't yet put in their contact lenses, and trundled over to the kettle. She retrieved one of the previous user's tea bags from the draining board and made herself a mug of weak tea, and wandered over to sit on a stool leaning back against the bar.

'Morning,' she yawned.

'Who are you?' Sam asked her.

'Juice,' she answered, and sipped some tea.

'What do you do?' he asked.

'I'm composing a symphony of found sou . . .' she

began before trailing away and, receiving an inkling of what amnesia might mean in practice, Juice not only took her tea downstairs but never flirted with Sam Caine again.

When Rebecca arrived soon after and diagnosed within minutes that Sam had forgotten while asleep everything from yesterday, she explained who she was, who he was, as far as she knew.

'You're like a fairy tale character, Sam Caine,' she surmised. 'You mustn't fall asleep. If I let you nod off, the monster'll get your mind.'

From then on Rebecca began each day with the same routine, bringing Sam up to date with his identity. Then while she went off to work Sam stayed in her flat reading magazines; watching crazed women run around supermarkets or chiselled actors suffer on day-time TV; staring into space, gazing at the sporadically populated street, at its coming and going, mostly Afro-Caribbean, residents. He began to acquire the straggly look of a moulting animal. During the free times in her erratic work schedule Rebecca devoted herself to reviving Sam: she quizzed him on the history of his lifetime in case some event might exist, or arise, in which he himself appeared. Frowning into Rebecca's crossed eyes, Sam drew blanks.

Evenings that she used to go out Rebecca now stayed in with Sam and watched TV or played Scrabble: she had a prodigious vocabulary of words irrelevant to everyday life owing to the number of books she'd read, words useful only for reading more books and for playing Scrabble. What's more she couldn't understand why being beaten by at least a hundred points every game was dispiriting rather than an uplifting educational experience, and considered Sam's dejection ungrateful.

Rebecca spokeveryfast, her brain nimble enough to let her tongue coast along. It wasn't that words were spat out, truncated syllables you had to strain to catch; more that there were no pauses between words, that she did without the punctuation most people use to marshal their thoughts, plan the next part of the utterance, check we're doing OK so far, make minute adjustments to the construction of the sentence at present under way. With Rebecca the words came streaming out of her mouth; not with breathless enthusiasm, though, but measured; like a swimmer she'd worked out how to breathe while embarked upon lengthy monologues.

'Cos if it's not a disease Sam if you're sure there's nothing wrong with your brain and it's something else a philosophical response to the human condition good God or an attempt to ignore your mortality then if we can just find the key we could maybe unlock the whole thing.'

Sam had to take a second or two after Rebecca had finished speaking to process what she'd said: he had to spool it back through his brain, editing in the commas, colons, dashes Rebecca had done without.

'All I know is,' he deliberated, 'I was just beginning to get a sense of what it's all about, you know? Like I was on the verge of great insight, that life's elusive meaning was within my grasp. But it slipped away.'

Rebecca scrutinized Sam's activity in her flat for any lodging of the habitual in his memory. She was unable to discern improvement. Each day Sam Caine awoke on an unfamiliar island of experience with no context, no reference.

'Take him to the police,' Juice advised.

'Give a fake address,' Davey cut in. 'Better still, leave

him outside. Ring the bell and run. Best of all, take him back to a hospital.'

'No,' Rebecca said. 'I don't know why; I have to help him.'

'It's like', Sam tried to explain, 'the sense driving to the sea of the land opening out up ahead, being aware of the sea before you can see it.'

'Amnesia's like that?' Rebecca asked.

'No, it's like the opposite of that.'

The days passed, bled into weeks, with no progress. The depth of Rebecca's feelings for Sam, however – what she took still to be pity – deepened. While Sam grew mangy and ill-tempered like a zoo animal, so Rebecca became listless and heavy with the burden of unrequited love. Diarrhoea, swooning pulse, sweating or shivering unconnected to temperature, came and went undiagnosed. Her laugh disappeared: Rebecca used to utter a breathless, yelping laugh, yaffling like a charmed woodpecker; now she found little funny. And the outgoing party girl stayed in all the time. The change in her behaviour was so extreme that Davey and Juice, like South Sea islanders unable to see Captain Cook's unprecedented ship in their bay, didn't notice it. She cut a slip of paper for Sam's plastic wristband with her name, address and phone number on it.

'Like you belong to me,' she said.

'Maybe I do.'

Thus identified Sam could safely leave the flat, explore the streets, stretch his legs in Brockwell Park, though he showed scant desire to venture outside.

'I don't know where I come from. I don't know where I'm going. Why am I here?' Sam moaned. 'Who am I?'

'Yeah, that's the problem all right, mate,' Davey agreed, trying his best to look as disconcerted as Sam.

6

THE TATTOO

Ben O'Brien may not look it, but he's a carefree child. With his white hair, his calliper, his tongue working as he stumps along, as if it's a vital aid to balance. But he has only to pause, Ben, for his face to recompose itself, for a clear and careless eight-year-old's smile at the world to return.

'Spasimodo!' is yelled in a Mancunian accent.

Ben O'Brien stumbles through the estate on a cold February morning. His father watching restrains himself: from clipping callous kid around the ear, from accompanying his son to school.

Solo knows he has to stop observing too but twice a day he plays a pantomime, says goodbye, Ben (or, later, hello). Got your sandwiches? Swimmers? Typewriter? he asked this morning, as he tied on Ben's Ankle Foot Orthosis, his lightweight, knee-to-foot splint. Ben nodded, smiled, set off from their ground floor flat. Solo closed the door and waited, thinking he doesn't say much because he doesn't need to. Can your child be your guru? Ben my Buddha boy, he teaches me and all I do is protect him. Inadequately.

Solo slips out, climbs stairs and stealthily follows his son to school. He knows he shouldn't, that Ben has to look after himself, but when Solo's clamped himself inside one or two afternoons it's been only to spend the period of Ben's stammering perambulation home staring at the door, terrier tense, bangs thuds car horns prompting throbs of fear in his bowel. He's not once been able to resist tracking him in the morning, as now.

Solo was able to observe his vulnerable son unseen owing to the layout of Crapton Towers. It was a vast mid-rise estate sprawling over acres of cleared bomb-sites: old soldiers haunted by the guilt of survival feared being killed by the Jerries twenty years on, by cunning time-delayed, or freakishly unexploded, bomb; as time passed their fear, unrealized, began to transmute, and the spectre dreaded became an event which had once occurred, so that successive influxes of incomers – Bangladeshi, Caribbean, Somali – lapped up Mancunian veterans' delusions of families torn apart in Tower Twenty-Five. For there were now twenty-four six-storey blocks with walkways connecting them to each other and to the shopping centre, schools, church, health clinic and library at one periphery. Keeping to the walkways on the first level Solo soon caught up with Ben, white hair easily discernible, and furtively tracked him.

'Alky!' a child shouts and Solo smarts but Ben himself plods on, no doubt smiling still. Two girls skip past him: 'Dipso, Dipso, Do the Calypso.'

Solo slips along the walkway, almost trips over the prone unconscious body of local soak Dixie McCord. Solo pays him no heed: he looks dead, desperate lying there in filth but surely he will rise, Dixie, a tosspot Lazarus, with his floating memories, his platitudes and his exquisite thirst.

Ben's footpath crosses another and he stops to observe the Highway Code as if it's a road: turns his whole body right then laboriously left then back to centre and launches forward. As if in a reminder of the wisdom of Ben's caution Solo is surprised by two boys whishimming past him on rollerblades. Bent, intent Olympians, up ahead they cross a finishing line discernible only to themselves, relax and rise, the one in front pumps his arms in victory before spectators he imagines at every broken window, their applause erupting from the quiet blocks.

Finally Ben totters off the estate. Watching from a corner Solo clutches concrete balcony, Ben at his most vulnerable in the open space in front of the school, kids criss-crossing, it's not fair not to make him wear a cycle helmet, he's a fragile atom on the crowded concourse. Solo watches, helpless, irresponsible kids dashing with their immature radar, their robust limbs, and Ben stolidly stumbling through, white-haired and smiling, towards the high-fenced, razor-wired, uniform-guarded gate of the primary playground, which he reaches unscathed. Solo breathes again, praise the Virgin, turns around.

Solo O'Brien sailed through youth with an open, boyish face, quick black eyes, an ebullient flop of hair. People could be endeared to or annoyed by Solo without his saying or doing anything very much at all. Nature had aligned his thin lips at a subtly flirtatious angle – or was it a mocking one? Women found themselves unsure whether they wanted to mother or smother him; men would open Solo a bottle then unaccountably want to hit him with it.

Solo had walked into his twenties with a sprightly stride, was now coming out of them at a lesser, more wary pace. Experience had slowed him. Forsaken, the responsibility and anxious love of a single parent had drained his face, paled his skin; had creased his eyes and given Solo the gravitas of disillusionment.

By the time he gets to his friends' flat on level five of Tower Seventeen, though, Solo's in another frame of mind. He rattles a tattoo of greeting. The door is opened by Luke Savage who stares transfixed at Solo. Solo stares back. Luke blinks, gulps; the scar that runs down one cheek does a serpentine shimmy.

'It's you,' he says blankly.

'Who else would it be, Scouse?'

'Hughie Green?' Luke wondered. 'I had a dream. Forget it. Hey, Solo, you know how to identify an Irish aristocrat? His tattoo's got no spelling mistakes.'

'Luke, man, it's too early for Irish jokes.'

'That's all right, O'Brien, I'll tell them slowly.'

'It's always too early, Luke. Zip it.' Solo pushed in past him and straight to the sitting room as if perversely drawn by its stale odour. Bottles, cans, shoes, plastic bags, plates, cutlery, mugs littered the floor, wreckage of a catastrophic party. Solo sat on the back-broken sofa of a mismatched three-piece suite. Luke followed him in and stood attentive as a novice butler.

Solo spied lipsticked dog-ends. 'Robbie got company?'

'Why do Crapton girls smoke?' Luke shot back. 'So they can smell like ashtrays. You should be a fuckin' detective, Solo. What's the difference between the women and the Rottweilers in Crapton? Eh? The Rottweilers wear lipstick.'

'Robbie's with a dog?'

'No. Wick's with a floozie.'

'How?'

'How?'

'Why?'

136

'For sex, wack. You've probably forgotten.'

'I mean how could Wick pull a woman? He never says anything.'

'Eh, don't sound impressed, O'Brien. You've not met her. I'm not saying she's thick, but the only way I could've got a smile out of her yesterday was to tell her a joke the day before.'

'You weren't her type, man.'

'I'm going to get her phone number, just so's I can give it to Billy and Wally.'

'Drop it, Luke. You live in Manchester now. Pull yourself together. Forget her.'

'I heard them clicking.'

'Clicking?'

'Yeh. She was as skinny as he is. Must have been their bones rubbing together when they did it. Like insects. Like the clackin' of dominoes it was.'

'What are you on, man?'

'Nothing,' Luke shrugged, but he stared at Solo defiantly and his right leg twitched as he stood. Luke's face was creased and blotchy and weathered, but not by nature. His eyes held too much information. It wasn't that he looked older than Solo or the others, exactly, but he sure looked like he had less time left.

'You been up all night?' Solo asked.

'Couldn't sleep, wack. Went for a walk. Bumped into Dixie. He only had one shoe on. I said: "Lost a shoe, Dixie?"'

Luke paused, stared as if daring Solo to respond.

'He said: "No, found one."'

Solo refused to smile, to encourage Luke, though it made no difference.

'So is Robbie still asleep?'

'Is the Pope Catholic, O'Brien?'

'I'll make tea.' Solo put the kettle on and set to

cleaning up his friends' kitchen, a thankless yet thera-peutic task. Before he'd finished a bowl of washing-up Luke was hovering behind him, hopping from one foot to the other.

'What's a girl in Crapton use for protection, O'Brien, eh?' he demanded, his Scouse accent toothier with his mounting agitation. He stepped closer. 'A bus shelter.'

Solo ignored him, but Luke carried on.

'Only come to think of it they've stripped all the roofs round here not to mention the side panels. The bus shelters are used for footie goals now, Solo, the kids play games from one to the other like in that village or that school, Eton. I never went there, like, but if I ever 'ave kids—'

'Luke—'

His mouth in Solo's ear: 'Sounds like an urban myth but it's not, it's the beginning of a folk tradition on our estate, mate, Ben can tell people in fifty years' time it began in Crapton, footie matches from one bus shelter to the other—'

'Luke—'

'You got any jellies?'

Solo turned, shook his head. 'When did I ever? Here, have some grass.' He dried his hands on his jeans and pulled Rizlas pouch lighter from his crotch pocket.

'Go to work on an egg. Remember that? Ha, that's a laugh. Giz a job. Remember that, Solo, you Mancunian toerag? My people.' Luke sat down and concentrated on skinning up with trembling fingers. Solo collected rubbish in carrier bags and took them out and down to a pile at the front of the block. There wasn't a single dustbin left on the entire estate; any there had ever been were long since stolen, a crime hard for any copper to solve since it was impossible to get his head round. The mound of trash leaked and blew its contents every which way: black bin bags had been scratched and bitten by cats rats dogs and slit open by small humans ransacking them for tin cans, which aluminium dealers would buy for one penny each.

Solo took a mug of black tea two sugars to Robbie, who groaned awake. Solo watched his blind hand grope the carpet beside the bed, fingering sock, alarm clock, empty glass, until he found what he was looking for: round spectacles and his current book: a TV repair manual. Other men needed caffeine, tannin, nicotine to start the day, Robbie Stiles required something to study. Pulling himself up sufficiently to sip tea without spilling it down his chin he opened his dopey red eyes a slit and through the thick glasses he began to read.

An hour or two later Robbie was in a state capable of speech, though his voice issued from behind the receptionless TV: 'It's going to happen this year, Solo, it's just a question of when,' he pronounced.

Solo fancied Robbie's face might just as likely come into focus on the screen as next appear round the side of it. There was an electronic squeak, and a hiss.

'Careful, man.'

'Relax. I've told you lads, I've never had a shock in my life. I'm immune to electricity. My element's wood, see, in terms of Chinese medicine, like, and—'

'What's the difference between you and Herbert von Karajan?' Luke, who was kneeling on the sofa with his back to the room, drawing with felt-tips on the wall, demanded. 'He's a worse fuckin' conductor than you.'

'Luke's right,' Solo agreed. 'One mistake and it'll be too late.'

'Too late for what?' wondered Robbie's disembodied voice.

'You think you're untouchable, man. So did Icarus.'

139

'In a magnesium flash an electric sun'll melt his wings,' Luke enthused, little realizing how prescient he was. 'The shock'll throw him across the room, out the window,' he declared vehemently. 'To plummet to the ground five floors below.' And all he really got wrong was that Robbie wouldn't be the only one.

Holding defiant yellow hands above the TV set Robbie waved them like a puppeteer revealing the secret of his trickery.

'Marigolds. I'm protected,' he declared.

Luke sneered. 'Sure. Know how Solo told the Black Queen he wanted her to be the mother of his child? "The rubber's split, darlin'."' He turned back to the wall, resumed filling in letters with various colours that spelled out: ONCE WE WERE SCALLYWAGS.

The set went snap, crackle, pop and the screen flickered with the phantoms of breakfast TV.

'You got something, Robbie,' Solo exclaimed. 'Only it's gone.'

Robbie Stiles rose behind the TV set. 'Getting closer,' he told Solo and disappeared again, saying: 'I may not agree with what my enemy broadcasts, but I shall defend to the death my right to receive it free in my own living-room.'

It was one of Robbie's projects: he intended to obtain every terrestrial, satellite and cable channel that came out of anywhere into the north of England. There was no doubt television had become an unhealthy obsession for him, and the only saving grace was that he refused to watch it.

'Television is the opiate of the masses,' Robbie proclaimed. 'It's the greatest educational tool in the history of mankind,' he averred in the next breath. 'The better it is, the worse for us: the more time we'll spend watching it. It's a passive activity, a secondary experience.'

'What?' Luke asked. 'Like reading a book, you mean?'

'No, you illiterate Scouse dipstick,' Solo told him, 'reading's active. You create the thing inside your head, in collaboration with the writer.'

'Telly's like radio with eyestrain,' Luke said. 'I like it.'

'The question is,' Robbie declared, 'is it better not to watch at all, and remain ignorant, than to learn all about everything – global news, the natural world, classic cinema, laugh the sofa sick, live the soaps, pick up cookery tips and fall in love with the weather girls with their steatopygous rumps and their kissable lips – and yet become a vegetable?'

The trouble was Robbie found it impossible to ignore his enemies. In order to achieve supremacy over television he had to gain access to as much of it as possible: he measured his victory by the number of channels he was able to receive and not watch. The way Robbie's mind worked was one of the things Solo valued in his best friend, and his mind had always worked that way: they were friends from primary school playground, when Robbie collected the same 1974 football stickers as the other boys but instead of swapping duplicate copies of one player he'd amass them; in Robbie's album each team was represented by a page of images of the same player, Sheffield United by Tony Currie, Arsenal by Sammy Nelson, Burnley Martin Dobson, Martin Chivers for Spurs.

Robbie had been eight years old at the time, the same as Ben now, which gave Solo hope. If that insane child could grow into the success that Robbie had become then why not Ben too with his handicap? Apart from the fact that Robbie was a consummate failure.

Solo despaired, will it not always be like this? The longer Ben lasts, the closer he gets to normality, so the more he'll stand out and be picked on. If Solo and his friends hadn't coddled and cradled him, hadn't caressed and coaxed improbable movement with home-spun therapies in his immobile baby's body, he'd be a slobbering spastic in a wheelchair now in the corner of some safe sad ward, and be left alone. If Solo hadn't besieged the education authority and local headmistress with letters phone calls visits Ben would attend a special school and be one of the brighter pupils, looked up to, curried favour with.

But no, Solo drives him on, makes no allowances for Ben's disability except about a hundred a day, just none that Ben can see and it can only get worse, with comprehensive, puberty, youth. Solo and his able-bodied buddies have so little, just what is it that Ben's supposed to hope for?

Robbie's television project was handicapped by lack of money, but then again this was also, he pointed out, the only thing that made it a worthwhile challenge. He had to cobble together mismatched old sets, co-incidental spare parts, broken satellite dishes, suspect decoders, from car boots and jumble sales.

In the early days of satellite TV the nouveaux riches thereabouts proudly clamped the dishes to the wall outside their windows and boys threw stones, scoring points for smiting the transmitter in its middle – less vandals than critics, some said. So the owners moved their replacements up onto the sixth floors of all the blocks, paying peppercorn rentals to their loftier neighbours, some of whose windows were thus ringed with dishes from which cables hung so that they looked like patient moony sperm clustered around a fenestrated cervix. Then, however, crack dealers took to shooting out the transmitters when they felt like target practice; which they certainly needed, often missing the dishes and studding the walls or even shattering windows instead, at which point the elevated residents unscrewed dishes in double-quick time and everyone was back to square one.

'It's going to happen this year, Solo, it's just a question of when,' Robbie repeated.

'I'm glad you're so confident,' Solo replied.

'We're all going to be thirty or more some time this year. It's just a question of whose birthday is most propitious in terms of planetary influences.'

'You won't catch me falling for that star sign crap,' Luke contributed.

'A typical Gemini attitude,' Robbie said. 'If you can change your name by deed poll,' he conjectured, 'maybe you could change your birth date. They're both on the birth certificate, aren't they?'

At that point Wick, third member of Solo's trio of flat-sharing friends, slouched into the room, ducking to avoid the lintel. As he loped over to his decks he winked at Solo with the white-toothed grin of a lanky shaven-headed black man who knows that his friends know that a woman stayed the night. As he strapped headphones to his ears he said: 'What's the story?'

Before Solo could answer Wick had switched on power, pulled a twelve-inch from its rack and sleeve, spun it between palms, plugged it unerringly onto the turntable and placed needle; and like a dentist asking how was your holiday before thrusting drill and fingers into mouth, Wick forestalled Solo's reply with the deafening beat of techno.

One of the reasons Robbie had to scour junk shops for TV spare parts was that, although he'd have had little compunction about shoplifting, one of the group's

143

pacts concerned the restriction of petty theft to ventures that would further Wick's career i.e. money for records – though not stealing records themselves because the ones he needed were produced in living-room studios in Detroit, distributed by fleeting anarchic labels in London, sold in Underground Records and Eastern Bloc.

Wick and Luke had met years earlier, one a funky teenage DJ, the other a Scouse street poet in exile, and they formed a musical duo. Wick mixed, scratched and sampled records, while Luke declaimed gobbledegook over the top: he wrote one called '(Praise Be To) God Rap' which came to him in a burst of divine inspiration, he told Robbie and Solo. Employed on a Manpower Services scheme, Wick and Luke were enabled to go into a studio and cut a record of their song just in time to have it banned: 'God Rap' brought them instant notoriety in Manchester.

The record, praising God while attacking organized religions with the coarsest rhymes a Scouse rapper could come up with, had a unifying effect: religious leaders from all over the city – rabbi, bishop, cardinal, imam – gathered together for a press conference at which they issued a joint statement denouncing this scurrilous profanity and pressing charges of blasphemy, libel, inciting racial hatred, obscenity and many more against its creators. 'God Rap' was censored in rapidly succeeding stages from radio airwaves, record shops and finally existence, the last remaining copies being seized from the distributor by police acting on orders from the Director of Public Prosecutions. As a result, pirate copies of the *cause célèbre* disc circulated, its value rising with each new ban.

Faced with the prospect of going to prison in defence

of free speech, Luke and Wick made a profuse public apology, and the charges were dropped, as did the price of black market copies of the record. That Christmas one music magazine voted it worst single of the year, a risible example of what happens when a white English vocalist tries to copy the rap style of black Afro-American culture.

One Saturday in mid-February Solo took Ben round to the flat, and after Wick had been at the turntables for a while Robbie rose from his corner and yelled: 'Let's ankle into town, lads.'

Solo and his son and his friends filed out of the flat. 'Little did they know, those pioneers,' Robbie began rambling, 'Alan Turing with his theoretical digital computer; the boffins at Bletchley trying to crack Enigma; the Pennsylvania nerds with their machine filling a whole room, with its vacuum tubes and radio valves—'

They descended the concrete stairwells just as the sun came out on a late winter day.

'—or Shockley and Bardeen with their transistor, or the geeks and gooks who came up with printed circuits, and silicon, and microchips, man, did any of those respectable scientists know that all their inventions were leading up to digital computerized music? Which'd then find its ultimate expression in Wick here's mixing genius. Could they have possibly foreseen that this was what it was all for?'

Wick – head lolling on his shoulders as if he was on the back shelf of a Ford Cortina – grinned, vacantly, less impressed by praise than by the rhythmic patterns imprinting themselves inside his skull through ever-present headphones. Ben, with his unarticulated joints splaying out, could have been taking the mickey.

'See that flat there with the tinned-up windows?' Luke asked, nodding towards a block to their left.

Which one, Solo wondered, scanning the equal number of windows glazed with steel plate as with glass; not just empty flats at ground level but on all six floors, since convicted young thieves from round here had been sent from Borstal on tough outdoor courses in North Wales, where they'd been forced to learn to abseil.

'An old bloke lived there, no-one knew him, hardly saw him. He died and his body rotted and of course he stopped payin' his rent. Council wrote and called but he never paid 'cos he was dead, like, but they kept pestering him. Finally he was so far in arrears bailiffs moved in to evict him. He wouldn't open the door, which he wouldn't 'cos he couldn't, so the police had to batter it down. Hell of a scene it was. They'd talked to the neighbours and one said he was a quiet old bloke, kept himself to himself so of course they thought here we've got a fuckin' paedophile, dunno what we'll find in there, porno kiddie pictures and that. Called in vice squad. Then someone else said they never saw him so that made coppers think it was a drug thing. Specials come in tooled up. Hell of a spectacle there was. They're shouting: "You're under arrest, Mr Birtwhistle. Come out quiet!"'

There was a pause.

'Yeah, so what?' Robbie wondered first.

'Nothing.' Luke shrugged. 'Death, eh? There was an advert on the notice board in the post office yesterday: second-hand gravestone for sale. Ideal for man named Derek William Crabtree.'

'You can trace criminality through religion sure enough,' Robbie agreed. 'Remember when we were kids and they nicked the lead off the roof of St

Aloysius? Then a bit later they went inside and took crucifix and candlesticks. With each recession another degrading step's taken.'

'The steps to Hades,' said Solo.

'Now that *was* a good club,' Wick said, shifting the others into silent nostalgia for a moment.

'There'd be Dad prising the collection box off the wall,' Robbie resumed, 'Mum lifting the votive candles, little Jimmy nicking the flowers off someone's grave to give to his girl and sweet Jenny cutting the cloth off the confessional curtain to sew a black skirt for the disco.'

'That's my point,' said Luke. 'They're nickin' the tombstones: what's that leave to rob, eh? Think about it.'

'Da da da dum, da da da dum,' Wick intoned *The X-Files* theme tune.

'I remember when my mother-in-law died,' Luke lied. 'The wife asked me what sort of tombstone we should get. I said: "Something very, very heavy, love."'

Ben laughed and took Luke's hand.

'That was the first time she smacked me one,' Luke added wistfully, bending down to offer Ben a piggy-back.

Ben cuffed Luke's arm as he climbed on board. He knew Luke had never been married.

The boys walked into town, heading – according to Robbie's directive – for the central library, a four-mile walk: it was exercise, they had plenty of time that didn't need saving and the bus money stayed in their pockets; Solo's car had no fuel, as usual. There was little point in going to the branch library off the con-course by Crapton: the only books left there, Solo knew, were reference ones, as defined less by content than by the fact that they were chained to the wall; *reference* meaning: you cannot take them home. It was a lending library in name only. There was a periodicals room resonating with snoozing dreamers and stocked with local newspapers from which *Sits Vac* and *Items Wanted* had been torn and tabloids divested of their topless models, leaving behind what looked like frantic failures of origami on the shelves.

The librarian and her assistant were two tough veterans of the bibliophilic business who'd learned to distrust readers, especially keen ones like Solo O'Brien. They fielded enquiries as obstructively as possible unless a person knew exactly which book they were looking for – author, title, publisher, date of publication, ISBN – in which case the librarian helped them fill out a request slip, which after they'd left she filed in the bin. People learned not to mess with Mrs Malone.

No-one could blame her, Solo conceded. She knew she was the last of the line, holding the fort in hostile territory, patrolling the battlements until reinforcements arrived to either close the library or privatize it; that free reading was no longer tenable, an absurd, anachronistic notion; that the Iron Lady and her ilk had stopped time and – like some infernal astronomers of Jack Knighton's rather than Solo O'Brien's imaginings – turned it backwards. We were spinning through Victorian England and the philanthropic wave of free meals, schools, travel that people didn't trust or value so they had to be charged until they understood again.

Solo fondly remembered Mrs Malone's antepenultimate predecessor, Miss Winifred Seed, who when Solo was fourteen came from neighbouring Bolton via the University of East Anglia and the British Library back almost home, with a faith in the power of the printed word barely rivalled since the days of William Caxton. Winnie was a missionary among her own people and every book was her bible. She organized an adult literacy programme, delivered large-print books in her bicycle basket to housebound pensioners on her way home, and started up a mother and child reading session in the children's room for which four generations of entire families squeezed in.

'Give us a winnie!' people greeted her sunny visage cycling past, except for Solo O'Brien, who gazed in dumb open-mouthed admiration, as he suffered the crushing swoon of a scraggy adolescent.

The library became a welcoming salon. It ceased smelling of must, ammonia and body odour, and was filled instead with fresh air that had been smuggled into the city. The sound of loveless men snoring was replaced by the expectant silence of concentrated minds. Winifred excavated whole sections of neglected books and rearranged them according to Italian bibliophiles' theories of colour, attracting hitherto incurious visitors and turning them into compulsive browsers and borrowers, and she displayed booklets and *bouquins* on coffee tables in the foyer along with free cups of tea.

Winifred's energy was vast and her zeal infectious. She brought oral storytellers, local authors and foreign literati to the library for readings sold out in advance to members of her newly initiated Crapton Literary Society, inspired by the Catalonian subscription concerts of Pablo Casals (as mentioned in his auto-biography, shelved under C).

Despite her projects, Winifred always had time to expend passionate advocacy on Solo, suddenly the most precocious youth on the estate. He read overnight books she recommended to him, so that he could pester her again the next day, could stare with sleepless eyes as she persuaded him of the superiority of George Eliot to Tom Robbins, of Kurt Vonnegut to Miguel de Cervantes. He agreed readily and read obediently. Solo was madly in love, despite Winnie's librarian's myopia, her commanding height, her non-existent breasts and her enormous arse. 'She was the one and only older woman I fell for,' he now confided in Robbie half a lifetime later as they walked. 'Now, I realize she were only in her mid-twenties. She had sex energy, and she poured it into doing good to everyone. Course I didn't know it were sex energy either. I were only a kid. And my desire for that lovely, wonky woman became attached to books. It's why book sniffing's got an erotic charge.'

Winifred Seed badgered the Chief Librarian of Manchester for extra funds for this vital branch in an *area of multiple deprivation* as Crapton was defined by the European Commission (in tasteless if appropriately medical jargon, Winifred thought, suggesting both sclerosis and fracturing of a community) and money bypassed Whitehall direct from Brussels.

It was an extraordinary winter. Boxes of books were delivered by Securicor and they poured straight out of the library. So few ever came back that Winifred and her assistants stopped bothering to stamp them, but what did it matter if people were reading? And some of them were. The truth was, Solo reckoned, that it hung in the balance for a while. There were rumours that truants were staying home from school to finish the latest Roald Dahl, that young mothers were not only reading but writing Mills and Boons, that men redundant since the steelworks closed down were motivating themselves with Charles C. Handy and Henry David Thoreau, that on the corner of Sanderson

Crescent and Thompson Close you could get a sachet of smack for an OUP poet and a New Order bootleg for a Philip K. Dick.

Yes, it was a close-run thing, Solo claimed. If it hadn't been such a cold winter maybe a critical mass of readers over and above the oddballs like himself might have built up.

'Get out of it,' Robbie told him.

'No, really,' Solo maintained. He'd voted for the Natural Law Party in the last election because he'd been impressed by their mathematics. 'Maybe if one per cent of the square root of the population of the estate had been reading for twenty minutes twice a day, it would have had a benign effect on the rest, some of whom would themselves begin to pick up books from the library.'

'It wouldn't have affected me, wack,' Luke boasted.

Whatever might have been, Solo had to admit, never was. People took books because they were there to be taken. The little bonfires began appearing with the first hard urban frosts, soon after Christmas. Winifred saw them early, as it happened, but hampered by the myopia of her optimism she misinterpreted the image: she misread the picture. She was just an old-fashioned girl, Solo would recall; an avid reader, yes, but visually illiterate. Winifred saw the first bonfires and they warmed her heart because she thought people with handfuls of books were reading by the light given off.

Robbie, who knew more about religion than Solo, was of the opinion that Winifred could have coped if the books had been burned for a reason. She'd have been distraught, of course, but not heartbroken. 'These proselytizers, apostle types, they thrive on opposition,' he reckoned. 'Opposition is what proves the need of their mission.'

He was probably right. Winifred would have understood books being burned because people thought them sacrilegious or subversive: after all, they should be. She understood the burning of the Talmudic Academy library by the Brownshirts of Lublin, the tossing of heretics' false scriptures onto their own autos-da-fé in the Inquisition, the melting down of lascivious vinyl by the Moral Majority of America, the use of white noise by Chinese soldiers to drown Tibetan monks' chanting, the slashing of modernist paintings by insane academicians, the ripping apart by Muslim fundamentalists of novels riddled with the apostasy of humour. Winifred understood all that: for art to be censored was proof of its vitality – not to mention, moreover, of the need for libraries. What she couldn't understand – until she did and then it broke her – was people burning books because it meant they could stay outside a little longer a bit warmer one English winter evening; choosing to glean more nourishment from paper's fleeting flames than from the words printed upon it.

'She were a honey,' Solo reflected, at the memory of them carting her away.

'There's beats in flames,' said Wick. 'Crackles and whooshes and sparks.' His head started bobbing as he walked; he could hear fire sounds inside it and was ordering them into repetitive patterns.

They strolled towards town through Gaylord Towers, a cluster of rusting blocks which the council had emptied in response to young mothers' hurling themselves and their babies through sealed windows of the fifteenth floor, the endless disabling of the lifts by low-living vandals, asbestos poisoning, vertigo for which Valium was mis-prescribed, rats who adapted to vertical communities, and the non-specific nervous disorders suffered by children there. The council took the enlightened step of moving all the families out to a neighbouring new development, low-rise Law Village, and replacing them in the Towers with university and polytechnic students.

The families who moved out, meanwhile, got their relieved feet back on the ground in Law Village, through which Solo's group now strode. Named after Manchester United's legendary goalscorer (whose most notorious goal came after he'd moved to local rivals Manchester City – a regretful, desultory backheel into an empty net against his old alma mater that relegated them to the Second Division), Law Village was a show-town sprawl of semi-detached chocolate-box council houses with their own gardens, fruit trees planted on the wide pavements, verdant lawns and ornamental borders.

'I applied for us to move here,' Solo told Ben, now being ferried on Wick's back. 'They had all these glossy brochures. Urban planners came from all over to ogle it admiringly. They turned us down.'

'Why?' Ben demanded.

'This lot didn't want us to leave Crapton. They wrote the council a load of lies.'

'Yes,' said Robbie. 'Thank Christ for you we did.'

Within months of its completion, requests for housing transfers from tenants in Law Village started mounting up, demanding to move back out. A housing officer drove out there to investigate: the place had been sacked, not by a marauding army but by its own inhabitants. He found the fruit trees stripped as if by packs of arboreal prosimians roistering through the forest or else uprooted by juvenile Samsons in trials of strength and returned for cash refunds to the garden centre they'd once come from. He found the lawns and flowerbeds not only trampled to sludge but sculpted with trenches, foxholes, craters and even tunnels. (This re-enactment of the Battle of the Somme by local gangs may also have been, incidentally, a factor in what a group of Ph.D. students in the Department of Climatology at the university discovered in a research project to be a higher than even local average precipitation: it was always raining in Law Village.) He found the parade of shops gutted and bus services redirected after repeated hijackings for delirious double-decker joyrides, after which bus drivers refused to come off the main road, which explained the antlike procession of women heaving bulging carrier bags – strained plastic biting into their palms – from the Mall in Crapton three miles away. Some pushed supermarket trolleys, vehicles more precious than bicycles there – people owned their own, took them inside and chained them to a radiator.

The council housing officer found he'd misplaced his car when he returned to where he thought he'd parked it. He wandered identical nameless streets for many hours, his gradually enfeebled mind teasing him with the notion that he was walking through a pastiche of a fictional character's dying dream, catching occasional glimpses of a car similar to his own screaming over junctions in the distance.

The group were brought to a respectful halt on their own constitutional by a funeral cortège passing at right angles behind them, for which they turned.

'My life is passing in front of my eyes,' said Solo. 'My whole life.'

Ben nodded gravely. 'And me, Dad,' he said.

The slow procession continued, with many people following on foot four black cars.

'Wonder who died?' Robbie mused.

'Probably the one in the hearse,' said Luke.

Wick hummed Beethoven's funeral march, embellished it with tickatacker rhythms tapped with his fingers on Luke's bald spot and a solid bass beat with his boot on the tarmac.

'Hey, whatever happened to that council bloke?' Robbie wondered.

'He found his car wrapped around the last remaining tree trunk in Lawless Garden City,' Solo recalled.

'With the corpses of four young grief riders in the mangled chassis,' Luke added.

'That's right,' Robbie nodded. 'Still on a trauma pension today.'

Families left Law Village whenever they could. Asylum-seekers occasionally replaced them: no-one ever moved in out of choice; no-one lived any place bad enough they wanted to transfer to the middle of Passchendaele. As soon as houses were vacated middle-aged men hurried in to strip them of the roof tiles worth thirty pence each, of copper water pipes and gas ones of lead. They ripped out the fuse boxes and stripped cables of their copper wire, they chipped away putty to remove window panes intact and demolished walls to resell the bricks, rushing off up the street pushing wheelbarrows; redundant men picked the houses clean to their bones like frantic vultures, in order to get what they could before their delinquent sons went in after dark to sniff glue in the empty buildings, then burn and destroy them.

The boys sauntered into town under the railway bridge on which one could still just make out faded graffiti Luke himself sprayed there long ago: PUBLIC NOTICE: OWING TO FINANCIAL CUTBACKS THE LIGHT AT THE END OF

THE TUNNEL HAS BEEN SWITCHED OFF, its lack of originality compensated for by the impressive legibility considering he'd been leaning over the edge and so working upside down as well as doubtless off his face.

They traversed a bridge over the canal that had brought cotton and taken fabrics from the textile mills, rubber, paper, chemicals, flour and a thousand products of engineering plants to Liverpool docks and thence out to the world.

It was only when they got to the central library and Robbie obtained an A4 sized booklet from ENQUIRIES that he explained his latest scheme to his confederates, seated at a table in the local history section.

'Lottery Fund Application,' Robbie enthused, taking his round spectacles off and cleaning them with the corner of his shirt. 'They want arts-based projects that's going to involve young people. Perfect, eh?'

'Brilliant,' said Solo.

'You're a fuckin' genius,' said Luke.

Wick stood his full gangly length and high-fived his friend front back and sideways, body-popping.

'Sshh!' hissed an elderly gentleman trying to focus at a microfiche screen not far away. The boys leaned into a conspiratorial scrum.

'So, er, what's the jangle?' Luke wondered.

'Yeah, like: how?' asked Wick.

Ben stared at Robbie with a patient expression.

'I guess what we're saying is, what did you have in mind, Robbie?' Solo articulated.

Robbie crumpled; his crest fell. 'Why do I bother with you guys?' he demanded. But then he put his glasses back on and bucked himself up and launched into: 'We're going to create events using our unique skills. Wick'll DJ, obviously. And Luke'll paint Day-Glo backdrops as well as a stand-up comic routine in the interval between Wick's sets.'

'What are you gonna do?' Luke challenged. 'You've got no legal aptitudes whatsoever.'

Robbie closed his eyes and contemplated. 'I'm going to create multimedia whatjamacallits, of course,' he said upon opening them. 'Televisual . . . computerized, er, digital, like, interactive sort of cyberspaces.'

'You've really thought this thing through,' said Solo.

'You want me to dictate everything?' Robbie pleaded. 'This should be a co-operative venture, lads.'

'What about young people?' Luke demanded. 'Where do they fit in? Apart from through the front door.'

'Where do I fit in?' Solo asked.

'You can run a crèche,' Luke suggested. 'That might attract some young people. And Ben can bring his friends, can't you?'

'What are you on about?' Wick suddenly erupted. 'We're the young people. Us. We're only twenty-nine.'

The other three adults looked at Wick with his wide brittle insect grin and at each other.

'Ah, screw it,' Robbie spat.

'Sshh!' someone hissed from a distance.

'Stuff the Lottery,' Robbie said, ripping the application form in two and dropping it on the table as he rose. 'I'm sorry, lads, I don't care what you say, but I am simply not prepared to be a part of a project that encourages people to gamble. Come on.'

Robbie led the way out of the library and the group went home – home also of the most avid of Lottery punters. On the way they said little. Solo considered his companions: Wick technopurist DJ playing music so harshly minimalist one in a million recognized it as the final triumph of the avant-garde, the dark pulse lurking in the heart of the universe, while the rest of humanity it gave a headache to; Luke lacerating his soul with humour; Robbie could have made done been anything he wanted to, he just couldn't quite decide what that was, and step onto the first rung. That was true for all of them: if they could just get onto the bottom step of the ladder there was little doubt they'd each and every one go skimming to the top. Their time was surely coming; they were almost thirty years old, damn it. A bunch of losers, the friends he had and himself, a fine shambolic parade of father and uncles for a disadvantaged boy to be saddled with.

Some days in the week Robbie and the others went with Solo to surprise Ben coming out of school. The days seemed to be growing dark and colder. They eyed up twenty-year-old mothers waiting for their kids or younger girls, meeting siblings, carrying their own junkie babies on their slender hips or in their tight bellies; others in miniskirts and lip-glossed, already dressed for the game later on.

Over here was the window-grilled chemist out of which tranquillized housewives were followed and mugged for their prescriptions. Over there the pub.

'Can you remember when the White Horse had windows?' Solo reminisced. 'Sean Gallagher used to come and reglaze smashed ones on a Monday morning. Regular.'

'Aye,' Robbie agreed, 'then it were twice, three times a week.'

'One week Jock had to call Sean out every day. He said, "Sorry, son, that's enough." And he got a brickie instead, to fill them all in.'

'I don't know what you lot are gripin' about,' Luke exclaimed. 'In Liverpool we *never* had windows. Not since they were taxed, like. Not in our local, anyway.

Funny lot we had round our way. I remember once a bloke walked in with a pig under his arm. "Where the fuck did you get that?" the landlord asked. And the pig says, "I won him in a raffle."'

'Old ones are the best,' said Robbie.

'Don't worry, he's not talking to you, love,' Luke told the nearest teenager.

'Here they come,' said Solo.

Kids with gaudy plastic rucksacks burst from the primary school and scattered like Smarties from a tube. They came pouring out of the playground with their strange stop-go mixture of enthusiasm and tentativeness, Ben in the middle, his white jerking head prominent, then his walk of a stumbling marionette and his beautiful smile. Solo let his mates greet his son: Wick swung low and scooped him up in his phasmidic arms and spun him round till he'd messed up his balance before placing him the right way up with a buttock on each of Luke and Robbie's shoulders. They paraded him homeward like a victorious rugby captain. Ben's disorientated face rediscovered equilibrium and his smile returned. Other boys glanced up at him enviously and Solo allowed himself to appreciate the fact that his son was not yet embarrassed by him or his friends' antics.

'Grow up so quick now, though,' he said to Wick as if his preceding thought had been voiced.

'Know more about music than we ever did, kids,' Wick replied.

They carried Ben aloft past the playpark children never entered, with its needles in the sand, its last remaining swing hanging on one chain like a severed puppet, its dog turds, its used condoms and its broken glass. At the boys' flat Luke made tea and Wick hit the decks. Ben lay on the carpet while Solo moved his legs and Robbie his arms in a residual bout of trunkal patterning: for the first five years of his life – since the Black Queen left, when Ben was six months old – Solo and his friends had performed therapy on Ben for two hours in the morning and two in the afternoon. They used techniques, developed by the British Institute for Brain-Injured Children, of patterning, which entailed replicating movement of a normal child through rhythmic manipulation of the limbs. Some of the exercises, like homolateral patterning with which they'd helped Ben to creep forward on his stomach, required three of them working on him at once. It was the great blessing – the benediction – of Solo's life that his friends were such worthless, idle losers: Ben's progress had so outstripped the paediatrician's prognosis that she grew more and more annoyed and threatened to stop seeing Ben; eventually relenting, and incorporating the techniques into her practice. Ben was used intermittently for publicity for the therapy; Solo agreed to let his beatific smile greet millions from boxes at the bottom corners of the front pages of broadsheet newspapers, beside captions appealing for donations, less for the cause than because he hoped even now somewhere in his hidden heart that his Black Queen would buy a copy of the *Guardian* in a little newsagent in a small street in some strange town, would, reading it on the bus, recognize the face – however little it ever resembled hers – and be belatedly, for ever, smitten.

'Eh, Ben, what shape's a dead parrot?' Luke demanded as he placed hot mugs on the table. 'A polygon. What d'you call a man walking through leaves? Russell. What d'you call a man with a seagull on his head? Cliff.'

Ben, despite looking as if he were being held down

by the brute at each end of him, responded, with a groan.

'What d'you call a man who always smells sweaty? Jim.'

Ben groaned again. It sounded like a juvenile version of the same groan Solo was making (having heard these riddles before) but in Ben's case it was the sound of laughter.

'I'm wasted on you lads,' Luke complained. 'Here's one for Robbie: what d'you call a man with a wooden head? Edward. What d'you call a man with two wooden heads? Edward Woodward. Honest to God, Ben, you're a hopeless case,' Luke accused. 'You don't like none of my jokes,' as Ben squirmed on the floor, pleasure twisting his limbs. 'You're too stuck-up to live here, you are. We're not good enough for you. We're stupid, we are; we're like that couple down the road in Tower Six what were in the paper, like, who've adopted a Roomanian baby. Mrs Hedges told me they're learning Roomanian themselves so that they'll be able to understand him when he starts to speak.'

Luke peppered Ben with jokes: he sprayed them from his Gatling gun mind; bullied the boy with one-liners. As far as Luke was concerned it was laughter therapy, and if it contained cruelty, which all his humour did, then that was the agent of disease in the inoculation; it was an anti-illusion jab in Ben's arm to prepare him for the shortcomings and disillusionments ahead.

'One day he'll start laughing, Ben will,' Luke used to say. 'And when he does he'll never fuckin' stop.'

Luke was about right: Ben rarely stopped smiling, anyway. Solo almost preferred not to see him made to laugh: Ben looked so peaceful smiling, whereas a laugh was awkward, uncomfortable, like speech. When Ben spoke he had to strain to express each word, his mouth an uncontrollable sphincter; reluctant, odd-shaped syllables. And each word too an almost identical groan, as if still preverbal or like the utterance of an acutely deaf boy, incomprehensible to an unpractised ear. Solo liked to convince himself Ben was a visiting dignitary, his son a VIP from some other country; some other continent. How good it occasionally was to interpret for Ben with someone – on bus, in shop – who'd been ignoring him as he pestered them for conversation until Solo deciphered; to see their creeping amazement that the idiot child was not at all, he'd just been speaking in code, a verbal disguise to make *them* feel foolish, chastened, improved.

'Look at this.' Robbie's voice brought Solo from his thoughts. He was parting Ben's white hair.

'Not nits again,' Solo moaned.

'No, come here.'

Solo peered at Ben's skull: there was a balloon-shaped face drawn in black ink with narrowed almond eyes.

'Yeah, they do that every now and then. Don't they, Ben?' The boy smiled. 'It's the Alien symbol. We're used to it, aren't we, chuck?'

Ben smiled back at his father.

'Look closer,' Robbie persisted.

'Yeah, we know. It's in indelible ink. It'll wash off eventually. It always does. It's funny, isn't it, Ben? One or two of the older lads; all part of growing up, Rob, you remember. Ben tries to see the funny side, don't you?'

Robbie, irritated: 'No, look closer.'

'What is it?' Solo shrugged.

'Bloody hell. Here,' said Robbie, reaching for a magnifying glass from his electrical tool kit still

162

on the floor by the TV set, and handing it to Solo.

Solo held the glass above Ben's head, adjusted it to and fro till the Alien face came into focus. He peered for a second or two.

'See?' Robbie asked, and then Solo did: he could make out tiny puncture marks in the black lines. They'd gone beyond indelible ink on Ben's skull. Now they'd begun to tattoo him.

7

SUPERSYMMETRY

Have aliens walked the earth? That's the kind of question that sneaks up on Jack Knighton when he's driving. Anything can trigger one, but in this case the cause is trailing him up the motorway, being towed along behind him. There it is again: a sheep bleated. What a weird unworldly sound that is. And what an unnatural animal, when you think about it. Best not to.

Have aliens walked the earth, though? It's hard to believe not: there are so many people sure they have and do. Jack Knighton doesn't know, he keeps an open mind as he drives (that's why so many things float in and out of it, Miranda says). It's like Stephen Hawking's argument against the possibility of time travel: if *Homo sapiens* should ever manage such a thing, if our descendants should master crossing time, why haven't we met them already? Why aren't we visited by our distant offspring; by time tourists on daytrips from the future?

It's clever but not, Jack reckons, conclusive. Perhaps they are here, but in a slightly different dimension, we just can't see them very well. Like illegal immigrants smuggled in in lorries. They're ghosts. Or angels. Jack Knighton doesn't know. But he ponders. Physics . . . astronomy . . . He does have a fully qualified HGV driver's Zennish ability to let the mind go blank – to think about nothing – for fifty or a hundred miles at a time, but Jack's natural inclination is more towards rumination. He can't help it. Often of course he's considering the road before and around him, obliged to only because there are so many abysmal drivers. Roads are like microworlds: his own lorry is an atom, himself its intelligent nucleus, but there are plenty of vehicles that are more like subatomic particles, moving according not to common sense and the Highway Code but rather Heisenberg's uncertainty principle. At the basis of quantum mechanics, this principle states that all physical quantities are subject to unpredictable and uncaused changes. This is very true. Such vehicles – a car full of kiddies driven by a harassed housewife; a de-regulated coach steered by a barely trained beginner; a smoke-spewing lorry from some cowboy outfit; a three-wheeler that should have been scrapped years ago; pensioners in a shiny saloon brought out of the garage for a leisurely Sunday, as if they still had the road to themselves on the Sabbath; a souped-up GTi, behind its mini steering wheel a tailgating teenager with a subatomic-sized brain – why, they're exasperating. But they also make the roads of England into the recurring enactment of a physics seminar. Maybe some of these surveillance cameras you see are not recording speeding cars but making videos to be screened in lecture halls with professorial voice-over. Because – with some of these irresponsible drivers – such a vehicle's trajectory is fuzzy and jittery, it's impossible to say precisely where it's located and how fast it's moving. There's no reason why a particular fluctuation in position or motion occurs as it does; it's not caused; it just happens. Such particulate cars seem to spontaneously come into existence: right sudden in front of you's a little Ford Fiesta trundling along in the middle lane of the motorway. There it stays, oblivious of your klaxon, your flashing lights, your bumper so close to its bumper you couldn't fit a cigarette paper between them; until it just as suddenly vanishes.

As for the roads of Europe – French drivers chasing ambulances through Paris; Neapolitans, wearing T-shirts printed with seat belts for the hell of it, accelerating through red fake traffic lights; Hanoverians conducting unofficial speed trials on the Autobahns; Greek and Turkish migrant workers ploughing their way somnambulistically home across the old Yugoslavia, drifting into oncoming headlights on the three insane lanes of the Motorway of Death – why, it'll take another Niels Bohr, Jack reckoned, to explain all that. To which a telepathic sheep bleated agreement.

Often, however, Jack was able to cruise along on automatic pilot, mind occupied but some appropriate part of his brain (in the motor area, presumably; that itself was a phenomenon he'd have liked to hear Melvyn Bragg discuss with someone on the radio) taking care of driving the lorry. And then he thought of one thing: his wife, Miranda, and their house, their dream home. Well, that's two things, but they were subjects inseparable from each other.

Miranda, my love, my Venus, I'm the luckiest man alive. He thought of his wife in majesty, no, in their humble detached, not fit for her really but still, it was for their home that he pushed his rig to the speed limit up and down, to and fro, across the motorways of England Britain Europe towing anything and everything that had to be towed. Jack earned the money for home improvements that she poor thing had to oversee when she should have been reclining on pillows, not surrounded by builders' rubble; fanned by Nubian slaves not making tea for chippies and sparks. Her nubility should have been fed by exquisite *cuisiniers*, hymned by enchanting eunuchs, in regal luxury. I'm sorry, Miranda, I'm sorry, you deserve so much better than me. With which a number of sheep agreed. They must be thirsty; not far to go now. Here we go round the M25 (the M25, the M25; here we go round the M25, at six o'clock in the evening).

Soon be on the M40 and up to Brum. Where poor Miranda was supervising plumbers and decorators, administering a complete overhaul of the second bathroom. The two of them discussed home improvement ideas he came up with on the road but Miranda was boss: she made the decisions and had the final say. She'd plumped for a top of the range power-shower with a free-floating rotating head with self-regulating temperature and water pressure controls that gauged the needs and wishes of your skin; a spacious two-person sauna; and a scallop-shaped Jacuzzi so large that – at the push of an underwater button – currents could be used to swim against in an exercise pool as might have been built, according to the glossy catalogue, by the imperial plumbers of Rome.

He imagined her now, overseeing dilatory workmen with their dawdling lads, tops off outside in the sunshine if you let them, and she with the stress of keeping them at it, a hopeless task when Jack had omitted to insert a time-penalty clause in the contract. Paint-spattered toshers come and go, stretch it out on the lawn, take advantage of a woman, of a sweet-natured woman, Miranda, my curvaceous queen. But it's hard to think, to imagine, for the motorway traffic slows down as it does nowadays and a chorus of bleating invades Jack's head, the sheep are all at it now, a melancholy accompaniment.

He doesn't like driving animals. It's just there's so much work, especially long-haul stuff with the common agricultural policy. Miranda doesn't want him to be away so long any more than he does, but they just have to both be brave and put up with it, like these sheep should. Baa! Baa! But she's right, he's got to take the work while it's there to pay for the house in which he spends less and less time, driving round and round in circles.

'Why don't you bring back more?' Miranda suggested recently. 'It seems like wasted opportunities, all these incontinental trips Phil Scritt's arranged.'

'What do you mean, my love?' Jack wondered. 'I'm taking a lorry load of sheep from Scotland, via Portsmouth–Le Havre, to southern Italy. Phil's got me picking up a bunch of goats to bring back up across and down around to southern Spain. Fill up there with sheep and come up, via Santander–Plymouth, back to that halal abattoir just down the road. What else could I do, my love?'

Miranda pondered. 'Gold? Currency? Drugs? There must be something comes from Africa up through Spain.'

'But that's smuggling, pet,' Jack pointed out. 'It's illegal.'

'Mention it to Phil,' she frowned. 'See what he thinks.'

It was typical of Miranda: if Jack could only make money more quickly, he could spend more time with her at home.

By the time Jack had got through the traffic jams,

embarrassed by the looks he got on account of the raucous misery broadcast to the world he passed through, unloaded slowly at the abattoir whose calm Muslims with their razor-sharp knives resisted the indignity of hurrying death, unhitched the animal trailer at Phil Scritt's haulier's yard, scrubbed it out and hosed it down with disinfectant, beetled in his rig through Brum suburbs to nouveau riche avenues of Woodgate and finally squeezed into the sloped parking slot between garage and pavement (which conjunction made both house and lorry cab look like toys), Miranda had long since gone to bed.

Loath to disturb his love's repose Jack checked progress on their bathroom. They already had an en-suite, but once the new improved one was operable the door between bedroom and old bathroom was to be bricked up and a new doorway knocked through in the opposite wall. Sure enough, the porcelain bed of the shower was laid and tiles attached, and the huge scallop shell bath in place. Looked like it needed little more than wires and pipes connecting; Jack suppressed a chuckle, anticipating a Polaroid of Miranda his Botticelli beauty stood in the bath, one hand unconcealing her breasts.

Jack tiptoed downstairs and without a second thought set to cleaning up: the kitchen suggested the aftermath of a children's party that'd gone horribly wrong, except that they didn't couldn't have kids. One thing Miranda hated was washing up. The sitting-room was little better. Every now and then Jack would point out their labour-saving gadgets and gizmos – like all-in-one hovercraft vacuum cleaner that sucked up dirt, washed carpets, dusted, polished and cleaned the windows in response to a computerized keypad in the handle; or their dishwasher that to others' envy

169

accepted every bone-handled knife, burnt pan and crystal glass. Miranda glared.

'Do you want me to suffer housemaid's knee? To have rough calloused hands? You big oozy-woozy bully, Jack Knighton, I thought you liked Mummy's hands too soft to do dishes, I thought you liked Mummy's fingers smooth when they hold you hard, naughty boy.'

Jack melted in the warmth of Miranda's affection, and now he cleaned up without complaint. In the early hours of the morning he sneaked into the bedroom. To judge from her breathing Miranda slept deeply. Jack crept around to his side of their king-size bed and slipped under the sheets. The salesman at Sweet Dreams promised that even as big a man as yourself, sir, could get in without waking the missus, on this separately sprung mattress. No matter where you've been, sir, the cheeky lad. Within seconds Jack snoozed content upon it, dreaming spumous, frothy, foamy, soapy, bubbling, lathery dreams.

Miranda awoke to find Jack asleep at her left breast, his lips latched on to the nipple, hovering slack and dumbly. Miranda pushed and pummelled him away from her. 'Get oorrgh, you horrible creature.'

Jack stirred groggily.

'You pathetic joke of a man,' Miranda scowled, getting out of bed, making her way across the deep pile carpet towards their soon to be superseded bathroom.

'My love,' Jack mooned, drinking in the sight of her wobbling arse before she closed the door behind her, at which point he sighed, got up and trudged downstairs to fetch breakfast.

While he put frozen croissants in the microwave, poured double cream on a bowl of muesli, fried sausages and scrambled eggs, and whisked a frothy hot chocolate, Jack mused on the different ways they'd each put on weight: he lost his male shape with flab, but Miranda became more womanly. She simply had more to adore; ampler charms to disarm him.

After breakfast in bed they sat back each plump and replete. 'I am stuffed,' said Miranda. She let out a decorous belch. 'Oops!' she squeaked, and Jack giggled. 'I couldn't eat another thing,' she declared, and by pressing against the mattress with hands and heels Miranda raised herself up a fraction and emitted a dainty fart.

'Whoops!' she exclaimed.

'Remember the first time we met?' he asked her.

Miranda lowered her head a little, the way people do recalling the past. They look up when imagining the future, and stare straight ahead making concrete plans. 'In the bikers' bar,' she said. 'I was there with my girl-friends, Sue and Marie.'

'You'd all got milkshakes, taken out the straws and competed for the quickest to down the first in one.'

'We liked to do that,' Miranda agreed, eyes glazing over and head tilting upwards because nostalgia does that too. 'I always had banana to start with.'

'I walked in with my mates just as you three finished together—'

'Rubbish! I won.'

'Yes, you won, my love, and I was greeted by the sight of your face lifting from the glass, a yellow circle of froth around your mouth.'

'And I saw you, dark and handsome and tall in black leather, I was that embarrassed.'

'Our eyes met.'

'Time stopped.'

'The whole café stopped. They could all sense it.'

'All I could do was gape. And then I let out a milky burp, and everyone laughed.'

Jack and Miranda chuckled at the memory, making the bed shake.

'You looked like Gary Cooper,' Miranda sighed.

'And you were a blonde bombshell.'

'Oy, put a sock in it. You never said a word. Just stood in amongst your mates. I thought it'd been a mistake, you hadn't noticed me at all, 'cos you just stood there.'

Miranda gave herself to the memory. Soon softened, gone gooey like fudge in the sun, she gazed glassily ahead, her nostalgia spreading, her left hand stirring the sheet at her lap.

'I'd said to Sue and Marie, hid behind my napkin which I was wiping my lips with, that's the man for me. They knew who I meant. Oh, yes. I was just a girl but a woman all right, all my juices flowing, and I knew because as soon as I saw you, well, like that Montrose song, "your heart is sweet and sticky", and mine was.'

Jack felt Miranda's right hand reach for his and invite it to verify.

'I said I'll be on the back of his bike, with my thighs wrapped around him, leaning my face against his leather.'

Miranda pulled two of Jack's fingers out straight and slid them inside her juicy sex, beneath her own left index finger.

'I ignored his mates who came to chat us up, let Sue and Marie have them, they all came over except him, stood tall and glowering, I waited and waited till I had to accept he'd no interest and then, only then, he looked in my direction and his eyes smouldered. I thought I was going to faint.'

172

Miranda took another finger.

'He was different. Like made from another substance, cast on a different scale from other men. Had an animal beauty. Never said a word he was so arrogant, so proud, just every now and again Gary Cooper glared at me, in the end I couldn't stand it, I pushed back my chair and walked over to him. I never said anything and neither did he, he just walked out of the bar with me following behind.'

Miranda spoke quicker now, gasping between words, eyes closed.

'I didn't care what the girls were thinking or what they'd say, slag slut scrubber, I was hypnotized by him. And I knew it was only envy. I went for him and got him and the other girls could kill. He straddled his bike and I climbed up behind him and squeezed his legs with mine, felt the seat give a little to my arse, put my cheek to his shoulder and hugged my arms round his waist, and when the engine roared into life I swear I started to come.'

Miranda trembled with dispersed, anticipatory spasms, her own engine catching sparking not quite yet roaring alive.

'We went to his place and we had it three times before Gary ever said a word to me, oh yes, we did—'

Now she juddered.

'We did—'

She shuddered, and let out a senseless howling vowel of gratification: it undulated to an end and Miranda abruptly gasped to get her breath back. Mercurial beadlets of perspiration had broken out all over her face.

'You can have me now,' Miranda uttered.

Jack swallowed hard, and as if under anaesthetic felt

173

himself to confirm what he suspected. 'I'm soft,' he whispered.

Miranda didn't hear him as she sank into the pillows. 'Shag me,' she moaned.

At a loss, Jack panicked and dived head first under the sheet, where Miranda seemed to be spreading across the mattress. He nosed into the folds and declivities of her ample flesh.

'Frig me,' he heard muffled in the aromatic darkness as he grunted like a boar sniffing out truffles in the forest.

'Fuck me,' in annoyed tone through gritted teeth far away as Jack snuffled deeper into the mysterious regions of his wife's interior territories, as he explored her swollen subterrain till his softness became hard and expanded. Finally he clambered aboard and entered her and they rocked and rolled with each other, testing their beating hearts and pummelling the bed frame to the limits of its tensile strength.

Afterwards Jack, empty, sated, lay back and let his mind follow whatever course it chose. And he found himself thinking about the recent discovery, in the Hamburg microscope, of the long sought super-symmetric particle. Electrons were fired deep into the nuclei of simple hydrogen atoms where, as expected, they were deflected by the electric forces of quarks, the hard centres of nuclei.

So that he didn't notice Miranda beside him quietly stewing; had no idea at all that she was thinking he was long and lean, he was strong and silent, and what a fool I was to think that behind that reserve lay moody magnificence. Oh yes I caught you in your prime, your brief virility. How long did it last? The length of our courtship. From the day of our wedding your steep

174

decline; letting go on our honeymoon already if I had but known it. Is a woman expected simply to forgive a man for trapping her?

While Jack was pondering how, in some cases – an absurdly small number, like a dozen in ten million or so, but still, occasionally – an electron was not deflected but recoiled violently. And the most likely explanation for such an event was that an electron and a quark actually overcame their mutual electrical resistance: they entwined together for an albeit brief union, before splitting apart again.

The electron was then all the more fiercely rejected. But a dance it is they must have had, Jack thought. In their fleeting conjugal union they transcend their separate selves, and attain the inexplicable unified state of supersymmetry. Or perhaps, he mused, we physicists should call it love.

'You sheep,' Jack heard in his ear.

'Paaardon?' he bleated, turning.

'You heard, you spineless worm of a man I'm wedded to.'

Jack winced. 'There's no need for such words.'

'What are you going to do about it, then?' Miranda demanded. 'You going to shut me up?' She climbed out of bed but leaned forward towards him. 'For once in your life are you going to stand up for yourself?'

Jack simmered, head down.

'You can't shut me up, can you?' Miranda taunted. ''Cos you're not a man, that's why.'

Blood swirled around Jack's head: veins swelled, skin ruddied, brain boiled.

'Because you're a worm, aren't you?' naked Miranda breathed in his face.

Jack raised both head and palm-open hand.

'Go on!' Miranda said. 'What are you waiting for? Are you a man? Prove it. Prove it!'

But instead of erupting into action Jack only began to shake. He let his trembling hand fall. He couldn't strike her; couldn't bear to bruise Miranda's flesh.

Miranda sighed and stood up, her pendulous breasts swinging. 'Ah well,' she tutted. 'It's a funny life, eh?'

Jack looked up at her.

'I'm off to the bathroom, get rid of this muck inside me,' she told him, and turned.

As Miranda made her slow, swaying way towards the bathroom Jack watched her wide backside describe such beautiful volutions, such swagging ogees – shaded by delicious additional shimmies of white flesh – that by the time she'd reached the doorway he'd attained a state of urgent re-arousal. Miranda paused, with one hand on the door frame, and looked back suggestively over her shoulder.

'Tell me, you little boy scout, you,' she murmured, barely mobile lips augmented by expressive eyebrows. 'Is that a tent-pole there, or are you just pleased to see me?'

To which Jack let out a swooning croon of desire.

8

WALKING

Jack Knighton knew how lucky he was. He had a Venusian spouse, while others had no-one, and to have no-one is to be forlorn. At least, that is, if you're a man. He'd heard on the radio that a conclusive study of elderly people showed bachelors dwindled, spinsters thrived; widowers faded away, while widows blossomed. A man alone loses interest but a single woman sends her energy outwards and it shines around her. To Jack the study made sense of his fear, that Miranda should do well to leave him, that he might be again left alone.

If Jack had met her now, rather than later in the year, Penelope Witton in her retirement would have proved the point perfectly. The Yorkshirewoman would, indeed, have agreed with it herself. In the Bradford Animal Sanctuary shop a flamboyant youth and girl picked through items in LADIES' WEAR with jackdaw eyes. They held garments up against each other and giggled, as if discovering an entirely new comedy, a stand-up routine in which anomalous items of out of date clothing had taken the place of jokes. Penelope kept half a beady eye on them.

A familiar middle-aged man entered the shop wearing a disappointed expression: he made for the books and scrutinized the shelves. An enormous woman waddled through the door. The evidence of such self-indulgence made Penny wince. The obese woman aimed for the shoe racks.

The girl came over. All her clothes – pullover, coat, skirt, tights – were faded kaleidoscopes. She had a ring through one nostril. 'May I try on that dress in the window?' she asked.

'Wouldn't you prefer the privacy of a fitting-room, dear?' Penny replied.

The girl stared back, her face a blank screen across which much mental and emotional activity flickered. Do such old women crack jokes? Is she making fun of me? Should I laugh, sneer or snarl? The unsettled weather of youth.

'Of course,' Penny smiled. 'I'll fetch it for you.'

It was a slow morning. Penny Witton possessed still the briskness in her limbs of the four-mile walk here from her home. She was pricing toys, writing figures on self-adhesive labels she then stuck on tarnished plastic. An extremely old man sorted through grey and dun jackets on the MEN'S rail as if looking for one of his own that had been hung here inadvertently.

The shop had a musty air, imported from the homes of dead people along with their possessions. When someone came in or went out they let in a chill blast that made goose pimples come up on Penny's arm, which she observed without shivering. An Asian woman bustled in, scanned displays through histrionic spectacles, and rummaged determinedly through a stack of children's shoes, groping and poking them like vegetables. Deciding upon a pair abruptly she paid and left.

The bookworm came in most weeks. He'd declared himself to the shop ladies as a bibliophile, and a proper one, who only valued books that were out of print: he prowled the charity shops of Bradford seeking rare first editions. Now, empty-handed as usual, he moved across the shop and prodded items in a wooden tray of cutlery: odd knives, forks, spoons; a stained tea leaves holder, a bent can-opener; brown plastic potato-masher, inefficient corkscrews. As if he couldn't bear to leave empty-handed, without a consolation prize at least. In a charity shop you saw acquisitiveness at its most naked. People eagle-eyed for a bargain would gladly haggle over five pence, Penny had discovered, then be off and spend fifty pounds on something new.

There was a kerfuffle in the corner. 'Let me see, go on,' the young man said.

'Push off,' the girl told him, retreating to the cubicle. Penny caught glimpses of her young flesh squeezing out of the tight antique dress.

The old man stepped onto some bathroom scales, waited for the gauge to steady itself. Peered at the result a while; stepped off again impassively. Those scales had been here a good month or two, Penny figured: maybe they needed adjusting. Perhaps they were too accurate. People resent the truth, don't they? Or maybe weighing yourself is not as popular as it used to be.

The young couple came over with a vermilion feather boa draped around the grinning youth's long neck. 'It says five pounds. What'll you take for it?'

Penny stared up at him. Brown lustrous hair falling on his shoulders, green limpid eyes, the remnants of acne. 'What does it say, dear?'

His smile tightened. Self-doubt clouded his eyes. 'It's marked for a fiver. Will you take three?'

Penny held out her hand. 'Let me have a look.' The young man removed the boa from around his bending neck and gave it to her. Penny saw her own writing. 'It says five pounds.'

He started to speak, yeah I know, closed his mouth, was crumpling. The girl, sneering, turned away. He followed her out of the shop. Without a by your leave. Not a smile, not a word.

'No manners,' she said. Mavis in the room at the back said, 'Pardon?' She guillotined old greetings cards in half, glued the pictures onto fresh cuts of coloured card.

Penny bought her own clothes in Marks and Spencer. Otherwise you'd be distracted when you came to work here. Penny took care of her appearance. Had a wash and blow dry once a month, a manicure; put on make-up each morning whether or not expecting to see anyone. She was slim, still elegant, she thought. A woman those a little younger patronized admiringly: she looks after herself. Though robust, a walker, she was almost petite compared to these youngsters you see.

Each generation increased in scale. Was it just their diet? Those careless hippies just now. The brutish youth in town with Edwardian haircuts. Amazonian girls loose-hipped, big-limbed. Plasters on their feet from unsuitable shoes, strumping along in wedges and heels. They eat in public, drink walking along the street, sprawl on the pavement. With their mobile phones. They loll and smoke; the sauntering young. What have they done to deserve their loutish beauty?

Mavis came through to the counter, saying, 'Our kids, they call Ern Grandead, the cheek of it. But what upsets him is they can't do their sums, haven't a clue. Can't add up, he says, or take away, never mind multiply. Never learned. Nor divide and slide rule neither.'

'They don't know how to operate a compass,' Penny agreed. 'Use a protractor? Dividers? Don't make me laugh.' It was true, such instruments of calculation washed into the shop, jetsam from another age. 'It's all done for them now, Mavis. Calculators. Computers. Our ways are obsolete.'

Mavis nodded. 'I never could do logarithms, mind.'

'We're almost extinct,' Penny said. 'Dead as a dodecahedron.'

A smile hovered uncertainly around Mavis's lips. 'You make me laugh, you do, Pen,' she said.

'We're squares, set in our ways,' Penny told her.

Even now, though, she could outwalk most of them, their slouching childhoods squandered before TV. She could have caught a bus or taxi here but preferred to walk, with her spinster's proud imposing stride, despite – because of; ignoring – the discomfort of her troublesome feet, her woody legs, the occasional bolt of pain that stabbed her heel. Who was that man who invented a kind of bubble-wrap for people in shops and factories to stand on, stopped varicose veins, made his million? Wished she'd had one.

The old man in the shop was leafing through a rack of records. Penny noticed for the first time a row of medals pinned to his lapel. Why? There was no remembrance today she knew of. A funeral, perhaps. Or maybe he was a kleptomaniac, had just picked them up, indeed. They often had medals given to the shop. She thought of the celebrations a couple of years back for the fiftieth anniversary of VE Day. It had struck her that the old men around her must have been the youngest combatants of that war: callow conscripts, immature volunteers. The generals and brigadiers and the old career soldiers were long dead (save for one or two decrepit relics whom it was hard to believe had once possessed authority). The war was being commemorated now by its amateurs. Recalling the heyday of their lives, of course. The marvellous deceit of such remembrance: shrouded with piety to honour the dead, but for survivors the war of their youth the deep, defining experience of their lives.

Along with Mavis and other animal welfare delegations Penny had also attended a special service, in the church of a sympathetic vicar, to salute the fallen animals of the war. Some had received Mitchell Medals for Bravery, the animal equivalent of the Victoria Cross. 'They Also Serve.' There was a stuffed donkey in the Imperial War Museum who'd received the Mitchell in the Somme during the Great War. In the Second, a pigeon in Scotland that had flown with bombers headed for the Baltic and northern Germany: if the crew got into trouble beyond radio range and were forced into the drink, homing pigeons were despatched with the news.

It was a chaotic service. People brought their pets, like the Christmas mass which St Francis of Assisi celebrated with real sheep and asses. Dogs barked and howled during the hymns, cats spat, children let go of hamsters and guinea pigs, which scuttled under the pews. Someone carried a chicken, who regarded the proceedings around it with beady-eyed jerks of its head, in a somewhat self-conscious and superior manner.

Some of the humans seemed to have even less idea of what to do than the animals. Looking as if this was probably the first time they'd stepped into a church, they copied other people, and so stood up, sat down, knelt to pray, in long drawn out bustlings. They shuffled up to the altar rail for communion with the blood of the lamb of God like schoolchildren lining up for a measles jab from matron. The young priest remained cheerful and calm throughout as the service kept dipping into anarchy and out again. Penny, at the age of sixty-six, had to stifle giggles like a ten-year-old.

She thought it even odder, though, that in our nation of sentimental animal lovers most churchgoers, not to mention clergy, in the city had shunned this service. The fear of you and the dread of you shall be upon every beast of the earth, as God told Noah. And upon every bird of the air, upon everything that creeps on the ground and all the fish of the sea; into your hand they are delivered, according to Genesis. Every moving thing that lives shall be food for you.

'Animals were put on this earth for man's benefit,' Mr Barton, the churchwarden of her own church, St Bartholomew's, where she was a server, told Penny. 'That's what it says in the Bible.'

'You're probably right,' Penny agreed.

'Yes, it does,' Mr Barton confirmed.

'And it says an eye for an eye, a tooth for a tooth.'

He nodded. 'That's what it says.'

'And it says turn the other cheek.' Penny chuckled to herself at the image conjured up. It reminded her of a television programme she used to enjoy watching, a martial arts drama in which a doe-eyed actor managed to turn the other cheek and extract an eye for an eye in one beautiful flowing movement. Hardly Christian, though.

Mr Barton shook his head. 'I'm a simple man, Miss Witton. We're not eggheads. That's why we've got priests, to explain the finer points of the scriptures. Can you clean the altar cloth next week?'

The last generations who put a Sunday joint in the

oven before going to church, to roast and crackle at home while we worshipped together, were bound to be hostile to vegetarians, Penny reckoned. So in general fundamentalists are threatened less by divergent belief than by a perceived, or implied, moral superiority.

Penny found such hostility baffling. It blinded people, made them indifferent to the sufferings of dumb animals at the hand of man. One hardly needed to regard animals as equal to wish that cruelty be avoided. She worked in the shop three days a week and visited the animal sanctuary itself a few times a year. It was run by people she considered to be secular Franciscans. They never refused refuge. Many were unwanted pets brought in by the families who couldn't cope with them or by strangers who'd found them on the street. Others were beasts of burden that failed to make the grade, that farmers would otherwise put down: runty piglets, lambs with curved spines, horses too old to ride.

But there was a third category: these were skeletal copies of family pets; heartless parodies of their species' domestication. Famine victim puppies, anorexic cats, ribs, joints, pressing against thin rubber skin. Dogs cowering from human contact, flinching from endless blows. Released from some death camp out there, except that this death camp was always moving, from one house to another.

You had only to see them, surely, to know that they were among the oppressed and wretched of this kingdom. Mavis had given Penny a book that contained the hidden apocalypse of the apostle Luke, kept for two millennia by a secret order of monks he founded and ordered to preserve his true teachings. These revealed that in his youth Jesus the Christ of Nazareth had travelled to the Himalayas in search of enlightened masters. St Luke's apocalypse showed clearly, Mavis said, the eastern inspiration for much of Jesus's teachings, which were suppressed by the early Christian church. They included an entire chapter on our relationship to animals, as well as the true beatitudes. Blessed are the animals, who are dumb and downtrodden and suffer now in these days of anguish. Rejoice in this day, and leap for joy, for behold, your reward is great in heaven. As low as you are now so as high shall you be at the side of the Lord.

Unlike this old man in the shop, with his precious medals, there were no animal survivors of World War Two to mark the fiftieth anniversary of its end. Were there? Mavis said Ern reckoned there might be a venerable Indian elephant or two.

Penny's own father had always refused to take part in such commemorative occasions – human or animal. 'I'm not a poppy wearer,' he'd annually decline, munching a meaty breakfast. 'I'm not the saluting type,' he said. Penny never quite knew why not. Her parents grew up on a silent farm eight miles from Bradford, outside Ogden. They were brother and sister. Penny seems to have known this for ever, this unsharable secret. This unatonable sin. Unsure whether or not they were twins, they were of similar age but looked different and ever less alike with age, thankfully. And quite different temperaments. Her mother regretted leaving the farm, while her father had always been drawn to the city, he told her; at night its lights blushed the sky, an eternal dawn just over the horizon. As if he planned it, with her pregnancy they were hustled towards the anonymous industrial metropolis.

Penny's father was a squat, pugnacious man, sensitive to dupe or slight, quick to defend himself. Her mother, timid, nervy, spoke to people with her eyes screwed up as if dazzled at the danger of another person seeing into them. Scarcely less anxious indoors.

'When guests arrive, say, "At last,"' she recited to her daughter. 'When they leave, say, "What, already?" And mind,' she added with a querulous smile, her own daughter's approval needed, 'you don't get them mixed up, Penny.' Not that they ever had guests.

Her mother's gestures: would rest in her palm one elbow, the hand at her throat in a restraining posture, as if ready to hold back some awful expulsion from her oesophagus, or to hide a trembling there. Sitting, towards the end, rocking slightly, hands loose fists in her lap with the thumbs wedged between first and second fingers, thumbs guilty of something, ashamed of them.

The old soldier meanwhile steers himself towards the door. Bet the skinflint was using the shop as a place to pass the time; too mean to pay for a coffee somewhere; has contributed nothing to the piggy-bank conspicuous on the counter. Penny glares after him. Then as he reaches the door and puts a hand on the knob he turns and with a sly smile inclines his head a fraction towards her. It's not a bow, it's shorthand for a bow, an indication of chivalry. It's sardonic. He did steal those medals! But does he really think that he could escape if Penny pursued him? A walking chase through the shopping centre would ensue! She follows him in her imagination. Shoplifting pensioner collared by charity shop have-a-go heroine! Not that she'd have to arrest the man herself. Would simply trail him at a distance, dog his footsteps until she saw a policeman or burly citizen to recruit. Walk him into the ground, she would. Is it not the marathon in which female athletes will first gain parity with men? Is it not true that had races been devised by female Olympians there'd be far longer, endlessly arduous ones?

As a young woman Penny had a high-stepping gait, pushing up off her toes; she felt she'd like to leap, knew she looked like a girl with joie-de-vivre and a dash of madness, cared not a jot. Inherited the walk from her mother, oddly, who scurried like a terrier on the tips of her toes, like a jittery dancer dashing point across a stage to her brother's beck and call.

Mavis locked up the shop. 'Did I tell you, a chap came in yesterday?' Penny asked her. 'Said he'd lost his dog.'

'Why did he come in here?' Mavis wondered.

'Exactly. I told him to put an ad in the paper.'

'Good idea.'

'He said, "Don't be silly. She can't read."'

'Get away, Pen. I'll see you on Thursday. I'm off to the bus.'

Penny tutted, and said goodbye. She walked home that afternoon, back to the home of all her sixty-eight years, with her head high and the straight back of a server in St Bartholomew's, passing the collection bag down the pews, back up the aisle. St Bart's church where she was till recently still young Miss Witton. Her father never went. 'Me and God don't get along,' he scoffed.

It's best not to look down when you walk. Pavements look like they've developed a skin disease in recent years. Concrete measles. It's chewing gum. Old age, however, makes Franciscans of us all, Penny reckons, our spines will bend, our heavy heads droop, and we'll all be able to see the worms and other insects our footsteps are about to crush. Not St Francis himself, however: he died at forty-four. Imagine how much the shambling mystic had achieved – his disorderly brotherhood already established across Europe – so young. Still, it's best to hold off the depredations of dotage as long as possible, Penny thinks as she strides on her exemplary, solitary constitutional through streets whose possession has changed utterly in her lifetime. She returns towards the flat above the corner shop her father ran, assisted by his daughter from as soon as she was able – her mother rarely intruding, remained upstairs cleaning, cooking, sewing, ironing. 'The devil makes work for idle hands, Penny.' She didn't stop until her brother lover husband died.

Penny strides home along the terraced streets that look because they're cold and empty now almost identical to her childhood memory of them. At the height of summer, however, they will parade in full their transformation, she'll pass through another language, another dress, another race, step into a different dimension. Except the same old Yorkshire accent resurrected from young brown faces.

Her father was harsh, unbudgeable, mean. It was he not her frightened mother who resented each intruder, every deserter. 'Pakis have squeezed Althorpes out,' he told his women when another polite family inspected their new shop. 'They're ruining us,' he said through gritted teeth. He saw the value of his business and property fall, his customers disappear. But the obstinate bulldog stood his ground, gave none. He initially refused to stock the spices, pulses, nuts, that even in the fifties were available from wholesalers. 'They come over here they can eat our food,' he averred, a stubborn rule he relaxed surreptitiously over the years, sneaking new ranges onto the shelves when his daughter wasn't looking, affecting surprise when a customer found garam masala, a terrible actor fooling only himself. He wouldn't, couldn't shift. 'What's wrong with British?' he demanded, forcing a can of Heinz beans into a customer's basket she'd filled with lentils, Basmati rice, chick peas. She took it back out with a rough hennaed hand, cursing him in Urdu; 'No, please, please, Misser Witton,' in English.

Always grudging. Until in the nineteen-eighties, with rising unemployment, in his seventies, white-haired, stubborn, the old curmudgeon's racism turned nostalgic, 'The first Pakis, Penny, who came here, you remember, they were good hard-working people, nothing like this crowd, rabble on the streets.' With obstinate irony he had kept hold of the immigrants' first target, the corner store, and they had come in all around him until WITTON'S GROCERIES was the last white incestuous Christian enclave in a Muslim sea of streets.

Her father died at the till. Penny kept the shop going – by then she did most of the work anyway – and was bemused to find its fortunes dwindle. Her customers, to whom she'd always been polite, friendly, Christian, for God's sake, now her rude father had died carried their shopping bags a further block or two to Muslim stores, or drove out to the supermarket.

Helplessly she had it crumble around her, till within a year the shop was little more than a confectioner's frequented by sweet-toothed shoplifters, delinquent smokers. When the break-ins started, Penny's fury astonished her. Her body hummed with anger. She was even sure she knew the culprits, boys she'd watched grow up; but, it turned out, not quite sure enough.

Her local community policeman sympathized. She told him she knew the names, he hazarded a guess that he knew them too, they wrote them on separate pieces of paper like a parlour game, create-your-own-Snap, 'cos there they were, the same names, Gufaz and

Sultan. But he needed fingerprints, a witness, stolen goods in their possession or, best of all, in fact the only thing, to be honest: to have caught them in the act. The lads themselves know that, of course, he told her. He would arrest them, just to let them know he knew they did it. They'll be a little anxious at first as they're hauled in for questioning, until they get the picture. It's all part of the game.

And if by chance someone did see them stealing out of Penny's back shed laden with worthless goods, someone who doesn't know them happened to be passing by, a remote chance in itself never mind that they'd come forward as a witness, then the youths' solicitor will delay the identification line-up on this and that pretext for weeks, while the lads grow beards, cut hair . . .

'Why do they do it?' Penny asked. What she meant was, They have no justification at all, do they, it's an absolute outrage? Yet articulating the question seemed itself to enliven her curiosity, so that as soon as she'd expressed it Penny genuinely sought an answer. 'Why do they do it?'

'There's no one reason,' the policeman answered. 'How many reasons do you want? They need money to feed their drug habits.'

'Heroin?'

'They're bored and meaningless kids. There's no jobs, of course, but I'm not allowed to say that.'

'What are you allowed to say?'

'There's bad apples and always have been. If we took a hundred and fifty known youths into custody tonight,' the constable reckoned, 'kept them in the cells a week, then burglaries, street robberies, car thefts in Bradford would drop by ninety per cent overnight.'

'Why don't you?' she said.

190

He smiled, nodded, sipped his tea. 'Who would we go after then?' he asked, nodding at the insolubility of the riddle that his question implied.

Penny leased the shop to a Pakistani tailor, retreated into the flat above with her mother, vaulted beyond the immediate community for the church and charity shop, for her retired life. This was just the area of partition she strode through. Past the sullen young men, sleek-haired, sly-eyed. She carried a snarled barb in her belly, thoughts snagged in her head: the mother culture's invaded by outsiders. Lovers unsure whether they are entering exile or coming home, gaining all or losing all, filling or emptying themselves. The invader insinuates himself in, the invader is invited in, soils the carpet with his muddy footsteps. He seduces, he is seduced, he slips into the fertile motherland.

The fury gradually contracted, diminished. Penny looked after her mother, humoured her, rocking in the armchair. 'Electricity's chased away elves that used to live in the shadows,' her mother complained of the light that had beckoned her brother to this lonely city. But she had a point. 'Machines have drowned the silence we used to sense God's presence in, Penny,' she maintained, growing both feeble and sapient in her dotage. Her daughter humoured her, nursed her, to the end: when her mother drew her last breath, to the attendant nurse's disconcertment Penny's first words were, 'What, already, Mother?'

And then before she knew it Penny was old herself: she began to succumb to both nostalgia and the chiropodic complaints of a career shopkeeper. It seemed to her that the speed, the bustle of our trivial lives had robbed us of the contemplation in which we once perceived our place in the generational procession of history. So that we were now people who skimmed over the surface of time. As for her feet, Penny had always had problems, suffered all the ailments there are names for: verrucas, corns. Bunions, chilblains. Kibes – oh so painful, ulcerating on the heel, in winter. Ingrowing toenails, athlete's foot, fallen arches.

Doctors were for hypochondriacs, pain was a test of one's virtue, a Christian privilege, and she wasn't a whiner. 'But why me, Lord?' in times of the greatest discomfort. Do you want me to crawl again, is that it? Would you rather I prowled around the woods on all fours, most merciful Father?

Penny walked every day, though, so as not to stop, to master the pain, to put it in its place. Her feet were her martyr's wounds, her suburban stigmata. This stabbing in her heel lately was simply an extreme manifestation.

She walked home from the sanctuary shop that cold afternoon through quiet streets with her shoulders back, spine erect. She knew that pride was a vice and she tried hard to thank God rather than congratulate herself for her bearing. Penny didn't even know now to whom she spoke in her mind as she walked. All she knew was that the words (their imaginary sound carrying a disagreeable reminder of her mother's jittery voice) were a cross between a poem and a walking prayer, a mantra changing little from day to day:

In the old days, it's true, you had only to glance up at the night sky, crystal clear, to see a shower of shooting stars.

Roses were bright and richly scented, and tap water tasted like dew.

We had thick deep white snow every winter, not this slush.

Never got these ridiculous droughts you get now, reservoirs empty in May. No wonder, with all the people.

Words in her head, insistent footsteps on the pavement home.

When then the pain stabbed her heel. Her ankle buckled, her knee gave, and Penny fell. Hit the ground with a bump. Lay on the deserted pavement, winded; surprised. She'd felt the stab in her heel, yes, and then it was as if the whole earth swiftly tilted, and fell upon her. Time stopped. Now Penny moved her limbs tentatively, testing each hand and foot, exploring the ground. She moved slowly in a world that had stopped turning. She felt as if she'd lost her intelligence: the impact had made her stupid.

Just as she began to try to raise herself up, a slow hand gripped her arm. 'Let me help,' a man's voice said. Part of her wanted to resist, to flap him away. She felt his other hand on her side, and his strength lift her to her feet.

'I'm all right,' she nodded. Saw brown hand, yellow trousers. Embarrassed and suspicious both, Penny kept a knuckle-tight hold on her handbag.

'Fear is the last thing to go,' he said softly.

'I'm all right,' Penny rasped, glancing at his bald head, young smile, pulling her wrist, body from him, out of his yellow-trousered orbit. 'Let me be. Thank you.' Penny trembled, stumbled, and then entered her stride, and with little more than acidic nausea rising from her stomach she walked on home.

9

LOVE MUSCLE

Back in London, meanwhile, on a sofa bed in Rebecca
Menotti's Brixton flat, Sam Caine was nosed awake
each morning by a pure white cat, for caresses she
claimed as her regal due. He called her Cat until a
human being appeared who addressed her by her
name, Gemma, which information Sam registered less
as news than confirmation of data dimly recalled.

Gemma was an even-tempered, sweet-natured
animal who spent most of her life asleep. She had a
basket of her own on the bottom landing, and it was the
one place in the flat in which she never slept. At night
she curled up in the television armchair Rebecca had
vacated, but in the daytime she invented a hundred
spots in which to doze: climbing into cupboards or
drawers left open and nestling amongst clothes; on the
tops of wardrobes; on window sills, her ears pinkly
translucent; perched on the rim of the bathtub,
absurdly, or atop the rickety clothes horse on the landing. Or simply striking a Sphinx-like pose, eyes closed,
pretending to be asleep, in the middle of a room –
suggesting by her feline serendipity and taste a

specificity to the spot, as if it was where two ley lines happened to interconnect, or that nature itself was somehow in secret collusion with Gemma: colour, light, space arranging themselves around her.

Sam slept in the daytime, too, badly. He was startled by car alarms, unaware they warned of no crisis, were to be ignored, their owners vilified rather than any thief. Lorries trundling over traffic calming ramps made the house shudder. Pigeons purred loudly outside on the window sills, as if parodying the white cat who couldn't catch them.

Gemma ignored them. Her afternoon naps were deep oblivions from which she seemed to leave her body behind. Eventually she'd stir, lift her head, perform a long drawn out yawn, then close her jaws abruptly and look around her with mild surprise, as if insulted by what she saw. She then uncurled herself and stood up tentatively, before embarking upon a series of hideously impressive stretching exercises that Sam mistook for the contortions of some feline ashtanga yoga.

When she eventually padded away from a briefly hallowed spot Gemma left behind a scrawl of moulted white hairs Sam took it upon himself to pick painstakingly from the rugs. He also fed her: Gemma wasted no time in working out that whenever this new tenant took a nap she had only to miaow once for food and he refilled her bowls of meat and biscuits. She never, on the other hand, drank from her water bowl, preferring to jump up into the basin in the bathroom and lick from the cold tap dripping there.

That spring, even in the city, the weather was neurotic. It'd be all bright and breezy then suddenly burst into tears; weep a brief shower then pull itself together and put a brave face on things. Rebecca had to leave home armed with a ridiculous array of paraphernalia – sunglasses, umbrella, gloves, sunblock, scarves, lipsalve – wrapped in layers of clothing she could peel on or off as the whim of the climate dictated.

There was a cat-flap in the door out to the small balcony at the top of the first short flight of stairs, but Gemma rarely went outside; neither was she besieged by suitors, having been spayed. She liked occasionally to go and sit underneath stationary cars – sustaining oil stains on her unfeasibly white fur – and even more rarely brought small rodents into the flat, not to torture and kill them but rather to set them free and watch mice scrabble terrified around the skirting boards, with the air of an amused zoologist. Now however she stopped going out at all, other than to evacuate the prodigious quantities of Science Plan Sam served her, and grew fat snoozing on his knee. In Sam's lengthening periods of depression he let Gemma curl up in his lap and stroked her for blank hours at a time: sometimes she kneaded her paws in his groin, a clumsy masturbation that hardened him; or her eyes narrowed with drowsy pleasure and her purring made her body resonate with hypnotic contentment.

'I don't like this,' Rebecca observed. 'Gemma's never been fat. She loses her appetite every now and then. I give her Diazepam to stimulate it.'

'I assumed she was always this impressive shape,' Sam said.

'Not that there's any left,' Rebecca shrugged. 'Davey used the rest of it to bring someone down off a bad trip.'

Gemma possessed the annoying ability to walk directly in front of a human being, tiptoeing disingenuously into the footsteps they were about to take, so that they had constantly to readjust to avoid squashing or tripping over her; they were forced into performing abrupt little dances. It was a trick particularly effective done on someone going downstairs.

She also liked to scratch on Rebecca's bedroom door at six o'clock in the morning: Rebecca had to stretch resentfully out of bed, placing one hand on the floor, in order to reach the door and let Gemma in, before reversing awkwardly back to bed. Half awake, she was then anyway unable to return to sleep as Gemma padded around the pillows and over the hillocks of Rebecca's prone body, nudged Rebecca's crooked nose with her nose, finally coming to rest some millimetres from her semi-buried ear: into which Gemma's expectant purring rumbled, until Rebecca cursed upstairs, tripping over her, to the feeding bowls.

With Sam now on the sofa bed upstairs, however, Rebecca was spared this daily ordeal: Sam was both accessible and responsive, so Gemma left her mistress alone. Rebecca was able to sleep a little longer each morning, to doze unpestered by that pesky cat, who when Rebecca did finally emerge would be lying in feline snugness under Sam's duvet, her white ears sticking out, slit eyes gazing back at Rebecca enigmatically.

Oh, welcome slumber snuggled up to oneself in the voluptuous embrace of mattress, warm duvet, down pillows in that languorous interval between alarm clock and the latest possible moment for the act of self-expulsion. Rebecca luxuriated in this unexpected catless bliss, undisturbed, growing steadily more annoyed as each day passed. Until one chilly morning at the end of March she'd had enough, snapped aside the duvet and slapped up the bare wood stairs in peremptorily grabbed and garbed towel and goose-pimpling flesh.

Davey munching toast with teeth-chattering speed and tossing back a shot of coffee like a Spanish artisan his antelaboral donkey kick of liquor, and lazy-lidded Juice sipping weak tea, Rebecca ignored, striding instead stiff-legged to the sofa bed. There Sam Caine's lacklustre blond hair protruded between duvet and pillows, beside it two white triangles stuck up like tiny fins.

'You mister are a weasel,' Rebecca blurted. Sam braved a glimpse of her, saw Rebecca's cross-eyes clearly. 'Yes it's you I'm talking to, Sam Caine. And that capricious cat,' she spluttered at the forms that froze beneath their visible tips, perhaps slipped a little further under.

'Over two months I've fed and watered you looked after you given you refuge. You've given me nothing. You have done nothing. All you've done is take my horrible cat away from me.'

Rebecca paused, took a deep breath and then another with which she launched into, 'And why have I done this? Will you answer me that? Am I your mother? You think I'm a social worker or something? Well I'm not. I've a very busy life that I've put aside for you and why? Do I get any thanks? The smallest hint of gratitude? No. All I get's this "Who am I?" every day, your bullshit amnesia, well I just don't know how I ever fell for it you must have been trying it on for years you bloody fraudster. Preying on stupid women with your blue eyes just for somewhere to stay in bed with their damn cat for God's sake you asexual creep and I just . . . can't . . . won't . . . bloody well stand it, you hear?'

Once stopped, Rebecca felt instantly foolish. She turned and in the four steps taken to reach Juice had burst into tears. Four wary eyes emerged from the sofa bed to watch the falling of the hot salt of frustration on Juice's shoulder. On the far side of the bar Davey fidgeted, his gaze shifting between one pair of people and the other while nodding his head in an I-told-you-so manner, Dave Imran Golightly warned the women, but a prophet is not a prophet in his own flat, forget it. Just heed us next time why-don't-you. He came to the bar and leaned towards Rebecca, her sobs abating now, and said: 'Let's go down the Fridge Saturday. Bring him too. That's what you need, girl. Him even more.'

They sauntered down Effra Road. 'Davey G. treads the mean streets of Brixton.'

Butterflies squabbled in Rebecca's stomach. 'I'm always nervous before we go out,' she told Sam. 'Don't know why. Always.'

'I'm not nervous,' he replied.

'Oh, get away,' she said, whacking his arm.

'I feel like a prat. It's gonna be cheeeeesy,' Juice lugubriously intoned. 'Can't we wait for Lost, Becca?'

'Loosen up, woman,' Davey reproved her. 'Your face is like a chimpanzee's arse. Relax. Like me.'

'Because you've got the discrimination of a leech. You're like a mental tick on the bloated hide of house music. Hey, that's good. Beat that.'

'Jeezus, what a buzzcrusher.'

'Guys. Please,' Rebecca pleaded. 'Saturday night? Going out? Having fun?'

They'd spent hours getting ready, bemusing Sam Caine with the procrastination of their preparations. Juice and Rebecca tried on a hundred items of clothing with frantic dexterity, as if in a shop about to close, only to abandon a mass of PVC hipsters, animal print shirts, shiny tights, pink feather boas, gunmetal padded jacket, blue transparent plastic dress, lace

199

trousers, littering the floor, and come upstairs and sink into armchair lethargy watching Cilla Ulrika Xena, making phone calls, cigarettes and tea. Davey broke off from cooking fish stir-fry to hand Sam a black silk shirt. 'Yeah, suits you, mate. Chill.' Such was the convoluted rhythm of the evening. The cooking and consumption of dinner at nine p.m. was an intricate affair because the apportioning of calorific values, proteins and carbohydrates seemed to be of crucial significance.

'Look at him gobble,' said Juice. 'It's true what they say: the way to a man's heart is through his chest cavity. With a sharp knife.'

There followed a lengthy period of digestion during or perhaps after which Juice put tapes on – 'Night Time World Vol. 1', 'Red Planet 6', 'Dark Energy': the flat's open space felt more than ever like a factory. Davey sat stiller than Sam had noticed him all day, as if sitting an examination, at the food bar separating pills into tiny self-seal bags, compartmentalizing powder into twists of aluminium foil and cutting up sheets of paper into miniature squares. Rebecca greeted John and Fuyuki and other friends and acquaintances who dropped by, made them tea, poured mineral water and Coca-Cola; they stayed, chatted, looked at Juice's tapes, conducted transactions with Davey, asked Sam questions he didn't understand, left or stayed.

Sam hid his ignorance of everything and had to admit to himself that he'd got it wrong: a night out here actually meant a night in and it had been quite enjoyable really. Rebecca and Juice disappeared downstairs again soon after eleven and Sam yawned. Three or four strangers sat around Davey saying nothing, the music having got louder through the evening until now they had to shout to be heard. Sam imagined himself lying down and falling asleep. He considered pulling out the sofa bed, and turning off the music at midnight if they didn't get the hint. Though they'd surely want to be going home themselves soon.

When Rebecca and Juice came flouncing back upstairs transformed. To whistles and hoots Juice strutted her stuff: John, with poppy-red hair, substituted an Abba CD for the techno tape. To the accompaniment of 'The Name of the Game' Juice catwalked across Rebecca's lofty boards in seventies gear that made even the amnesiac Sam Caine nostalgic: knee-length white PVC boots, tan tights, pink velvet hot-pants that snuggled her every fleshy inch, a white wraparound halter top, tacky rouge and thick mascara and a hairpiece that extended her blond hair towards her waist.

Rebecca patiently awaited her turn, knowing male eyes in the room were darting and shifting towards her even as Juice held centre stage. John anticipated then conducted events by cutting to 'Hold That Sucker Down' by OT Quartet, and Juice sidled off. Rebecca was sheathed in a white fishnet catsuit over black bra and knickers, a studded black collar, black belt with zippered pocket around her waist, shod with a pair of Adidas trainers. She danced into the middle of the room in a manner Sam Caine was sure he'd never seen anyone dance, like a robot out of control – except that Rebecca retained a sensual grace while thrusting bumping pumping eight different parts of her body to the monotonous music, bizarrely, as if she were responding to eight different beats when in fact there was only the one deadly repeated thump. The others, however, leapt forward to join her, a cluster of spinning satellites, and Sam watched them blankly, confounded.

At the end of the track someone said, 'We're ready to go,' and they almost were. Rebecca spilled some capsules into Sam's palm.

'Vitamin E,' she said.

'I'll wash them down with beer.'

'I shouldn't drink anything. Just water. And put these in your pocket,' she said, passing him folded tissues. 'You may need to shit and there's never paper.'

Wrapped in fake furs and velvet jackets, Juice in a coat that changed colour in front of Sam's eyes, they crossed Brixton Hill at midnight. The queue for the Fridge was residual. Black unsmiling bouncers, breath condensing in the cold spring night, let them pass between metal barricades to the foyer where they paid for tickets which a man beside the booth immediately took from them, and they stepped on through swinging double doors, in from the cold into a deafening furnace, hot, dark, crowded, crammed with bodies. Sam Caine let his coat be taken from him and deposited at the cloakroom counter, and stood deserted, and jostled. Juice reappeared with plastic mineral water bottles. Rebecca leaned close and yelled in Sam's ear: 'I'll get you orientated, so you know where you are,' which seemed an ambitious idea, but he let her take him by the hand and lead him through a world he knew he'd never inhabited.

The club was both dark and vibrating with colour in which as much could be seen as was hidden. Rebecca led Sam in slow motion past stunning black trans-vestites by a long bar and into a café where shaven-headed men interwove and lolled against each other on the plastic seats and spilled tea on Formica tables. She showed him up stairs: people passed them, some dreamy, others manic. On the upper floor a balcony stretched round the walls. Rows of seating looked down, through a view obscured by gantries, onto the dance floor below.

The music was deafening and deadening. Rebecca squeezed Sam and herself into a space and gave him a white pill.

'You have this, and if you want more later you ask me,' she breathed in his ear, and downed one herself with water. Sam glumly gulped his, winced from the taste of its toxicity, and followed her back downstairs, to the loggia into which they'd first entered.

'We'll base ourselves over near those speakers,' Rebecca pointed. 'You do what you want: wander, dance, watch, sit in the café, go your own way or stay with me. Just remember, if you want me, I'll keep coming back to that spot. OK?'

'Thanks,' said Sam. 'I'll be fine.'

'And don't forget to drink plenty of water.' Rebecca stood beside him for a while, watching as he did the crowded dance floor, almost entirely male – some women around the fringes – jerking their pumped-up bodies. It looked as if they were working out without weights. Above, beyond them was a stage on which the most exhibitionist men strutted: some made furious patterns with their arms as if trying to communicate to someone across the heads of the crowd. Their wild eyes showed both the urgency and the impossibility of ever doing so.

'Where's the sound coming from?' Sam yelled, and Rebecca pointed out the inconspicuous mixing booth barely yards away.

'It's good here,' she explained. 'Some clubs you have the DJ up front and the whole crowd facing him, it's like a Nuremberg rally.' She paused for breath. 'Here, everyone's facing every which way, the focus is where you are on the dance floor.'

A short while later Rebecca vanished from Sam's side and, relieved, he worked his way back upstairs to where he'd taken the pill, finding a space to stand leaning against the wall around the front of the curved balcony. Dispirited, he gazed at the writhing mass of bodies below, gratified that he had keys to the flat in his pocket, hopeful he could find his way home alone, with the insurance of Rebecca's address still on his wrist. The music was awful, pallid disco songs, with this thumping beat clamped on to kill off any fitful life they may once have had. And why had they brought him – why indeed had they come – to a gay club? What was the point? He didn't mind but he was bound to do or say the wrong thing, and he felt dislocated from reality and maybe that was Rebecca's idea, some kind of trauma therapy. But all it did was to deepen his depression. He yawned. Well, he'd watch for a while, he'd pretend a little interest. Sam eyed those around him: how curious their uniformity, the ubiquity of commando haircuts and muscle-toned torsos, the rigidity of this gay identity strange even if its aggressiveness was less so. The odd thin or flabby man stood out, hopelessly out of place, and here and there much older men, chaste survivors. A gay man, Sam Caine ruminated, must be intrinsically prone to narcissism since he is of the gender he finds attractive: he can use himself as a model of what he desires. Do opposites attract? Not on this dance floor. Here the Platonic ideal is a mirror image. But why such awful music? So loud? Why so crowded?

Sam yawned again. He could feel himself sweating, and his legs ached. He wanted to sit down. No, he wanted to lie down. Time soon to go. It all comes back to the body, doesn't it? he thought. A moment ago I was thinking abstract thoughts, but discomfort pulls me down; and sure it's something physical wrong with me, deep inside, a virus in this computer brain. But then he came back to thinking of his body, here and now: of his tired feet. Of his aching head. Of his stomach. Which seemed to be warm, for some reason that was not the heat of the club, or the bodies around. It was warming up from inside. A hot glow, which spread out, and up. A wave of anxiety overrode, overtook the chemicals. 'What's going to happen when they reach my brain?' the wave asked. I'm watching an experiment, Sam thought; the trouble is, it's going on inside me.

Sam Caine felt weak: his legs turned to jelly, a nausea hovered in his gullet, his head went giddy. Sam leaned forward, rested his weight against the balcony parapet and acquiesced to the warmth as it invaded his whole body. Muscular tension evaporated; his limbs relaxed. And his brain effervesced. He had the sensation of an imminent launching, like a ski-jumper or parachutist, and then it dawned on him that the launch had already occurred: he had just taken off.

As with tension in his body so too did fear in Sam's mind ease away. His mouth smiled by itself and he looked again at the men lounging on the balcony around him; he grinned at their fresh retrospective beauty. He remembered deciding some time before – was it a minute or an hour? – to go home, and the idea now seemed absurd, illogical, for this was where the present was, nowhere else, and he Sam Caine was in it.

But there was something else too in the becoming pleasantness of Sam's perception: the awful beat of the music broke up, letting through different rhythms from within it, and Sam couldn't help his head from nodding in greeting to these unexpected arrivals, nor his toes from tapping, nor hands from gesticulating, as if seeking the rhythms in the air. The beat was mesmerizing, the wit of a melody made him laugh out loud, the gorgeous melodrama of a disco diva's voice, hypnotically, electronically, repeated, gave Sam a rush of sorrow that left him feeling happy.

The music became magnetic: Sam had to get closer to it. Just then the DJ stripped the sound of all its thumping rhythm and brought the crowd below to a standstill, leaving only lush electronic piano chords to massage their minds while they got their breath back and rested gyrating bodies. And then from far away, from deep down in the depths of the speakers, a drum machine pulsed and rumbled. Calling to Sam Caine, to him alone. He set off down wide crowded stairs and tripped along concrete corridors in which bewildered soldiers necked pills, snogged each other, gawked at Sam as he passed by. Sam smiled his way through, dragged by the drums that were coming to meet him: beyond, he could hear the DJ teasing the crowd with thumps and chops and slabs of sound. Frenzied revellers hooted and whistled. Sam pushed through swing doors just as the drums cascaded over a thousand other people too, they crashed over the dance floor and all the crowd were in the beat and on it again with a great surge of relief and release, as if in celebration of Sam's arrival the whole dance floor jiving pumping joy.

Sam insinuated himself through to the heart of the throng, found a small space surrounded by fierce bare-chested men drenched in sweat, T-shirts wrapped around waists, and he danced. He let the music come in and take over, it entered his body, infiltrated every cell. Yet he was inside it, too, and the body of the

206

music duetted with his body, tentacles of sound entwined themselves around his limbs.

Rebecca watched him: she saw he had a madman's grin slashed across his face; sometimes his eyes were closed, surrendered to the overwhelming ocean; at others he luxuriated in the secret pleasure of his tingling tactile body. He didn't see her but he saw others, and when he caught their gaze he knew they understood what was happening to him, and he to them, and smiles of complicity were bartered.

Sam was drowning, in a sea of chemicals. He gritted grinding teeth, tried to keep his head above the surface but it wasn't possible, the only thing to do was relent, to let go, let the hot toxic ocean claim him. He sank into it. He knew the top of his head was going to blow. He'd not felt such intensity in his unremembered life before, it branded itself into his being with a synaesthetic tattoo of heat, sweat, cigarette smoke, loud sound, perfume, amyl nitrate. Intoxicating in the crammed air-conditioned space.

He could dance for ever, such energy suffused him. But his water bottle was empty. He hated to leave this place in which he was safe, surrounded by men who had accepted him, but he pulled himself away and forgot them. He traipsed upstairs where the toilet was dark and full of bodies, and slipped back out. He wandered into a chill-out room, where much gentler music made it seem like time had slowed down. On the way downstairs he passed Davey intoning, 'Ease. Trips and whizz.' Davey clocked Sam wide-eyed and clumsy, and grinned.

'You up or what, black eyes?'

Sam tried to formulate a reply but found words were fish in his mouth, his tongue a blunt hook to catch them. Davey freed him from embarrassment with a hug.

207

When he returned downstairs Sam realized that
Rebecca had vanished. He wandered around the club
searching for her, growing distraught, convincing himself he'd never see her again. It was a devastating
prospect. Finding himself back in the loggia, people
jostling past him, Sam gazed forlornly at the dance
floor. People were slumped around the edges like dolls
wound down: some, after devouring more chemicals,
sprang to life again and re-entered the chaos, manic
once more. Sam spotted Juice near the speakers: a
stranger sidled up behind her and danced ever closer,
adapting his hip sway to hers until he'd got it, then he
put his hands on her hips and pressed his groin into
her bottom and they writhed. Then each twisted
around the other until their lips could meet, and they
kissed long and slow. Sam Caine stood there for a
couple of minutes more, or it could have been hours;
time was not linear, neither was it circular, exactly, it
was a wheel spinning along a road. Sam Caine felt himself slowing down, he was one of the mannequins
losing vitality.

All of a sudden Rebecca was there beside him. She
hugged him, gave him half another pill, and dragged
him into the café.

'You OK?' she asked.

Sam nodded inanely. He thought he must be shivering, although he was hot not cold, and he concentrated
on not spilling his trembling tea.

'I've been keeping an eye on you,' Rebecca smiled.

'Really?'

'Come on, let's get back on the floor.'

Davey was dancing with his head bent and hands
out, looked to Sam as if moving things around on a
surface, or parodying work on a factory line. A life
others had that he had avoided? Or an allusion to

everyone's working week, from which dancing to mechanical music was the newest form of escape?

'You've come up again,' Rebecca told him, grinning.

'How do you know?' he asked, but she was dancing.

Juice gave Sam some chewing gum. Rebecca regarded him with a demonic smile. Cross-eyed, crooked-nosed and sweaty, Sam realized how beautiful Rebecca was, a belladonna with dilated pupils. He thought he shouldn't stare at her but he couldn't help it, his gaze kept returning to her. So with an effort he closed his eyes and once more the music.

Sam surrendered. He heard the music not only with his mind: he had turned to liquid and the sounds were swimming through him. He and everyone else was riding, surfing along on the crest of the rollercoaster music; awash with chemicals; drenched in music.

Got me burning up. And the music poured through Rebecca, too, through the chemicals inside her; the rhythm, the remorseless magical beat gushed through her, and she rode the music. It occurred to her that a childhood promise was being fulfilled: that we might pass through the wardrobe, through a door in a wall, a tunnel in a mountain, into another, enchanted, realm. Is this what we've done? she wondered.

Juice passed Sam a popper and he inhaled and the intensity was amplified with a sauna surge of heat. He opened his eyes and there was a totally shaven-headed guy in front of him, skull glazed with sweat, wearing only yellow dungarees; it was clear he'd been smiling, and once Sam had focused on him the man leaned forward and hugged him. Time stopped. Was it the music, or the drug, or a stroboscopic lighting effect? Time ground to a halt. But people could still move within it.

'You know,' the young man said in Sam's ear, 'in a sense, every parent is a sacrifice to their child.'

Sam and the man released each other from their embrace. Sam tried to work out with his messed-up mind whether the man had just mimed the words to the song in their heads. He wanted to know, and he also wanted to hug the guy back, so he did so, closing his eyes.

'What?' Sam asked.

He heard, 'Life spins around,' and he broke their clinch again to see the young man smiling at him. Mouthing the same words, 'Life spins around,' then nodding as he began to dance again.

Sam turned to get Rebecca, to introduce her, he pulled her over. But the man had gone. 'This guy hugged me,' Sam began to explain.

'Yeah, that happens,' she yelled.

Sam gathered himself to tell her he thought the man recognized him, had a message for him; it took a moment to formulate this in a sentence, though, by which time Rebecca had told him, 'I love dancing!' and pulled away. This time he didn't stop himself from watching her. Rebecca flexed and shimmied her body and limbs. The air was like water. Her back, shoulders, hips in motion became marvellous means of self-expression. She swayed her head this way and that, she looked at Sam with drinking-in eyes, her mouth pouted, 'Whoo!' and on top of all those different movements her whole body, whole being undulated in one overriding serpentine shimmy.

Suddenly there was an explosion of sound, of red light and of heat above their heads: a great red ball exploded, like the sun bursting, like a revolution of the sun.

And now Rebecca's body was against Sam's, still; she caressed his arm, it was like velvet.

'I've never been so happy,' he told her.

'How do you know?' she smiled.

'I know,' he averred. 'I would have remembered this. I'm sure, somehow.' He was drawn into her eyes which were looking at his, until he could glimpse hers closing as he closed his eyes, and they delicious kissed each other's lips.

Floating (2)

It was warm in the stone cottage now. Condensation on the walls, as if they were sweating.

Contractions came every twenty minutes. I gasped through them. 'Try to sleep in between,' Jack, the bald, corpulent Brummie who had appointed himself my birthing partner, suggested. Impossible. As soon as I was gripped by a contraction I could only bear to be standing. So in between I had to perch on the edge of the bed, ready to heave to my feet at the first twinge. And lean forward against the bedroom wall, Jack trying clumsily to support me. Hours dragged by.

'Seventeen minutes,' Jack announced. What was the point of timing them? It wouldn't change a thing. How could it help?

'Fifteen minutes now.'

I didn't even have the energy to tell him to shut up.

My back ached. Weary, I just had to lie down between contractions. But they arrived without warning, besieged me and were excruciating. Jack helped haul me, already in the brutal grip of one, back to my feet.

It helped to rotate my hips, rocking the discomfort around in a circle, cradling the pain. Moaning all the while, an awful lullaby to myself. Women tell you how painful childbirth was and a few months later they're already planning another: does a secret enzyme erase the memory? In a Moroccan tent is where I would have liked to be. I'd read descriptions of nomadic births, of the pregnant woman dancing and then, in the final stage, being surrounded by a circle of fiercely undulating Berber women. Their thrusting movement encouraging, coercing her contractions. A muscular empathy. The pain exorcized by the sound of their hair-raising zagareeting.

The white-haired boy, Ben, stumped into the room now and again. He didn't say anything. Stood and watched with a look of alarm on his round face; scarpered, on spindly legs.

I moved around the cottage, from my downstairs bedroom into the sitting-room, where Jack kept a fire going and put more candles along the mantelpiece as dusk approached. I struggled upstairs to the bathroom: it was impossible to tell whether the urge to expel was coming from womb or bowels. Halting on the stairs for unstable contractions, Martha now with us, holding on to me with her reassuring strength. Her wiry blond hair, her apple-like complexion. She had the ability to materialize beside me when I didn't realize she'd been in the room at all.

The contractions became increasingly severe. Acute backache. Legs like jelly, I was so tired. Unstable. Exhausted. 'I want a bath,' I said.

'You're not ready yet,' Martha told me.

'Fuck you.'

'Wait a while. You'll really want it soon.'

'I want it *now*.'

'Wait.' To Jack, 'Make her a honey sandwich.'

'Should she eat?'

'I'm not hungry.'

'You need to eat. At least try, Rebecca. Get her a drink, too.'

I rocked the pain with my hips, around in a circle. Don't fight, I ordered myself. And don't push either: don't resist these contractions. Welcome them, that's what I tried to tell myself. The memory of clear instruction in a calm antenatal class, with a woman who invoked the generous authority of all the women who had ever given birth. An incontrovertible accumulation of experience, with every generation, that felt of no use at all in the extreme duress of this present, with two unpractised strangers.

Martha rubbed my aching back. 'Get your hands off,' I snapped: her fingers felt like insects. 'Don't touch me.'

Pregnant women dream of giving birth to a cat, a dog, some other animal. I hadn't. Maybe I should have.

'What's happening?' I heard Jack ask Martha in the corridor.

'I don't know.' Martha spoke as if she resented wasting breath on words, in an accent that still had more West Country than I ever had.

'Tell me.'

'I said I don't know! I'm not a bloody midwife.'

'Could it be the wrong way round?' Jack asked. Out of sight but I could imagine the panic on his face. Jack would have offered up his own pot-belly for a Caesarean if it would have helped.

'A breech? Of course it could.'

The contractions occurred every ten minutes. They came as waves, waves from the dark heart of an ocean, tidal swells of water-muscle looming, to crash and mash me into a mangle of tissue and blood and bone on the beach. Waves rearing up from inside. It was like an awesome riddle, but one I couldn't solve because I was being pounded: my mind was hardly free to attempt a solution. My only hope was to keep my nerve, and concentrate, and surf the pain; to climb up and ride these waves. Otherwise they would surely kill me.

10

PERI-NATAL, POST-NATAL, HAZARDS AND DISASTERS

Which came first, story or history? Just as advertising uses the means of telling the truth in order to tell lies, so a historian views fiction as duplicitous embellishment of fact. But how else to enter consciousness? We look back along the stretching perspective of human record and see, beyond its end, storytellers around a fire; imagine bards and balladeers. But were they ever without contention? Did some scrupulous listener not decry this singer's glorifying rhetoric? Didn't a swell of snoring greet that contented pedant?

Myth, ancient or modern. The narrator's same vexed question: story or history?

In a small, untidy flat on a Manchester housing estate Solo O'Brien woke with a jolt, from the mild electric shock insomnia intermittently administered. Sprung wide awake he lay in the dark, thoughts scattering. There were times when he went to sleep during the day, not out of tiredness but in the hope that he might dream of his wife, because his unconscious retained a more lucid image of her than his conscious mind — and so then replenished it. While at night he'd put off going to sleep, preferring to slump in the lounge drinking, swimming in memories, drowning . . .

Now Solo lay, reluctantly alert to the building in whose gut he stewed, as the tower stirred itself and came to terms with another day: ceilings sighed, girders groaned, lavatories gargled, fridges hummed to themselves. From Ben's room came the sound of tapping keyboard. Solo flicked aside the duvet and launched himself into the morning.

In the bathroom he sighed at his caprine reflection, considered shaving off the goatee beard; reminded himself that without it he just looked weaselly.

'And how's Ben doing at school?' stern, the woman asked.

'Fine,' Solo nodded. 'Great, really. Top of the form. As they say.'

'How about bullying, Solo? Still calling him names? Spaz, and—'

'Oh, no, none of that, Pat, thank God. And the Blessed Virgin. Good kids round here, they're, sort of, protective towards him, you know.'

'Because it's common, even natural, members of a group picking on the weakest. If we detect it early we can get in there and sort it out.'

'Oh, yeah, sure, Pat, I know, that's right.' Solo raised nervous eyes from coffee cup to interrogator. Pat had been visiting him three, four years now – he'd been on her first roster of clients when she moved up from London – and he suspected her feelings for Ben were nobler, purer, more useful than his own; relations between them made him intensely uncomfortable. Because all she wanted was to use the entire panoply of state resources, colleagues' expertise and her own

218

righteous anger for Ben's welfare. And Solo spent each visit – after scouring the flat clean, scrubbing all ashtrays, expunging the smell of dope with joss sticks, aftershave and furniture polish – trying to convince her that he needed little or nothing, everything was dandy, no problems, none. That for a single father bringing up a boy with cerebral palsy on job seeker's allowance and child benefit in an inner city slum was a bed of roses. He could never quite bring himself to trust Pat, though, because her social worker's loyalty was that of a surrogate mother's, to the child not the lone father, and if she judged it necessary she'd scoop Ben up and spirit him off into the labyrinth of the state's nursery.

It didn't help that there was a police constable standing outside, even if he was only an escort: council bailiffs came into Crapton accompanied by titanic bodyguards, doctors refused to make home visits here at all; ambulances hurtled in with panda car outriders – though often too late: few residents had telephones and the public booths were wrecked. When someone had a heart attack or stroke, a relative ran down to the ground in search of a black BMW, to beg from a dealer the use of his mobile phone.

'We're like detectives nowadays,' Pat said. 'Have to be, but we need eyes in the back of our head, too. We've got abusers in front of us and bureaucrats behind. Some of what you see, Solo . . .'

Pat spoke as if there was a stone in her mouth obstructing her voice; she managed to move it around with her tongue in order to get words out, but it strangled her pronunciation, making her accent throttle and shift, tortuous, between standard English elocution and Cockney; as if she couldn't quite bring herself to fully relinquish the middle class she came from for the proletariat with whom she claimed allegiance. Anger lurking in the twisted syllables.

'Any problems with his diet?' Pat asked.

'No, none, he eats like a horse. No sugar of course. Never! I mean, he doesn't eat too much either, Pat, that's only puppy fat. I don't let him scoff or graze, movement's difficult enough for the lad without extra weight to drag about.'

Solo was sweating.

'No more toilet problems?'

He shook his head vigorously. 'Oh, no, never now, Pat. I mean I put a diaper on at night just to be sure but I hardly need to any more.'

'And—'

'And before you ask he's sleeping fine. Right through. I have to wake him up.'

'I'm sorry we couldn't get the nappy allowance back, Solo,' she said through gritted teeth. 'It maddened me they got away with that one. Where were the media? They're not interested.'

'Never are,' Solo agreed.

Pat nodded towards the corner of the room. 'When's the last time he used the walking sticks?'

'Can't remember, to be honest, Pat, so long ago. Don't know why I keep them. Sentimental reasons, I s'pose.' Solo wondered whether she could hear his teeth chattering. He wanted to throw himself at her feet and say help me Mother of God please help me. He needed a woman. In fact, Pat wasn't unattractive; she was short, stocky, with a round flat face, and her anger inflamed her. It crossed Solo's twitching mind that he might throw himself at her feet, yes, but only to climb from there to her generous lap. To hug her girth, weep into her pillowing thighs, have her stroke his head and soothe him with burbulent words. Except he'd be

220

surreptitiously unbuckling belt and buttons, and she would be covertly shifting arse and slithering hips even as he wept and she soothed still, and he'd slide off her knickers. And by now weak with weeping he'd swoon, bury his face in her bush, and her strangulated voice would break free of its impediment, her soothing utterances would lengthen; words lose linguistic meaning but attain another, transmogrifying from English into the groaning esperanto of pleasure only it never was, was it, it was always individual, every woman registered her abandonment uniquely. Forget ewes identifying their own lamb's bleating; forget handwriting, fingerprints, DNA; this was the most personal expression of identity – or at least, *pace* Einstein, the most beautiful; as would be Pat's. Oh Mother of God he wanted to provide and hear her angry orgasm—

'I mean with walking sticks, I ask you,' her annoyed voice reached him.

'Sorry, pet, Pat, I mean, what were that?' Solo asked, shaking himself.

'I said they've privatized the Motion Aids and Artificial Limbs Department, divided up the various' – Pat air-quoted with hooked fingers – '"goods" as they call them, and put out their provision to tender. As well as giving the various "customers" (doctors or social workers like me) who procure goods for our "clients" (which means Ben), giving us the "option" of purchasing goods – crutches, wheelchairs et cetera – from the cheapest bidder. If Ben needed a ladder-back, f'rinstance—'

'No, he doesn't.'

'I know he doesn't, Solo, but if he did I'd get it from, I don't know, Aberdeen if that was where they're going cheapest. But the thing is we used to have a group of carpenters at the Clinic for Partially Sighted Artisans

221

over in Stretford making walking sticks – out of beech, incidentally, from a wood in Cheshire. Now, a company's put in a lower quote to the Social Services Finance Committee to provide walking sticks which they import from Ceylon. Can you believe that?'

Solo shook his head. His erotic reverie had faded, the quick tight tide of blood receded.

'*Probably* produced by child labour. *Certainly* carved from hard woods cut from the rain forest. But if they've offered a lower price forget ethical, social, environmental considerations, Solo, our committee's obliged by law to purchase from them. It makes me seethe.'

As she was leaving, Pat turned to Solo on the doorstep. 'No sign of the . . . ?' In the pause he saw her countenance cloud. 'From your . . . ?' It wasn't only injustice riled her. 'No word from the boy's mother?'

Solo shook his head, Pat left, he shut the door, leaned against it, closed his eyes; let his knees buckle, and sank. The boy's mother. Strange how her image swam in and out of focus, while certain conversations resurfaced seemingly entire. They used to kid about her colour.

'I'm a Negro,' she maintained.

'You're a mongrel,' Solo told her. 'Like all of us. You're a Manchester mulatto, love.'

'I'm a daughter of Africa,' Syreeta laughed. 'And don't you forget it, you Irish runt.'

'You think you're a princess, just because I worship you. You're all mixed up, a mish-mash, half-Hulman and half a potent mixture of under the influence influences, sweetheart.'

'You Mancunian mick!' Syreeta exclaimed, pushing Solo onto the sofa and casting her ample charms upon him. 'What am I, you Paddy poltroon?' she demanded.

Solo spluttered, trying to heave her off him, failed, and slumped. 'You, Syreeta,' he murmured, 'are one pure and gorgeous specimen of female negritude, acushla.'

'What am I?'

'You're black, woman.'

'And even though you're a pale imitation of the human ideal, me I look beyond the skin: I love you, Solo O'Brien, don't ask me why. And if we ever have a child, what will it be? I ask before I deign to let our colours mix and mingle in the palette we call a bed.'

Trying to keep a straight face, Syreeta pressed her solid knees once more upon Solo's wiry pectorals, then bounced off once astride him, and came down onto her elbows, her body atop him lengthways, so that their eyes zoomed in towards each other.

'If we have a child, it'll be one little black mother-fucker, Syreeta,' Solo acquiesced, before she kissed him, giggling.

Except, of course, that he wasn't. In the hospital Syreeta recovered from the natural shock of childbirth and gazed at her snow-haired son in the cot beside her unable to believe her eyes; she suckled him with a look of stupefaction on her face – this tiny albino baby at her full brown breast – eyes glazed as his, trying to work out what had happened. In the turmoil of this genetic engineering age we had embarked upon could it have been some other woman's egg? Or – Syreeta suffered for irrational seconds that dread male suspicion that nature shielded women from – had Solo been messing around? Or was the hospital using her as an incubator for some infernal experiment – horror movie to follow based on a true story? Or was she simply the victim of a cosmic practical joke?

'Albinos are rare, which means they're special,' Solo tried to reassure her. 'About one in twenty thousand, the doctor said, in this country. That means there's three thousand altogether.'

'When's the last time you saw one?' Syreeta coolly demanded. 'Among black people?'

'They're common in Nigeria,' Robbie informed her when the boys came round to visit back home. 'We looked it up. You see them in any Nigerian town.'

'When did you ever go to Nigeria?' Syreeta eyed him suspiciously.

'There's a whole tribe of albinos in the highlands of New Guinea.'

'Make great musicians,' Wick maintained. 'The Winter brothers, Johnny and Edgar both. Yellowman in Jamaica: Mr Sexy with his shabba ragga music.'

'He's even whiter than Salif Keita,' said Luke, having picked Ben up from the chair in which Syreeta had laid him.

'The way you mispronounce African names shows your racism, Scouse,' she said, in her guttural Mancunian accent.

'Honest: the white Negroes of Africa. An esteemed and honoured category of people,' Robbie claimed.

Syreeta was unmoved. She provided Ben with a minimum of mothering for survival. After feeding she put him down and ignored him until his bawling irritated her enough to stop it with her nipple – though even that seemed to Solo more to relieve the milk from her swollen breast than to nourish the baby. He came home from work to find Ben's nappy unchanged in hours, the boy lying still and blank as his mother sitting on the sofa, two remote idols estranged from each other and the world.

Solo quit his job at the petrol station. The health

visitor explained post-natal depression and Solo looked after Ben, only brought him to Syreeta sat massive and unconcerned for feeding. He looked after Syreeta too, my black queen he called her at her throne when he brought Ben back from walks in a sling.

'It's not right,' Robbie told him.

'It's very common,' Solo explained.

'There's something wrong, man,' he persisted. 'I suppose as long as she's feeding him. He sounds hungry now.'

'I've got a bottle.'

'She expressed some?'

'I made it up. Syreeta says it's good to start weaning him gradually.'

'From a month old?'

By six weeks Ben was weaned for good, and Syreeta no longer touched him.

'He's special,' Solo beseeched her. 'Noah were an albino. Maybe Ben will build an Ark, survive some other flood.'

Syreeta eyed him flatly, disinclined to waste words.

'He'll have to wear shades is all, our prince. He'll be the coolest kid around.'

'I am a Melanesian,' said Syreeta enigmatically. Maybe she considered it suitably mysterious a pronouncement (Solo had never heard the word before) and at the same time perfectly clear (for Ben suffered precisely a lack of melanin) for those to be the last words Solo would hear her utter. That night Syreeta vanished.

'The Black Queen's gone,' Robbie told Luke.

'Thank fuck for that,' Luke confided in Wick.

'The kid's got a chance now,' Wick nodded to Robbie.

And after she'd gone Solo wondered whether, while

he'd been out of the room, Syreeta had considered their son. Had in fact been already or about to be coming out of the blues but seen the same signs Solo saw: only gradually making themselves apparent, being the very absence of a baby's motor skills that were due. Could it really have been just Ben's skin colour (surely no woman could be so unmaternal, so heartless, certainly not his regal love) or had she noticed as had Solo something missing? There are things one perceives without really hearing them: a part of one's brain glimpses and lodges that knowledge but the mind as a whole does not accept it. A splinter, it works its way towards the surface, but then sharing it is itself another block to acknowledgement; and given Syreeta's reluctance to engage with Ben it was hardly surprising Solo's doubts never expressed themselves. But after she'd gone and Solo had finally admitted to himself his own concern and voiced it to the health visitor, and he'd been to hospital, and a specialist had examined Ben and explained what was wrong, Solo wondered whether Syreeta had sensed it too.

Solo was told that when a child is not suspected of being at risk from cerebral palsy there can be a delay of a year or more in detection. Much of babies' movements, after all, are a continuation of their reflex paddling and kicking in the womb. Their first movements look uncoordinated and disjointed, because they are. What Solo detected was something different: a helpless eagerness in Ben's early smiles, his carriage, his reaches for objects. Once his condition was diagnosed, Solo became an avid parental expert. He wanted to know everything so he could look after his baby, but he also rehearsed explaining it all to his Black Queen on her eventual, penitent return. Solo began by memorizing the dictionary definition of cerebral palsy: spastic paralysis from brain damage before or at birth, with jerky or uncontrolled movements.

'The exact location of the damage inside Ben's brain', Solo imagined he would explain to Syreeta, 'determined the type of disorder, the parts of the body affected. Ben was diagnosed as having spastic hemiplegia.'

Solo did the research and then he scripted his own lines. He wrote them in an exercise book and fine-tuned them in his head, where he committed them to memory. It was important, somehow, in understanding Ben's condition and coping with it himself as well as preparing to tell Syreeta; and it was vital too to get it right. To equip himself with authority as well as com-passion; with as much honesty as understanding.

'Spasticity, Syreeta,' Solo envisaged himself saying, 'is caused by damage – a trauma, an insult, a peri-natal hazard or a post-natal disaster; words that make you appreciate Ben's and all of our perilous passage into existence – by damage to cells in the motor cortex.'

Syreeta would come home recovered from her depression, embrace her man and beseech his forgive-ness and reconciliation. Then he'd reintroduce her to their son and now with the blue devils exorcized she'd adore him as nature, her own and life's, intended, his now evident disability only triggering Syreeta's damburst bond to flood through her.

Later, as she and Solo sat together, Syreeta holding Ben sleeping across her lap – on his face the Buddha smile that emanated from him at rest – then Solo would take Syreeta through the whole unfortunate process from the beginning.

'See, to start off with, love, everything were fine,' he imagined. 'The single cell formed at conception, in one

227

beautiful fuck, by the fusion of your egg, right, and my sperm, began to subdivide and multiply. Within a couple of weeks, cells that form the central nervous system were making a ridge on the back of Ben's tiny embryo. By the end of a month his brain began to form: new cells, neurons, migrated to particular areas of it, where they took on specific functions.'

Syreeta was no scientist but neither was Solo, and she'd follow what he said, because it wasn't the dull biology of school but the creation of this unique child before them. When Solo rehearsed his speech he found himself repeating pauses and gestures; ums and ahs, loves and sweethearts; carefully scripted hesitations. He was working on the rhythm but he also understood that when you're providing technical explanation there's a balance to be struck between authority and ostentation: if you make people feel stupid they'll switch off.

'Each neuron has a simple structure: there's a nucleus at its centre, controlling its function. Then there are axons, they're tiny sort of threads, which process impulses away from the neuron. They're often covered by a myelin sheath which, like giving a computer extra RAM, can increase the workload of the axon and also determines the speed of the conduction of the impulses.'

'RAM? Computers?' Syreeta would ask. 'What are you on about, Solo? You know I'm a technophobe. Couldn't work the answer machine, never mind set the video. You making fun of me?' No. That would be a mistake. No similes needed; keep it simple.

'Now. The neuron also has dendrites, branches like the axons, right, except they receive the impulses that come into the cell from the axons of *other* nerve cells. The spot where axons and dendrites of different

228

neurons contact each other is called a synapse: an impulse passes through the synapse. By about the sixth month of pregnancy, Syreeta, all the neurons have been produced. From then on, till the child reaches around the age of five, growth of the brain is due to the formation of new synapses. Each neuron of a large vertebrate, and that's what Ben is, may bear several hundred synapses. There are a hundred million neurons in the central nervous system of a human being. That's as many trees as in the Amazon rain forest . . .'

No, no. Stick to the point.

'The growth of the human body, in particular the brain,' Solo would continue, 'is so infinitesimally precise that it's only amazing any of us emerge as other than hideously mangled and mutated monsters.'

'Like Luke,' she says, and Solo laughs.

'Yeah. Now, the growth and survival of living cells depends upon the right supply of oxygen and nutrients and hormones. In the womb, which is where Ben were brain-damaged, oxygen is diffused from the maternal to the foetal red blood cells through the mother's placenta.'

In Solo's imagination Syreeta's regal brow furrows; irritation creases her countenance. 'What, it's my fault? I starved Ben of oxygen? Is that what you're saying?'

'No, listen,' Solo says and rushes on: 'Hypoxia – that is, oxygen deficiency – is only one cause of brain damage. The nutrients that the foetus needs are supplied in suitable form, such as glucose and amino-acids, that the foetus can't produce for itself in sufficient quantity yet.'

'Yes,' Syreeta says, warily. 'So again it all comes through my blood, right? It's my placenta in my womb that fed Ben. Or failed to feed him. It's my fault.'

'It's no-one's fault,' Solo wants to say. 'This is not about fault. It's information; it's just the facts. The placenta acts as a barrier to toxic substances,' he continues.

'So I had the occasional drink, yeah, I smoked some cigarettes; less than anyone else I know. And I kept off drugs, you know that, while you had good times. Don't lay that Irish Catholic guilt on me, my boy, 'cos I was a good girl. All speed trials were postponed; all trips were cancelled. Sod off, Solo.'

'Forget the reasons,' Solo will continue, trying to keep calm his imaginary lover and his own flustered mind. He can't even get the rehearsal right, and he's directing the damn thing. 'The reasons are many and various, sweetheart. Let's look at the effect. The cells in the motor cortex of each of his cerebral hemispheres control the opposite side of Ben's body, and they're responsible for conscious voluntary movements. All the parts of the body are mapped out in the distribution of these cells, all the intricate components of Ben's movement and speech.

'Axons from cells which control the trunk and limbs extend into the spinal cord and activate or inhibit the cells there that form the nerves going to individual muscles; while axons concerned with eyes, tongue, face and palate are much shorter, and terminate at nuclei in the brain stem.'

Solo knows Syreeta's pulling away. He stumbles on, because the only thing worse than losing your audience is drying up; corpsing on stage.

'Now, this is where it begins to make sense. With someone like Ben—'

'With someone like Ben? Who is this someone, exactly? Anyone I know?'

'Yes, right. With Ben, impairment of his body's

functions results from damage to neurons or their axons. Such interference with the message-relaying ability of the brain causes a stiffness and slowing of movement, or spasticity. Affecting, in Ben's case, his left-sided limbs.'

What started as enlightening explanation, with Syreeta intent upon every word, has, even though it's only imaginary, deteriorated. She's not really listening any more, sits surly, arms folded, a barrier between her and the baby on her lap, and Solo rushes on to complete the picture:

'Ben has severe difficulties in all forms of move-ment: with arms, legs and trunk, with sucking, chewing, swallowing and speech. That's our boy. That's Ben's condition. Some children afflicted like this are never able to walk. The unequal tension in many different groups of muscles is liable to lead to deformities. Other difficulties may be encountered, like fits and seizures. And as Ben grows up, his increasing size will bring him growing discomfort, and risk.'

Solo let the implications of his failed speech sink in. As he thought about it, he realized that his imagination erred: Syreeta would not get angry. There was no need for her to do so. It became clear to him that she had already seen the same signs as Solo and intuited Ben's disability, his diagnosis. She blamed herself and left; wanted to do no more damage: her leaving, the removal of herself – it was obvious, now – a monumentally selfless act.

For Syreeta denied herself the parental privilege of seeing her child grow up. An engrossing parade of small unexpected development. This last winter Olympics on TV Ben got hooked: the boy in his awkward body sat spellbound by speedskaters and waltzing ice-skaters; terrified by the hurtling bobsleigh.

'Look, Dad, look,' he beseeched Solo, 'flying. He's flying.' Solo turned to see a skier slither down a ramp and take off into engulfing space, shooting his hunched body out ramrod stiff, as if scared rigid as Ben was for him.

'He's flying, Dad.'

Soon after the full diagnosis of Ben's cerebral palsy came the offer of residential care, which Solo rejected. Then someone put him in touch with the British Institute for Brain-Injured Children, and his friends enabled him to initiate the institute's regimen of therapy, their daily repeated hours of patterning exercises. His ragamuffin musketeers – whose only fear was that the Black Queen might one day return – gave themselves over to Solo's assistance. They set targets and kept meeting them: they had Ben roll voluntarily, creep, crawl, sit, stand and finally walk – if with a calliper on his left leg. He learned to read, and to talk – if with a limited range of sound.

'What do you stuff a parrot with? Polyfilla,' Luke fired at the boy. 'What's an alligator's favourite card game? Snap.' Ben grinned and groaned and jerked his head in pleased response. Luke believed in the therapeutic value of jokes. Wick on the other hand believed in the improving quality of music; or, to be more precise, techno.

'It's the repetitive beats, just like these patterning exercises, and every time Ben hears techno his brain'll be mending those axons and filling the gaps in the nerves and making extra connections.'

'Could be true,' Solo conjectured. 'Like the way music brings back the high in your brain.'

'No drugs,' said Luke. 'We're getting this boy off all his anti-convulsive medication, Solo. Just you see.'

Which was rich, Solo reckoned, coming from Luke.

Robbie, Solo's best mate, was his chief ally. 'Ben, he's all right,' Robbie would tell their neighbours on the estate, 'he's an angel who clipped a wing on his way to earth. He's a giraffe with neckache is all; Ben's a bird with vertigo; he's a zomophobic fly.'

11

RATS!

'Deformed animals, mum?' Joe Snow repeated, aghast. 'Monstrous mutations? I'd never work on experiments for drug companies, don't you worry,' he promised over breakfast. 'They're multinational, those pharmaceuticals, and they repeat the same experiments all round the world. Which isn't right,' he opined, hurrying out of the door.

Outside the organology department, Joe U-locked the bike his mother had given him for his birthday to a signpost, plucked the lights off front and back and unsnapped the chinstrap of his bicycle helmet. He was aware that this headgear looked nerdishly ridiculous, and would do until a certain ratio of cyclists adopted the habit, at which point bicycle helmets would be all of a sudden hip, a de rigueur accessory. Just as with his radioactive-yellow anorak. Such was the tyranny of fashion, its gift to behold, to bestow: to define whether or not safety was attractive. Until that day, Joe knew, he'd continue to look like a dork – though he had no choice, having promised his mum he'd wear it. Despite this self-consciousness there were some days Joe – it was hard to admit, but true – actually forgot to take the helmet off. He'd scurry in, rocket to the top floor, get stuck into work. And it could be mid-morning before a double-take in a mirrored surface would alert him to the realization that he'd been walking round the labs and talking to people with a bright blue blob on his head.

Freud certainly had something to say on these matters. The way we forget to zip our flies; say the one word in our huge vocabulary we'd determined to avoid saying. Though Joe reckoned no-one would be able to diagnose with certainty whether in his case it was self-destructive or merely absent-minded behaviour. He reached reception and greeted the tired-looking night porter. 'Freezing fog on Woodstock Road,' he informed Monty. 'Blooming mist floating in from the Parks,' he declared, placing the upturned helmet with the lights in it on Monty's desk.

Monty stared at it and said, 'Looks like a fruit b-b-bowl.'

Joe put his finger in the air. 'Nice image! I've got yesterday's crossword here somewhere,' Joe said, patting his pockets. 'Ah, here we are. There you go. Can't stop, Monty. Must rush. Mr Bone in?'

Monty inspected the torn corner of newsprint. 'Twenty m-m-minutes ago,' he relayed towards Joe's lift-aimed figure, his eyes meanwhile swelling with disappointment. Joe had cut out the easy crossword by mistake.

There was the danger nowadays of rushing his work: as senior lab technician, Joe was overloaded with grateful graduates being granted research fellowships in this the fastest growing department of the university. Some late nights in the lab, truth be told, Joe boosted himself with a little alpha-methyl-phenethylamine stimulation, a nocturnal nip to which he'd been introduced by Willem van der Bierstoonk.

'Just don't tell that bleddy Magenta,' Willem whispered. 'She thinks I'm this accomplished on fresh air and doughnuts? Naive or what?'

This morning, though, Joe had to be composed. He was conducting one study entirely on his own: Mr Bone said they needed it done and there was no fellow qualified like Joe was. He'd get going on that experiment this very morning, as soon as he'd fed his rats. He pushed open the door of their dormitory, was greeted by the nutty sweaty pissy boyish skin smell, and by the quiet scrabble from a thousand cages stacked round the walls of the room. They were hooded rats, hybrid albinos, able to breed all year and put on weight rapidly. Most were male, being more consistent in their responses than female ones. Sociable creatures, they were caged in twos or threes: any combination got along, which was something Joe liked about them, most animals being territorial and aggressive towards their own kind. They could screech when they were upset, an awful noise, but mostly young rats made high-pitched squeals and peeps beyond the range of human hearing, like bats, while older males were in the habit of lying on their backs and singing ultrasonic songs to their females; or quite possibly each other, Joe fancied. One of the composition students in the old Musical Studies down on the third floor had come up and recorded this singing, then processed it somehow through his computer and brought it back into our auditory sphere, made the rodents' serenade sound like it'd mewled from some instrument related to a violin. Very odd it was.

These hooded rats couldn't see as well as wild ones, not like the more widely used Agoutis, but then neither could Joe and he liked them for that as well. He'd discovered they were fond of Smarties, and often picked up a tube from the canteen at lunchtime, came and spoiled a few in a quiet moment in the afternoon.

After feeding his rats Joe went to room 27 where he anaesthetized three white cats he'd prepared there the day before, made a single hole in their skulls with a straightforward dentist's drill, and implanted a tube into their brains. He then came back along the corridor and unlocked his workshop – the distillery, as researchers called it – for more of his daily duties, while the anaesthetic wore off. Joe filled working bottles of Histoclear, which smelled of orange peel, and acetone, like his mother's nail polish; he checked the chloroform, small quantities of which were constantly being spirited away, much to Mr Bone's annoyance.

'They sniff it,' the boss whined, 'at their parties.' At least they no longer used formaldehyde solution, not since, before Joe's time, it was discovered that formalin was carcinogenic. 'Now there was a joke,' Mr Bone told him without laughing. 'Imagine it. They'd be looking, say, for a cancer cure, and the chemical they used for sterilization was giving *them* cancer. They were heroes in my book. Like the helicopter pilots over Chernobyl who received radiation. Should have been given medals, really.'

Joe returned to the room where his experiment was situated. This entire side of the top floor had now been partitioned into discrete rooms: on the other side, the old Veterinary Studies had been given over to purely chemical experiments. With no behavioural component, isolation for live animals was no longer required there, so space was best exploited by one open-plan workshop. A different senior technician was responsible, and Joe was glad he rarely had to cross the corridor into the place, with its rows of benches and sinks and its pervasive aroma of acetic acid, just like a school laboratory.

'You should have smelled it years ago, Mr Snow,' Mr Bone told him. 'In our early days, the late eighties. Some of the cookery experiments we conducted for dog and cat food companies,' Mr Bone said, wincing from the very words he uttered. 'Waste products you wouldn't believe. The stuff that came in here from abattoirs. I'm here to tell you, Mr Snow, there's nothing in the bovine body that can't be minced, pulverized, ground down. We tested possible dog foods on retired greyhounds, to see what they'd eat. Half starved, but they had their pride: sniffing at offal and sticking their noses in the air. Revolting.'

Joe preferred the separate rooms on his side of the top floor, where each experiment was distinct and valuable, like this one in room 27. The three cats had recovered from their anaesthetic. Joe inserted thermometers into their rectums and then injected a mustard drug through the tubes to their brains. He picked up pencil and paper to record what he saw. With each cat in turn, shivering began within a minute or two and quite soon became vigorous and wide-spread. The next effect was vocalization, he noted; periods of miaowing became more frequent and of longer duration and gradually gave way to growling and yelping. This was followed by rapid breathing (tachypnoea, Joe noted for Mr Bone), panting and salivation. Their hair stood on end (piloerection, he wrote) and ear twitching could be observed.

Joe enjoyed writing reports. He might have preferred the challenge of translating English into Sanskrit or Swahili, but failing that, tinkering with his own language was a reasonable substitute.

As time went on, he wrote, periods of intense excitation alternated with periods of a more restful condition. Yes, that sounded right. The cats – or, rather, the preparations, Joe reminded himself – would suddenly charge blindly ahead or jump up and cling on to the roofs of the cages with splayed claws. Their eyes were wild – or, better, their pupils were maximally dilated. In addition, they showed compulsive biting: Joe had to distract them from chewing through the leads of the rectal probes by offering them instead pencils on which they could clamp their teeth. They eventually gnawed through these, soon after which event Joe subjected them to euthanasia, prepared their bodies for dissection and took the lift down to the canteen for lunch. While queueing for pie and chips, plus side salad with Paul Newman dressing, Joe spotted Mr Bone on the far side of the refectory, in the executive area, with Mr Ben Ali Al-Shalir.

Joe wasn't the only one. Individual attention all over the canteen was directed subtly towards that corner. Students, teachers, staff kept looking over their shoulders, sneaking a peek at the two men deep in important conversation. Sages, heads locked. The whispers of the powerful. People snatched glimpses of the pair as if with a glance they might capture the essence of genius, of wealth, of nobility. Or was it that they couldn't help themselves, such was the magnetism of Ben Ali Al-Shalir?

It was a source of satisfaction to Joe that he worked so closely with, in fact was directly subordinate to, Mr Bone; he was fortunate that Animal Studies on the top floor was the nerve centre of the department. But Mr Al-Shalir he knew not at all. Joe doubted whether Ben Ali had a clue who he was. Unless Mr Bone had mentioned him? The bright young spark?

The two men finished their meal and their conversation, and rose together. For a second, Ben Ali looked as short as he really was, but then his charisma reasserted itself and swelled him in every viewer's eyes to a more heroic stature. They exited between the tables, Mr Bone walking behind Ben Ali, who nodded to and helloed senior figures in the department. One day, thought Joe, he could be greeting me. Reading a journal while she ate, Magenta Hroichkova, directly facing Joe Snow a few tables away, was one of the few people who seemed unaware of the procession. Ben Ali slowed down as he passed behind her, and bent to confide something in Magenta's left ear. Joe had a clear view of her face: he saw there displayed a tableau of Balkan acting, shock succeeded by outrage, replaced by lascivious interest, followed by a heavy-lidded flirtatiousness, culminating – all within six or seven seconds – in haughty disdain. Joe thought he also caught a glimpse of Ben Ali's chubby fingers slipping between Magenta's arm and side and giving her right breast a brief squeeze, before he continued towards the door.

People's necks craned towards Ben Ali, Joe observed. Hands hovered, disembodied, seeming to realize how presumptuous a proffered handshake was. They now twitched in mid-air, making ready, perhaps, to stroke the hem of his jacket; to pick off a stray hair or wisp of fluff.

How pitiful people are, Joe thought. As deferential to wealth as ever they were. Then he realized with a jolt that Ben Ali Al-Shalir had just veered, with a ninety-degree turn, in his direction. He arrowed straight towards Joe! Joe's pulse rate accelerated with every step Ben Ali made. His armpits exuded sweat. He began to tremble. The great man was about to say something, what a wonderful moment was upon him, except that Joe sensed that he was going to faint before it arrived. And even if he didn't, his throat was bone dry. It was a certainty that when Mr Al-Shalir addressed him he'd be incapable of reply. Unforgivably rude. Could Joe get away with nodding? Here he was, yards away. Or would Ben Ali fire him on the spot, as he had done to countless grovelling others? Hyperventilation was imminent. Heart palpitations.

Ben Ali swept past Joe and on towards – of course – the side exit behind him. What relief. What disappointment. Joe took a gulp of air, and tried to restore his breathing to normal function, before returning upstairs. He was determined to conduct the present experiment to a standard of which Mr Bone would be proud, even if it was a little soon to hope for another promotion. But you never knew, the way things were going. Mr Bone seemed to be off supervising the conversion of another section every other week these days, as The Laboratory Ltd spread virus-like through the building. Joe appreciated the way that Mr Bone left the names of the sections in place. He'd actually got Joe to help kit out Human Behaviour: to deal with carpenters, plumbers, equipment salesmen; to take responsibility for choosing a water dispenser that delivered an electric shock each time an animal took a drink from it, to test how long before that animal becomes anxious enough to stop trying to drink; as well as a treadmill for giving jolts to the animal not working it fast enough. Joe had found one with both variable speed controls and an adjustable current for less than ten thousand pounds, for which Mr Bone warmly congratulated him.

Such machines and many others were being put to valuable use at this very moment in Musical Studies, with the interesting addition of a carefully orchestrated playing list of muzak broadcast through the speakers for the benefit, as Mr Bone explained the previous month to the higher education inspectorate, of musicologists involved in radical research. 'Music', he opined, 'unquestionably affects our mood. Ambient music in supermarkets and so on. We're researching the possibilities of using it as an aid to learning in schools, as well as to increase productivity in the workplace.' He had a weird sense of humour, did Mr Bone. But he was always alert. Leading the shuffle of bureaucrats from Musical Studies to Human Behaviour, he whispered to Joe, 'Make a note of that flippant jest, Mr Snow. There may actually be something in it.'

Then as he took the inspectors round Human Behaviour, Mr Bone convinced them that it was the graduate students, apparently carrying out vivisection on animals, who were in fact themselves the subjects of the real experiments being carried out there. What were they prepared to do to these animals when it was demanded by science; by a white-coated figure of authority; by truth's eternal imperative; and their own career ambition?

'These are the issues under scrutiny, gentlemen; the cut-up animals are simply a ruse – these young humans are the animals under a microscope, did they but know it.'

Mr Bone had celebrated the inspectors' departure that afternoon with a glass of wine for everyone on the top floor, which they drank out of glass beakers and plastic jugs. After Willem and Magenta and the others had gone, Joe helped clear up.

Mr Bone remained in convivial mood as they took the lift down. 'You see, Joseph, Mr Al-Shalir,' he said, 'and his brother,' he tacked on, 'and myself,' he added modestly, 'have great dreams for this place. A palace of scientific discovery. Remember: through happiness, wisdom. And you're a part of those dreams, young man.'

'I'd never do experiments for beauty products, Mum,' Joe assured his mother the next morning. 'Mr Bone says we should not and we do not have to.'

'But I read about it, Joey,' she worried. 'Those placard people were outside the post office again with their petition.'

'That's lies, Mum. What they say about cosmetics, make up what they want. It's not right.'

At work, Joe began the histology of his white cat experiment. He sterilized equipment in the autoclave and attached a frozen brain to the cryostat. He found a small bolt had worked itself loose again, and fixed it in place with a blob of Blu-Tack, before settling down to the gentle, painstaking task of shaving off sections forty microns – four hundredths of a millimetre – thick. He picked each one straight off the blade onto a glass slide, the temperature of which was enough to defrost the tissue so that it slid on easily. It was auto-mated yet concentrated, methodical work and Joe lost himself in it – a watchmaker in reverse, deconstructing a brain into notional if not outright fictitious component parts for statistical analysis – and in filing the glass slides in racks in long thin drawers like photographic slides, each one a portrait, it seemed to Joe, as valuable as any framed in an art gallery.

While downstairs that morning members of the board were engaged in an actual photographic enter-prise, in which Roderick Pastille took a leading role.

What with a battery of typists transferring the contents of the library on the first floor onto

243

the Department of Organology's site on the World Wide Web, and books journals bound theses then shipped to a scientific institute in Jordan, some of the space opening up in the stacks was used to construct a small occasional television studio, in which three avant-garde video artists from the Oxford Film Co-op were today paying the rent by hiring their services for corporate work.

A make-up girl touched up Roderick's blusher; he reassured the knot of his tie.

'Sound running.'

'Camera running.'

'Just get the bloody autocue right this time,' Roderick barked at the editor or director or whatever the rank amateur in the control booth wished to call himself. A red light throbbed on. Roderick focused straight into the camera, imagined a viewer on the other side of the lens, was undisturbed by a suggestion of his own convex, diminished, reflection in the glass. You're addressing a child, he reminded himself, as ever. Speak slowly. He let his facial muscles relax to form an expression of intimate concern, concerned intimacy, then raised his eyeline the merest fraction to the words in large type on a screen above the lens.

'Those with vested interests in putting a stop', Roderick enunciated, 'to progress in science, medicine, biology – the very cornerstones of our civilization – are those shouting loudest for the banning of the necessary use of animals in the cause of that progress. The insurmountable problem they have in persuading us, however,' here Roderick smiled indulgently, 'is one of logic; nay, of plain common sense.'

Roderick paused, inclined his head a fraction to one side. '"Speciesism," they cry on the one hand, and say we humans have no right to impose our will upon

244

other animals that are quite different and separate from us. But ask them why not, exactly, and they will say it is because animals are *like* us: they feel pain, they suffer stress. Well, which is it? we wonder. They do not know. All they can do is shout louder.'

'Crowd cutaways here,' the editor whispered to Ben Ali Al-Shalir in the control booth.

'We, however, do know. Everyone here at the Department of Organology in Oxford values, nay, cherishes, animals. Why, I myself have a golden retriever at home I count as one of my dearest friends.' Roderick paused, and the autocue paused with him. 'I claim spiritual kinship with the composer Edward Elgar, who when staying in London used to telephone home to Worcestershire so that he could listen to his Labradors barking.'

Mr Bone frowned. He found it unsettling when Roderick strayed from his carefully worded script. Even though, he had to admit, the politician was good at such extemporizing.

'My wife is extremely fond of cats,' Roderick resumed as written. 'Our children adore their horses.'

'Insert family snaps one and two.'

'We don't want anyone to work here who is not an animal lover. We demand people who understand the difference between compassion and mere squeamishness. If admitted to hospital for an operation, do you want a surgeon without compassion? Of course not. But do you want a squeamish surgeon? No, you most certainly do not.

'There is pain, there is suffering, unavoidably inflicted upon animals here, and the point is that we take the greatest care possible to keep it to a minimum. Why, only last year we closed down the sub-faculty of Veterinary Studies because we felt we could no longer justify experiments that did not have a direct and identifiable benefit to the human race.'

'Cue models.'

'For that is what this entire department is about, finally. The good of the human race.'

'Model one forward.'

'If you have any doubts, answer for yourself this question: which do you value more highly, the life of this beautiful child?'

'Close-up on child. Model two forward.'

'Or this nasty brown rat?'

'Close-up on rat. Hold. Pull out to group. Hold. OK, cut.'

Ben Ali Al-Shalir rose to his feet. 'Brilliant. Absolutely fucking brilliant, Rod.'

His brother Mohammed clapped his hands. Mr Bone sang, 'Superb. Quite superb.' Dr Horlock shook her head: 'Excellent. First rate.'

Roderick came out from under the hot lights and stood looking scary in his make-up in the comparative cool of the doorway, where the make-up girl wiped viscous beads of sweat off his forehead.

'But somehow,' Ben Ali frowned, 'I can't help thinking there's something missing.'

'H'm,' said Mr Bone. 'I know what you mean, sir.'

'Yes, there's certainly *something* missing,' Dr Horlock agreed.

Mohammed Al-Shalir nodded his head.

'Why don't I mention Descartes?' Roderick suggested. 'And his assertion that animals lack a soul. This video's mostly going to be seen by post-doctoral students, after all. We could do with injecting a little philosophy.'

'But most of them will have been educated in America,' Ben Ali pointed out glumly. His brother then leaned over and whispered in his ear. Ben Ali's eyes lit up. 'Tears!' he exclaimed.

'Tears?' Roderick wondered. Mohammed looked rather pleased with himself. Dr Horlock leaned forward in her chair. 'Tears?' Mr Bone enquired.

'Tears,' Ben Ali affirmed. 'As my wise brother says, this talking heads nonsense works best with a bit of feeling. You!' he barked in the direction of the make-up artist dabbing Roderick's blushed brow with cotton wool. 'Stop messing about with the poor fellow and fetch something to make his eyes watery.'

The young woman's own colouring faded. 'I didn't bring glycerine with me,' she quaked. 'No-one said anything about crying.'

Ben Ali reddened without any help. 'However many minutes it takes you to obtain some, you brainless young twat, you've got half of.' He glanced at his watch. 'The clock starts now.'

'May I suggest?' Mr Bone interjected. 'I could buzz up to my senior lab technician to bring down some pipettes and a bit of hairspray or detergent from one of the rabbit rooms. We employ the Draize Eye Irritancy Test every day. Take but a moment.'

'Good idea, Mr Bone. Thank you,' said Ben Ali. 'You're a lucky girl,' he scowled. 'You should thank him too.'

'Hey, hey, hang on,' Roderick interjected. 'Wait a minute. I'm not sure about this. I have my own image to think of, chaps. I'm a man's man. It's fine to be known as an animal lover, but I don't want to be seen weeping over the bloody things.'

The editor, who'd been a silent witness all this time, spoke up. 'I've a suggestion,' he ventured. 'Do you have any dogs in the building?'

'Dogs?' asked Roderick.

'Of course,' Mr Bone affirmed. 'Hundreds.'

'Any with particularly photogenic eyes?' the young man asked. 'I mean, like, puppies?'

'Take your pick,' said Mr Bone. 'All ages. All sorts. Beagles, naturally. How about them?'

'What's the idea?' Ben Ali Al-Shalir demanded.

'Could we do it again in wide shot?' the editor wondered, making a parallelogram out of his thumbs and forefingers and pointing it at Roderick. 'Mr Pastille with a puppy on his lap all the way through? That might appeal.'

Ben Ali got up, stepped over to the young editor sat in a swivel chair and grasped him in an affectionate head-lock. 'Now this young feller,' he told the others, 'I like very much.' The young feller flushed and squirmed. Ben Ali ruffled his pony-tailed hair with his spare hand. 'He's got ideas in this skull,' he said, rapping it so that it sounded, paradoxically, hollow, before letting him go. 'You are the type that will go far,' he surmised.

'I'll get some appealing beagles sent down,' Mr Bone grinned.

A number of those to whom Roderick referred in the recruitment video, meanwhile, shouting for an end to vivisection, did so right outside the department's front entrance. The night security porters like Francis Montagu were warned to look out for letter bombs in the morning post. So far, these terrorists, in their black combat trousers and hooded sweatshirts, had restricted themselves to poison-pen letters, insults and occasional eggs hurled at staff coming in, plus the tuneless shouting of slogans that penetrated the double glazing of Ben Ali Al-Shalir's office. Occasionally the animal rights activists ('bloody Zionists, Mr Bone!' Ben Ali called them) coincided with peripatetic groups of black-gowned, crow-like undergraduates who were finding their voices, rusty after generations of silence ('lounging scroungers expect the best education in the world for free, before graduating to astronomical salaries in the City. Where are yesterday's student pro-testors, Mr Bone? They're all bankers now.' 'Bonkers?' 'What?' 'Did you say they're all bonkers, sir?' 'Of course they're bonkers, Mr Bone, that's what I'm say-ing'). On such days staff in the Department of Organology wished for triple glazing to shut out the racket of 'NO IFS, NO BUTS, STOP THE EDUCATION CUTS!' clashing horrendously with 'ANIMALS HURT, ANIMALS FEEL, WE WANNA HEAR A VIVI-SECTIONIST SQUEAL!'

Poor Mr Bone bore the brunt of such activity: as well as overseeing the expansion of The Laboratory Ltd through the corridors of the Department of Organology, taking over less profitable units within it as pure gave way to applied research, he was saddled with respons-ibility for security. And of course the two went together, as with any expanding empire: as its boundaries spread, so there were more vulnerable frontiers to defend; the perfectly natural response to which was to spread wider; so inviting further threat, and inducing more anxiety.

Security wasn't helped by the innate irresponsibility of junior research fellows who despite the regular despatch of memos to their pigeon holes continued to lose security lift keys or leave windows open. Which so far was less a problem during the day than it was at night: Monty, having endured early evening hours of town lads' skateboards' slap, crack and whirring on the concrete outside, would later be stirred from a slumbering vigil by the sound of caterwauling tomcats or howling dogs outside. Sometimes both, clashing as horrendously as human protestors. And he'd trudge up to the top floor and work through the rooms of The Laboratory Ltd until he found a window open of a room where female cats or dogs were dormed and one or more had come on heat, the olfactory rumour of their ovulation teasing into the night air of the city.

Joe Snow worked late again that night, till each of the white cats' brains was neatly shaved into countless sections and filed, for analysis he'd begin as soon as he was told what the experiment was for. He pulled tight the chinstrap of his crash helmet and unlocked his mountain bike. As he wobbled home towards Jericho, his fluoro anorak aglow in the dark, Joe rehearsed something he planned to tell his mother over breakfast the next morning. 'I won't take part in any weapons testing research, Mum, you can be sure of that. I'm a pacifist.'

12

DEEP FIELDS OF SPACE

'Any intruders, rip their throats out, you beauties.'

On a Texan-style hacienda in the heart of the Black Country, Phil Scritt fed his dogs before going to work. The Alsatian and the Rottweiler gobbled steak in their compound as he closed the front door with one remote control and opened his Land Cruiser doors with another. He drove along the avenue lined with the rusting hulks of juggernauts, flatbed trucks and low loaders, left through the wooden SCRITT RANCH portal and joined the A458 towards Birmingham, England.

Phil's office was a Portakabin in the middle of a vast yard. He gave the thumbs up to the nightwatchman as he drove in. Ranged along one fence was a fleet of forty identical lorries painted red and green, with the words P. P. SCRITT HAULAGE CONTRACTORS signwritten in black on the sides. The rank of lorries looked ready at a one-two-three-four country music intro to launch forward into a vehicular version of line dancing, forty extremely short drivers just waiting for the fiddle to scrape into action. This whimsical notion – the only addition needed was the sight of stetsons poking up above the steering wheels – was probably suggested by the vertically challenged stature of Phil Scritt himself, now climbing down from his Land Cruiser and negotiating puddles in the rutted yard. He was five feet four inches tall in his cowboy boots and he didn't have a complex about his height at all, except for when he'd had a drink: then he picked fights with men over six foot. He had to leap up to land a punch on their jaws or else wind them with a right hook or left uppercut to the stomach in order to bring their head down to a reasonable level. Usually he was swatted irritably away, occasionally beaten up, but sometimes over the years he'd managed to pick on someone who didn't understand brawling and gave himself something to brag about for months.

'He was giving me the eye, like,' he'd tell his drivers. 'He was a lofty great cunt. I went up and I whacked 'im one. He never knew what 'it 'im: went out like a light and never got up. I felt ten foot tall I can tell you.'

Over the rest of the yard were ranged assorted P. P. SCRITT pantechnicons, tankers and articulated lorries, as well as anonymous containers to be attached to the cabs of such freelancers as Jack Knighton, to whom he gave work for reasons of loyalty, flexibility and tax evasion.

Phil unlocked the Portakabin door and entered the small reception area where drivers collected their papers, greeted by a stale reek of yesterday's fags, cheap perfume, oily clothing and powdered coffee from the machine. He carried on along the corridor past two toilets and kitchenette to his office, which took up three-quarters of the Portakabin's entirety.

The office resembled the war room of an incompetent army. Walls were covered with road maps of different sizes of various parts of Britain and Europe peppered with vari-coloured pintacks, some with flags that had nothing to do with any national symbol. There were calendars and charts relating to drivers' shifts, lorries' trips, maintenance schedules, clients' orders; information posters detailing countries' visa requirements and import/export forms. Jutting from grey battered metal cabinets, misfitting drawers held files of B&Bs, hotels, ferry companies, Le Shuttle, vehicle rescue services. A trestle table sagged with the weight of computers, fax, printers, answer machines, while the one vast desk was covered with a scrumpled litter of papers that looked as if it'd been rifled in the night by an industrial spy wearing mittens.

It was the nerve centre of a disorganized rabble, Phil Scritt surely the adjutant-general of an army in retreat (this perhaps the English offshoot of some multinational whose French and German partners had already failed to make a delivery to Moscow and here was Phil overseeing a hat-trick; doomed to failure come the Russian roads in winter). His own outdated uniform of gelled quiff, denim shirt, shoelace tie, Levis and cowboy boots only reinforced the impression given by this officer's mess. And it was entirely misleading. P. P. SCRITT HAULAGE CONTRACTORS was the fifth largest in the country; Phil Scritt was one of the more unlikely-looking of Birmingham's millionaires.

His one and only assistant, chain-smoking secretary and nail-polishing receptionist Vera Semithwaite, regularly urged him to take on more daytime admin staff, but Phil refused.

'I'd rather relegate than delegate,' Phil chuckled. He was an affable boss. He hung his hat on a hook, checked his hair in the mirror and began planning the day ahead. Soon after Vera arrived, the lads started entering the reception area, and leaving with keys and itinerary. This morning a new boy was starting work, second driver on one of the small vans. On building sites, apprentices get sent to the yard for tartan paint or a left-handed hammer. Here the new boy, a peroxided and unfortunately tall youth, was told by colleagues that the boss liked to be referred to by his initials, being a J.R. kind of a character as anyone could see. There were three or four men in reception when Phil came through with folders of loads, routes, schedules.

'All right y'all, lads?' he greeted them. 'Looking chipper, Jack,' he said to Jack Knighton. Then, spotting the new boy, he reached over to shake his hand. 'Welcome, Justin. Bob here show you the ropes?'

'Yes, thank you, Pee Pee,' the nervous youth replied, provoking grown men's suppressed giggles.

This was, needless to say, another thing that made Phil punchy. The hapless boy's chin was in addition at a height Phil was used to: instantly intoxicated with anger he drew back his childish fist and leapt up, aiming his swing with fine precision at the pimply, inexpertly shaven jawline looming there. Only to punch air and flounder, as Jack managed to yank Justin out of the way. Phil staggered, regained his balance and, the peak of his fury passed, only reached up and grabbed the shocked youth by the scruff of his neck and pushed him back against the unsteady, shuddering wall of the Portakabin.

'I don't care who told you to call me that,' Phil snarled. 'But if I ever hear it again, I'll fucking throw you out on your ear. All right?'

Young Justin nodded faintly.

'Good,' said Phil, letting him go and turning. 'Now, Jack,' he said, 'I've got a good long-distance job for you, mate, running the north-east coast of Jockland, then off to Eastern Europe.'

* * *

Five days later Jack Knighton came back from the
Continent with a truck full of heifers. He was carrying
them from Holland to the Republic of Ireland. There
they'd give birth and their calves be reared to adulthood before being shipped live for slaughter to North
Africa or the Middle East: Irish farmers could obtain
EU subsidies for exporting outside Europe; for being so
good as not to add to the EU meat mountain.

'Why don't they give them subsidies for not having
cows in the first place?' Jack had asked Phil Scritt.

Phil regarded Jack sceptically. 'You angling to get
paid for carrying empty loads around?'

'Course not, Phil.'

'Next thing you'll be wanting subsidies from me for
not driving. So's you can spend more time on that
machine you call a house.'

'See you later,' Jack smiled resignedly, stepping out
of the Portakabin, letting the door bang flimsily behind
him. He'd started carrying animals when Phil Scritt
first entered the trade on the back of the Lamb Wars of
1990, in which French farmers hijacked lorries carrying British sheep. The gendarmerie stood well back
from barricades of burning tyres: they only stepped in
to help round up flocks let loose in town mayors'
gardens and in government offices, whose carpets the
sheep nibbled and littered with droppings. British
drivers, forced to take their freight to local abattoirs
and then watch Gallic celebrations around bonfires of
the carcasses, were put off the whole business; while
hauliers were defeated by the frustration of their
lorries blockaded in Godardian queues on tree-lined
roads in the unreachable centre of rural France.
Consequently less timid souls, like Phil Scritt, took
what they relinquished.

Jack disembarked from the ferry at Harwich, and processed through the gauntlet of Customs. It was always a hit and miss business bringing livestock into Britain: on the one hand it wasn't good for anyone, not least the animals themselves, to have the truck standing on hot tarmac for long; on the other, only rigorous import controls had kept these islands free of rabies. Then there was the question of contraband: what better place to hide illicit cargo? He'd been shocked by Miranda's suggestion but maybe she was right. What Customs officer fancied searching through shit and straw and stinking bovine bodies for a small packet of pills or powder? What uproar would a sniffer dog cause, a spaniel sent in for junk snapping at the flanks of distraught cattle; looking for grass and yapping at hay? Then again maybe the truckers' rumour's true: that they get their dogs hooked – canine addicts aching for a fix better motivated – in which case the hounds'll be nipping the livestock to get out of their way.

Jack handed over duplicates and triplicates of fading information as he crossed the docks – the heifers' passports, in effect, as well as his own. Phil Scritt was so distrustful of his drivers' competence he treated them like young footballers and kept their passports in a file in his Portakabin, handing them out as required for particular trips along with the other travel documents.

Almost at the end of the bureaucratic procedure Jack sat in his cab waiting for his passport to be handed back. Time seemed to stop for good. One of the Customs or Immigration functionaries stood close to his wound down window, dirty yellow overalls suggesting that he was saddled with much of the donkey work.

'Look like you've looked underneath a fair few

vehicles today, like,' Jack said, instantly regretting his affability: Customs had to be slipped through anonymously; the worst thing you could do was draw attention to yourself. Jack Knighton wasted quite enough time in queues from accidents, breakdowns, roadworks; he had no time to give away.

'We're all searching for something,' the shaven-headed young man smiled back, and Jack relaxed a little. He had no interest in fashion but he'd noticed the recent increasing prevalence of cropped haircuts. It pleased him greatly. His own hair had been receding, it seemed now, since about the day he reached manhood: Jack's premature hair loss had robbed him of a period of hirsute maturity to which every man was entitled; his nascent quiff sad as a collapsing soufflé. Miranda had a point: no sooner had Jack entered his prime than he was exiting it.

Ever since then Jack had fought a losing battle against an ineluctably expanding bald spot. He had wiry brown hair and so for some years he encouraged it to grow around the edge of the crown of his head like a hedge, enclosing the inner absence, which at least by this means was only visible from above. Each year, though, ever shorter people could ridicule him, and by the age of thirty it had come to look foolish to all, as if someone had placed a wreath on his skull; as if Jack was mourning the loss of his own hair, as Miranda wittily put it. At that point Jack changed tack and bullied what remained of his hair flat with Brylcreem, plastering it from all sides in across his unwanted tonsure, a monk resentful of his faith. He applied gel regularly but still gusts of wind and sudden movements trifled with his esteem. He watched Yul Brynner movies and Kojak on TV with bitter admiration, wishing he had the courage to stride through Northfield

257

shopping centre with proudly shaven skull. Except that he, Jack Knighton, could never pull it off, would cringe and feel like a cancer patient on chemotherapy or an overgrown hooligan or the victim of a stag night caper. How he'd love to have the confidence to burlesque his own condition – to wear a cowboy hat and boots like Phil's, the black shirt and jeans of a gunfighter; to suck lollipops – but he was incapable of such extroversion. Jack knew the first thing he'd do after shaving his head would be to buy a wig. Now that *would* be ridiculous.

'Everyone knows there's only one cure,' Miranda remarked in the bathroom as Jack rubbed another useless tingling potion into his scalp. 'The way you performed just now you might as well take it. There's a rusty pair of scissors in that cabinet.'

But then came this fashion for skinhead haircuts, baldness not shied away from and covered up but chosen freely, demanded even, that started in gay circles and was now rippling out wider and gave Jack hope. He was forty-two years old and knew he looked well over fifty. He was almost ready, like a wallflower waiting for the dance floor to fill before insinuating himself into its shadows, for a critical mass to be reached after which he wouldn't be conspicuous if he took that drastic step of erasing what to be honest was the minimal remaining tenancy of hair upon his pate.

So that Jack had a hopeful, complicit attitude towards this smiling, shaven-headed young man at Customs, as to a bona fide member of a club from which he awaited news on his own anxious application, even before he'd replied, 'We're all searching for something.'

'I bet it's knowing where to look in your job, isn't it?'

Jack responded, throwing caution to the wind. The heifers were mooing behind him.

'In my job?'

Maybe the man wasn't so young, actually, Jack reconsidered. It was the very smoothness of his skull that rendered him so youthful. Jack vowed to follow suit as soon as he got home from this trip. 'Yes,' he said, 'like the parts of a chassis or even the engine for stashing stuff. You lot and smugglers must be trying to outwit each other all the time, like fruit bats and flies matching each other's radar and sonar abilities. Evolution, like.'

'I wouldn't know about evolution,' the man in yellow overalls said. He nodded sideways: Jack looked in his wing mirror and saw a uniform approach. His passport was handed up to him without a word and he took it, and the uniform disappeared. As Jack prepared himself to set off the bald young man said, 'It'll be fine.'

'Hope so,' Jack replied, leaning forward and looking out at the sky. It was all the blue at the bottom of a flame, not the smokiest whisper of a cloud anywhere. Time stopped again. 'I've got a lot of driving to do.'

'It'll be fine,' the young man repeated. 'You'd be surprised. Take care of the child.'

Jack clicked his seat belt, saying, 'Not me, mate,' then turned sideways, 'we haven't got—' to see empty space: the young man had moved on. Jack leaned out of the window, but there was no sign of him. He shrugged and gunned the engine into life, drowning out the sound of the heifers.

The important thing is, Jack thought as he drove down the A12, to get things in perspective; to grasp the scale of things. There are, after all, a hundred thousand hairs on an average person's head; maybe there are too many hairs in the world already. Astronomers around the globe, using the most mind-boggling technology, have barely begun to probe the extent of our solar system – of which there could be about a hundred thousand *million* in our galaxy, the Milky Way; which itself is so vast it would take a beam of light – the fastest moving entity we know of – a hundred thousand years to cross.

The Milky Way is in turn but one rather small galaxy in the universe. The Hubble space telescope has taken pictures of the deep fields of space (a phrase that made Jack visualize space as an enormous cricket pitch) revealing so many galactic clusters that astronomers have upped their estimates of the number of galaxies in the whole universe to some two hundred billion.

You have to grapple with the scale of things. Jack wasn't even sure if when astronomers spoke of billions they still meant a million million, or whether everyone had now adopted the American procedure of having a billion represent a thousand million, without telling the rest of us. But there, you see, was an example in itself: two hundred thousand million or two hundred million million – both such unimaginably large numbers there was no point in a layman like himself splitting hairs over the difference between them. At which conclusion it came to him from nowhere – from the deep field of his inner space – that Miranda was ill; and that it was her heart.

It came upon Jack as a startling revelation, in a sudden floodlit image of Miranda lying inert upon their lounge carpet as if his mind's eye could instantaneously see clearly the scene two hundred miles away; which image then blinked out of his vision once more. He telephoned home only to get the answerphone – not just Miranda's voice speaking from beyond the grave but the words, 'I'm afraid I'm unable to come to the phone right now,' mocking her lying incapacitated yards feet inches from the receiver so close so far from help. Jack yelled: 'Miranda! Can you hear me?' just in case she was simply screening calls, but of course she didn't pick up. 'I'm coming home!' he shouted to the patient spooling tape.

Although Jack was a rational man who poured scorn on astrology and zodiacal starsigns (whose constellations anyway – as any amateur astronomer could tell you – were out of whack, owing to the slow retrograde motion of equinoctial points along the ecliptic); even though he worshipped at the altar of reason, Jack trusted his sudden premonition. This was on account of honouring the memory of his mother who was said to be psychic, and from an early age Jack had awaited evidence of his paranormal abilities as proof of the sundered bond still underlying between them. Abilities which never showed themselves; Jack had never had a psychic experience. Until now. So that his dread at the plight of his beloved, her ample gorgeous limbs spreadeagled, was mingled with a profound, regressive gratification at this connection with the mother he'd barely known.

The heifers would have to suffer a detour. Jack drove at full speed up the M1 towards Birmingham, telling himself he had to be calm. He had to keep things in perspective. It was Edwin Hubble himself who with his Mount Palomar telescope confirmed that other stellar systems, other galaxies, are receding from us at a speed proportional to their distance; we probe deeper and deeper into space to observe what is moving away from us faster and faster. With our divine hunger for knowledge we pursue the eternally elusive.

Then it came to him, too, from Sunday School it

must have been, long ago: if I have prophetic powers, and understand all mysteries and all knowledge, and if I have all faith, so as to remove mountains, but have not love, I am nothing.

The universe is becoming less crowded. And colder.

But eternal expansion is not the final word: astronomers seek explanations of the end of the universe in its beginning. They discerned the Big Bang after all only in the detection of radio signals, its distant echo, in empty interstellar space. And now they posit that the density of the mass of the universe will eventually slow down its expansion, and then begin to pull it inward, back in on itself towards a Big Crunch. Or else it's possible that the mass will be insufficient for such a theophanic change of mind, such celestial suicide. He whose breath made the heavens luminous, of whom a whispered echo is what and all we hear, realizes the folly of creation and reverses it in an act of repentance? No, the mass may simply slow the expansion down to a comfortable, possibly eternal, equilibrium.

Love never ends, Jack thought. For our knowledge is imperfect and our prophecy is imperfect; but when the perfect comes, the imperfect will pass away. And the end of the universe is irrelevant to us. Long before that fateful day, that eventful nanosecond, our sun will have swollen into a huge thermonuclear sphere, swallowing the earth, and then itself collapsed into a tiny white interstellar speck, extinguished and sterile.

You have to put things in their proper place, he considered, with such speculation diluting the bilious dread in his gut. For if I speak in the tongues of men and of angels, but have not love, I am a noisy gong or a clanging cymbal.

*   *   *

In a break in the motorway traffic a car went gliding past. Perhaps it flashes its lights in greeting; or, signalled space by the lorry to complete its overtaking manoeuvre, re-enters the inside lane and winks its indicators left and right, and even left again, with that flirtatious courtesy beloved of HGV drivers.

It could have been – though not yet – Penelope Witton. She was still in Bradford. Today was not one of her animal sanctuary shop shifts: she was arranging flowers in vases for the window sills of St Bartholomew's church. A task whose defining feature, Penny acknowledged, was its intrinsic competitiveness. Not just with the other ladies on the rota, but also with the weather at this time of year, when rainy April days alternated with early summer sun. During the previous Sunday's meandering sermon, a vivacious display of flowering cherry and phacelia bursting before a dim window suddenly, with an annoying burst of sun outside, clashed with brilliant light pouring through the stained glass.

Penny was now cleaning out one of the vases when the vicar bustled in. He seemed to rustle as he walked, whether or not he was wearing a cassock.

'Good day, Miss Witton,' he said, scanning the chancel windows. 'You're doing a lovely job.'

'Those are last week's,' she replied. 'I haven't replaced them yet.'

'Oh, I see,' he grimaced apologetically. 'You're not stuck, are you?' he asked.

Penny looked down. She'd stopped what she was doing as the priest approached: her arm disappeared into the mouth of a slender green bowl.

Adopting an American accent in what she imagined was a reasonable impression of Katharine Hepburn, Penny said, 'It's got me in its vase-like grip, vicar.' He frowned at the swallowed limb, then up at her. Penny pulled her arm free.

Relieved, the vicar asked, 'How are you, Miss Witton?'

'Very well,' she said. 'Apart from the pain,' she added.

'Pain?'

'Oh, nothing. The usual. Ankles. Arches. A lifetime standing up. On my feet, serving people.' She had an impulse to call him Father, though he was years younger than her; and neither of them Catholic, after all. 'What can you expect?'

'You must take care of yourself, you know.'

'How?'

'Well, I don't know. Massage? And don't forget to pray.'

'I thought', she teased him, 'I was supposed to pray for other people, vicar.'

'I'm sure the Lord will allow an occasional plea on your own behalf.'

'I've spent a long time learning to pray for others,' she laughed. 'I don't think I know how to pray for myself.'

'Ah, you're an example to us all, Miss Witton. No, really, you are. Do you know, a friend of mine came off his bicycle the other day. He was racing up to the hospital to give blood, would you believe? Head down. Rode straight into the back of a parked van. He was taken to the hospital, where he had to be given blood himself.'

The vicar shook his head with admiration at the irony, then looked up and saw Penny's expectant face.

'Oh, no, there's no point to it,' he admitted. 'Just a story, I'm afraid. Not a parable. I took the bike to be repaired for him, told them what had happened. When he went to collect it yesterday they showed him the cracked frame. A write-off. He told me he hadn't been treated with such respect in years.'

Penny frowned.

'Going uphill as he was, you see. Quite a feat.' The vicar smiled. An afterthought struck him: 'He is Scottish,' he said, as if by way of explanation, and headed towards the vestry. Penny resumed another floral arrangement.

The car driver could have been, but was not, Penny Witton. Soon it would be. The unearthly silence of her saloon's engine would make time around it settle, so that it felt as if it were moving in slow motion. Penny, though, wouldn't notice the numb landscape soothing past her: she'd be cruising; inside the warm sealed capsule of the car interior baroque sonatas from the stereophonic, one hundred watt speakers would wash through her body and her mind.

Or it might, and really could, have been Martha Polkinghorne driving a grey, anonymous Transporter van on the other side of the central reservation from Jack Knighton. The van was not in Martha's name. Neither was its insurance. Nor was income tax, council tax, national insurance. Such things aren't easy to fake or do without. Martha had no bank account or credit cards. Odd lockers and keys, dotted here and there. No web site or e-mail address. A mobile phone whose number no-one knew.

Most nights Martha camped, sleeping in her van or out under the stars of a summer sky. She came in from outside the cities to stay in large, featureless hotels, the sort with a gym and a pool in the basement, a bar through which other transients passed. Martha always requested a room with thick curtains. 'I sleep badly,' she said. 'The light wakes me.' It didn't seem like much to ask. After registering, under an assumed name, Martha luxuriated in a strange clean bathroom. Miniature soap bars; sachets of shampoo, bubble bath; white towels.

In the bar she'd give the same fake name to men bold enough to introduce themselves, and take one of them to her dark room. As she'd heard whores say, all men like to be hurt a little at least. Their skin. The sensation, the tactile confusion of pain and pleasure. Some she'd sense their surprise at a fantasy inexplicably come to life, popping out of place and time.

'I like it,' she said. They might have seen her split eyebrow, scar tissue the badge of a warrior; her Prussian officer's duelling scar. 'Can you feel how I like it?' Getting off on their resistance, suffocating with a kiss: neck squeezed, nose pinched, they reluctantly ejaculate.

She'll let them leave. Lie sleepless. Later, at three in the morning, swim slow, silent lengths in an empty pool in a hotel basement.

Jack skirted the underbelly of Birmingham on the M42, joined the M5 briefly, came off it again at Junction 3 and tore along the Quinton Expressway. He careered through the suburb of Ridgacre as if aiming to crash through a police barricade. Other drivers saw his lurching load coming towards them or looming in their rear view mirror and pulled over on either side, cyclists fell off their bikes in fright and pedestrians hugged walls to let the bovine cacophony on wheels roar past. The agitated animals pawed the chaffy floor of the lorry and kept planting and replanting their feet to regain balance, so that dust rose and escaped through the slit windows, transforming the noisy vehicle into a bellowing cloud in hurtling motion.

Sharing the animals' lamentation Jack thudded the truck to a halt askew the kerb outside his house and dashed to the door. He fumbled with the keys, stumbled inside, to be greeted by a pre-recorded, 'Welcome home, darling.' In his haste Jack forgot to disable the house alarm, and when it went off he elected to ignore its grating insistence: instead he set forth on a journey through his dream house, with its telepathic technology, its responsive gizmos, carrying his forlorn heart on his sleeve, and having shrieked at his entrance the house now opened its arms. Calling, 'Miranda, my love,' answered only with, 'Welcome home, darling,' Jack raced along the corridor with doors flapping open for him and shut again and open. Lights blinked on and off, startled at the rapidly moving shadow of his bulk. He looked in the kitchen where the kettle clicked its heel, the microwave winked at him, the retractable towel rail saluted. In the empty lounge the smart CD player diagnosed his mood and accompanied his desperate procession with Chopin's Funeral March – competing with the burglar alarm and the heifers' moos that entered from outside. Jack rushed upstairs to their bedroom, also empty, where was she? She was here, he could feel her, and the sensitive thermostat recognized the icy terror in Jack's mind and by the time the video had paused him with its whirring initiative and begun to play 'It's a Wonderful Life', and he'd then pressed himself fast forward to the bathroom, he was already pouring sweat.

Of course. She would be here, this is where it happens: where we sneak in to perform the humiliating burdens of our corporeal condition, to wash away the daily cavalcade of matter through us, so it is here that the body betrays us, staggering us with the effrontery of cardiac arrest, clutching our breath and beaching us on white tiles and porcelain.

Jack prodded open the new bathroom door with squeamish reticence. The light came at him like a flash bulb to reveal the bright bathroom disturbingly empty, like a police photograph showing the place where a mysteriously vanished body had last been seen. Miranda's customary fleshly mess of soggy towels, smudged cotton wool, discarded sachets, scrunched-up toilet paper, damp flannels, littered the surfaces. As if she were already dead this intimate memorabilia struck Jack senseless with sudden grief. The toilet flushed itself; the jacuzzi bubbled as if murmuring sympathetic information. Jack's gaze lifted to the mirror ahead of him and he saw his sorry reflec—

There was something written. He stepped closer and read in crimson lipstick: YOU HAVE DRIVEN ME AWAY FOREVER.

Miranda had then signed this message but not with her name. She must have been seized with temptation and been unable to resist such an opportunity: she'd signed the message with her lips. Their gorgeous imprint on the glass her parting endearment, her last kiss goodbye.

Jack walked slowly downstairs and collapsed on the front steps. All about him was bedlam: the cumulative noise of the heifers' voices and his house alarm had set off each of the other burglar alarms around the close, as well as a couple of parked cars, all of whose electronic caterwauling combined to create a modernist masterpiece of strident discord. But Jack barely heard it. It mocked yet failed to disturb the depths of his stunned mind. After a while he rose heavily, shut the house up again, climbed into his cab and set off for Ireland, wondering what the hell that Customs chap had meant. 'Take care of the child.' Child? What child?

13

A GIRL WITH AN APPETITE
FOR LIFE

Sam Caine woke in an alien bed, in a foreign room, and stared aghast at the naked stranger beside him. He leaned over her sidelong body and saw on her unfamiliar forehead a yellow self-stick note on which was written: 'My name is Rebecca. Make me tea and toast.'

Sam traipsed vainly down, and then up, stairs till he found the strange kitchen, where he clumsily obeyed the instruction. He returned with a tray he placed on the floor and opened curtains introducing murky light, to which the unconscious figure responded with a groan. He redrew them almost to a close, allowing an archery slit that resisted the invasive rays.

Rebecca woke up like a tired actress miming a long recovery from illness. Groggily pulling out an extra pillow from under her body she heaved herself up to a sitting position. She tasted the coiny dregs of sleep on her tongue, then, opening one eye, turned to look at Sam Caine. He waited for her to say something. But speech appeared to be beyond her: Rebecca closed her eye and turned back. Sam placed the tray on her lap, and she proceeded blindly to swallow tea and scrunch toast. He studied her visage, listened to extraordinary noises her tummy made – liquid gurgles, quizzical squidges. He removed her empty plate. Eventually, cupping mug in her lap, Rebecca peered at him, again one-eyed. He winked at her. She scowled.

'I'm a member of the kuklōps clan,' she mispronounced sullenly. 'Don't look at me like that. I'm having a bath.' Handing the mug to Sam (which he assumed to be empty and took from her too fast, so jerking an inch of tepid tea over his torso), Rebecca drew aside the duvet and got up. At the sight of her naked body blood sped to Sam's groin, the flow slowing as she exited the room, leaving him with the fixed semi-erection of a Kalahari bushman. It was still there when she returned ten minutes later wrapped in towels. Her eyebrows bobbed. 'I see your . . . *reputation* precedes you,' she said Maewestern style, the lasciviousness of her gaze at his cock provoking it to fulfil its potential. A smirk carnalized her mouth; with an indiscernible shimmy the towels about her began sliding to the floor: the tumescent head of Sam's phallus throbbed.

Rebecca indicated the bed. Her glance, however, took in the alarm clock. 'Damn,' she said, 'I'm late. Piano lesson.' She threw on some clothes and was gone, with only, 'Read that, see you later,' tossed over her shoulder and cursory gesticulation towards paper pinned to a wall.

Upon half a dozen A4 sheets Rebecca had typed Sam's story, hers, and theirs together, so that she wouldn't have to explain everything every day, and he could become acquainted with himself while she was out. In fact it took her a little longer to write each evening what amounted to a diary entry than it would to have given a verbal account the next morning. But

271

Rebecca justified the enterprise as an investment in a future when the story would become longer to recount than each day's entry to write.

So that Sam spent a lengthening period every day reading his biography. The only one there was. He had none the less before that to discover that Rebecca was one-eyed in the morning. That the puffiness in her face was temporary. That her black mane of hair needed a concerted effort to untangle, as if taming a wild beast of the night, and some mornings when she wasn't in a hurry she let him brush it till it shined and crackled with static. Then he'd watch as she used her hair to define her appearance for that day: gathered up on top of her head, perhaps with strands left sluttishly, elegantly adrift; in a motherly bun; scraped back and tied ready for action; plaited with wit, pony-tailed for fun, or with the pigtails of a naughty schoolgirl; or some days just ignored, letting passers-by or fellow tube passengers pray this madwoman wouldn't approach them.

Strange it was for each of them to wake up together, the habitual as great a novelty for Rebecca as the fresh unfamiliarity was for Sam. Nights were something else again. Sam slept deep and loudly, he snorted like a disgruntled hippo, snuffled at imaginary flies on his nose, snored with a sound like the slow approach of thunder. Rebecca whispered, 'Ssssh,' but to no avail. She murmured, 'Wake up, Sam,' in vain. Muttered hoarse, ill-tempered 'Stoppit!' only for his snores to amplify, driving her eventually to sit up in bed exasperated and cry, 'WILL YOU SHUT THE FUCK UP!?'

Sam ceased snoring, hummed briefly, smiled in his sleep, and resumed twitching like a dreaming dog.

Rebecca snorted with envy. The trouble was that anything woke her: not just the way Sam shifted position during the night, less rolling over than bouncing, clutching the duvet as he did so and taking it with him, yanking it clear off Rebecca's body. When she tried to pull it back he grunted and held on tight. He didn't even bloody well need it, had a furnace of a stomach that burned up everything he ate: Rebecca lay there planning to smother him with a pillow but made do with pouring mineral water from glass to glass until Sam was woken by the need to piss, and stumbled somnambulistically to the bathroom.

Rebecca could be woken by Sam's merest whisper: 'Rebecca?'

'What?' Instantly alert. An eternally vigilant woman; a sentry who'd slept on guard duty and let the city be taken in a past life, she mused. Sam thought he had only to open his eyelids to wake her, so that it was literally impossible for him to be awake without her being so also. It wasn't, of course: Rebecca slept unobtrusively, curled up like a hibernating animal around her extra pillow, silent except for an occasional quiet purring.

By morning Sam was replenished by eight hours of uninterrupted dreaming, while Rebecca had been disturbed from her light, quiet, motionless sleep a hundred times. By neighbours' domestic bust-ups, by insomniac joggers pounding the pavement, by housebreakers running off with TVs and videos. As the days grew longer, lighter, warmer, and windows opened, air thinned, so her sleep was wrecked by raucous drinkers going home, cackling women, football supporters singing nostalgic beery classics of their genre like

Two nil two nil two nil two nil two nil two nil two nil

Dogs bawled, tomcats squawled, and distant loco-motives could be heard leaving Clapham Junction. Then before Rebecca knew it dawn was breaking. A milkman whirred into the empty street on his clatter-ing float and dustmen banged dustbin lids with the enthusiasm of Kodo drummers. Rebecca lay fuming imagining riot police and water cannons to cleanse the borough of such scum; of herself as merciless vigilante, a Catwoman stepping out of the shadows to punish them for ruining the sleep of the just.

So that Rebecca woke tetchy and petulant, slightly more tired than when she'd gone to bed eight hours earlier. She had to catch up, and could spend whole weekends doing little more than sleep, waking occasionally to make a mug of Ovaltine and a toasted sandwich which she took back to bed with her, and slept some more. Until, replete, she smiled tiredly at Sam, her sleep-swollen limbs tattooed with the in-dentations of the sheets, felt herself falling into the clear blue sky of his cerulean eyes, and invited him to bring his *uccello* home to her nest.

For she too had to come to understand him, her dumb lover. Not knowing what to say he took off his clothes: she saw his penis begin to grow, thought my God is even undressing enough to arouse him? But it was something more tentative; his cock unfurled like a blind and sleepy subterranean animal uncoiling into

274

the light. Sam came through the sleep-turgid air, crawled beneath her warm duvet, nosed towards the tangy odour of her pungent cunt. She closed her eyes, lay back again as if to sleep once more. He mouthed her vulva, licked into the margins of silky hair each side of her vaginal lips; he inhaled the tart ammoniac aroma, tasted the salt of her sex, and addressed her with his tongue, slowly, in long leisured sentences that wound around the subject without ever quite getting to the point, luxuriating not in sense but in the sounds engendered, her moans of pleasure as time slowed down, time curved, round and around, her pleasure became the centre of a slowly turning world. He could feel her body amassing tension, as if absorbing impact from outside. When he hoped that she was ready he pushed the conversation on, probed deeper towards a secret, like a priest into sacramental liturgy, like an adept for the first time allowed into the penetralia of life's mystery; and he could taste her clitoris as she groaned, and he felt chastened, with a hard, masculine humility. Unable to express all he wanted before her arousal his hands kneaded her breasts, massaged her buttocks, as her vagina swelled, gushed, she shuddered and moaned and pushed him away.

'Come in me,' she gasped. She looked down his body, his back, its bony ridges, bunched muscles, Sam's compacted male strength. 'Come in me.' Her eyes had gone smoky. They made love.

As the days passed they fucked deeper, longer, more wantonly, so that as well as their lascivious cries so smells emerged from the bedroom, animal aromas, driving first Gemma the cat out into resentful slit-eyed siestas on the uninviting balcony and then Davey and Juice on excursions any place other than here. Those two almost overcame the discomfort each felt at witnessing sex such as neither had given or taken, and attained a rare camaraderie in indignation towards their overbearing landlady and this parasitic squatter. Not that either Sam or Rebecca noticed their door-slamming departures, their lengthy absences, their sullen presences, nor indeed the hunch-shouldered recriminatory posture of Rebecca's beloved cat as she sat on a nearby surface pointedly ignoring them. Everyone they saw looked happy to them.

Sam would raid the kitchen and arrive back in bed with a tray of food just as Rebecca realized she felt faint from hunger. 'How did you know?' she asked with her mouth full, reviving as instantly as a diabetic with sugar.

'I could see,' he said.

'You could see I needed food before I felt it? I . . . I . . .'

'What?'

'I think I . . .'

'What?'

'Nothing, Sam Caine.'

He sat dumb, patient, with his neon blue eyes.

'Don't do that,' she said. To return the favour Rebecca brought Sam lunch in bed in uniform: one miniature pinafore tied round her waist. 'I'm your morning tease maid,' Rebecca breathed.

It was always going to happen. A man and a woman, a woman and a man, they met and fell in love. Rebecca Menotti for the same Sam Caine. Sam for a strange woman every day, poor sap; the lucky lover's memory left him when he slept, and in the morning again a dizzying intoxication. Rebecca's eyes he had to gaze at to make sure they really were crossed. Her crooked nose, her scatty brain, her affection. He suffered the light-headed silliness of sexual attraction for the first time; making love, every orgasm meant a convulsive, revelatory ejaculation. If only life was like that: each cigarette the first of the day, with a coffee in a foreign café strolled to; each footstep revealing gravity's miraculous earth underfoot as if one had just disembarked from days at sea.

But if Sam suffered love's vertigo each day anew, then surely he should have felt it the moment he met her. Which hadn't happened, Rebecca admitted to herself as she struggled with the diary, accepting the obligation to go back and rewrite odd bits. In the beginning, Sam declared no feeling for Rebecca; so how come now, she had to ask? And the answer she found was the power of reciprocity. Rebecca fell in love with Sam for her own abstruse, serendipitous needs, and maybe Sam now fell for Rebecca in response to what he saw in her eyes, voice, body: her adoration. His heart was flattered and fluttered; Rebecca cooed and Sam took wing; thus were these lovebirds borne aloft.

It may have been only because they were wrapped up in each other that Rebecca no longer tried to jog Sam's memory; but it wasn't only that. Like this he was hers, entirely: he had no past she was no part of. Rebecca's jealousy was a furious anomaly in her character, inappropriate, atavistic. One night while he slept she found him hard and woke him, demanded to know of whom he was dreaming. When once he seemed to recognize a woman in the street Rebecca felt her pulse race, mind rage, nearly ran to strike the bitch, pulled Sam and herself away. Afterwards, after encouraging him to let it go, a meaningless flash of confusion with some figure on TV, she admitted to herself how rare and pleasing his blank slate was.

She asked him to explain what his amnesia felt like. Sam pondered. 'You know how every now and then there's a house on a cliff somewhere round the coast that crumbles into the sea?'

He paused, until Rebecca nodded. He continued, 'For a moment we wonder whether the whole island may be vulnerable. And then with some relief we recall how large Britain really is.'

'It's like that?'

'No, it's not like that at all. Better, like this: you know that England was once covered in trees. Chopped down to clear land, to build Elizabethan ships, to stoke insatiable fires of industry. And you suspect the country, the landscape, retains a memory of the trees that covered it, like a phantom limb.'

'H'm. I think I know what you mean.'

Sam spoke slowly. 'No, I don't mean that. I mean this: you know that dislocated sensation you have when you wake from daytime sleep? Like something momentous happened, you missed it, what was it? That fleeting sensation. Then it's gone: the world and oneself fit back together again.'

'I know, my love.'

'I feel like that all the time.'

'Really, Sam? That's amnesia?'

'I don't know. I think so.'

And Rebecca would tell Sam about her father. 'He was – and is – always redecorating one or other of the rooms in the house. The thing is, I picture him sitting down as he paints a wall. I mean, you know how it is for the rest of us: you're arching your back or bending low or twisting a knee to reach that awkward bit in the corner. But I remember Daddy, always, sitting down,

278

talking to me while he painted the wall. Comfortable, you know? With himself. I wish I'd learned it for doing up this place. You'll have to meet him, Sam; we'll visit soon.'

She meant it, though her feelings scared her. When she looked into his bottomless blue eyes she wondered what would stop her falling. 'One of us has to wear shades, Sam Caine,' she said. She was in freefall, or something else perhaps, remembering rare winter days her father drove brothers sledges Rebecca out of Exeter and up to Haldon, where in a snow-covered field below Lawrence Tower they careered out of control towards the Teign Valley, over and over again, insatiably, until their father anticipated the brink of their exhaustion and ushered them home.

'Head over heels, I guess,' she admitted to herself. 'A tobogganing love,' as weeks passed, a month.

While Sam Caine was drawn towards Rebecca, into her physical realm. Magnetic, she pulled him towards her. As if he belonged to her, bodily, the smell and heat of her his home in this world, and to enter her was to return from exile. Rebecca's face making love became more beautiful: was it his perception altered by hormonal urging; or was she clearer to him then, elucidated by the act of sex? His self dissolved behind him, a computer virus eating him up. He dwelt as much in Rebecca's thoughts, inside her mind, as in his body on this earth.

'Don't you think we're all trying to remember something of where we came from?' Rebecca asked him. 'Who we were before?'

'In another life?'

'When I was a child I had memories, vague images of people, a place. I think they might have been

279

residual memories of my previous life. I've a hunch a lot of children have that.'

Either Rebecca or her father telephoned the other customarily on a Sunday evening. Updates on their health, news of her brothers, gossip from her father's street; Sandro ended each conversation by asking whether Rebecca needed anything. It was easy to put off telling him about Sam.

One evening John and Fuyuki came round. Davey cooked up a stir-fry and afterwards Fuyuki started taking Polaroids of people across the detritus of dirty plates and half-empty bottles. When the glossy dark square whirred out of the camera she grabbed a fork and distressed the image.

'You've got about ten or fifteen seconds,' she said, scratching squiggles into the wet surface.

'Look, you've messed up Juice's face,' John rebuked Davey. 'Let me have a go.'

They took it in turns to snap, then filigree, each other's portraits. Rebecca did the washing-up.

'Try it,' Fuyuki said, bringing dirty glasses over.

'I don't like photos,' Rebecca told her. 'They make me uneasy.'

'What, do you harbour one of those obscure superstitions?' Fuyuki ribbed her. 'Has some jungle cult come here I haven't heard about, been revived in Brixton? "The camera steals your soul."'

'Seriously. It's just me. You can do what you want.'

'It's important to document the present. More rather than less, as it hurtles past us.'

'We should *live* in the present.'

'I thought you were the historian, Rebecca. Hey!'

Fuyuki yelled back towards the room. 'My turn. I want to take one of Sam.'

A few moments later was captured the one and only known image of Sam Caine. Wiping her hands dry on a tea towel, Rebecca came over to watch his medium-close-up face against a plain dark wall emerge from the chemical plane of the Polaroid. And maybe it was seeing that happen that would trigger the thought, whenever she looked at the picture in the future, that Sam had just come rising out of meditation. Such, Rebecca thought, was the expression of ease and self-effacement in his face; of contented emptiness in his eyes.

Hours, drifting days in bed, around the flat. The moronic, mutual sufficiency of lovers. 'Fuyuki told me about Yakuza,' Rebecca said. 'When they're in prison they sew a pearl into the shaft of their penises, one for every year they're inside.'

'Am I in prison?' Sam asked her.

'Are you?' she countered.

'How long have we been together?'

'In the biblical sense, you mean?' Rebecca laughed. 'E messes up the memory. Sex drains it. Five weeks.' She sank her teeth in his neck, planting a tattoo of tooth marks in his skin.

Sam went shopping with Rebecca, expeditions to the King's Road, to Knightsbridge, where she rarely bought anything but tried on clothes as if auditioning them, comparing herself in countless mirrors to some interior self-image that was neither more nor less attractive than the real her but somehow both. Sam became light-headed in the shops, from hours on his feet and from too much womanhood, understood that he adored

281

women in a shy, furtive, hopeless way. Back home, thumbing through an encyclopedia, looking for clues, Sam came across an inventor.

'Jules Léotard was an acrobat,' he told Rebecca.

'I thought he was a philosopher,' she said. 'A post-modern—'

'No, he invented the leotard,' Sam frowned. 'What a monument. Whenever that word is read or thought or spoken, so – as well as an image of the garment, describing, hugging, a woman's body – so that man's name is being evoked.'

'You're nuts, Sam Caine.'

'No. Look, it's like instead of a statue, ridiculed by pigeons, rotted by car emissions, he's got real women with their real bodies commemorating him.'

'I think you're confused. You think that's post-modern?'

'What? No . . . Why?'

'Forget it, Sam.' Rebecca shook her head.

In May the weather turned suddenly warm. Walking the short distance to Brockwell Park one Saturday at noon, after making love, Sam dropped back, watched the sway of Rebecca's bottom, the weaving of her shoulders, the swish of her hair. She walked like two different kinds of dancer: both a belly dancer settled in her hips, feet full on the ground; and also pushing upward from the small of her back, a straight spine, jazzy shoulders flat, bosom firm afront her. Having read as on every morning Rebecca's lengthening account of their lives Sam wondered whether something yet resided with him – intimacy creating some coagulant to stay the out-pouring of experience. He suddenly perceived – felt rather than saw, somehow – a four-dimensional picture of Rebecca's body. Not just her outer form but inside, too, he felt he knew her, cherished her organs as much as her face, understood that she – her mortal form – was precious, as nothing else could be to him.

In the park Rebecca lay on a towel and took off clothes before the sun. Her Italian skin blushed brown. Her shaved armpits were peppered with dark granules; inner thighs scribbled with black hairs. Sam's white dazzling skin threatened to reflect the sun's rays back into the sky.

'Sam,' Rebecca said, 'I'm pregnant.'

'With me?' he asked.

'Of course with you, you sap. I know it's unbelievable,' she said, breathlessly. 'I mean, we've got so many contraceptive options, and when you add them to the drop in male sperm count caused by pesticides, pollution and the prevalence of oestrogen in the drinking water, not to mention the precarious architecture of our reproductive systems, it does seem incredible anyone ever gets pregnant at all.'

'How long?' Sam asked.

'Six weeks.'

'That's good,' he said. 'Is that good, Rebecca?'

'It's fine,' she nodded. 'I'll have to add it to the story.'

Davey and Juice, meanwhile, had called a conference that very lunchtime of themselves plus Fuyuki and John in Café Pushkar.

'She's broody and moody, man, messed up,' Davey told them.

'You look in his eyes,' Juice said, 'these vacant eyes, they make you feel you're not there. Looking through

283

you. I'm like, excuse me, am I hollow? You feel like a ghost. You have to stop and remind yourself that *he's* the ghost.'

'He's a scam artist,' Davey said. 'We've all seen his sort before.'

'It's like a kind of brainwashing technique,' Juice reckoned. 'You know how bright Rebecca is. Just look at her now.'

'We've got to save her,' Davey declared.

'From happiness?' Fuyuki wondered. 'That's Zen.'

'From him,' Juice emphasized.

'You have to talk to her, then,' said John.

Some Sunday afternoons, when Davey hadn't chased E with whizz, gone on to Trade and back to DTPM, stalked his own tail all round the weekend, he prowled around the flat in a slightly less agitated state, attired in outdated blue football shorts and nylon socks revealing wiry legs. He bounced a football as he sat at the food bar – thus waking anyone in the flat still sleeping off Saturday night.

'Remember it, Sam?' he asked. 'One of the defining moments of growing up, one of the rites of passage, when you can pluck a football with one hand. You ready?'

'I don't think I ever played,' Sam protested.

'You can be in goal.'

'Can't Rebecca come?' Sam pleaded, but Davey tugged him outside. Juice made coffee, joined Rebecca still in bed as they hadn't done in months, overcoming the fetid stench of the couple's self-absorption.

After beating-around-the-bush feminine preliminaries Juice asked, 'What's going on?'

'What can I tell you?' Rebecca smiled.

'Rebecca. I have to say it. He's a quote idiot unquote.'

'How can you say that?'

'He's draining your money, time, independence. Your vitality.'

'I'm happy. Be happy for me.'

'It's not his fault, Beccy, but he's a sap. A goose. Even his name's an anagram. He's an imbecile, woman, you can't be serious.'

'What if maybe this is it, Juice?'

Juice understood she was and would be getting nowhere. 'Davey claims in Sicily they say eternal love lasts two years. You're Italian, right?'

'It's too late.'

Davey came in and bounced on the bed. 'It was un-believable,' he exclaimed. 'This guy' – as Sam loped in shyly behind him – 'says "Oh I can't kick, I never played, let me watch," he won't knock up, and we're all there with those Ghanaian guys I told you about, shit hot and all and we kick off and someone rolls Sam the football and he takes it and it's like *Terminator* meets *Shine* or something, he caresses the ball like he's being introduced to an old friend. Who he suddenly recognizes. Transformation I'm telling you, flicks it up on his chest, on his shoulders, neck, head, there's guys shouting, "Oy! We started, mate!" So he brings it down, thigh, knee. Passes it he like strokes it to me and I'm dumbstruck.

'And *then*: it's like I mean this guy here can *dribble*. Can't be English, Becca, he's Gianfranco Zola, Pat Nevin, Charlie Cooke the Prince, I mean of course he's slow now look at him but he must have been hot once girls and we fucking thrashed them.'

Davey finished, leaned over to Sam and kissed his forehead. 'Wicked, man.'

'Good grief,' said Juice with lonely resentment.

'I didn't know I could until I did,' Sam confessed.

Rebecca regarded him with parental pride.

'Too late,' Juice lamented, 'too late.'

14

OUT OF THE BODY

Roderick Pastille was right on time. He was being driven in the ministerial limousine. He relaxed in the back with a drink in hand and a folder on his lap and he was gloating. He couldn't help it: was it his fault that he was a Secretary of State? Or that one of the things about being a government minister is that you can order confidential reports carried out by a civil servant sworn to secrecy? If you don't like what they produce you can shred it and they'll not leak a line. Think they want to jeopardize their pension? Never mind risk the Tower or its equivalent; a Clive Ponting comes along once in a decade. Roderick held the folder to his chest, flirted with a tight frisson of delight. It was a beauty, this one, truly. He raised it to his lips and kissed it. Oh, yes, he had the old bastards over a barrel.

They'd resisted homosexual soldiers and he'd let them. He'd given assurances that his government would never countenance a European army. Nor allow British servicemen to sue for maltreatment or discrimination in a civil court. Spineless, but effective. He'd softened them up. They thought he was on their side now, after years of suspicion that he was intent on privatizing them. Which of course he was – in the next parliament if by some miracle, Roderick sighed, we obtain another term.

The report was bound in distasteful grey with a small window through to the first page, where the title addressed one: *Women and War – A Study of Females in a Combat Role*. Roderick opened the folder and reskimmed the report, the most far-reaching one ever compiled on this subject, drawing on hundreds of case studies, foreign accounts, academic research, interviews and observational experiments. The final structure, however, was simplicity itself: a comparison of male and female performance in a wide variety of roles in time of war, both front line and back behind the lines. Out of one hundred and thirty-seven separately specified tasks, men and women performed equally well (given a plus or minus margin for statistical error of five per cent) in fifty-six tasks; men performed better in fourteen; women performed better in sixty-seven.

There were, it was true, according to the report, supposedly masculine qualities with which men in general were endowed more generously than women, e.g. lifting heavy weights, imagination in written debriefs, a sense of humour under duress and one of honour in the field. It was just that when applied to military efficiency in modern warfare the overall value of these traditional male qualities was negligible, and pretty much confined to the foot soldiers of the infantry. What the report indicated was that, individually, trained male and female soldiers (already, it was emphasized, superior, untypical citizens) came out roughly equal judged by almost every criterion, and that it was specifically female generic qualities that tipped the balance in their favour: brain-eye-hand co-ordination for the operation of hi-tech weapons systems; calmness and co-operation displayed by mid-ranking officers, in the military equivalent of middle management in industry where the case was long since proved; greater competitiveness and ruthlessness; less obsessive but more efficient, routinely pedantic attention to detail.

In short, the report concluded that there was no doubt about it: women made – or would make, if and when given the chance – better soldiers than men.

What a bombshell. Explosive stuff. A catastrophe in the making. Roderick could hardly contain himself, didn't know how he was going to wait for the next meeting of the joint Chiefs of Staff. There wasn't one scheduled for days. But he was ready for it: here comes Roddy Pastille, gentlemen, to mess you up, remember the name, Rod Pastille, subversive agenda bender, the politician of your military nightmares.

There was only one caveat in the report, one morsel of consolation which Roderick wondered whether he should try to suppress. But then decided that in fact it was a boon, a sop to their vanity that would render the report palatable. It suggested that there was no evidence that enough women possessed that peculiar combination of arrogance, deductive logic, lateral thinking and daring for more than isolated entries into the upper echelons of leadership.

'In other words, gentlemen, *your* jobs are safe,' he'd pacify them as they absorbed the implications of the report. 'You chaps can keep the club intact; top brass will not be breached,' Roderick would reassure. 'It's just', he'd conclude, 'that apart from the foot-sloggers you'll be leading an army of women.'

* * *

It doesn't matter how strong a woman is or tries to be, Penny Witton reflected, she can be undone. The pain in her heel moved: it migrated around her body. She relented eventually and took herself off to visit her local and hitherto nominal GP for the first time in her adult life when the pain was a searing burn in the middle of her back. The surgery was like a cabin on board ship, inversely wainscoted with dark wood panelling on the top half of the walls. Assorted silent, glum people slumped, too sorry for themselves to browse through old magazines on the coffee table. From four small black speakers in the top corners of the room excitable muzak exhorted the listeners to 'Do the Twist' or 'La-La-La-La La Bamba': Penny anticipated someone snapping the excruciating contrast between bouncy music and morose patients by going insane. Dancing in the surgery. Maybe she would herself, should a Scottish reel come on.

The doctor referred her to a specialist at the hospital, a non-committal young woman who sent her off for tests: Penny allowed a nurse to take various of her bodily fluids, and from then on things happened fast. Every few days someone telephoned Miss Witton to ask her to come in for further urgent tests about which they were unable to say more.

'More, dear?' Penny asked. 'Can you say more if no-one's said the first thing yet?' But she submitted herself to progressive indignities: she consumed a barium meal; let evasive technicians take X-ray, ultrasound, body scan; probes entered her, fibre optic cameras filmed the innermost secrets of her undefiled body.

By the time she met the consultant oncologist, Penny was suffering a hysterical, or frozen, shoulder. Studying her file he affirmed, 'There's no next of kin?'

'There's no kin at all,' Penny told him.

'I'm afraid it's not good news,' he sighed. A handsome, pensive man in early middle age, he wore the pinstripe suit, pink shirt and spotted tie of a dandy banker.

'No news is good news,' Penny smiled through the gritted teeth of her discomfort.

The oncologist made a determined effort to look her in the eye. 'We think you have a malignant growth. More than one actually, we believe. A number. Many.'

Penny glanced round the room, wondering whether they'd been joined by some invisible presence. 'We?' she asked. What did he mean by we? He and his wife? The nurse? We? Did he discuss Penny's case with the taxi driver on his way to work, and they came to the same conclusion? Goodness gracious, young man, she thought, talk sense. Plain English.

'The peculiarity in your case', he was meanwhile continuing, 'is that we don't know where it is. Or they are.'

'You don't know where it is?'

'No. We're pretty sure you have an inoperable tumour in there somewhere. It's just that we can't quite find it.'

'Maybe it's hiding.'

'We can find numerous metastases, secondary growths, of course. Unfortunately. But not the primary site.'

'But you know it's in here somewhere?'

'It's a bit like trying to pinpoint the enemy's HQ in wartime, when he's deploying battalions all over the terrain like decoys. And the truth is we're somewhat outnumbered here.'

'It sounds awful,' Penelope frowned.

'Rather bad news,' the oncologist agreed. 'I'm terribly sorry.'

'Should I take something for it?' Penny asked.

'Oh, yes, of course. Pain relief. That's the first thing we should concern ourselves with.'

'I'd better go to the chemist on the way home,' Penny suggested. 'I did take an aspirin last week, though I prefer not to. You never know what these things are really doing to you, do you?'

'You realize what we're talking about, Miss, er . . . ?' He scanned her file.

Penny shook her head. 'No. Do you?'

'Cancer, Miss Witton.'

'Now we're getting somewhere.'

'The question is which one of your organs is it that's been besieged.'

'Ah, an organ. I might have known one of them would be at the root of this.'

'It's a mystery.' The consultant frowned. 'You haven't by any chance taken clomiphene citrate at any recent period?'

'What?'

'Fertility treatment. No, of course not. We need to get in there to have a good look.'

'I thought you had already.'

'Oh, no. Don't worry. We've hardly started, Miss Witton. You can have a laparoscopy if you want.' He smiled. 'We could give you a gastroscopy.'

'Thank you.'

'A computerized tomography scan. Visceral mapping. I tell you what,' he said excitedly, 'we've just taken on an artist.'

'Really?'

'A painter. She can sometimes pick up things before technology can, would you believe? The earliest indicators. Unconsciously, of course. We look at the portraits she does and, perhaps, just maybe. Spot something. Occasionally.'

'Surely that's an old—'

'We've revived it, Miss Witton. We're more open-minded about these things than people realize.'

'But what you're saying is, I have cancer.'

'Yes.'

'H'm,' she puzzled. 'Of the ovaries, you think?' Penny surmised.

'That I'm afraid we can't say with certainty. I suspect so. But it could still be the liver, or a kidney.'

'I see.'

'Lungs. Breast.'

'I understand.'

'Colon. Rectum. Throat.' The consultant had become gloomy again. 'The vital organs. Our dynamic centres. These are the places where the madness begins.' He gazed out of the window. 'We still don't know why the body goes berserk inside, in this way we call cancer. Intestine, pancreas. The brain, even. Uncontrollable growth of malignant tissue. Why? We don't really know.'

Penny found she was gazing at the oncologist's tie. 'And what's my prognosis?' she managed. 'How long have I got?'

'Oh, Miss Witton. No. Don't take that attitude.' He brightened up again. 'There's a whole range of treatment at our disposal. Cancer may be more widespread; yes, it's more common nowadays. But it's not the killer it used to be.'

Beyond a biopsy of metastases the surgeon Penny was referred to refused to operate, saying the tumours were widespread even if he didn't know where they were, exactly. He couldn't find the primary site, either.

The strange thing was that after Penny's

appointment with the oncologist, the pain magically vanished. For a month. Then all of a sudden in the middle of May it re-erupted in her stomach. Penny was felled by an agony intense, she imagined, as childbirth. Her belly ballooned. Doubled over, she had to dress in ill-fitting smocks in the hospice where it took a week to juggle different cocktails of drugs, of analgesics and opiates, to find out what best kept at bay the pain. Penny carried her distended stomach like a pregnancy, the disease mocking her barrenness, poking fun at her virginity.

People don't talk to each other in the waiting rooms of hospitals, Penny discovered. But in the hospice, conversations rambled and meandered. People would say things and then be interrupted – by visitors or nurses, by their own discomfort or sleep, by woozy distracting thoughts – only to return to the point hours later. Penny was drawn into a dialogue two old men in fresh dressing gowns seemed to be rehearsing in a faltering way.

'People live to a hundred and fifty in this place,' one had said.

'What, here?' Penny interrupted.

'This place he read about,' the other man said. 'A remote Scottish fishing village.'

'No,' the first man said. 'Japan.'

'That's it. Japanese fishermen. The protein.'

'In Japanese fish?' Penny asked.

'Or was it Georgia?'

'Atlanta, Georgia?' the second man laughed. 'America?' he coughed. 'Lucky if they live to twenty with the guns.'

The trio were interrupted by the arrival of lunch, but found themselves sitting close together at teatime three hours later.

'Soviet Union Georgia,' the first man declared. 'The USSR.'

'As was,' said Penny.

'Communists,' said the second man, nodding his head. 'Look at their presidents. Keep people alive. But at what cost?'

'They're not communists, they're rural people,' the first man said. 'Live up in the mountains.'

'Wait,' said Penny. 'I think you're right. I heard that, too. Ossetia.'

Mavis must have told the others at the shop about her, because on the Wednesday Penny was visited by one of the girls from the animal sanctuary, who brought a dog with her. A large brown boxerish mongrel, with a face that had not yet quite come to terms with itself. The sister, 'against my better judgement, mind you,' let the girl bring the dog in, and so witnessed what she would otherwise have had difficulty in believing. The dog detached itself from the girl and wandered from one bed or chair to another. Patients responded as if honoured, and petted the boxer-Labrador cross with the bunched-in face. The dog, for his part, calmly sat beside each one and offered himself, his body, his fisty, spiritual visage, to be appreciated. The girl who'd come to see Penny ended up spending more time with the sister than with her, and arranged to return on a weekly basis.

Once Penny was out of the hospice, clinical tests continued as an outpatient in the Department of Oncology at the hospital. Samples of the human body. Blood, urine, stool. Her sputum and mucus and saliva. Specimens, smears. Not just once and for ever but repeatedly, one nurse or another or the same all over again. Drained, worn down by the relentless questioning of medical interrogators, these detectives of organic corruption. At church on Sunday, kneeling clumsily at the altar rail, it occurred to Penny that she'd rather have a child's blessing than communion; wanted to say, 'Lay your hands on me, Father. Heal me gently.'

The oncologist put her on a course of chemotherapy that may have been responsible for Penny's stomach contracting – as if it had been no more than a phantom cancer – but which certainly visited upon her the indignity of being unable to stop herself breaking wind, and also made her feel so toxically and thoroughly sick she was only surprised to acknowledge that she had no wish to die to escape it. Penny came home from the last session of the first series determined to live.

A neglected delivery van sat in her garage, and a car dealer took it in part exchange for a new Vauxhall Cavalier two-litre automatic. It was smooth and sublime a drive as a hearse at seventy miles per hour, and needed little more than steering in the right direction. Day after day Penelope drove up and down and across the motorways of northern England. Out of Bradford on the M606, up to Leeds, around the infernal triangle of the M1, the M62 and M621; off towards Hull and back again. She got into the car after breakfast each morning, belted herself in and set off. Diagonally down to Greater Manchester, orbiting it and shooting off beyond, up the M61 or M66. Setting out with unspecific destinations, a road map and a vague sense of direction, interconnecting via A-roads, returning to Bradford at different times of the evening. She spread further afield, and the first night Penny spent in a motel she slipped into an open-armed hedonism.

Pain came and went. When it was bad she lay on the sofa at home or in the bed of a strange neat room and fought what felt like gremlins roaming around inside her body and squeezing knots of tissue and nerves with malevolent force. They relaxed their hold and she'd breathe again, then they'd take another handful and grip it tight. But there were whole days of respite and she drove. Joined the furious procession of cars lorries coaches, became a participant in the human race. She saw all the single drivers, men in shirt and tie with their jackets on coat-hangers behind them: she flashed her lights at them out of recognition and solidarity; sometimes they flashed back and she'd wave. Crawling through snarling rush-hour traffic and through sheeting rain Penny in her sealed environment was at the still moving centre of storms. Or she drove at night communing with the hi-fidelity radio, enjoying a peculiar, sociable solitude.

One morning cruising along the nearside lane of the M65 past Burnley, with the sun warming her through the driver's side window, Penny noticed that she felt strange, and rapidly more so: light, insubstantial. Suffused with light, she felt, as if all the molecules of her body were motes of dust in a sunbeam shafting through a room; dancing atoms. Her mind, though, calm and yet alert. 'This is the meaning of the word sublime,' Penny thought to herself. 'Is this a state of grace, Lord?' she wondered, as she became aware deep down inside herself of a distant wave of bliss rolling in from far, far away towards her, towards her heart, and it dawned on Penny that for the first time in fifty or sixty years – since she was a child, indeed – she was going to cry. Flipping the indicator she pulled over to the hard shoulder, came to a stop with her guts churning, switched off the engine, broke down, and wept with fury at God's ingratitude.

Penny cried so hard and long it was a mystery where all the liquid – what little, after all, the nurses had left behind – came from. Maybe her anger manufactured it. Or found it in unknown zones of her body. The sweet and upright woman – misbegotten but good, dutiful, happy, wasn't she? – once Young Miss Witton with her overlooked lips, her disregarded countenance, her sad breasts, her nubbly, unsuckled nipples, her unexplored vagina, her unvisited clitoris, her neglected womb, wept for the unread story of her heart. Her heart like a walnut, the only one of her organs untouched by disease because it was so withered not even cancer could penetrate its defences. Penny Witton wept her body dry.

Others dreamed of love, and power, and overcoming death. But they all had obstacles to overcome. There was a worrying trend, for example, in the scientific establishments of higher education, Ben Ali and Mohammed Al-Shalir noted: the number of post-graduate research students setting up their own companies, and taking out patents. Look at the field of biogenetics: every other week some quiet as a mouse bespectacled boffin was floating himself on the Stock Exchange, throwing off his white coat to go live in the Bahamas. They'd have none of that here, they decided, which was one of the reasons they'd sent a recruitment video around the world: Brits were getting a little too cute. No, those given generous allowances, superb working conditions and the privilege of being at Oxford University signed contracts handing all in-tellectual ownership of their research over to The Laboratory Ltd, in return none the less for potentially lucrative one half of one per cent royalties of any profit thereby accrued by The Lab.

The important thing for The Lab, as Mr Bone under-stood, was to maximize resources. Each new generation of students, for example, was given the opportunity to learn for themselves how to carry out the LD 50 test: to determine the toxicity of a given substance, a group of animals are allowed to swallow measured amounts of it until such time as half of them have died; thus the 50 per cent Lethal Dose is ascertained. Mr Bone made sure that each time a student learned the procedure it was on a product The Lab was being paid to test. Anti-freeze, say; brake-fluid, bleach. Church candles or oven cleaner. Deodorant, bubble bath. Crayons and paint. Suntan oil. Fire extinguishers. Hairspray.

That was all well and good but more could be done: when an animal was shaved to attach electrodes, Mr Bone made sure the razor was a new model being assessed; if they had to test a pen manufacturer's ink Mr Bone procured enough spare biros to write up all reports for a year. The aim was to reach a stage where they never had to pay for a product, only for services, though even that could be cut down on if Roderick helped them win a contract to test independently the local water. It was Mohammed's idea, however, for the Department of Organology to take a stand on an environmental issue: a memo was sent to each student, researcher and member of staff announcing that as a contribution to the city of Oxford's worthy anti-traffic policies, the department was no longer going to provide car parking in the basement. Instead – as photographs and accompanying articles in the *Oxford Times* and *Mail* and even one or two nationals then witnessed – rows of bicycle bars were planted all round the building ('Tie your horse to one of these,' Ben Ali joked to the young member of staff dragged out for the photographers, his first words addressed directly to Joe Snow) while shower units were installed in the ground floor toilets for sweaty commuters.

'Scientists used to be thought of as being a little out of touch,' Ben Ali told the papers, 'but here in Oxford we like to think that, on the contrary, we've always led the way. We understand better than anyone, after all, the subtle interconnectedness of our ecosystem; how could we not care about the environment, the environment we all share?'

By this simple expedient was a vast space in the basement liberated for The Laboratory's expansion into experiments with human beings. Mr Bone had long been envious of Psychology's practice of offering impecunious students money to take part in behavioural tests, while the brothers looked to America where guinea pigs queueing up to volunteer for a cure for HIV were so numerous they had to take part in special lotteries for selection.

The basement was speedily transformed from concrete gloom to bright offices and workshops. A showcase experiment was set up, initially entitled *A Study of Extreme States: Bliss in the Guise of Torment*, to be carried out by the internationally acclaimed, award-winning team of organologists Willem van der Bierstoonk and Magenta Hroichkova, lured back from the brink of Johns Hopkins by a generous grant from the Research Council.

Magenta was intrigued by the way people went through certain experiences which from the outside looked like the utmost in suffering, but which afterwards they reported as having been pleasurable. Epilepsy, for example, in which in one short fit of a few minutes' duration there occurred a day's worth of nervous activity – an electrical storm in the brain – which utterly exhausted the subject, yet which they could describe only with words more appropriate to mystical religion.

Pretty soon she had make-believe astronauts hurtling beatifically around a room in a machine that simulated the G-force, while their faces were distorted by horror unimaginable; in another a group of the Yogic flyers of Skelmersdale bounced like ecstatic, hiccuping frogs; in a third a trio of weightlifters from Blackbird Leys went through their companionable paces towards transcendent moments of grunting self-torture.

Magenta succeeded in sending Willem out to conduct experiments in the field: he handed out questionnaires to kids playing Laser Quest and rode the rollercoasters of Alton Towers, and he visited nightclubs to observe the terrible suffering of bleddy idiots who couldn't hold their beer so they took drugs and look what 'appens to them. Bleddy sad, really, yet the Bulgarian bint's right, they do *think* it's enjoyable. Weird.

The last of these experiments were among those that fed into The Laboratory's first medical trials in the basement of the Department of Organology. 'We're getting there,' Mr Bone told Joe. 'Organology, that's what it's all about, ultimately. The lure of everlasting life. Through wisdom, immortality.'

Mr Bone's eyes seemed to look inwards on those rare occasions he had the time to share his optimistic vision with Joe, in his office up on the top floor. 'It's a chemical future and it's ours, Joseph. The boffins are cracking the code of the brain all around us, but we're the ones who know what to do with the information. This is HQ, Mr Snow.'

'It's the brave new world, Mr Bone.'

'Nonsense, Joseph,' Mr Bone assured him. 'A few

301

selfish liberals and intellectuals think that because *they* mistrust the implications, everyone else should.'

'And they shouldn't?' Joe asked, because he wanted to be sure.

Mr Bone's smile revealed his well-manicured teeth. 'Joseph, most people will be queueing up outside to hand over what the elite told them was their most precious possession, the so-called freedom of individualism, which is nothing more than the freedom to suffer in your own unique way, for the greater freedom we offer. Mark my words: Mr Al-Shalir will be ripped to shreds by the press. But if we can beat death, if people think they might live for ever, he'll come to be loved in the country.' Mr Bone got up from his desk. 'But we can't sit around all day chatting when there's work to be done, Joseph. We've fabulous creatures to engineer.'

'Yes, Mr Bone.'

'Mythical beasts, Mr Snow. Transplants soon. But first, treatment.'

It was tobacco companies that put up most of the initial money, though soon brewers and distillers gave donations too. As Ben Ali pointed out to the press, the largest companies gave the most to charity. 'The richer the man,' he explained, 'the more generous his heart, you'll find.'

The work began with the quiet granting of a licence to test the effects of cannabis in its various forms on certain illnesses, and if the tobacco companies had a stake in a time when cannabis might be legalized that was no more than a scurrilous suggestion and a purely speculative coincidence.

No-one, fortunately, made any such libellous connection between donations from the alcohol industry, pharmaceutical experiments conducted in the old

Veterinary Studies unit on the top floor, and the resultant substances being discreetly administered to voluntary patients who began to enrol in the new basement surgery; one of whom, Penelope Witton, had been referred by her oncologist in Bradford, who'd been one of the Department of Organology's first postgraduate students.

'Don't worry,' he assured her. 'Whatever they're developing, you won't become addicted. Thousands, millions of patients have received opium, morphine and other narcotics as painkillers, without ever emerging with a drug habit. We really don't know why.'

'I'm not worried about that,' Penny admitted. She drove eagerly to Oxford, stayed in a bed in the small ward, and had intriguing nocturnal experiences during her week's stay. She was given regular drinks of something like a revolting milkshake that made her feel woozy and then sink into her body as if into another substance. It reminded her of something she couldn't quite identify, a nostalgia for a time before memory, until she sensed that it was inducing in her the gorgeous tranquillity of breast milk. Had Magenta Hroichkova but known it, she could easily have slipped from her office in the basement to the infirmary next door and seen Penny's body, her face in a grimace of apparent agony, while in her mind she was off some place else. On a journey, as it happened, upwards: a levitation, of sorts, in what seemed to her like an unworldly lift. Up, up (towards the light, she rather hoped, although in truth the vision remained unromantically murky). Up past the 1st, 2nd, 3rd, 4th floors, coming to rest at an unmarked floor above, at which point the lift doors opened and she, well, the illusion was that she floated. Through a large open-plan laboratory that smelled of childhood at Bradford High School for Girls, over porcelain sinks, test tubes, Bunsen burners Penny floated. Across a corridor and into a maze of rooms and smaller hallways. Penny was seized with an eagerness to reach out and open each door to see inside the rooms, an eagerness that turned to reluctance when she discovered that each one held a human being, sleeping much as she appeared still to be five floors below.

Penny knew she'd left the present behind, and was grateful. What she couldn't yet know was that she was visiting the future.

The human beings looked peaceful, so much so it could have been a mortuary, they could have been corpses, until she floated closer to one and saw that attached to it by an intestinal tube was a snoozing dog. In another room a sleeping woman lay holding hands with a comatose monkey: Penny saw that their wrists were bound together at a mutual sewn-up wound. A fat naked man was covered in leeches; a child and a lamb lay spine to spine; an Asian woman with extravagant spectacles had her toes inserted in the gut of a wolf; a man resembling Penny's father smiled in his sleep as snakes slithered out of his nostrils and other orifices.

Each hallucination Penny backed away from, out of the room and into an empty corridor, only to be impelled, despite her mounting dread, towards and into the next room, where a yet worse vision awaited her in a Boschian catalogue, a bestiary of medical nightmares. She entered a room where a long thin man lay on a table. Penny couldn't see an animal there, or anything attached to the man's body. Yet she sensed that something awful was being done to him, and she had to move closer to find out what it was. She was hovering above him when he opened his eyes, bottomless blue eyes, saw her, and whispered. Something Penny couldn't hear.

'What?' she asked, bending closer to him. His lips moved again.

'Help me,' the man whispered.

With a sudden electric jolt Penny snapped out of the future and woke up back in her bed in the basement.

Floating (3)

'I need a bath. I can't wait any longer,' I said as a contraction receded.

'Run the bath,' Martha told Jack. He dashed ahead. We heard the water gurgling through old pipes and filling the cottage's cast-iron tub: some way short of the luxurious plumbing Jack had left behind, and wouldn't see again.

Martha helped me struggle upstairs. 'It's dark outside,' she said.

'What?'

'I only just noticed,' she said. 'Night's fallen.'

I clambered in: they helped me lower into warm water that soothed instant relief from the back pain that burned even between contractions.

I lay there a long time. The labour seemed to steady itself, slow down.

'It doesn't want to come out,' I said, calmly.

'Why would she want to come out?' Martha asked. 'She's in her own flotation tank in there.'

'Of course he wants to come out,' Jack demurred. 'As soon as he's ready.'

'Have you ever been in one of those?' Martha asked. 'I have. And I wouldn't have got out if I wasn't obliged to.'

'Neither will I,' I said.

Jack kept the bath topped up with hot water. Contractions themselves were as painful as before but in between I began to doze, slipping into inviting sleep. Jack pulled me up, or else I'd be squeezed awake by another contraction, and come to, spluttering scummy water.

'What if it doesn't come?' Martha asked outside on the landing.

'Of course it will,' Jack assured her. 'How do you mean?'

'I don't know. Maybe she'll need a Caesarean.'

'Can we do that? I mean, you.'

'Of course not.'

I wept. Salty tears slid into the bath water. Inside me a narcoleptic baby waited, lolling in the livid cavern of my womb.

'This baby doesn't want to be born,' I moaned. Blue veins ridged my swollen breasts.

Jack put candles on the window sill and the shelf along the wall at the side of the bath. 'He or she chose you, Rebecca.'

'Why the hell would anyone choose me?'

Jack looked at me, no longer embarrassed. 'Anyone would choose you.'

Ben leaned against the door jamb. He nodded his head in agreement. 'Uuh,' I heard him utter, interpreting a 'Yes'.

'Get out of the bath now,' Martha advised.

'No.' I lay still in the dirty water.

'I can't see,' she said calmly.

'You don't bloody need to see!'

'That's right. She doesn't need to see,' Jack agreed. 'But you've been in the bath for hours. You'll be wrinkled as a pot-bellied pig if you stay much longer.'

'It hurts enough in here. It'll be worse if I get out.'

'It'd be good to walk around now,' Martha told me. 'Walk about a bit and let's bring this baby down.'

I understood that my position was untenable. I began to sob even as I gritted my teeth. 'Help me up,' I demanded.

15

THE WINKER

Along with most of his cabinet colleagues through the spring of that year, the Rt Hon. Roderick Pastille, Secretary of State for Defence, was begging the PM to stop dithering. The putative chief had been biding his time praying for an upswing in the government's fortunes. Months, however, went by with barely a bung or a blunder yet the PM's and the party's standing in opinion polls remained at an all-time low. In one group, the number of respondents who thought the Prime Minister was the best of the leaders on offer amounted to a mathematical negative; the panjandrum was hardly helped, Roderick sniffed, by the fact that he looked every passing day as dithering a decision-maker as Hamlet vacillating in the halls of Elsinore.

A general election was finally called when the full term of the government's office hove into view and one could be delayed no longer. The Defence Minister heaved a sigh of relief, only to be then gripped by panic: Roderick had no idea what outcome was to be preferred. A comfortable win, of course, the retention of his seat in constituency and Cabinet, followed by immediate overdue promotion to the Exchequer or Home Office – but that was clearly impossible now. A narrow win, then, and the same objects achieved. Defeat, however; that was the issue: if they were to be trounced, then to be identified as a close colleague of this wretched PM would be disastrous, obviously, but what if there should be a narrow defeat? How best to align oneself in the ensuing struggle for succession, bearing in mind that there's nothing riles the party faithful or the slippery powers behind the throne more than disloyalty? Unless of course it brings power.

But there was no time left now for reflection. The hour for battle had arrived. Onto the hustings. Into the studio. Bring on the hecklers, the do-gooding whingers, traducing hacks of the gutter press, the poison pens, the mockers and knockers and scoffers of this green and envious land. When the blast of war blows in our ears, then imitate the action of the tiger. Yes. Stiffen the sinews, summon up the blood, disguise fair nature with hard-favoured rage. Once more into the breach!

It was indeed on Europe that HM government decided to fight, on the subject if not the soil. Roderick's good friend and rival, the junior ministerial Under Secretary of State for Foreign Affairs Cyril Blunt – with whom at Oxford twenty-five years earlier he'd drunk foolishly, fallen out of punts into the Cherwell, climbed over the wall at night to avoid the bulldogs, debated, dropped acid but not hallucinated, competed for a Blue in real tennis (beating him to that but yielding to Cyril's First in Greats) – had few of the customary political virtues: hypocrisy, venality, duplicity, nepotism, greed. No, Cyril wasn't a bastard. He was, rather, a raving lunatic. He was clinically insane; any psychiatrist was able to explain that to a tabloid newspaper for a small fee, and his condition belonged to a category of madness known as the shadow syndromes: in Cyril's case, in an excited state mild paranoia and idealism could chemically combine, apparently, to produce delusional thinking. Those afflicted with such syndromes, however, posed no physical threat either to themselves or other people. In fact some physicians believed that a significant proportion of the population suffered from one or more.

Roderick knew that Cyril Blunt was a lunatic all right with an obsession about Europe. Even in peacetime he showed no sign of modest stillness or humility but campaigned tirelessly around the country giving speeches in stale halls to twos and threes of doting strangers like some pathetic novelist. Why go to hear a politician claim that a single currency was merely a German interim measure before the Deutschmark invaded Britain or that the Mafia were planning to relocate from Sicily to the Isle of Wight, when there was some nutter in the family or failing that the pub spouting likewise? Come the election campaign, though, his every pronouncement was listened to with forensic attention; each gathering Cyril addressed rammed with cameras, tripods, flashes, microphones, notebooks.

Journalists were keener on being assigned to Blunt's campaign trail than Pastille's because Cyril was urbane, convivial company on the train coach plane; then on the rostrum he became insane and all they had to do was stifle their giggles and catch him at it: a significant feature of the election was that it resembled a radio panel game called *Catch My Gaffe*© in which politicians had to talk for a minimum period of time without saying anything that could embarrass their leader, while journalists listened with fingers on buzzers for just that slip-up they could splash across the front page. The same rules applied to mainstream politicians of every persuasion and such gaffes included referring to sex or drugs without censure, forgetting to criticize teachers, and offering the possibility of spending taxpayers' money on anything at all.

Cyril Blunt provided a number of gaffes, less in his carefully doctored speeches than in impromptu answers to questions afterwards in which he gave his opinion that the French planned to apply to the European Court in Strasbourg to outlaw the Sunday roast and that the Spanish proposed to censor the BBC because it was too impartial. He was a growing embarrassment to the government.

It was a strange campaign. An esteemed grouse-shooting, fox-hunting, secretary-inseminating backbench Conservative had died just before the campaign began. After the resultant by-election in what was regarded as one of the safest rural constituencies in the country one newspaper made a semantic gaffe of its own and ran the headline: STANDING TORY LOSES SEAT SHOCK. But the paper had inadvertently given the correct impression of the confident Tory candidate's parliamentary chair's being whipped away from under him as he went to sit down in some sort of House of Commons schoolboy prank, and landing painfully on his coccyx.

Schisms opened up within the Cabinet not just over Europe, but over economics, too. Roderick was amongst those who advocated the announcement of a large cut in income tax a month before the election, the tactic, he pointed out, that always works; but the Chancellor of the Exchequer, with the Prime Minister's backing, explained that taxes were already so low it was impossible to cut them any further. Much better, he argued, to concentrate on the inevitability that Labour, with their traditional commitment to unbridled social justice, would raise taxes. This, Roderick would reckon with hindsight (lamenting – on behalf of his party as much as himself – that he could not now become Chancellor, a job eminently suitable for him), was a monumental blunder. For the Shadow Chancellor promptly launched the Opposition campaign with the promise that *his* party in power *would cut income tax*. Not only that but this was in fact a part of their Big Idea, as the Leader of Her Majesty's Loyal Opposition explained: what he promised the British people was what they'd always wanted, always needed, but never had. Improved management of the country. The government had been a bunch of sleazy cheesy, lazy wastrels in power, money had leaked and flowed not just out of corrupt water companies' pipes and tunnels but everywhere else too. Labour would save money by belt-tightening here, cutting waste there, slashing bureaucracy in front of us and incompetence behind, and with the banner of good management above us we'd all come marching home again, ta-ra, ta-ra.

The Shadow Chancellor and Shadow Minister for Health vowed to cut the budget of the NHS, yet proved with the use of computer graphics and holograms that the money this saved would enable them to significantly increase the budget of the NHS through (and here they spoke slowly, enunciating clearly) New Improved Management. Their lead in the opinion polls increased a point or two, as it did again a few days later following the same arguments for education.

Whatever Roderick and his government did or wanted to do, it seemed, the Opposition got there before them. Surefire winners were missing the target.

On law and order, the Shadow Home Secretary promised to be Tough on Crime and Tough on the Causes of Crime. The Home Secretary pounced on this waffle, pointing out that Tough on the Causes of Crime was old socialist-speak for Soft on Crime itself and declaring that HM government would make sure that from now on violent criminals would serve the full extent of their sentences.

'We', said his Shadow, 'will arrest squeegee merchants, and while they're in prison they can clean the windows.' The polls swung further the Opposition's way.

'We shall impose tougher sentences on drugs dealers,' the Home Secretary promised.

'We shall lower the age of imprisonment for juvenile offenders,' said his opposite number. 'Let them learn discipline.'

'I blame the media,' the flustered Home Secretary said.

'I blame the schools,' said the Shadow. 'Bring back corporal punishment: bad teachers need a good caning. Detention for unruly children must be imposed. For those who refuse to spell properly we advocate longer sentences.'

'We have to reassert traditional values,' the Home Secretary blustered. 'The break-up of the family's to blame. Feckless absent fathers; irresponsible single mothers.'

This time, though provoked, he'd gone too far. Tabloids cheered but the broadsheets jeered; there his words were greeted with a howl of protest: feminist columnists were offended, old hippie pundits outraged, by his remarks.

The Shadow Under Secretary of State for Home Affairs, who might have been expected to respond, was oddly silent. Edna Wartwhistle was a chaste, plain, scruffy, straight-talking lesbian Lancastrian who wore her heart on her sleeve, was almost as naive a politician as Cyril Blunt, and was an old adversary of Roderick Pastille: she'd been a Shadow Junior Minister at Defence for a time – until she was shifted for claiming that tanks and torpedoes were inefficient phallic inventions of male engineers and that if girls were encouraged in science at school it would all be quite different – and had a way of expressing her moralistic contempt with a sneer that had annoyed him unduly.

'Would the honourable gentleman reassure us', she'd refer to Roderick in the Commons with sarcastic stress on the first syllable of *hon*ourable and a loud sniff that implied a reek of *dis*honour about him, 'that on his recent and we hope not too *arduous* trip to our *friends* in Oman, amid the talk of *small* arms for their internal security forces, there was no link made between those sales and any aid package?'

She got under his skin, somehow, as he admitted to Russell Crowe, his confrère and confidant. 'That bitch has it in for me, she knows something she won't let on.'

'Relax, Paz, it's our distaste for bull dykes is all. They remind us of that creepy rugger-bugger master at school who watched us in the shower; who knew something about us before anyone else did. Including ourselves.'

'I'm *not* one of us,' Roderick disavowed. 'I wish you'd get that through your thick queer Negro skull.'

Russell Crowe was an odd, shadowy, flamboyant figure himself, who'd made his name by his ability to remain anonymous: he was unknown to all but those in power; was so often the only black in a room full of whites that he'd remained invisible while developing a

316

high profile. He was on first name terms with the Governor of the Bank of England, swapped freemasons' handshakes with members of the 1922 backbench committee, belonged to the same club as the chairman of the CBI, had his own key to the back door of certain buildings in Whitehall and met junior members of the royal family without genuflection. It was just that no-one knew what he did or where he came from, not even Roderick, his best friend. He had the old-fashioned air of the offspring of a Commonwealth diplomat who'd creamed off enough of his country's assets to send his children to board in England, one of whom had stayed here. But Russell had no known address, no visible means of support other than pink braces beneath his pinstripe, no apparent family, and a CV writ in fog.

'That Edna Wartwoman looks like a horse,' Roderick exclaimed peevishly.

'Why, Paz,' Russell responded, 'some of the most beautiful women in history have looked like horses. For most of our benighted civilization the steed has been exalted, man's most noble companion. For centuries men would far rather ride the splendid beast than a woman.'

It was true, Roderick conceded: of course our notions of beauty reflect the changing values of our times. Look at the fashion models in magazines today, skinny adolescents everywhere, monstrous really. It's quite clear. For the first time the widespread sexual abuse of children has been brought into the open, the sad sorry stories bubbling out of Borstals, orphanages, schools, choirs. Cauldrons of sin unheeded for generations. And that's good, yes, I mean go practise if you please with men or women: leave a child alone. It's good, but our shadow side cannot help responding: the devil is helpless in his energy. Where good flourishes, evil is surely skulking through the undergrowth. So fashion throws up for us these images of child-women, young girls in their faux innocent allure.

The hopefully future Under Secretary of State for Home Affairs was silent, however, on the subject of the family not out of personal reticence so much as that she was nowhere to be seen. Edna Wartwhistle was absent, uncontactable out in the middle of nowhere somewhere: for it happened to be her turn for a visit to a certain health farm nestled in the home counties where legions of female Opposition candidates were required to attend on a strict rota basis, on pain of discipline from the fearsome party whips, rests from which they emerged reassembled. Stepford Wives with Attitude, Russell Crowe called them. Even the ideological veterans like Edna Wartwhistle were obliged to make the trip along with their young colleagues in the new sorority.

So that the furore had died down when, two days later, Edna reappeared in public transformed from her makeover, in a well-cut trouser suit, her hair cropped gamine short, doe-eyed with full make-up including vamp red stop-go lipgloss, in a pillbox hat, switched butch to fem, now a lipstick New Lesbian, ten years younger, accompanied by leaked rumours linking her with a straight female soap star and with even – the masterstroke – with even her name changed, the first part of it excised for ever like some awkward clause. She was now Edna Whistle. The change seemed to suggest that like Tony Benn she'd dropped an aristocratic appendage, except that unlike that old deadwood socialist here was a modernist, a people's politician that women could relate to and men could, well, what else could men do but what her surname now invited them to? And when they did, Edna turned out to have become a good sport overnight, and pouted sultrily back at them.

Edna, however, brought the subject of the family up again of her own accord: her first audacious announcement was that single mothers were a bane of society and that her party promised to cut their benefits.

There was silence while this sank in, though not stillness, at least not in one area. For, watching the news, Roderick Pastille felt a jolt in his groin. Edna (née Wart) Whistle now doubly unsettled him: it was already bad enough that he suspected she knew not only of his Indonesian escapades but also of the parties Russell Crowe threw, with cavalier whores to his friend Rod's taste – hoydenish, tomboy girls; with the hysteria of this election, the looming catastrophe exerting a weird electric thrill, pulling all towards it as to an abyss, so Roderick's libido was overcharged. He didn't go home to Heather for days on end, caroused incognito at Russell's secret Mayfair apartment with a different girl each night, ever younger, indulging recklessly, led on by the danger of potential exposure, the unstable conviction of invincibility, the desire for voluptuous punishment, with the image of Edna Whistle now pouting sarcastically into his face as he collapsed upon the boyish girl beneath him.

Roderick emerged from inadequate hours of snatched sleep with rings under his eyes that an assistant powdered before studio appearances and photo opportunities. In truth their vestige conferred upon him a useful gravitas and evidence of unstinting commitment to the cause. As a young man Roderick had had a silly face, with exaggerated features, and he'd grown more handsome, dashing even, in his thirties; now in his mid-forties was approaching on his way to the pinnacle of power his physical prime. He was spoken of as a future party leader more often every year, more with each rabble-rousing speech he gave at the party conference. PUGNACIOUS PASTILLE, they called him, as he lambasted foes of every hue; THE HOUSE-WIVES' CHOICE, with his flamboyance, dishevelled by his own rhetoric, his hair all over the place and mad eyes like a troll on a pencil end, 'with lead up its arse,' Russell teased him. Rumours circulated – was he really gay or not? – but the libel laws restricted them to metropolitan dinner parties. Did R. Pastille have too much testosterone or too little? Was he a macho man or parody of same, with his pouting snout, his lascivious lips? At conference he aimed (like Zero Mostel, Russell crowed, appealing to the drunks in the back row) for the old people, older, ever older, in a party leeching youth; his standing ovations had recently begun to totter, and arms would rise here and there tentatively as if to ask a question of him, only to adjust their hearing aids.

With three weeks to go to election day the Prime Minister decided that his Ministers were competent honest paragons of government, all that was needed was to get this across to the electorate. He demanded a spotlight put upon the individual officers of his crusading army and one directive from central office was the attachment of a photographer to every Cabinet member. Roderick found an inscrutable young Devonian accompanying him on the campaign trail at all times, sat silently beside the chauffeur. He snapped the Minister unobtrusively and on rare occasions would say, 'Excuse me, sir, ideal opportunity, if you don't mind.' This usually involved domestic pets, which the young man – or maybe he had orders from

the advertising guru in charge of the party's image —
seemed to think shaded babies as the pictorial key to
political success. He was there when Roderick made a
visit to The Lab for a board meeting, and grabbed the
chance to take a whole series of Mr Pastille grinning
with monkeys, dogs and cats.

The image, that was the secret, Roderick conceded.
They had, in fact, tried with Heather, his wife, the
fragrant Heather, a passably handsome aristocrat when
they married who as soon as she gave birth had
collapsed, aged as rapidly as a Mediterranean peasant
woman. It's an ancient truism in politics that a wife on
one's arm clears the air, but Heather had grown dowdy,
frowsty, uberous female flesh spilling as she suckled
squalling infants. Attempts to glamorize her had mis-
fired: blue-rinsing her prematurely white hair ten years
earlier had made Heather look at thirty-five hideous, a
caricature, like some kind of weird performance artist
parodying the party faithful. For her weight problem
someone suggested bulimia, which had been made
fashionable by royalty; she ignored that treatment but
went on other diets and turned yellow, began to smell,
repelled not only her husband but others too. 'The
colonic irrigation's backfiring, darling,' people
whispered behind Roderick's back. 'Wonder if Paz'll
bring the Scarecrow tonight.' Defeated, relieved,
Roderick left Heather at home with her children, her
lovesick whippets, her garden in Highgate. It was only
a shame she didn't spend more time further away at
their cottage in Herefordshire.

Now ten years later Roderick wondered briefly
whether Heather might not be slipped through this
health farm of Labour's for one last try, such advances
had experts in these matters made. Certain senior
female figures in the Opposition had been given plastic

surgery and during Prime Minister's Question Time they sat on the facing front bench with a look of astonishment at the government's effrontery. Could he not? . . . Well, there it was, you see, in a nutshell, that was it precisely. Modernization. He was thinking of his loyal spouse, his better half, his helpmate. Over there the wives *were* the politicians. A distaff army of candidates, to spread their arses across the Commons benches come the election.

Cyril Blunt, meanwhile, continued to embarrass the government at every opportunity. The PM's men tried everything they could to stifle him short of a kidnap, until in an Oddfellows Association hall in Leek one Tuesday evening Cyril came up with the biggest gaffe of his political career: following an anodyne, neutered speech (and restraining himself from reassuring those present that the preservation of the Peak District wallabies was a government priority), in response to a question concerning unemployment and the social chapter Cyril noted that people in the UK who had jobs worked longer hours than in Europe; he pointed out that the UK, in resisting EC legislation for a minimum wage and maximum working week, had no allies whatsoever and could expect none since every Continental country already possessed domestic legislation more stringent than that proposed by the EC. The journalists frowned and yawned. Cyril was in intellectual mode, crawling through labyrinthine argument towards some obscure point, something he was quite capable of doing without saying anything interesting. Then all of a sudden he leapt out of the deep end and onto the diving board.

'What we should beware of,' he said, 'is the Channel Tunnel. It's a ploy. It's winching us towards Europe.'

Cyril stepped down from the platform and journalists scurried off to tape phone e-mail the quote which appeared on TV, radio and in newspapers the next day.

MORE BLUNT TALK: CHUNNEL IS A PLOY, one broadsheet proclaimed, while a tabloid trailed his latest nonsense with CYRIL TELLS IT HOW IT IS.

A surprising portion of people around the country had as much affection as derision for Cyril Blunt. He reminded them maybe of that oddball kid in class or the crazy cousin they caught up with once or twice a year. Many more, however, regarded him as the only politician of any substance. The psychiatrists were right: an enormous number of ordinary people out there were nuts. So many, in fact, they formed a political constituency of their own, with Cyril Blunt their chief representative in Westminster.

For the first time in the campaign the government's position in the opinion polls stopped falling. Right-wingers came rushing forward to acclaim this brilliant metaphor from their esteemed colleague, and at the sight of them the following day's polls slipped back again. So Cyril Blunt called an unofficial press conference to announce that he'd been misunderstood. It hadn't been a metaphor at all. What he'd meant was that the Channel Tunnel was a winch by which the French and the Benelux countries, anchored by Germany, aided and abetted by all the rest, were pulling island Britain back towards the Continent.

'Am I the only one to have noticed how train times keep getting fractionally quicker?' he demanded. 'They're the same Shuttle engines. Ergo: the Tunnel's getting shorter.'

This time the party's standing not only stopped falling but stabilized, hovered, and then began unbelievably to winch itself back up. At last someone in the party had found a Big Idea.

'The bastard!' Roderick exclaimed at Russell

Crowe's that evening. 'Posing as our sweet idiot savant, our untainted holy fool, and all this time he was placing himself in the frame for the leadership. Mendacious little sod!'

What really irked Roderick, of course, was that he'd not come up with a Big Idea of his own. He rather supposed they'd all been used up back in the eighties: electoral boundaries had been changed by true blue cartographers; party actuaries had devised improved methods for measuring unemployment figures; we'd gone to war with a tinpot dictatorship – and with a bigger one in the nineties. Wait a minute! War! Perhaps it wasn't too late to overtake Cyril. Ride the public mood and grab the reins. I'm Defence Minister, after all, he reminded himself. Political leader of the armed forces, pretty much. Let me attack.

And so with a week to go to the election Roderick Pastille delivered a stirring speech in which he thanked his close colleague Cyril Blunt for alerting us to the real danger of Eurostar; for bringing to public attention the threat of the Winch. As Secretary of State for Defence, he invoked the spirit of Dunkirk and the Battle of Britain and rashly paraphrased Winston Churchill, promising to lead his forces on seas and oceans and beaches, in streets and hills, in defence of the realm and the security of the nation.

Applause rang round the hall where Roderick spoke live, but the TV electorate was less impressed. The trouble was that, as astute commentators recognized, Roderick and his colleagues had been employing euphemism for so long that it was difficult now to untangle the language. Defence? Security? Far from invoking our finest hour long ago such terms recalled embarrassing episodes in the Gulf War when Americans shot at their British allies by mistake because our trucks were the same as the ones we'd sold to Iraq for *their* security – with which they'd then invaded Kuwait. It was for Indonesia's *defence* we'd sold them the Hawk jets they'd used to slaughter East Timorese. So what did that smoothie Pastille mean now? Was the RAF to defend us by sending so-called Transporter planes on low-flying bombing missions along the Champs Elysées? To strafe the home ports of Spanish trawlers? Should the police interrogate Dutch tourists with electric shock batons?

It didn't help that Labour's Shadow Defence Secretary seemed to have public support for his novel proposal to use morality as a measure of foreign policy. On Europe, though, the Opposition kept quiet. Domestic policy was their battleground. It was where they'd discovered the real *Big* Big Idea, though the Idea wasn't made public: it was the Leader's Idea which he shared only with his inner circle, but it determined strategy on all domestic issues.

The *Big* Big Idea was imported from the United States, where the Leader had been impressed by the Communitarian Network philosophy behind the present president's success. This was the realization of how painful it was for conscientious decent-minded fair-playing social-democrat-leaning people to ignore the reversion of society to its pre-war divided state. Of course it had to *be* ignored, everyone understood that: the post-war project was long dead, the consensus of socialists liberals one-nation Tories on the uplifting from the bottom of British society; it had to be ignored since, of Britain's two nations, one no longer voted, and pandering to its occupants would not alter that fact overnight. A compact had been accepted, an unspoken contract signed by the rest: that the ghettoes, the slums, of this post-industrial age were the sacrifice

325

we paid for our affluence. The underclass – the unemployed, ill-educated, single mothers, riotous families; the boorish, chain-smoking, hard-drinking, highrise-dwelling, homeless begging, pimple-squeezing, junkfood-eating, freewheeling, crack-dealing, beer-drinking, sweat-stinking, vomit-sicking, cash-nicking, rap-riffing, glue-sniffing lost generation – had to be ignored from behind discreet window grilles, burglar alarms and private security patrols.

The *Big* Big Idea was, like all the best, simple. ('Socialism answers needs, not wants,' the Leader maintained, and he meant it: the path to social justice was now a bureaucratic one, glacial, Nordic; a penny in the pound here, a change of punctuation there in the letter of the law.) The underclass as a whole was our conscience, but when you had the courage to lift the lid what did you see? What did it house but the guilty, those who made it uncomfortable for conscientious decent people to go about their daily lives in peace of mind? That was why the Opposition targeted juvenile criminals, homeless travellers, city centre beggars, heroin-addicted burglars, sponging mothers, pound-an-hour casual workers in junk food Mcjobs on standby time. It was no good the middle class (the new, modern, New British middle class) ignoring the poor: it was high time we punished them.

So began the final dying days of this administration, which came none too soon for Roderick Pastille. A party worker was editing video material on the night of Roderick's intemperate fighting speech. In the fast-forwarding and rewinding of a section, determining the in and out points, rocking back and forth the manual control, she was disturbed by a barely visible glitch on the tape. When she played the tape at normal speed, however, although she saw it was there when she looked closely – as Roderick proclaimed, 'The armed forces are in better shape now than they were when we came to power' – she couldn't actually identify it on any single digital frame. And then it happened again a little later in the speech, when the Defence Secretary said that having undergone commando training himself . . .

It dawned on the video technician that the problem was not a technical one but rather that Mr Pastille was suffering the most fleeting of facial tics; a wink at audience or camera but infinitesimal, the merest most minute spasm no more than the hint of a shadow flickering across his countenance, all but invisible to the naked eye. Thus alerted, she kept watch on the Defence Secretary's speeches over those following days – she kept an eye on his eye – sharing her suspicions with one or two colleagues in the central office media centre.

So it was there that the rumour which floated around in the hysterical pre-election atmosphere began, there where party workers gathered at the end of each hectic day and squeezed into the studio to watch the Defence Secretary's speeches and laugh, just as the public were doing when sections of his speeches were broadcast on the news into the living-rooms of the country: because they were funny; unaccountably, mysteriously, mountingly so. The Secretary of State for Defence made statements of fact, promises for a Tory future, assurances of the government's accomplishments and personal pleas from the heart, and viewers found themselves weeping with delight as Roderick, unable to help himself, winked at the nation every time he lied.

16

RAVING

Volcanic eruptions, the shifting of tectonic plates. Glacial melt. Lightning-struck fires in a dry forest. New stars tumbling from nothing into being in the gaseous expanses of the universe. The impregnation of a woman. Egg released from ovary, sperm ejaculating into vagina, darting towards Fallopian tube, meeting egg; spermatozoa detach the egg's outer layer, and a solitary sperm pushes through alone, reaches the nucleus of the egg; the egg attaches itself to the uterine wall; twenty-three chromosomes meet twenty-three chromosomes to form the central part of a single ovum, which meeting triggers the process of abundant cellular multiplication, the process of growth. Rebecca's pelvic girdle become the cradle of an ocean, a warm salty sea in which life could grow. Her womb swelled, a new Mediterranean, while organs shifted like islands to make way, her bladder shrank, the winding promontory of her colon let itself be rearranged around the edges of the rising uterus.

And when she walked, Rebecca was a planet, cradling the primeval soup inside her. She reminded

Sam Caine of archaic images of our earth being carried on the back of an elephant, or turtle.

'What you lack in memory you seem to be making up for in imagination,' Rebecca told him. 'I'm not four months pregnant. There's hardly a bump yet.'

'I'm patient,' he assured her, and she knew he was, he had a ruminative placidity, a constancy, that was surely his nature. No matter that each day she was a stranger to him, she was convinced that he would remain beside her. And that she would want him there.

One Friday afternoon in July they struggled in John's car out of London, westward. Davey, squashed in the middle of the back seat, appeared to Sam to have reformed overnight from the character Rebecca described in her diary, which she'd made him read that morning, as ever. Although, like other characters, he was being filled out. Pregnancy was the reason or excuse Rebecca used to give up work, except for the odd piano lesson, and she not only spent longer writing the diary each day but went back over it, cut and pasted, refined and embellished. Back then she was still, however, writing it for just one reader, Sam Caine. She had no idea the diary was also an early draft of something else; would become the notes for a novel.

'E's crap, man,' was what Davey was saying. 'It's a terrible drug, it shouldn't be allowed. I mean I know it's not, but if they wanted to stop it they could, but Interpol let through a certain amount of shit, just enough to stop the people rising up, and apart from rock E's what they're happiest to let through.'

'I don't miss it,' Rebecca said. 'Much.'

'No, it's bad,' Davey ranted. 'Weak shit. Gives pathetic people delusions of love and empathy and belonging, fake and thoughtless, and they yap yap gibberish.'

'He's still on the big comedown,' said Juice. 'The longest in history.'

'It's not me I'm talking about, it's kids. They're the ones who are being fucked over. The bastards who sell kids E should be shot. The trouble is when can we honestly say we're grown-up? Adults entirely responsible for our own actions? Sixteen, eighteen, twenty-one? I'm thirty-four and am I grown-up? All right, Juice, I said that myself so shut it. I say legalize, yeah, everything, but don't sell to anyone under thirty. I won't, cross my heart. Bastards who sell drugs to people under thirty, shoot 'em.'

'Did he snort a line at that petrol station?' Fuyuki wondered.

'Whereas, on the other hand, as proven aids to personal pleasure and spiritual growth, we should consider making certain hallucinogens compulsory for anyone *over* thirty. Especially pensioners, they've got the time to enjoy it. In their tea, maybe. I'm on nothing, as it happens, Fuyuki: you can forget coke, it doesn't make you feel like God at all, it makes wankers act like fairground bullies, mini megalomaniacs; like Balkan fucking warlords.'

'Who said anything about God?' Juice demanded.

'I'm glad you mentioned God,' Davey said. 'DMT makes a person feel like God, you know why? 'Cos it apes existence. 'Cos what existence is is God inhaling and exhaling. On a vaster time scale than you or I could imagine. God exhales and a universe comes into existence; goes through its evolution and civilization and shit, which he enjoys. Then he inhales it, he sucks it back in, 'cos it's like smoke to him – it's like maya, right, an illusion, a smoky veil? – he savours it in his lungs. And when God exhales again a new universe comes into being, the same stuff mostly but in a new

330

configuration. Each time God draws he gets a slightly different hit. DMT helps you see time properly. Our eternity is just one breath of God: the Big Bang was his exhalation; one day all this will disappear in a puff of smoke, one good toke, the Big Crunch.' Davey shrugged. 'What the hell? It's cosmic. We can't be expected to understand.'

'Right,' John nodded his startling magenta-dyed head from the driver's seat. 'Like you can look at life as either a race or a rave.'

'A dance,' Rebecca mused. 'Me, I think the world danced itself into being.'

'I agree with you, Davey-san,' said Fuyuki. 'Except for one thing: don't forget there is no God. That's all.'

They drove along the M4. Agricultural sprayers ejaculated water into the air. Cornfields blushed with poppies. The synthetic peppery smell of rape infiltrated each passing car. Beside one yellow field was a purple-blue one of flax, and then white clover, as if colour co-ordination consultants had transgressed from farmers' wives to their susceptible husbands and recommended here along England's silicon valley an arable mix'n'match, a patchwork quilt along with wheatfield mazes and corn circles for the tourists.

Once upon a time, Davey explained to Sam on the journey, a law was passed decreeing it illegal for people to hold a party where rhythmic music was played or that went on past midnight or was attended by more than three people.

'This would be in the fifties?' Sam guessed.

'Almost,' Davey agreed. So parties became illegal, unless a licence was obtained. Now applying for a licence was perfectly straightforward, Davey said, it simply had to be requested from the local police. On the whole, applications were considered on a strictly fair and even-handed basis: every one was refused. Not point blank. The police kept the organizers on tenterhooks till the last possible moment, announcing the refusal as everybody stood poised with lorry loads of amplifiers, marquees, food, drink, DJs.

Before long those who enjoyed organizing parties, for pleasure or profit or both, got the message and started arranging them clandestinely, and the police were happy: they hadn't enjoyed employing the cowardly, bureaucratic expedient of banning social gatherings with the stroke of a pen. They were much happier chasing people around the countryside.

Davey broke off to reminisce with John about treasure hunts through English villages, stopping at phone boxes to pick up clues then using mobiles to receive and convey coded messages, hounded by keystone cop county constabularies, coalescing in extempore convoys, converging upon woods, fields, quarries for alfresco all-nighters in the early nineteen-nineties.

The police responded with the full force of the law. 'The nanny state turned on her kiddies with a suffocating pillow,' Davey claimed. With the Berlin Wall down, spies came home and grew dreads to infiltrate underground sound systems, establishing their credentials by smuggling in Albanian techno and importing impressive arcane customs, like that of the remote Koryak tribe of Siberia, who boiled fly agaric with water; poorer people outside the tent held wooden bowls for the intoxicated shamans and chiefs to piss into, which they then drank, and the effect could be passed through four or five more people; a habit that proved popular in the home counties.

'Remember that guy Don, with the beard?' Davey

asked John. 'I always reckoned he was an undercover cop. He got his acid from the postman.'

'Postman?' Sam interrupted. 'Is that a hip expression for an LSD dealer?'

'No, it's like the man from the Royal Mail. Who delivers our letters in the morning. This Don bloke got his acid on postcards, a microdot lurking behind the stamp.'

Having won the Cold War, the spies' code-breaking colleagues knocked their heads together at GCHQ cracking the enigmatic anagrams and riddles of party organizers. And with peace looming in Northern Ireland, crack anti-terrorist squads were returned to England to stop people dancing. Road blocks were set up; riot squads hunched together in Transporter vans, adrenalin hissing through their veins; helicopters with blinding spotlights buzzed the roads, night birds of prey, and when they swooped on parties, off-their-face revellers incorporated the flashes and sirens into the chaos of their extravagant perception.

'Disco lights from heaven,' Fuyuki reminisced.

'If there's one thing we hate it's other people having a good time,' Rebecca mused. 'And when *we're* the ones having a good time, it's even better when we know other people want to stop us. Hey, do I sense a certain reciprocity here? A meeting of needs and desires?'

Davey told Sam to ignore Rebecca and concentrate on the rest of his paranoid history: petitions were circulated demanding the freedom to party as a Universal Human Right, but fewer signatures were recorded than phone calls made to police hotlines, information on imminent party activity given by concerned citizens who could hear repetitive beats somewhere nearby. Unless it was a woodpecker. Or that branch tapping against the window. Or the hearing aid playing up again.

'It's a trip down memory lane for these guys,' Rebecca explained to Sam.

'A trudge down nightmare alley more like,' said Juice. 'Techno's an urban indoor music, it's for dark subterranean spaces. I can't believe I've come out of London with you hippies.'

They made their way to the smallest town in Britain. Dusk settled.

'Turn left at the bank,' Fuyuki read off a scrap of paper.

'Bank, what bank?' John demanded. 'It's all flat.'

'Some people, Sam,' Davey was suggesting, 'reckon say Simon Posford's like a reincarnation of Johann Sebastian Bach; that polyphonic music's come back through the computer.'

'How about Barclay's?'

They headed off into forested hills. 'Who's got the map?' John asked.

'I like Bach,' said Sam.

'I've got directions written down.'

'I can remember the way,' said Juice gloomily. 'It's etched in my psyche from last year. You turn right up here.'

'Trance music can be contrapuntal,' Rebecca agreed.

'And I like William Byrd,' said Sam.

'It says left on this bit of paper,' Fuyuki read.

'Yeah, but it's not harmonious.' Juice turned to Rebecca.

'Some reckon Tsuyoshi Suzuki's like Shakespeare,' Davey told Sam.

'Straight on at this junction, John.'

'In the early days, whenever you saw his name – in

Time Out, CD booklets, on flyers – it was spelled all kinds of different ways. Like this,' snatching paper off Fuyuki. 'Tsuyoshi. Tsuoychi. Syoshi. Tsyuchi.'

'What Jeff Mills say is doing is the opposite,' said Juice, 'stripping rhythm down to its fundamental components.'

'Carry on here. I think.'

'Detroit's got harmony, Becca. It's got funk.'

'We're lost.' John killed the lights, cut the engine. 'I knew it.' They climbed out of the car into inky silence, onto an empty planet, its surface deserted by humans.

'You go outside the M25,' said Fuyuki, 'and it all gets weird.'

'Listen!' said Juice. 'I can hear it.'

'Me too,' said Rebecca, pointing off to one side. 'That way.'

'No.' John bent his ear to the opposite direction. 'It's coming from over there.'

'I think it's back over behind us,' Juice said.

'I can't hear a thing,' Davey lamented. 'I don't know what you're on about.'

'What a surprise coming from a man who drops four tabs of acid and dances by the speakers,' Juice mocked, ''cos he likes to quote watch unquote the sound waves pouring out of them.'

'All I can hear', said Sam, 'is a disconnected beat that sounds like it's floating low in the sky somewhere.'

'That's it, you dope,' Rebecca chided him. 'Where's it coming from?'

'Right in front of us.'

They drove furiously round meandering lanes, stopping every now and then to lose their bearings, for an hour or more, before all of a sudden finding themselves sandwiched between other cars stuffed with eager passengers, and swept in an excited convoy over a bridge – where they paused briefly to hand over tenners – and on into forestry land. John hurtled them along bumpy tracks through the dust of the cars in front for miles. Then they slowed and parked on the verge at the end of a line of cars threading off into the distance. Purple light throbbed through pine trees up the slope above them.

'Shall we set up camp?' Rebecca asked.

'We've wasted enough time already,' said Davey.

'Yeah, now we're here let's neck a pill and party,' said Juice, leading the way.

They walked up the track through an overnight-assembled village that looked as if it'd been there since the Middle Ages, populated by hundreds of people. Bearded men in worn combat fatigues and wiry women with weary, curious infants hanging round them, new gypsies created by poverty and rebellion with their lined leathery faces and tinkers' tans, stood sat squatted at cooking pots by tents or at mobile cafés doling out chai, toast, stew. Here and there were stalls selling bright stretchy multi-coloured clothes; records tapes CDs; jesters' hats; pipes, lighters with a yin-yang symbol, T-shirts bearing Celtic mandalas; fluorescent headbands and bangles. Off in the forest men stood mesmerized at small fires.

'The druids meet Mad Max,' said Juice. They ate rice, drank tea.

Davey returned to the group from procuring fresh mushrooms. 'Organic,' he said.

'You take what you want, I'm fine,' Rebecca assured Sam, giving him a blotter of acid. 'I'll dance, and rest, and be around.'

The dance floor was a thinly peopled clearing that a few fairy lights pretended was a grotto, until Sam realized the lights were stars. The DJs' booth was the folded-open side of a van. Every now and then a blue or purple bulb pulsed like a hyperactive star, but otherwise the only illumination was the moon that bathed the clearing, a lunar field, in which a gradually condensing tribe stamped their feet on the earth. Sam Caine's group dispersed and he worked his way to a space and danced. The people around him were serious, intent upon a common task. It was as if they were working together, preparing something, stirring a stew, blending flavours.

Sam felt sick from the LSD strychnine in his stomach but held down food and danced through the nausea to music that was a series of interconnected stories in a narrative which built into the story of the night. Sam's limbs were spongy, his skin began to feel sensual to him, velvety, like a pleasing accoutrement to himself. The present DJ, a diminutive witch, Medusa hair bobbing, gave way to a man whose spectacles glinted from the light by which he worked, and the music grew darker, stranger, the hard beat filigreed with squidgy, squodgy loops and scrawls of sound. Sam closed his eyes. He knew he was tripping now, felt like he – his mind – was roly-polying down an endless slope. Fractals kaleidoscoped, masses churned and changed through his vision that some part of his mind tried to identify – or fabricate – as purposeful shapes: animals, plants, barely organic entities with almost human aspects. He danced in the dark for hours.

The first light of dawn was creeping around the horizon when the shaman of the tribe took over behind the record decks. And stopped the music. People came down from their chemical eyries and back to earth like the exhausted, unlikely survivors of some terrible siege and slowly looked around them and towards the DJ, wondering what had happened; there was no sound in the clearing in the forest any more except for odd squirly noises, and bangs and burps and fizzles.

The cauldron had stewed long enough, it was time to feast. The shaman gathered his sounds, began to build them up, and the baffled, insensible revellers became impatient for him to load the catapult of noise; they whistled and shrieked and bayed until he did and fired it at the moon, it came bursting out of the speakers and they had a party on their hands.

Sam Caine felt impelled to see everything and everyone; he couldn't get enough visual information in through his eyes. His eyes had an insatiable thirst in the soft morning light. A Red Indian chief in a waist-length head-dress, squaws with fluorescent warpaint. A bearded biker punching the air, a girl in a lime-green luminous skirt, a boy in a wheelchair.

Their group coalesced inside the tribe of people. Davey, with a complicit mischievous grin on his face, grabbed at the air, as if plucking the beat from sound waves as they passed. Juice danced twice as wildly as anyone else. Fuyuki squealed, 'I love acid.' John looked imperiously around him as he danced and waved his hands like an MC milking applause, conducting other dancers, or imagining he was.

Rebecca materialized close by and Sam gazed at her, enraptured. Her body moved in waves; Rebecca created waves with her body; her hands were the crests of waves and her feet projected each wave from the earth, as she told the same story with her body as the DJ told with the music. She followed the music on its journey through the shapes that it suggested, making those shapes real, yet she also led the music – it followed her. Just as, Sam realized simultaneously – while understanding somewhere that these were complementary illusions – he was making it himself. The DJ took his lead from him, somehow; tuned in to what Sam heard, and reproduced it on his decks; it really seemed so.

Until it dawned on Sam that his hearing, her dancing, the DJ's mixing, were simply happening at the same time. Now.

Sam danced as if reaching for something he couldn't quite get hold of. Rebecca watched him twisting and turning, his eyes closed with happiness that hurt, pummelling the air like a losing fighter.

Rebecca hugged him, squeezed Sam to her. 'Consolations,' she whispered. She let go, and he, they, resumed dancing into the day.

After mugs of tea and cigarettes and fruit, collapsed among others on the hillside, after the smell of pine sap and the sheer clarity of the morning, pine needles underfoot, faces, exhaustion and elation cohabiting limbs, ears reverberating from the terrible pounding they'd taken, the group stumbled to John's car, emptied the boot of tents, Lilos, sleeping bags, blankets, and – having to concentrate very very slowly – set up clumsy camp nearby.

In their dome tent Rebecca kissed Sam, she tasted like no woman all women had ever tasted before. His twirling mind.

'You're my salivation,' he murmured. 'If I sleep, will you still be here when I wake?'

Rebecca, yawning, laughed. He kissed her again.

'Glad we came?' Sam asked.

'It's a different place,' she said. 'It's outside of

society, isn't it? A fucked-up, innocent garden of Eden. Yes, I'm glad we came. And now: I am so tired, Sam Caine, I'm going to sleep for days. Bring me tea and toast in the afternoon.'

Sam Caine closed his teeming eyes, and entered oblivion.

A silence settled over the forest as over the scene of a massacre. In the hot early afternoon children wandered, carefree and derelict. In time, though, across the wooded hill half-asleep adults stirred sluggishly. They emerged as if out of tombs from yawning tents or came rising out of the undergrowth, returning to the anti-climactic quotidian, the everyday, with a *déjà vu* disenchantment of resurrection.

Fuyuki assembled a Calor gas burner from the boot of the car and brewed tea. Rebecca hauled herself out of her tent. 'You seen Sam?'

'Don't think so.' Fuyuki shook her head. 'Could be up there, one of the cafés is set up already.'

'I'll look in a minute. Got to pee. Again. Back in a sec.'

Over here, as if planted for runner beans to climb, the tent poles of a tepee stood bare, presumably abandoned by campers who'd rendered themselves unfit to complete the task. There, stragglers slumped and stared at smoky fires or lurched along the paths, heavy-lidded, vacant zombies, scooped out by the night. Children and dogs scampered to and fro. Bassy reggae drone-thumped out of a small system.

'I need a shower,' said Juice, leaning against the car.

'I thought we were going to stay all weekend,' Fuyuki countered.

'I hate to say it, but I'm with Juice,' Davey conceded.

340

'Maybe we could go and find a hotel with a swimming pool or something and come back. I'm sweaty, smelly, my clothes are smoked.'

'I could do with a shave,' John agreed, sipping his tea.

'We can't cope with the filth of freedom,' Rebecca lamented.

'But we'll come back, right?' Fuyuki worried.

'It's up to John,' said Juice. 'John's driving. And John needs a shave, right?'

'Sure, we can see how we feel,' John shrugged.

'Yeah,' Davey nodded, 'let's return to civilization first, and then we can decide whether we really want to slog all the way back to the crusties' convention.'

'Talk about slumming it,' Fuyuki despaired. 'Bloody weekend ravers.'

'Help me find Sam, and then we'll leave,' Rebecca told them.

The next entry in Rebecca's diary for Sam Caine would, were he to read it, confuse him. It would seem to be an instalment rather of the history Davey recounted on the way to the rave. But then paranoia was part of the territory. Just because they're not after you, Davey would have said, doesn't mean they're not going to get you.

It's like the first whispers from Stanworth Valley that balaclavaed bailiffs who dragged road-protesters out of the trees were too good; these hired hands neither doleful nor thuggish lackeys like the security guards below, they climbed like mountaineers, they were experts. This became common gossip as they reappeared at other camps and soon activists started voicing their suspicions in public – that proper climbers were taking silver pieces from the state to help environmental despoliation – an absolutely disgraceful slur on the British climbing community that turned out to be true. It cleaved that fraternity in two: outraged mountaineers rushed to the site of the proposed Newbury bypass, scampered up the trunks of trees and defended them against men whom weeks ago they'd have trusted with their lives on foreign rock face and ice.

So you couldn't be sure: no-one could write off the wildest freak's conspiracy theories, or gloomy dopehead's most morose prognostication. Suffice to say that that day was added to the catalogue of outlaws' persecution mania, in a subdivision marked *Paranormal Paranoia*, accounts from imaginative children of meeting scary masked hobgoblins; reports, from people who'd got up to go shit in the woods, of stirrings in the bracken and brambles which they'd dismissed at the time as scintillae at the edge of vision of their drugspun perception; and one self-proclaimed druid's belief that he'd seen a Green Man. Which was particularly rare in a coniferous wood, apparently. Stories all that any rational analyst would perfunctorily dismiss.

Rebecca and the others had searched for Sam Caine in a meandering manner for an hour or so before Rebecca's heartbeat began to worry her. They regathered and carried out a more systematic hunt through the camp, on Rebecca's insistence peering into vehicles and tents. No-one took much umbrage or indeed notice of them – a feature of a rave being the prevalence of people eternally searching for other people – as Rebecca's anxiety destabilized her gut, pulsed at her throat.

Davey caught up with Juice down on the dirt road. 'The bastard's done a runner,' he spat.

'Of course,' she agreed. 'Why didn't I think of that?'

Juice found Fuyuki. 'I reckon Sam Chicane met some traveller girl with a van, took off,' she told her.

'You think so?' Fuyuki frowned. 'Figures, I guess.'

Fuyuki pursued John's red-dyed head. 'Hey. Don't worry. You know what Sam Caine's like, easy come easy go, he's gone off with another woman.'

'Rubbish,' John sneered.

'No, really,' Fuyuki nodded. 'I think Juice or some-one maybe even saw him.'

'Really?' John pondered. 'But Rebecca's pregnant . . . I see. Of course. Yeah, it makes sense. You told Beccy?'

'Would you?'

'No, but I'll tell Davey. There he is.'

Davey was furious. 'But it was my idea.' He guessed the chain of whispers. 'Juice is stupid, man, she didn't have a clue.'

'Oh,' John sighed. 'You better tell Rebecca, then.'

Davey frowned. 'Course it might have been Juice who *saw* something. Maybe she should tell her. Like, woman to woman.'

Rebecca prevailed upon them and half a dozen strangers won over by her pitiful insistence to spread out in a line and trawl circumferentially through the woods around the outside of the camp. In vain. It was evening now, an hour or two left of becalmed daylight as Rebecca wildly implored the organizers to organize, for Christ's sake, get everyone into a search party and comb the undergrowth before dark. When they declined she threatened to call in the police, demanded a mobile phone. Juice and Davey pulled her away. They found the courage to tell her what they thought. She didn't buy it, was dismayed at their mistrust.

'He knows where you live. He's got the address on his wrist, right? He'll make his way back if he's lost,' Davey claimed as they stood at the car in the gathering dusk.

'What if he wandered off and lost his way in the middle of the forest?' she demanded. 'He could be out there.'

They were interrupted by a young crustie. 'Anyone seen Dosser?' he asked, barely pausing. 'He's disappeared.' They shook heads, and he passed on.

'I don't want to leave,' Rebecca decided. She began taking stuff out of the car. 'You lot go back. I'll stay on, I'll find Sam, we'll make our own way home.'

They tried to dissuade her. 'He's here,' she insisted. 'I can feel it. Imagine how he'll be when he comes back to the car and finds us gone. Imagine that.'

The others avoided eye contact with Rebecca, sought it with each other across her. Davey wondered whether hormonally a pregnant woman was like a premenstrual one for nine solid months: he figured it was Juice's job to deal with female volatility. Juice was figuring it was Davey's, that a particular patronizing male authority would work best at this moment. Fuyuki wanted to stay another night anyway. John suspected Rebecca was right: he had an intuitive inkling that Sam Caine was nearby. While Rebecca huddled her belongings to her chest, holding tight hope.

And Rebecca had been kind of right about one thing. They had gone out into and beyond the margins of society. So far outside that, as Jack Knighton might have observed, like an unpredictable quark one of them had vanished; to reappear, unbeknown to the others, slap bang in society's centre.

It was partly and inadvertently Roderick Pastille's

344

idea, sprouted at a Lab board think-tank brainstorming session in Oxford. The general election that early summer had resulted in a rout: the inevitable occurred – the Opposition were swept into power – although at the last minute it didn't seem inevitable, it seemed to everyone suddenly inconceivable that this government that had been in office in one form or another for almost twenty years could be summarily dismissed. All the polls promised the same result yet the possibility of a collective change of mind, a universal loss of nerve, shrinking from the new, better the devil you know, loomed. Witnessing the Prime Minister's final interviews and speeches, with their hollow, neutered optimism, was like watching a man step blithely into the void without a parachute and the public knew he was going to fall yet despite all reason they held their breath in case a wind current, a passing albatross, a magic carpet, might catch and float him safely to the ground.

It didn't happen; the government were routed; they lost all but their safest seats. Roderick Pastille, thankfully, occupied one of those. He gave a brief interview going into the polling station. 'I believe that despite what the spin doctors say, the people of this country will decide to trust a safe pair of hands and vote us back in,' he said. And then he winked at the camera.

In the early hours of the following morning it was hard to tell from television who was more stunned: the young Opposition candidate who when he realized what had happened looked delightfully guilty, as if he suspected that his vote for himself had tipped the balance, perhaps; or Roderick Pastille, whose magnanimous smile prepared for the privilege of victory had to be kept in place while behind it his brain, and beneath it his stupefied body, sustained the blow. On the TV soundtrack, too, there was an astounded pause after the declaring officer's announcement: the cheer of the victorious supporters took a second longer to erupt than in other constituencies; then a disbelieving roar surged into the vacuum.

BRENTWOOD & CRAPTON MP OUSTED screamed the *Manchester Evening News*. PASTILLE LOSES FLAVOUR. He did so, however, with good grace, recovering from the aberrational pronouncement to wish his opponent well and thank his constituents for having allowed him to represent them these last dozen years. The Commons, he addressed his conqueror, is like a fair house built upon another man's ground, and he winked at him in a friendly way. 'But I have lost my edifice,' Roderick bowed out, 'by mistaking the place where I erected it.'

He then winked at his constituency and stepped back from the limelight.

The truth was that Roderick felt betrayed and bewildered. His fall was so sudden – but then he'd flown so high. It was hubris. Aeroplane pilots suffer a higher rate of leukaemia than normal, he'd read in some in-flight magazine: radiation from UV rays; flying too close to the sun. As he took some weeks off to recover from the shock of it, what struck Roderick was not the punishment for trying to transcend gravity – not Icarus's fall itself – but how greedily the earth reclaims us. How sudden the fall.

Roderick understood, however, that it was all too easy for a politician to atrophy. Use it or lose it. Early astronauts, as Jack Knighton could have told him, on their return from the first American space missions, were found to have lost calcium in their bones, and were in danger of severe osteoporosis. NASA added calcium supplements to astronauts' diets, yet the same results were repeated, until they worked out that the problem was weightlessness: without exercise the bones needed less calcium and so the body excreted superfluous amounts. From then on, astronauts were given isometric exercises to do that put strain on their bones even in weightless conditions, and fooled them into retaining the calcium that would be needed after their re-entry into the gravity of earth.

Roderick had, then, to keep in practice, but it was easier said than done. A month later there was a board meeting at The Lab. Accustomed to being chauffeur-driven at high speed and gliding suavely in, the last to arrive, today he travelled to Oxford by train in good time and reached the Department of Organology early. The porter wouldn't let him through without checking with security.

'I'm sorry, sir,' the porter said. 'We've had to-to-to tighten up.'

Used to sweeping in, Roderick was irked. He felt his scalp tingle as the porter whispered into the phone.

'That's fine, sir,' the porter said, finally, replacing the receiver. 'You want the b-b-b-boardroom.'

Mr Bone hovering in the corridor seemed to take a moment to recognize Roderick, before ushering him into the empty room. Dr Horlock, Russell Crowe, Mohammed Al-Shalir arrived; Ben Ali was the last and when he saw Roderick he beamed.

'I wasn't sure whether you'd come or not, Roddy,' he said mysteriously, then promptly hugged him. Roderick was surveyed by the assembled company over the top of Ben Ali's head, his chin resting on Ben Ali's brown dome. He could smell the expensive eau de cologne rubbed into the scalp.

Ben Ali uncoupled himself and grabbed one of Roderick's cheeks. Roderick wasn't sure whether or not he should be letting this happen to him. Ben Ali let go the cheek and briefly slapped it. 'He may be a loser, but he's got balls,' he broadcast, to resounding 'Hear, hear's of agreement.

Roderick smiled weakly at his fellow board members, until he gathered that something further was taking place outside his control. Just when he was thinking, Well, yes, I have got balls, he realized that Ben Ali had hold of them.

'He's no use to us now, none at all, whatsoever, by any stretch of the imagination. And yet, gentlemen and lady, he comes back to us anyhow. To do his bit for science, education, learning. For a mere pittance.'

Ben Ali squeezed the grip. Roderick winced. 'I love the man,' Ben Ali proclaimed. He let go, and escorted Roderick – bent double by discomfort and now shorter than the chairman – around the table to his seat.

It took until Any Other Business for Roderick to clear his mind, but having done so he relaxed. He knew, after all, the rules of the game.

'The problem of the moment is these animal rights ruffians,' Ben Ali Al-Shalir declared with a dismissive flick of his hand, in his enunciatory accent which sounded less like a foreigner with a brilliant command of English than a RADA bad actor in brown paint and fake Arab moustache, his wrinkled nose and pursed lips making clear to those assembled how distasteful it was to have to even mention yet again these people. 'They're either plug-ugly lunatic anarchist elements who've escaped from a mental asylum or menopausal termagants,' he winced, 'but the trouble is they're devilishly persistent. Press coverage is becoming – incomprehensibly – more sympathetic to them; their numbers swell. There's no imminent threat to our security. But, gentlemen, and lady, we should look always to the future, particularly with the expansion we hope for. Suggestions, please.'

The members of the board were not, as types, bashful or retiring: brainstorming was a natural ping-pong process for them, stimulating, parliamentary.

'Take the gloves off,' said Mr Bone.

'Target the media,' said Dr Horlock. 'We have many friends.'

'Isolate the ringleaders,' suggested Russell Crowe, who on Roderick's recommendation had been co-opted onto the board following Dr Cologne's retirement into dotage.

'Yes,' Mr Bone agreed. 'Put the frighteners on the women, and frame the thugs for our friends in the police force.'

'I'm sure they'd be happy to help us if they could,' Ben Ali nodded.

While the others spoke Roderick Pastille sat back, played with his tongue around the inside of his mouth, as if feeling for words.

Dr Horlock brightened. 'Perhaps we could arrange for certain incidents with these people involving animals.'

'Cruelty?' Ben Ali responded.

'Neglected pets,' Russell Crowe grinned. 'Starved horses. Rabbit traps. I know! Bestiality!'

Mr Bone blushed.

'That sort of thing,' Dr Horlock approved.

'Do you remember', Roderick broke in, 'how at the height of football hooliganism we tried to persuade the PM that it was a wasteful drain on police resources keeping the armies of yobboes apart? That what we should do was the opposite: help bring them together, at suitable bomb-sites and patches of wasteland, provide them with ammunition — rubble, iron bars, bludgeons of wood – and let them get on with it.'

'Could have made it a spectator sport,' Mr Bone elaborated. 'Charge people for watching. Let the police force *make* money instead of spending it.'

'Quite,' Roderick agreed.

'It would have been more popular than the football,' Dr Horlock opined.

'There was one game I seem to recall,' Russell contributed, 'Luton v. Millwall, when both sets of fans went berserk, throwing seats, fighting all across the pitch. There were black and white hooligans all mixed up: one remembers thinking how tremendously encouraging it was, this vision of racial harmony.'

'Forgive me, gentlemen,' Ben Ali interjected. 'I fail to see quite where this is leading.'

'The point is', Roderick said, 'that we have to think laterally. There may be a simple solution.' He shrugged: 'Stop animal experiments.'

There was silence, broken after some perplexed moments by Ben Ali. 'Now we're bloody well getting somewhere,' he decided. 'Thank you, Rod.'

'I don't understand,' said Dr Horlock.

'Yes. Where's the fun in it?' Russell asked. 'Unless . . . One of the hunts I've ridden with's persuaded some cross-country runners to put a scent down for the hounds. The runners find it gives them an extra adrenalin rush, improves their marathon times.'

'What about the hunt?' Ben Ali asked. 'Don't they miss the fox?'

'Actually, no,' Russell mused languidly. 'They miss the sabs, though. Used to enjoy chasing them, cornering the odd one in a copse and giving him a good thrashing.'

Mohammed Al-Shalir nodded for the first time.

'Of course one doesn't wish to upset country people

any more,' said Russell. 'Lose them further jobs. Beagle breeders are already up in arms at the prospect of hunting being banned, after all; think how many they sell for vivisection.'

'Yes. H'm. What about the breeders, Mr Bone?' Ben Ali asked.

'Most of our animals are imported from abroad, sir.'

'That's a relief.'

'You know,' Mr Bone said, 'our scientists dream of using people. Not just volunteers. For the kind of comparative studies that could give us a breakthrough.'

There was an unusually long pause, a silence which itself seemed to contain some liberating property.

'We drag the animal rights protesters in off the streets?' Dr Horlock wondered.

'That's an elegant solution,' Ben Ali agreed. 'But not quite right. Too neat; too obvious a link to us.'

'That's true,' said Roderick. 'We need subjects that have no connection with us at all.' He used his fingers to number their requirements. 'We need to avoid all publicity. Therefore we need to procure individuals in secret, by force if necessary. And they'd have to be ones who wouldn't be missed by anyone.'

'Not simply that, Roderick,' Russell contributed enthusiastically, 'but ones whose absence will be particularly appreciated.'

'How do you mean?' Dr Horlock asked.

'Well,' Russell grinned, 'the sort of dross we'd all rather were not here. Certain people', he said, turning to Ben Ali, 'would surely be grateful for such a contribution to, let's say, the cleaning up of our streets.'

'Russell,' Ben Ali declared, rising from his seat, 'you are a fucking genius.' He hugged Russell – who, since he was seated, had his face thrust into Ben Ali's paunchy midriff – and ruffled his wiry hair. 'I love this golliwog,' Ben Ali told the assembled company.

So it was that Russell Crowe set up a meeting with a man who'd been an officer in the SAS and now occupied a featureless office in Victoria. Major 'Wild' Bill Jennings made a living out of Africa. He kept a discreet register of ex-SAS soldiers available for freelance employment, *Covert Operations* their customary mode; bongoes a speciality. In a twist of colonial history they could be hired by autocratic presidents of immature democracies that needed shoring up or by anxious tyrants who required assistance in quelling the voice of their people. Thus did modern British soldiers connect with their forebears in a distinguished litany of proud employment: with fourteenth-century men-at-arms, veterans of Poitiers who then formed the White Company and were employed by warlords throughout Italy; with Madras Engineers lieutenants in the eighteenth century and Bombay Artillery captains, officers of the British Army who stayed on to defend the interests of the East India Company; with Lawrence's descendants in the Arab Legion, who remained in the desert and led Bedouin companies in inter-tribal warfare in the nineteen-thirties Middle East.

For a black man to enter Major Jennings's office with lucre in his pocket, then, was not unusual; only that this one was a member of the English establishment. Russell relished employing mercenaries to operate with the utmost secrecy, you understand, of course, such is your clandestine reputation, we got your name from Brigadier Youknowwho. A quiet job in the heart of the country, oh, you've worked at home before? We didn't realize, so that's what happened to her, and as for him so it wasn't sex? Well, yes, bizarre, not tried auto-erotic asphyxia myself ha-ha, but we'd heard of the chap in Buenos Aires and, what, that was you too? Well I never. I believe, Major Jennings, you're just the man we need.

And the finest fighters in the world, who'd become dervishes in the desert or Arctic foxes in the Antarctic or camouflaged killers on the Falkland moors or resolute peacekeepers in the gorges of Bosnia, had no problem at home kidnapping a few insignificant civilians. One sortie was all, initially: once it was confirmed that the local police had decided to stand back from a huge rave on Forestry Commission land, it wasn't difficult to drive in from the other side, to park a mile away, to stealth march at night to the hippy camp and hunker down till late morning; then seek out what looked like loners, half a dozen, male, steal upon them, spirit them away. Stretcher them back to the vehicles and drive to Oxford.

Where that same Saturday night Mr Bone left open the side door of the Department of Organology, the one with a shrinking plate indicating THE LABORATORY LTD, and Joe Snow on overtime led steely mute stretcher bearers to the security lift and up to the top floor. There were delivered six male unconscious bodies.

Mr Bone rubbed his hands. 'Our first arrivals. This is a great moment, Joseph.' They placed the men's inert limbs in restraining devices. 'We'll be known as the Florey and Chain of our time.'

'Do you really think so?' Joe asked, as he clamped Sam Caine's floppy wrists down. 'Are we doing good?'

'Are we doing good?' Mr Bone's forehead glistened with sweat. 'We are instrumental in furthering science in the most crucial advance since that lot up the road discovered the therapeutic use of penicillin. *Now* we shall find that part of the brain we're looking for, Mr

353

Snow. Where the poison is manufactured; from where leaks this chemical that infects us with the intimation of death. That, you might say, makes us human. It's undeveloped in other mammals, and that's the only reason we've not been able to find it. Are we doing good indeed. Not only that, young man, but also Mr Al-Shalir has authorized me to double your salary. What do you think of that?'

'I don't know what to say, Mr Bone.'

'Joseph, if you say anything to anyone, and I mean anyone, I mean even your mother, you'll not only be out on your ear, you'll be in far worse trouble. This is tip-top secret work, it's of national importance. Tell no-one about it, Mr Snow.'

17

RISING UP THE SPINAL CORD

It was the hottest weekend of the year, the middle of August, England was in the grip of drought. Brown lawns. Melting ice-creams. Spontaneous combustion in back parlours. Boys playing football fainted, girls tried to remember what rain tasted like. In Cheshire reservoirs were cracked-earth mudholes from which humans not hippos sought sustenance. A hosepipe ban had been in operation in Cornwall for weeks, while in the Potteries a drought order outlawed car washing, sprinkling of golf courses and the filling of private swimming pools. Early morning anglers were greeted by the sight of fish gasping on the surfaces of rivers. Thames Water told off its customers for using water irresponsibly, and the Environment Secretary gave Yorkshire Water permission to pump emergency supplies out of the river Wharfe. The new Opposition quoted figures in documents leaked from the industry regulator's office to prove that every Briton could have his or her water needs met by the water criminally wasted by the ten hopelessly inefficient water utilities that they in power had themselves privatized.

The Meteorological Office scanned the skies in vain for signs of weather patterns that might bring rain, saw only the spectre of global warming loom in the next millennium. Sections of the M5 motorway melted: Phil Scritt despaired as lorries stuck in traffic jams for more than five minutes began to sink into the gooey tarmac. In the West Country, railtracks expanded: trains from Bristol Temple Meads had to be driven gingerly across the Mendips. Sunburned pigs grew bad-tempered, and refused to mate with their sows, preferring to lie down in any available shade. And when the sun went down, dusk brought little relief, because the world was well and truly baked.

Martha Polkinghorne could make herself invisible. She slipped through sultry darkness between the road and the house, planting each slippered step exploratively upon the ground for crackable twig or cinder, her breathing steady. There were dogs here, one Rottweiler on a chain, a caged Alsatian: she could have flung them doped meat but that was too easy. It was a hot, dangerous evening. She wore only the sheerest mini-mum but still sweat was inevitable, detection imminent. In addition, security lights kept sur-veillance, triggered by movement interrupting invisible beams. Martha had both to trust her daylight estimate of safe passage and to judge it now in the dark.

She prowled up the drive from cover to rusting cover and then, bent double, approached the house. The temptation was to hurry but Martha was practised, advanced slow step by cautious step, every sense alert, aware from climbing that minimizing risk, not reck-lessness, is the key. She smelled the first dog then heard it, gnawing on something, snuffling to itself; stopped until she had identified its precise position, unfortunately at or close to the end of the extent of its chain: she'd have to pass close by. Keep calm, breathe through the left nostril, let chitta energy flow and the senses predominate, prana energy subside, sweat little so he won't smell you. No need to be afraid. Hold more breath in than you let out. Because even if he does he can't reach you, will be yanked back by his collar. All he can do is bark, snarl, froth at his toothsome mouth as much as he likes, while you can run. Shorten the length of your expirations, this is no strenuous exertion; down, down, twenty, fifteen angulas. And anyway if he were to snap the chain, what then? You'd have to kill him, that's all: deflect his spring, tip him, break his neck, it's his karma not yours. Simplicity. Heartbeat slow and steady.

Martha was concentrating hard on what she had to do to evade the dog. She must have stood up too tall or stepped to one side, because the world all of a sudden photo-flashed white then arc-bright: turned into a film set. Cast in the leading role, Martha turned her eyes-blinded face away and froze, became an unblinking statue, a heartless pillar. As if her face were not turned away but looking back over her shoulder, she was turned to salt, leaving not entering the scene of transgression. To her relief only the furthest, caged dog barked at the explosion of visibility, and then desultorily, out of bored obligation: it must happen often — flies, air currents, leaves must set it off. But then: would they not see her? She remained in the position in which the light had fixed her and tried to breathe the way she had been taught, calm rhythm of the breath alternating between the chitta energy inhaled through left nostril with prana life force energy flowing through right; then longer breath through both together, invoking the force of her atma.

357

Like a busbyed guardsman troubled by an infantile tourist, like some robotic busker in Covent Garden, eyes closed, Martha hovered; awaiting growling, gnashing teeth. The muscles in her thigh nagged, burned, her neck began to ache. She held on, imagining herself inorganic, airy, clear. And, miraculously, the dogs didn't see her in the halogen glare. She was invisible to them.

She had acquired the ability painfully, patiently slowly. 'Invisibility is invincibility,' her teacher proclaimed. Guru Loop was a southern Indian of indeterminate age, with a spry moustache, the pot-belly of a tabla player, a jazz trumpeter's toad-cheeks, and foldable legs. His brick terraced house in the sooty, cindery shadow of a run-down Sheffield iron foundry – 'my ash-ram, indeed,' he called it – was as much of a home, a point of reference anyway, as Martha owned.

'What does invisible mean?' Guru Loop demanded of his two dozen pupils on the most recent retreat – in the Georgian house of one of his wealthier devotees on the edge of Eyam Moor. She'd persuaded Guru to hold them there rather than his small house where the old-fashioned smell of coke in the air disrupted novices' asanas.

'It means you are not visible,' one rash woman ventured.

'No, indeed it does not mean that,' Guru said, shaking his head. 'No. It means people can't see you.'

That teacher's trick of contradicting his pupil with a slight rewording was one of Guru Loop's irritating habits. Others included a tendency to affect the hauteur of a Brahmin, and the enjoyment of weak jokes.

'I'm not scared of superstition,' he declared. 'It can't hurt me,' he boasted. 'Touch wood,' he added, breaking into a high-pitched giggle. Having worked thirty years as a tailor, Guru Loop was, he admitted, what is known as a hidden master. He called himself a Swami of the school of swara yoga and taught simple meditation and breathing exercises, whilst alluding to arcane knowledge, a whole system of esoteric science which could harm the ignorant if improperly practised and so had never been written down. It was instead secretly preserved by adepts who only handed it on by word of mouth to worthy initiates, from guru to disciple, generation after generation. Thus ensuring, Guru claimed, its utter lack of purity, as any game of Chinese whispers will prove. It was knowledge, he regretted, for which most of his pupils were not yet ready, and they relished such scorn; it confirmed the urgent necessity of their spiritual quest, though they were less pleased with Guru's acceptance of the formal religions that had scarred their souls, as evidenced during the afternoon period set aside for Questions and impatient Answers.

'Hasn't Christianity imposed a tyranny of suffering upon our culture?' one pink-tracksuited lady asked.

'Why, no,' Guru laughed, as if she'd cracked a great one-liner. 'Jesus is a great guy. Make yourself useful, woman. Go and brew us all a cup of splosh.'

'In the name of Islam,' a second lamented, 'thousands of girls are mutilated by circumcision every year.'

'Well, kick my arse,' Guru Loop frowned, screwing up his nose. 'You've got a point there. Muhammad would be livid.'

'What is your opinion of the Millennium Dome's spiritual focus being mostly on Christian images?' a third woman wondered.

Guru Loop looked dumbfounded. 'What, did I miss something? Am I a hell of an ignoramus? Is it a thousand years to the day since Siddhartha gained enlightenment by the river? Or three thousand since the Prophet received those divine revelations that superseded all Allah's previous ones?' Guru Loop opened his arms. 'Is it four thousand years already since Krishna preached the Song of the Lord to Arjuna on the eve of battle?' He leaned forward. 'Or is it a million years before the first enlightened bloody Englishwoman? Good God, girl, you're celebrating two thousand years of Judaeo-Christian culture here, for better or for worse. In sickness and in health, yes, indeed, for richer for poorer. Why, people like me, we've only been here five minutes. Now for the next epoch we're all in it together. Ha-ha. The pick'n'mix millennium. A grab-bag of bhagwans, a mishmash of swamis. Then *we'll* be the ones to blame,' Guru said, raising a finger. 'Never trust a teacher,' he tittered. 'You westerners,' he said, 'you love to beat yourselves up. A few years ago the Church encouraged this flagellation business, and there were soon great bloody enormous epidemics of the damn thing. People attacking themselves with whips, seaweed, nettles. Hardly any work was getting done. Once the Church realized how much people were enjoying whipping themselves, they quickly banned it. Forbade it absolutely. Bloody good thing too,' Guru laughed, rocking backwards and forwards from his lotus position, his pot-belly quivering.

'But the secret of our unhappiness is in the past,' someone pointed out. 'In our childhood.'

Guru Loop stuck his tongue out. 'Spend too much time looking back you get neckache, woman. You'll bamboozle yourselves with all that déjà vudu.'

When someone got annoyed with him Guru whipped a mirror out of his pocket and held it up in front of their face. Not that he had a great number of pupils: he only took on new ones as old ones fell away, and although he never proclaimed himself as such his reputation was that of a healer. Few students left his circle voluntarily. If they were well they attributed their health to him; if ill he was the one person they needed to be around. When one of the week-long retreats came to an end it was the devil's own job to get rid of all the women. The weaker ones clung like limpets. 'Don't you run off,' he told Martha. 'Help me get them out of here.'

'But what do I do now?' one of them begged.

'Oh, get yourself a bloody dog,' Guru dismissed her. 'A Labrador, for example. They're empathic like a good friend, and better listeners than most therapists. With the advantage that you can give them a good cuddle at the same time, which you shouldn't with a therapist,' he concluded. 'Not outside Totnes, anyway,' he added, erupting into high-pitched delight as he slammed the door.

Guru Loop held half a dozen retreats a year for twenty or thirty people, almost all women, filling the house: the bedrooms became ad hoc dormitories, with foam mattresses and Lilos, and bunk beds that had served the same purpose in Guru Loop's own cramped Sheffield terrace; bunks subtly fragranced with the smells of spices. Cardamom, coriander. Though a long-established pupil, Martha chose an uncomfortable bunk each visit, for nostalgic as well as faintly ascetic reasons. The bunks were impregnated with the scents of caraway and ginger, and with the heat of her body it seemed the wood sweated them out, musking the air into which she awoke. Lingering aromas, like the stains of turmeric and chilli on the floors of warehouses in London Docklands. Had Guru once run a boarding house, she wondered, a funnel-through for illegal immigrants, before finding a calling more profitable?

This last time on the bunk above Martha was a new arrival, an old woman who ground her teeth in her sleep, Penny, Penelope, extremely unwell. The first day of the retreat, introducing herself to the group, the woman described the mystery illness that had eventually been diagnosed as cancer, of unknown type, origin, cause. 'Cancer of some kind,' she lamented. 'What do they know, these doctors? I've been fit all my life, a picture of health, now I feel lousy, lousy, and do they tell me what's wrong? They say, "You have cancer, Miss Witton." "What sort?" I ask. "Where? Why?" And they hold up their hands like this. Idiots! We pay taxes for that? They know nothing. It's a joke, that's what it is,' she claimed, 'a joke.'

Penelope Witton ceased railing when she realized – the last in the room to do so – that Guru Loop, sat cross-legged a few feet in front of her, was chuckling. Penny stopped talking, took a deep breath, swallowed and began to take on board the fact that here, now, under the harrow as she was, this small fat stranger was laughing at her. The affront was almost too enormous to comprehend. She just about managed it and was on the brink of responding when Guru Loop whipped a mirror out of his pocket and held it up in front of Penelope. She stared at her bemused, angry, wasting reflection and burst into tears. And no wonder, Martha reckoned; the woman was all skin and bone.

'So you're going to die,' Guru told her. 'Shall I let you in on a secret? We all are. It's just a question of when, you know.'

Now her work begins, poor cow, Martha thought. Not that she spoke to Penny or anyone else much. Martha fulfilled her duties on the retreat rota, cleaning rooms or preparing the terrible food – limp salads, soupy dhals, sloppy vegetable curries – that the bright-eyed aspirants ate slowly, chewing the cud with indifferent placidity. Martha kept to herself in the crowded house, applying her mind to the morning's yogic movement and breathing exercises at which she was more advanced than any of the others, to the silent meditations, and to the healing sessions at which she acted as Guru Loop's healthy assistant when he laid his hands on the bodies of those with afflictions.

Penelope pestered Martha throughout the week; the old bag seemed to have selected her to be her friend. 'Is that a religious mark, dear?' she asked, indicating Martha's split eyebrow. She brought cups of herbal tea Martha left untouched as a thank you for Martha's part in Guru's gift: the liquid heat of his healing was curing her, she was sure.

Martha put up with it all – the communal life, Guru's irritating habits, his flagrant charlatanism – for the fact that he'd succeeded in teaching her to be invisible. The end goal of certain spiritual disciplines is levitation, of others movement on the astral plane, Guru Loop explained; while his particular tradition promised, at the end of lifetimes of rigorous tantric breathing exercises, an ultimate reward of invisibility. Such ends were of course alchemical metaphors, he told Martha, images for the transmutation of the base matter of our personality into the goal of a realized soul. As absurd and fanciful as virgin birth or bodily resurrection. As if taking the baton from Christian priests, now yogis had to perform the tricky pedagogical task of convincing impressionable pupils to regard such myths as true without actually taking them literally.

The pranayama practised by Martha and the rest of Guru's swara yoga pupils involved nadi shodhana: aiming to achieve consistency and uniformity of something they did naturally, which was to breathe through alternate nostrils. Martha picked a spot in a back corner of the room. The other ladies closed their eyes and sat in as close an approximation to the lotus position as each of them could manage, while Guru – in the full lotus himself, with hands folded over his stomach as he spoke – explained that they should breathe in through the left, lunar swara, breathe out through the solar swara, then try the opposite. He explained that inhalation was pooraka which drew vitality into the body; exhalation, rechaka, eliminated impurities, including bad karma; while breath retention, kumbhaka, towards which they worked, generated greater vital capacity. He wanted to feel even waves of energy undulating through each person, he said, and all around the room.

Martha understood that the goal of invisibility was obviously in reality that of dissolving the ego, but its function as an image could only be fulfilled by believing in it, and so Guru Loop administered arduous sadhanas in which roomfuls of Englishwomen coughed and spluttered, held their breath longer than was sensible, went red in the face, sneezed, found their cramped legs locked in agony, rolled over backwards, almost asphyxiated themselves, and looked surreptitiously out of the corner of a closed eye for signs that they or anyone around them was becoming . . . what? Well, less apparent, perhaps; vague; ill-defined, kind of.

'I don't get it,' Guru confided in Martha. 'Metaphor is at the root of English bloody poetry. Don't they read any more?'

It had been an enormous shock to Guru Loop the summer's day five years previously when Martha Polkinghorne vanished from the room during one of his classes without exiting through the door. While he tried to lead them through meditating on the shadow, the other students making their usual advances – one dropping off to sleep here, another hyperventilating to herself over there – Martha in the bay window watched colours passing across her chidakasha, the screen of consciousness, the canvas of the mind; the inside of her eyelids. Yellow, purple, blue, flowed one into the other. Red, grey. Her breathing became balanced, the ida and pingala nadis by which she alternately breathed seemed to unite, and as they did so, so in the same moment they or something inside her separated.

At that moment Guru opened his eyes: he had been taught himself and now taught others that yoga is a method of achieving union, between meditator and object of meditation, between prana and mind, between energy and matter; if such union is achieved, then meditation occurs. The awakening of kundalini. And the purpose of yoga becomes attainable, which is paradoxically the separation of energy and matter.

Martha recognized in her euphoria that her spiritual energy, her kundalini, her serpent power, had been awakened, because she heard – as did Guru Loop, seated some twenty feet away – a sound like the hissing of a snake inside her. And she felt the movement of energy up her vertebrae.

Guru knew about beginner's luck. It sometimes happened that people in their first attempts at meditation had experiences far beyond their accomplishment or readiness: neophytes can be almost drowned in waves of inappropriate bliss that often set them ten paces back before they've taken one forward, being unlikely to repeat such experience for years, if ever. Even the most knowledgeable adepts were mystified at this phenomenon. It was like the whole store of a person's good karmashaya blowing up in their face.

What happened with Martha wasn't quite like that: she'd already been practising for some years. But even so neither she nor her diminutive guru were ready for the fact that her kundalini travelled straight up her spinal cord, through her chakras, to her ajna, the seat of intuition, her third eye. And while Martha felt herself evaporate in a warm mist of blissful light so it seemed to Guru Loop that in the blink of an eye his favourite student did a kind of hop, a bizarre dance, from one dimension to another. He saw and did not see her; she disappeared from view, he closed his eyes and promptly met her on another, interior plane, at which shock Guru blinked his eyes open in time to see Martha re-materialize in the bay window. Whereupon he did a kind of Oliver Hardyesque double take, to confirm what had happened, only for the object of his gaze to disappear again.

Later on, still not quite sure whether what he'd seen had been Martha confounding the metaphorical nature of his teachings or the experience of his own invisible body, or indeed a hallucination caused by something he'd eaten – hardly unlikely considering the crimes these women committed against Indian cuisine – Guru asked Martha what had happened. 'It was simple,' she told him. 'The world disappeared.'

Yes, it was worth putting up with everything for the lessons in invisibility, and for the sessions alone with Guru Loop. With other people she had met since leaving home half a lifetime ago Martha was tight-lipped, sparse, conflicted, but he put her at her ease. She knew she'd become his favourite; she was the one he enjoyed being teased back by.

'You have special gifts, my dear,' he assured her.

'It's a bloody shame you use them so irresponsibly.'

'I could say the same for you, boss,' Martha rejoined.

When she complained about Penelope, that old woman, the new arrival, who'd been harassing her all week, he said, 'Oh, grow up, girl, for God's sake. Would it hurt you to be nice to somebody once in a while? Especially someone who's dying, damn it?'

'She believes you're healing her, Guru.'

Guru Loop frowned. He took the mirror out of his pocket, held it up to his own face. 'As I thought,' he lamented. 'I'm still only a little Indian medicine man. Be nice to her, Martha. Take her out for a bloody cream tea or something.'

'It's not fair,' Martha whined like a child. 'Do I have to?'

'Yes!'

Guru didn't always give Martha what she wanted, but at least he didn't try to dissuade her from stealing from the rich. She sometimes wondered whether actually she didn't wish that he would forbid her, demand penitence, a stern confessor, and order her onto a path of righteousness.

'That's not theft,' he declared impatiently, 'a rich man losing money, his wife her bobbles, it's only suffering in the practical sense, an opportunity for growth. Just try not to hurt anyone, Martha. Don't mug some poor chap; don't snatch a lady's purse in the street. That's traumatic behaviour. If you steal from the poor,' he said, beginning to chuckle, 'I shall bloody well excommunicate you, girl.'

So that when a week later the halogen lamp snapped off with the dogs' jaws still slobbering unconcerned and in the thick hot darkness Martha resisted the temptation to relax, but inched forward to the house, crawled up the metal drainpipe above oblivious

Alsatian, she was unencumbered at least by guilt. She hauled herself up onto the roof, actually a geometrical tangency of original slopes, extension angles, annexe flats at whose centre was a single skylight. There was something excessively empowering about entering a house from above. Of course any orifice would do but to come in the basement was underhand, a ground floor door or window sneaky too, an upstairs one was stealthy and fine enough but, so long as not followed by entering clownishly down the chimney, a parodic Santa Claus, come to steal not deliver gifts, to gain the roof first was like storming the battlements. Martha atop the house felt it was already subdued, cowered beneath her. She took a modified, Z-shaped screw-driver from the belt around her waist and by the pinhead light of a pencil torch slid it between frame and casement to where she could see a perforated latch bar. Martha squeezed and jostled until the bar sprang, and she lifted the unhindered window up. Leaning into the gap, Martha shone the thin beam upon a small lavatory. She reversed, swung round, placed her bottom on the casement, pivoted, and lowered her legs until a foot reached the edge of the basin. Then she stepped easily into the house, bringing the window down behind her.

Martha had graduated from crawling over the labial slabs of Bodmin tors long ago to serious ascents. The itinerary of her kleptic life followed the mountains. She stayed in hotels, motels, B&Bs or kipped in the VW Transporter van in which all her worldly goods were stored. Who needs a home, or wants one? Martha escaped long ago, and had explored the monadhs, fells, drums of this extensive island; had bought maps for and ranged over Dartmoor, the Brecons and the

Berwyns, Snowdonia, the Pennines, the Lake District, and on across the great wilderness of the Scottish Highlands.

Her burglaries followed on from her outdoor pursuits. Every Friday night all over this country ramblers pour out of cities towards the open hills by train, car, thumb. Martha passed them, travelling in the opposite direction; going to work. She hiked in the week, and when she saw ahead a line of eye-catching bogtrotters grudging across heathery, tussocky moor, disturbed a flock of orienteering kids huddling and scuttling between cairns, or discovered joking climbers yoked together, then she swiftly plotted a fresh course and discreetly skirted them.

Martha Polkinghorne broke the cardinal rule of climbing: not to do so alone. She parked her un-obtrusive van in a lay-by and set off with flask, dried fruit, Kendal Mint Cake, spare layers of clothing, elastoplast, glucose, salt tablets, map, compass and torch for long circular walks. With possible extempore movements. She carried no whistle, though, left no responsible note of proposed route or compass bearing in Youth Hostel log book, pinned to sleeping bag in tent, tucked inside windscreen wiper.

Lone walkers are not such an oddity Martha worried she'd be taken note of; there are few busybodies on the hills, more shy anarchists with respect for others' privacy and freedom, almost as evasive as those self-effacing potholers who bury themselves in the caves of mother earth, as if they can't wait to return from whence they came. Martha didn't emulate them, could not imagine willingly forsaking the mountains. Scree-running down from conquered crag, swimming in icy tarn. The solitude of deep gullies, her voice echoing back from rock walls; snowbound bivouacs below summits from which she'd seen Christmas dawns: Aran Mawddwy, Carnedd Llewelyn, Bidean nam Bian. She relished the danger of pea-soupers that you had to grope your way through, obeying the compass however wrong you intuited its needle to be, learning to trust the magnetic fields; of will-o'-the-wisps on Dartmoor misleading the unwary wanderer to a hidden swamp; of the black cloud she stood and watched one calm blue day race across Plynlimmon towards her, rooted disbelievingly, awed, until it overcame her and she pelted for safety through a blizzard down frosted hillside to the track.

Her companions the spirits of unsung cartographers, the pedantic visionaries of the Ordnance Survey, Martha climbed solo, without ropes – forfeiting the joyous return to earth of an abseil – scrambling according to the guidelines given to Marines: standing upright, body well away from the rock, watching her feet; heels down, toeing into holds. Looking up to consider moves ahead and making them as smoothly, rhythmically as possible. She could wriggle or back up a chimney; make a hand traverse or pull herself up by her arms a few yards if she had to. You had to work with, and trust, pain. Success, her very life, depended on a willingness to tolerate pain in her fingertips and knuckles, but she had also to sense the point of imminent breakdown and judge when to make another hand or toehold, or retreat.

On the whole, though, Martha held herself back from rocky buttresses and sheer slabs, content with hard scrambles. The Snowdon Horseshoe, the Bristly Ridge, the Aonach Eagach in Glencoe.

Rigorous in reducing risk, still Martha figured that if she did get into difficulties, lost or fell, who would miss her? It'd be better, cleaner anyway, to perish alone, like a cat, than the mess of rescue, of ambulance, hospitals, police maybe. She was recorded on no computer and intended to keep it that way, saw nothing sad in the image of her lycra-covered skeleton being found in the future, bleached bones unknown, unclaimed, only better let them turn to dust in the wind and the rain.

Sometimes Martha hiked past isolated cottages and almost compulsively broke in. She was surprised by what treasures people kept in their holiday homes, but never took anything. She too was on holiday, the intrusion into someone's property no more than keeping limber. She did, however, take note of half a dozen around the country – in the Peaks, the Welsh Marches, the Yorkshire Moors – a mental list of bolt-holes, secret places she might run to in time of trouble, neglected refuges imbued with the unloved smells of mothballs and mildew, saucers with pellets of rodent poison. Spiders' victims webbed in the windows, dead butterflies on the sills. Sagging lace curtains.

Martha thought of them as hers, knowing it was nonsense; she might turn up at one to find it filled with an urban half-term family. She'd never actually had to try to return to one of these cottages and didn't expect to; but the idea of a fallback gave her a security no home would do.

Was there anyone in here? She stepped out of the lavatory by which she'd entered – unlike the thief of common dread had no need to use it – listened in the hall until she was quite certain there was no-one else in the house awake, at least.

The owner was a rich man, Martha knew, but she could hardly have discerned that from his furniture or ornament. Unless anonymity, characterlessness told of wealth. The same thick green carpet ran along these corridors, down the stairs, into rooms, as if it had over-grown from one landing, perhaps, and taken over the ground like ivy. Paintings on magnolia walls were framed reproductions of those masterpieces, those jewels of our civilization, become so ubiquitous and familiar no-one sees them any more. Martha surveyed the house: one fitted out vicariously, and looked after by labourers on immigrant wages rather than its occupant, it held the aromas – polish, bleach, hidden dirt – of a two-and-a-half-star hotel. Bedrooms bare, tidy, hard to tell apart from each other except for the master bedroom, which was a mess. Dominated by a king-size waterbed beneath a mirrored ceiling, at its foot an enormous flat-screen television, the video cases of Candy Samples, John Wayne, Cynthia Rothrock movies scattered around it, in the air a musky after-shave, traces of dope, amyl nitrate, the lair of a caveman.

One entire side wall was a concertina of walk-in cupboards, against its opposite a dresser. Martha rummaged through a drawer of male knick-knacks – cufflinks, lighters, foreign coins, dead watches, pens, scratched sunglasses – then opened the other, to find before her an array of sex aids.

It was the way women are attracted to a powerful man that annoyed Martha. To his superior physical strength, which will protect her. The same superior strength that will bully and beat her; her desire the same impulse – habit? hormone? – that makes her a victim. Martha escaped this cycle, loneliness her legacy, her parental inheritance, the hotel rooms, the solitary meals, companionless books read in the dead of night, sporadic loveless fucks, money spent onanistically, endless miles of long drives, jokes on the radio laughed at alone, the empty rooms of her life. And she doesn't hear the car approach up the drive until the lights outside flash on – her silhouette in the bedroom thrown against the slatted cupboard doors – and dogs bark, knowing the sound of this car, proclaiming the success of another vigil to their homecoming master.

Phil Scritt comes home alone this hot night. He's bushed from a long day's work then line dancing in a favourite bar, but rootles around downstairs for a while. Nursing a bourbon he scans the paper, channel hops, eases off his cowboy boots. Eventually he carries himself upstairs, the loping reluctance of fatigue, every few steps feeling the wall for reassurance. As he comes into his room he flicks the light switch and is a pace or two in before registering that nothing happened. No light. Strange, didn't hear the bulb pop.

Next thing Phil Scritt knows he's flying. He didn't do a goddamn thing and nothing he's aware of was done to him but he's tumbling through the air and now he hits the ground and sprawls every which way. By the time he's come to a stop and has got his bearings he's lost them again: the landing light has been switched off and the bedroom door closed. He hears the key turn in the lock. Phil looks to where he figures the windows are, but the curtains have been drawn. As he sits there and stares desperately, a rectangle of pencil thin lines appeared.

Phil Scritt leapt up and launched himself towards the window: he needed light. Halfway there, though, he went sailing again, this time hit the wall with his left shoulder, which stopped him pretty good.

'What do you want?' he moaned. Of course he had

enemies, doesn't everyone? 'You want money?' Silence. Scared spitless, he felt foolish too, not knowing where to direct his voice. 'If you're getting paid, I'll pay you more,' Phil croaked, from a crouched position. 'Double it.' Silence. Stifling night. He had a feeling the intruder was tempted, listening, calculating, fifteen feet away, a persuadable stranger on the other side of the room. 'Cash.' Boosted by a momentary injection of hope, he was about to project specific amounts when he felt himself yanked by his hair up from the floor and then squeezed around the neck and throat – by what object or part of another's anatomy he had no idea, knew only force and pain and dismay. Consciousness, already befuddled by shock and the continuing darkness, began to evict him. It occurred to Phil that he should leave it now, that would be best, he'd just drift off if nobody minded too much.

The sweaty grip loosened a little. Phil came woozily back into unwelcome awareness. Something else was happening. It was bad news. What was it, though? It was his belt. The buckle of his belt was being undone, and now the top button of his Levis.

This is going too far, I really must protest. Excuse me. But though he can breathe, just, his throat is too constricted to speak: Phil can barely express a spastic sound. It's only a plea for mercy and this bastard can't understand it. Is doing it for fun, anyway; it's one of those, isn't it? Phil recalls from articles he's read. Housebreakers high on crack. In a frenzy. Superstrong. Phil doesn't even know what position he's in, it's just impossible to move, whenever he jerks or flinches a little pain is inflicted, and he feels a hand undoing his fly buttons, methodically, one by one, and he can feel his own insane blood-curdling erection which is pushing into the gap, and the fingers are having to work around it now to undo the bottom buttons.

He never meant to intrude on anyone else's turf. No, of course he did. He shouldn't have. He shouldn't have dealt in illegal goods. Of course not. And why did he ever take on those government defence contracts? Did he really think a little guy like him could play with the big boys? Undercut them and get away with it? He'd driven up to London with Vera in the Buick, parked in Whitehall, met a Minister and suits in a room where nothing was written down, nothing signed, as he feels his throat constrict once again and sees the headlines in his Sunday paper, the ones like WORLD WAR II BOMBER FOUND ON MOON, yes, sure, ELVIS ALIVE AND LIVING IN BOURNEMOUTH, you never know, MY WIFE WAS AN ALIEN, why not? And next week MILLIONAIRE BRUMMIE HAULIER DIES IN BIZARRE LONE SEX ACT for all his friends to see. Except he realizes it's worse than that when his jeans and boxers are yanked down and he feels an unmistakable shape pressing against him. Phil Scritt begins to whimper only he can't through his lips so the fear splutters against the roof of his mouth and comes snorting out of his nose.

Then everything loosens for a second or two and he's moving, doesn't know how, staggering or carried or falling and then he and his assailant are bouncing, that's what they're doing, they're bouncing together on his waterbed, locked together, and with each bounce his face is oddly unimpacted and his hard-on is strangely untouched yet the other phallus, the one behind him, is ramming against and into his arsehole, the pain is bewildering. The ligature around his throat is loose enough for him to moan now, 'I am fucked, sweet mother, I am fucked.' And a honeyed woman's voice right inside his ear says, 'Yes, you are.'

All of a sudden – how? – the light comes on in the

room and Phil Scritt's staring at himself, at his reflection in the ceiling mirror above his bed, which he's bouncing towards and away from, each landing a grunt of pain, the limbs of someone else's body wrapped around him, a collar round his throat, a gag over his mouth, helpless as a baby. Beneath him Martha like a diabolical twin, a shape-shifting, shirt-lifting, cross-dressing heroine; an Elizabethan actress taking a male role or Lysistrata calling an end to the sex strike with a phallus taken from a member of the chorus. 'Is this what you want?' Martha fucking him, each landing a wrench of pleasure, and Phil wonders how long it will be possible for this torment to continue, before his sperm ejaculates out of his reflection and comes shooting towards him.

Phil Scritt poured Martha Polkinghorne a bourbon.

'What have you got for me, Martha?'

'The usual. Diamonds. Gold. Emeralds.' The whisky was smooth and warming. 'They're in the car, Phil. I'll fetch them. You've got cash here?'

'Plenty. In the safe. I'll open it.'

18

JUNKIES DON'T VOTE

Just once in his son's life Solo O'Brien had ventured forth from Manchester with only Ben and himself: the summer before last he'd driven south-west, down the M6 and then across on the M54 towards mid-Wales. Cader Idris looked like a chair on the horizon.

'That's where we'll go,' Solo decided. 'We'll have you sitting up there tomorrow.'

The volume of traffic kept dropping, thinning out as they drove into the west. 'By the time you're grown up, Ben, they say people might be back living in the country again, working from home. On line. Wired up.'

'We live in Manchester, Dad,' Ben told him, in case he'd forgotten. With his voice like a young calf's.

'You'll be able to live wherever you want,' Solo said. He drove right around the back of Cader, set up camp – which meant Ben sleeping on the back seat of the car and himself on the ground – between Bird Rock and Mary Jones's cottage.

'She was a young girl who walked over the hills from here, to a faraway town called Bala. To get a Bible from one Thomas Charles, the first person to translate it into Welsh,' Solo told Ben when they set out the next morning. 'Do you think you'd do something like that?'

'Yes,' Ben said. He stumped and stumbled up the track for a while and then Solo gave him a piggy back. Ben was a six-year-old bundle of uncoordinated bones and he got heavier, Solo swore, the higher they climbed. Solo was used to sharing the load, and he and the lads had never been insane enough to carry Ben up a mountain.

'We can go back, Dad,' Ben told him.

'I've started so I'll finish,' breathless, Solo stammered. His wiry legs on fire, lungs heaving, into the heat of the day. They managed it, eventually, scrambling up scree towards the hussocky summit, Ben bobbling on Solo's back, grim determination imparting itself from father to son.

And the struggle was worth it for a spot in the stream they crossed on the way back down. Gaspingly cold water poured over and rushed round smooth boulders. They stripped to their underpants and climbed into a pool. Supporting Ben like a lifesaver, Solo floated down, pulled up, the stream. The cool cascade gurgled, bubbled and pounded against their skin, revitalizing aching muscle, roaring in their ears. The oxygenated air made them giddy. Ben laughed, battered by sensations.

When he realized how much Ben was shivering, Solo scooped his son out of the water. Towelled Ben's hair furiously dry; they wrestled their clothes on over wet skin. Solo threw Ben over his shoulders in a fireman's lift and jogged down to their car in the valley. They made a fire, fried sausages, ate egg sandwiches, sipped hot tea.

'You know the country?' Ben asked in the dark, as Solo set him down to sleep in the car.

'Yeah, I know the country,' Solo whispered, as tired as his son. 'Here we are. This is it. What about it?'

'There's hardly any people, Dad,' Ben said approvingly.

The movement of people on Crapton Towers estate, in and out of their dwelling places, operated according to a timetable rigid as the old factory shifts. Pensioners rose early, impatient with the wasted time of sleep, to plod to newsagent, allotment, or simply exercise. Some doubtless felt still the optimism of the dream of this place: of old slums cleared, goodbye to communal taps and outside toilets, good riddance to TB and rickets, welcome easy-to-clean flats, with TV, washing machines, hot and cold running water, close to the factories around it.

Then the women and children, the men still with jobs, and throughout the day the toing and froing of baby buggies and shopping expeditions. Children came home from school and played football on the dirt quadrangles, skipped hopscotch on chalked tarmac, cycled round the carless drive on bicycles they heaved upstairs and into the narrow corridors of their flats at twilight. Then the dealers came prowling in black cars, and their strung-out clients emerged like vampires to score and steal.

The estate was an urban planner's dream that reality had soured into a nightmare: when the steelworks closed down, each flat was transformed from launching pad towards the satellite factory into a cell on the surface of a dying planet. With no job no money neither did inhabitants leave for holidays but remained trapped; redundant, hopeless men who drank indoors, sporadically violent, or summoned up energy but only enough to leave alone. And the one-time showcase

379

estate revealed itself to be in fact, and to have been all along, lurking disguised beneath a benign appearance, a maze designed by a master criminal-architect, with its labyrinthine walkways, its myriad escape routes. The police initially regarded Crapton Towers as having the ideal layout for surveillance – a few coppers' narks could keep an eye on a thousand suspect assignations and shady huddles, could keep order with East German ease – but at some crucial point the plan curdled. Everywhere the smell of piss, the grasses were scuffed out and information became impossible to obtain because everyone was scared of a baseball bat swinging from the dark, of a petrol bomb letterbox delivery. And, sat across the brazen bonnets of their idling motors, the dealers held court in the baileys.

'We're gonna get out of here,' Robbie Stiles confided in Solo one evening, coming by his flat.

'Of course we are,' Solo agreed. 'It's just a question of when.'

'No, really,' Robbie insisted. 'Is Ben asleep? No-one else here?'

'Yes. No,' Solo replied, squeezing the tea bag.

'Good,' Robbie whispered.

In the sitting-room Robbie reached into his rucksack and pulled out half a dozen videos in their display boxes, still wrapped in tight cellophane, and put them on the table.

'Wallace and Gromit? The Lion King? Tom and Jerry . . . What, are these for Ben, Rob?'

'Kind of,' Robbie whispered. 'In a sense,' he winked. 'Partly.'

'Why are you whispering, man? Ben'll be sleeping deeply.'

'These are how we're gonna escape,' Robbie confided.

Solo saw suddenly the nervousness in Robbie's demeanour. He raised a quizzical brow. 'Kids' films? Pirate videos?'

'Inside the cases are video cassettes, yeah. Only inside the cassettes are not tape and plastic cogs and wheels. What we need is for you to keep these here tonight and tomorrow. We leave the day after. All of us.'

A spasm swam queasy through Solo's gut. 'What's in there?' He guessed what was in the cassettes generically; what he wondered was the specific.

'Five thousand doves,' Robbie nodded. 'Worth over twenty thousand quid to us: that's enough to escape with. What I need—'

'Wait,' Solo interrupted. 'Hold on a second. This is Luke's crazy idea, right?'

'You off your rocker?' Robbie demanded. 'Luke knows nothing about this, man. He'd pop it. We'd be wiped out. Don't you think?'

The nervousness seemed to be jumping off Robbie, leaving him. Maybe Solo absorbed all that was available to them both in his juddering heartbeat.

'I . . . obtained them off a guy in Moss Side. I'm selling them via an unconnected individual in London, day after tomorrow. I intercepted a drop, Solo. I've been planning it for months, hatching my little plot, just keeping my ear keen, nose to the ground, eyes open.'

That's what happens with adrenalin: pumps you up and you're fit to explode, then later when it recedes you're mellower than with a beer in the evening sun.

'The beauty is, no-one in the world can possibly know I've got it,' Robbie beamed. 'There is no connection. You understand? No links in no chain. I'm the maverick. The cops' nightmare. The dealers' demon. I came in from outer space. So's we can escape.'

Solo wished his friend would disappear, grin and all. He fished around down the side of the chair for his charas and tried to remember whether he'd had a blow before Robbie arrived. 'I don't want to go among mad people,' he murmured to himself.

'We're all mad here,' Robbie twinkled telepathically. 'I'm mad. You're mad.'

'If no-one knows, why keep it in this flat?' Solo demanded. 'What's the problem with your place?'

'If Wick or Luke find it I've no idea what the problem might be. They may not be able to handle it. I dunno. It's better if they know nothing and we all just go. I'll make up some bullshit about why we're going and they'll tag along. Don't you think?'

Solo considered, and had to nod. It was ironic enough that Wick was excluded from such activity, though, never mind Luke. Ten years earlier, having just gone through detoxification treatment in a clinic on the other side of the city, and being then registered on a rehabilitation programme, Luke was drafted onto an independent review panel commissioned to look at the drugs crisis in the area. At the end of the dead years before he met Syreeta, Solo recalled, when all he and his friends did was hang around, lie about, tranquil, like a prematurely bedridden generation. On the panel were local Conservative MP Roderick Pastille, an Assistant Chief Constable, a city councillor, a GP, a lecturer in sociology at Manchester University and a senior social worker – plus the politically correct addition of a recently reformed addict, Mr Luke Savage of Crapton Towers.

The committee studied evidence of the alarming rise in all drugs use, the prevalence of harder drugs, the increase in medical prescriptions by GPs, the incidence of younger users and the spread of AIDS via infected needles. They then deliberated over options for a more effective future policy, giving special consideration to a Social Services report based on local drugs counsellors' recommendations, which the committee listened to, discussed, agreed with in private, and then refuted in public. To Luke's then uncynical surprise – before he and the social worker insignificantly resigned in protest – the committee rejected setting up a needle exchange, free testing of Ecstasy in nightclubs, police cautions rather than arrests for the possession of cannabis in amounts for personal use, the printing of posters encouraging addicts to chase the dragon – to smoke heroin rather than intravenously inject it and thus add AIDS and hepatitis C to their woes – and the provision of pure heroin on demand for registered addicts.

Instead Mr Roderick Pastille MP, the chairman, read out at a press conference that Luke watched on TV back with the boys the committee's conclusion that society must stand firm against the forces of evil. He announced its recommendations: increased funds to the police; arbitrary drugs tests for drivers; new powers to evict from council housing tenants convicted of drugs offences; custodial sentences for all such offences; and the automatic removal of entertainment and/or victuallers' licences from any pub or club in which any illicit pharmaceutical was proved to have been bought, sold or imbibed at any time.

Luke had confronted Roderick Pastille before resigning, argued that when you make illegal something a lot of people do you not only criminalize them, you're also gifting an entire industry to criminals, with all the ensuing consequences. The politician seemed genuinely bemused, Luke admitted to his friends:

Roderick couldn't work out whether Luke seriously expected him to throw away his future.

'Don't you realize junkies don't vote?' Roderick Pastille asked Luke incredulously. 'The electorate don't want to hear about free needles. They want to hear me pledge greater powers to the police to detain the trash and lock them up, shiver the junk out of them, stop them stealing law-abiding people's property to finance their habits. That's what they want, and I don't blame them.'

Luke had considered taking a swing at the Member of Parliament – *How'd that look on your swingometer, Peter Snow?* flashed across his mind – and wondered whether such would be a treasonable offence. Would he be locked up in the London Tower? Hadn't one of Solo's brethren, an Irish MP, yes the ex-terrorist Bernadette Devlin; hadn't she once laid one on Reginald Maudling on the floor of the House of Commons? Was she protected, though, by parliamentary privilege? They can say what they like without fear of libel, MPs can, so maybe they can attack anyone physically without being charged with GBH?

Such conjecture in Luke's not yet entirely focused mind had distracted him from throwing a punch which he doubtless would have mistimed anyway, his balance being somewhat disarrayed by recent derangements and rearrangements in his body chemistry.

'Ah, you should have had a pop, man,' Robbie lamented. 'A once in a lifetime opportunity.'

'Yeah, and what if I'd missed? Duffed up by a Tory MP! Imagine that. I wouldn't be able to show me face on Merseyside again.'

Roderick Pastille had been the Crapton Towers constituency Member of Parliament owing to a quirk of the electoral boundary, whose line looped out of a corner of Brentwood, the adjacent wealthy district of professional, detached, Edwardian residences, and lassoed Crapton. Common sense decreed that the estate should have formed part of a Labour stronghold but it was also true that it wasn't only addicts who'd become alienated from the political process. As few red posters appeared in the tenement windows of Crapton as blue placards on Brentwood's spacious lawns; each looked equally odd, political participation an eccentric or shameful activity. The difference was that on election day D-reg four-wheel drives convoyed bumper to bull-bar from Brentwood to the polling station, while in Crapton the silent majority remained mute. Maybe some even did vote Conservative, persuaded by the argument the Honourable Member espoused in one of his pre-election television appearances, back in 1987: 'What the loony left won't admit', Roderick said, 'is the fundamental truth of the trickle down process: lowering the higher rate of income tax, freeing money out of the State and into the market economy, will generate further wealth, healthier industry, higher employment. That means future jobs for the unemployed.'

'Lies! Lies!' Robbie had yelled at the TV – back in those days when he watched it. Now, ten years later, in this most recent general election campaign, Roderick Pastille still espoused the same measures – Robbie only heard him now on the radio – but few people were dumb enough to believe him: they'd come to accept that it wasn't happening, this trickle that promised to guggle and gurgle, to flow into an economic waterfall by the time it reached them at the bottom, a fruit machine jackpot cascade; that it wasn't going to happen, indeed, it never had been going to happen. Which was a shame, it was such a pleasant idea.

Robbie seethed with smugness on the one hand, infuriation on the other. 'It's not a shame,' he raged, 'it's bollocks. It wasn't a good idea, it was a lie.'

'But the thing is, Robbie, like,' Luke said. 'In the eighties, we were fed false hopes, right? In the nineties, today's youth are demoralized, hopeless, 'cos they've got no jobs to look forward to. Right?'

'Very true.'

'But in the seventies youth were demoralized 'cos they all had these brain-dead borin' soul-destroyin' jobs to look forward to. When the factories were closed, our older brothers thrown out, we cheered, man.'

'That's your problem,' Robbie told him. 'You lot understand sod all about politics.'

As Robbie left Solo's flat – the video boxes left on a shelf in a cupboard in the lounge – Solo paused with his hand on the door before opening it.

'What a shame, eh?' he asked Robbie. 'With all our dreams, all the ways we thought to make it, it comes down to dealing.'

Robbie's eyes held Solo's, shining. 'Pipedreams,' he replied.

'You're taking care of it, man,' Solo told him. 'Of us.'

'All for one and one for all, eh, D'Artagnan?' Robbie winked, and Solo let him out.

A rumour had been going round that people on the estate were having the same dream: of a construction team in black overalls and face masks erecting a high wire fence around Crapton Towers. It was a self-fulfilling urban myth, once started, since a certain proportion of people do dream about what is suggested to them. That night Solo realized he entered that category: he dreamed of floodlit balaclavaed men, hammers ringing, stretched wire zinging, German shepherds straining at the leash, watchtowers. He thought he dreamed it in World War II black and white: it had shades of Colditz, a dash of the Warsaw Ghetto. The odd thing was that Solo in the dream knew they were working more slowly than they should; he was less afraid than disgruntled. 'They'll finish a day late,' he was saying or thinking. 'Why the day's delay?' he demanded.

Robbie came round at midday. 'Help you get the car started.'

'Of course,' Solo agreed, and they set off, on a familiar, mile-long walk.

Solo possessed an olive green Ford Cortina estate of so venerable a vintage that when he drove it into garages mechanics, despite the fact that it had so many rust spots it looked like a camouflaged military vehicle, fell prey to nostalgia for the days when a monkey wrench was something worth passing.

There were no cars on Crapton Towers estate – apart from ones everyone knew not to touch. Solo parked his a mile away in the garden of a family he paid to protect it – they displayed it as a status symbol, and Solo gave them a quid whenever he took it for a drive, in effect hiring his own car. Their house was at the top of a sloping road. It meant he could push start the car even if alone, whenever the battery was low. 'Flattery'll get you nowhere,' as Luke told Ben.

Solo had bought the car four years earlier, to take Ben – and the boys – on excursions. They couldn't afford holidays as such ('What are holidays anyway?' Luke disdained. 'Just the times you find out where not to go next year') but drove out of the city once every month or two in Trigger, as Ben christened their juddering jalopy.

Solo wasn't afraid of his dermatitic car's theft. A 99p sticker on the back window that Luke had bought Trigger for Christmas, which said FREE ENTERPRISE WORKS, was worth more than the rest of the car. It was a mobile rubbish bin Solo left unlocked in the hope that someone might steal something from inside it without breaking a window, and save him the trouble of disposal. There were lads on the estate who'd nick any motor left unattended for longer than the blink of an eye. People hated them for it but they did it anyway for the respect of their peers and the rush of theft and speed. When caught they were vacuous, blank, as mountaineers. Why did they steal? It was there. That was all. Because it was there, their Everest, an unattended car the summit of their ambitions. But they would never have stolen Solo's decrepit Cortina: it'd do no lad any good at all to trundle along Stirling Road, revving in second, unable to gather sufficient speed to burn rubber hotting on the concourse.

No, the only threat was vandalism, that the same or other bored, glued-up kids would scupper poor old Trigger, smash, slash and burn him, finish him off for good.

'This is insane,' Robbie said when they were almost there. 'I bet you sometimes walk further to get the car than you end up driving it.'

They had to take an extra detour to get a litre of petrol – enough to fuel the car itself as far as the same garage – because Solo never left any in the tank. The family in whose garden Trigger was parked had insisted, since if the car should ever be torched and explode their home was perilously close. Which was no bad thing, since like as not the contents would have been siphoned off anyway.

They bump-started the car and took it for a spin to recharge the battery, stopped at the garage to check oil water air, fill up with petrol.

'Bloody hell,' Robbie cursed as they struggled back up to the parking place, 'this car's so old someone should do its life story.'

'Its autobiography,' Solo suggested. He switched off the motor; the car shuddered and sighed.

'No, that's when a book's written by the subject. No, shut up, Solo, listen: this piece of paper's got the name and address of the guy in Brixton. Dave. You don't need it but now you've got it anyway.'

'I don't know why.'

'Now, tomorrow: we ought to leave before dawn. I'll come over to yours, look after Ben while you collect the car.'

'OK,' Solo nodded, frowning because he knew he should tell Robbie to leave Ben out of it. Except that somehow there was no alternative.

Riots erupted on Crapton estate periodically. They were used – sometimes started – to square an account; flaming cars merely smokescreens behind which retribution was inflicted, rough justice meted out. Who could see anything clearly in the confusion? Because a riot was a carnival, a spectacle which drew all but the crawling and infirm beetling out of their flats and teeming along the walkways, criminal curfew lifted, to see the fireworks.

That night Solo went to bed early but he couldn't sleep with thinking about tomorrow; embroiled in his own, he didn't pick up on the tension that was in the air and keeping everyone else on the estate awake too.

In the early evening, over in Law Village a supplier passed a stash to a youth out in the open. A police squad car could hardly ignore what they saw in their headlights, and gave chase. As the youth's stolen vehicle sped up without losing his police pursuer so small objects began to fly out of the windows, as if obeying some rare lineafugal force. The police radioed for assistance, both to pick up the illegal litter and to head off the car, which they managed without mishap, and took two young men aged fifteen and sixteen into custody at the central police station.

Soon after dusk fell, a different police patrol at the edge of Crapton Towers saw a red VW Golf cruising ahead of them. Control confirmed it as one stolen from Brentwood that afternoon, and as the police moved closer towards it they saw that the car's two occupants wore black balaclavas: they appeared oblivious of the police presence following them and now drawing in, but with a sudden jolt of gear change and squeal of tyres the car shot forward and the police, uncorking their siren, gave chase.

The two cars sped into Crapton Towers like the front runners of a Grand Prix meeting, petrifying onlookers with their meteoric whine, till the police pursuers found themselves in a brand new cul-de-sac created up ahead by two overturned vehicles billowing filthy smoke. Their prey came to a halt, seemed to hover a second at bay, then the doors opened and the youths ran, one off to each side. Past other young men appearing. The police skidded to a stop, surveyed the scene, and the driver rammed his gearstick into reverse as stones bottles cans filled with dirt rained down upon them, denting paintwork, cracking glass. He twisted his torso, focused over his shoulder, and floored the gas pedal, juddering and veering backwards, the car wild as his desperate heart.

He didn't stop reversing for ten minutes, until his colleague had told him for the third time, yelling in his ear, 'It's all right, mate, stop, we're clear now.' And they came to a halt in a quiet, empty close with cherry trees on the verge.

That was how it started. Solo slept fitfully: he kept waking up thinking the alarm set for four was about to go off, only to find it still not midnight. It didn't occur to him that he was being woken not by his internal anxiety but by the same noises everyone else was.

There's the tension before the balloon goes up and the boys go over the top. Or at least that's what Robbie said at fifteen when he used to ruck in the Kippex Stand and the streets around Maine Road. It's like a peculiar silence that is actually one's own quickened hearing, smell of danger the manifestation of adrenalin fuming in one's nostrils. *Then* come the sounds: shouts, car door slams, sirens, sporadic footsteps along the balconies outside your door. The boys are out, the ragamuffins, hooligans and their hoydens, curse them all and the trouble they cause.

Ben slept with a smile on his face. Solo watched the flickering eyelids of REM sleep. His son was like a dream figure to him. He worried that Ben's smile would get him into trouble when he was older: that belligerent dolts would find it provocative. 'What are you smiling at?' Drunken numbskulls. 'Are you laughing at me?' And hit him before they saw his disability. Or after.

But listen out: tonight the sounds move onto another level. Isolated sirens accumulate, surely pleasing Wick, under- and overlaying each other, both more and less startling together as they create a weird harmonic. Male voices too yelling in terraced unison. The muffled explosions of petrol tanks in cars set alight. These are the Pied Piper's tunes and in response doors open and footsteps drum along the walkways.

And suddenly Solo hears it: none of the crescendo, only the riot in full fortissimo, as if it's erupted from a different dimension back into this one. And he knows at once that a riot is used to settle scores, exact revenge.

'Wake up, Ben.' Solo shakes his son, literally pulls him up out of sleep. 'I'm sorry, mate, but we gotta move fast,' though he need say nothing for his mood transmits itself to Ben who's instantly alert.

Solo panics. There's no waiting for Robbie but he daren't leave Ben here alone while he fetches the car. A folded wheelchair is kept in the cupboard in Ben's bedroom: the boy'll have to come in that. Having rapidly dressed and toileted Ben, Solo plonks him in it and wheels him through to the front door, where bags and suitcases wait containing clothes, Ben's typewriter and binoculars, certain videos.

'What's going on?' Ben asks.

'We're leaving, Ben boy, only heard last night after you'd gone to bed, good news, son, a long holiday for us, I'll tell you all about it. Only we've got a problem: I can't carry all this stuff and push you as well.'

Ben groaned something which Solo, rushing back to grab a jacket, ignored. Ben groaned again more desperately.

'What? Put them in the wheelchair? But we're in a hurry, mate, we've got to run.'

Mr Khan held his head in his hands as louts levered the grilles off the wall and clear of his windows, smashed the glass, clambered into his shop.

Launderette, library, chemist, chippie on the concourse suffered the same. This hadn't happened since 1991 the last time. Solo pushing the wheelchair piled high looked like a particularly enterprising looter, though why a boy clung to his back like a monkey was maybe a mystery: the son of a shop proprietor, bravely attempting to slow the thief's escape, perhaps. Except that as well as holding the man around the neck he seemed also to be sitting in a sling strung over the man's scrawny shoulders.

Solo didn't give a damn what he looked like, only prayed as they sped as fast as they clumsily could between campfires belching black smoke, through air swirling with petrolic fumes, that the unrest wasn't spreading like a forest fire in front of him, to reach his car before he did. They left Crapton and began the long slow climb. Halfway up Solo stopped to catch his breath, turned round leaning back against the weight of the wheelchair. And he saw – as did Ben over his shoulder – the big bonfire of which torched vehicles were merely satellites: an unprecedented conflagration. This time the riot was out of control. For one entire block was ablaze. It was Tower Seventeen.

'Robbie,' Ben moaned in Solo's ear. 'Luke.'

'They may be at the car,' Solo suggested. 'Could well be.'

'Binoculars,' Ben urged.

'Good idea,' Solo replied and pulled them swiftly from a bag. He raised them to his eyes. The fire had reached the top, fifth floor: he saw window panes pop out, flames shoot hungrily into the open air. The fire raged unhindered, for on the ground a mob were pelting fire engines and ambulance with motley missiles: police crouched beneath shields, caught in indecision between self-protection and dispersal. Most of the greater crowd were irresolute spectators, their attentions shifting between the emotional pull of violence and the hypnotic spectacle of fire. Though the latter was winning, for it was a bonfire with a difference: it had living Guys on top; it was a burning ghat, a funeral pyre from within which unwilling victims had climbed. But there were no steps or metal staircase on the outside of the building. And the fire engines couldn't get close enough for their extendable ladders, looking from here like insects' feelers, to quite reach the roof.

Solo focused on the figures discernible there through thickening smoke. Were those, were those not, his friends? Wick a black spider, scuttling to and fro, he was surely running but he could have been dancing. And that was Robbie was it not waving, as if at them, as if waving Ben and Solo goodbye? And there was Luke, crouched over on top of the cuboid stairwell ceiling that jutted up out of the middle of the roof. What the hell was he doing? Suddenly Luke was illuminated by bright light. Solo raised the binoculars, to discover a helicopter hovering.

'See chopper, Dad,' Ben telepathized, but Solo's leaping heart died as his magnified vision revealed no rescue service but a TV cameraman leaning precariously out of the door, filming the desperate occupants of the roof as the flames rose up around them, as the surface beneath their feet grew hotter, melting the soles of cheap trainers before surely melting itself and collapsing everything into the infernal centre of a concrete volcano.

Solo didn't know that images of his friends' annihilation swallowed by the camera were at that very moment – simultaneously! live! – being spewed into a million insomniacs' living-rooms in a historic news broadcast that would win awards at the end of the year in a London hotel with men and women in evening dress; images being bounced between cameras, studio, space satellite and dishes, some indeed on the walls of Crapton Towers itself, so that the old and infirm could watch what their young people, bless 'em, were doing just around the corner; images intercut with those from two other cameras. One was on the yobs still hurling whatever they could at police ambulance firemen sustaining casualties now, abandoning the trapped residents to their roasted fate because they needed to help each other, visored police carrying injured firefighters in their yellow helmets like Greeks retreating from an unsuccessful assault on Troy back to the paramedics.

The third camera stuck with a roving reporter conducting interviews with spellbound ghouls, orange flames reflected in wide eyes; with desperate spokesmen of the Fire Brigade; and with courageous ex-constituency MP, erstwhile Defence Minister Roderick Pastille, who'd rushed here from an abruptly abandoned official engagement and now strode into the disputed space between the astonished mob, the emergency services, and Tower Seventeen, reminding older viewers of de Gaulle entering Paris and marching towards Notre Dame; so too was Pastille invulnerable, louts' stones and falling masonry alike missing him by inches, as he cleared a way through for a fire engine to follow, his arrogance and grace bringing a respite to hostilities so that at last hoses could be connected and water aimed at flames, and ladders inch towards the roof. But, surely, too late.

Solo saw what viewers saw when the studio editor cut to the helicopter camera, the scene on the roof, though from an oblique as opposed to vertical angle.

So that it was only by flexing his arms hard against his chest to solidify the wavering binoculars that he was able to make out first that Luke the mad fucker was spraypainting graffiti onto the roof of the stairwell; and secondly what it was that the words spelled out, revealed as Luke stood up and stepped off into smouldering space: WE ARE A BASTARD RACE.

Luke Savage's final statement, seen by millions, his dying words, not spoken but sprayed for the eyes of a long-gone God.

Solo lowered the binoculars, filled his lungs and yelled, 'We are a bastard race!' into the Mancunian night, then turned and heaved the wheelchair forward.

'What happened, Dad? Where's Robbie?'

'We're leaving home, Ben,' Solo said over his shoulder, pushing hard, putting grief on hold, thinking of the car. There were people all up and down the sloping road now, gazing down on the fire, and Solo pushed past.

They'd given the car a run the day before, recharged the feeble battery, but still Trigger started like an old man coughing, clearing the phlegm from his throat in the morning: Solo pulled the starter and Trigger grumbled into life.

'Come on, old boy,' Solo urged, and they crawled out of the front garden, puttered across Salford and trundled along the M602, where it started raining. Ben fell asleep on the back seat. Dawn was breaking; black was relenting to grey. Trigger's windscreen wipers tick-tocked across the greasy glass, where it looked as if someone had smeared their fish-and-chip paper. On an incline the wipers slowed down, then speeded up going downhill, as if the old car were applauding itself.

In addition to livestock, Phil Scritt had established his

haulage company in the late eighties and early nineties shunting the components of ordnance hardware – shell-casings, propellants, fuses, cartridge cases, initiators – from one stage of the production line to another. In a business where secrecy was a prime virtue this one-man outfit's value was evident, allied to a flexible workforce. One contract had required moving a thousand tons of fuses and high explosives destined for Saudi Arabia between two factories in Scotland and a Royal Ordnance factory in Durham: P. P. SCRITT lorries, loaded with explosives, drove up to Glenrothes, where the charges were assembled, and to Cumbernauld, where the fuses were made; then back to a depot in England, where the charges were stored. Phil was shuttling his lorries twenty-four hours a day – often with fifteen-ton loads, three times the legal limit – for twenty weeks.

Occasionally arms were driven all the way to Portugal, but more often Phil's lorries carried shells to the docks at Hull, Aberdeen or Liverpool for shipment to Zambia, Morocco, Singapore, Cyprus; none of which countries had the guns capable of firing them. Everyone knew that most had been bound for Iraq; though since the Gulf War, the majority now went to Iran. Last night Jack had delivered what he was told were plumbing fixtures, huge pipes, on a flatbed lorry to Hull Docks, to be unloaded on a Greek ship bound for Jordan; a police escort had accompanied the long load south. Now in a grim grey morning Jack, having dropped the flatbed at Phil's storage depot near Knutsford, drove his rig back towards Birmingham imagining an ideal home in Baghdad, like his own just on a greater scale, with deluxe bathroom fittings, occupied by an oil-rich Arab with not one ex-wife but a whole harem in contented residence.

* * *

Trigger's windscreen wipers struggled to achieve pellucidity, pawing across the glass like a tired old charlady, and his engine sounded bronchial too, its lungs heaving. Every minute or two the exhaust belched, making the car lurch. At least the M6 was virtually deserted this early in the morning, thought Solo; because when your own visibility is poor you have to assume drivers behind can't see you; you distrust your car's lights.

Although designed for extreme simplicity of operation, the Ford Cortina's instrument panel was at present confusing: temperature gauge seemed to threaten freezing point, the petrol tank offered no fuel, and the speedometer needle had abandoned all pretence at accuracy and was swinging gaily between five and ninety miles per hour. The chassis meanwhile began to throb, causing the body panels and doors to shudder: they were visibly bowing; Solo half expected them to start whining like Rolf Harris pieces of wood. As for the rain it was finding its way into the car's interior through the ill-fitting windows, splashing up from the floor, and plonking through rust holes in the roof.

'It's only a couple of hundred miles, Trigger,' Solo whispered – as if his voice could be heard if he yelled above the vehicle racket, never mind actually wake up Ben.

When steam rising from the engine was joined by black smoke Solo pulled over to the hard shoulder. Leaving Ben still asleep in the back, he lifted the bonnet, leaned in, sheltering his torso from the pouring rain, feeling it soak his trousers and shoes, and studied the engine block. I wonder whether to check the carburettor? Or should I clean out the spark plugs? Or would it make more sense to dismantle the engine and look at the pistons in case the head gasket's blown? I've probably got a screwdriver somewhere: maybe it's the distributor cap? Perhaps if I'd taken a vehicle maintenance course or ever looked at a manual I'd have the faintest idea what to do but I don't. Why did I not join that environmental transport association? 'Cos I'm trapped in the cycle let's call it the car of poverty. Ben's asleep in the back and we're stuck on the side of the motorway with a kaput motor, no money and a stash of class A drugs on board. My friends are dead and I'm alone in the world. I'm an irresponsible fuck-up and I can only pray that Pat looks after him, it just requires a fork of lightning in the electrical storm that's about to crack to strike me and improve the boy's predicament, forgive me, Mother of God.

A sheet of lightning lit up the sky and Solo saw, in a heart-stilling flash, a slim bald man in yellow overalls stood beside him. For a second Solo believed he was dead. Then he thought he'd suffered what he'd always assumed was a myth: an acid flashback. Once his eyes had become accustomed to the downpouring murky light, however, Solo saw that the man was still there.

'It's a sad moment when a car dies,' the young man said.

Solo gathered his wits about him. 'Who are you, the celestial RAC? An angel from the AA?'

The young man took an abrupt breath. Then another. Time seemed to slow down as he did so. The rain faltered. Traffic noise receded. Then the man in yellow overalls sneezed. 'Do you have a tissue?'

'No, mate, I don't. Use your sleeve. Your motorbike broke down?'

'I have a message for you: look after her.'

'Her? Who?'

'You'll know. Both of you: look after her. Not for yourself, not even for him.'

Solo frowned at the man, then looked around him. 'Look, mate, I dunno what your game is but I'm up shit creek without a paddle. If you'd like to help us, if you've got a motor, I'd appreciate it. Otherwise kindly clear off.'

'Oh, this,' the man shrugged. 'This is nothing. Don't worry. You'll both be out of this in no time. She'll be in far more need of help. Look after her.'

Solo decided he was about to give the geezer a piece of his mind when lightning struck again and thunder rumbled towards them as if up the motorway from the south. And this time when it passed the man was gone.

Jack was ploughing down the motorway relentlessly, oblivious of the thunder that rolled past him, the inter-mittent lightning and the steady rain. He thought only of reaching home within an hour, measuring the diminishing distance, calculating the time, hoping that no accidental snarl-up or early rush-hour build-up should slow him. Nor the tachograph, the lorry driver's automated conscience, force him to stop before.

Jack never picked up hitch-hikers; Miranda forbade him, due to the potential insurance liability. Which was the very reason, a rebellious impulse, that he began to brake, even if at that moment he hadn't caught a glimpse of what looked like a white-haired child asleep in the back of the old Cortina on the hard shoulder. He'd decided to stop anyway for the sorry-looking little guy, thin as string, with hair and beard as straggly as his wet clothes, standing with his thumb outstretched.

The lorry cab indicated left and pulled over to the hard shoulder some hundred yards ahead. Solo hardly dared hope those were really its reversing lights, or that it was increasing in size, until he heard a robotically repeated woman's voice through the drumming rain: 'ATTENTION! This vehicle is . . . reVERSING!' Then two electronic notes, high low, beep beep.

'ATTENTION! This vehicle is . . . reVERSING!'

Solo ran forward, stepped up and pulled open the passenger door.

'You look like a drowned goat,' the fat driver said helpfully. 'Get your child in here, son, and let's get moving.'

Shortly thereafter Solo was being transported in dry miraculous warmth, wrapped in a towel, bags at his feet, son at his side, sipping sweet tea from Jack's Thermos.

'It's the wife's voice,' Jack explained. 'I had it put on special.'

'That's clever,' Solo said through chattering teeth. 'An articulate lorry.'

'Yes, well, it was so even when I was having to go backwards she could still be on my mind, like.'

'You must be very much in love.'

'You'd understand why I was, I am, if you met her, son. Any man would. Where are you heading?'

'London.'

'I'm going in that direction later. How about I take you home? You both need a hot shower and a good breakfast while your clothes dry out. A kip. Don't say a word, now. And what's your name, young man?'

'Ben O'Brien,' Ben replied, although Solo knew that to the fat driver, his gut spilling over the steering wheel, it sounded like 'NNNNNNnn A Buh.'

'Pleased to meet you, Ben,' their saviour said. 'My name's Jack. You got cerebral palsy, is it?'

401

Ben nodded.

'Yeah, my best mate had that. At school. 'Course, he died, even before we left.'

You can't pull words back out of the air, like miscast hooks. Jack cringed; Solo cursed him: even the kind ones cock it up. But Ben looked up at Jack unconcerned.

'I had a dream just now,' he said, in his slow, struggling manner. 'In the car. Someone's going to die, but it won't be me. Not for a long time.'

With one arm Solo hugged Ben to him.

'That's good,' Jack said. 'Here,' he addressed Solo. 'You'd be welcome to stay a day or two. We've got a couple of lovely spare bedrooms. And we never had guests. The house isn't finished yet, like, but I'll be glad to show you some of the features.'

'That's very kind, but—'

'Don't say anything now. Just relax. We'll be there in a minute.'

Jack parked by the side of the house and led Solo and Ben in through the front door. As he opened it a woman's voice, familiar, said: 'Welcome home, darling.'

Solo looked round for the voice's owner. His eyes reached Jack, who was grinning proudly at him.

'Had it installed,' he beamed. 'Can tell it's me from my weight on the threshold 'cos there's a touchpad under the mat, like.'

Ben stepped towards the doorway.

'Welcome home, darling.'

This time Solo identified with certainty the reversing voice.

'It shouldn't repeat like that,' Jack frowned. 'Can you come in off the mat, please, lad?' he asked Ben, who complied.

'That's better,' said Jack, shutting the front door behind them. 'Now, the kitchen's through—'

'Welcome home, darling,' the speaker in the hallway repeated. Jack dived embarrassedly into a cupboard underneath the stairs. His big arse stuck out, shirt and jeans parting to reveal builder's crack. The voice suddenly hurried out of the speaker at chipmunk pitch and speed. 'Welcome home, darling. Welcome home, darling.'

Solo and Ben looked at each other. The voice was speeding up. There was a bang in the cupboard and a following 'Ouch!' Then the voice once again, but droning slowly, like a battery-rundown, gender-swapping tape player: 'Wel . . . come home, dar . . . ling.'

Jack's backside retreated out of the cupboard and turned as he straightened himself up, with a creaking grimace. 'Driver's back,' he exhaled, rubbing it. 'I think that's shut her up.'

The height of Jack's eyebrows indicated that such minor malfunction was not the rarest of occurrences. He stood with the anticipatory posture of the socially inept, waiting for someone else to initiate conversation. In lieu of an order, maybe. A man perplexed by life; bewildered. Before Solo could think of something to say, though, the sky outside lowered, casting the house into increased gloom; to which a dimmer switch responded by mildly brightening the hallway. Jack nodded upwards. 'Fully automated,' he winked. 'Smart lights. State of the fart, as Miranda said. Come on, breakfast.' Overhead along the passage a line of small bulbs, strung along invisible wires, floated like the miniature spacecraft of dwarf aliens observing: each picked out Jack's bald spot, passing the honour one to another as he crossed the hallway towards a closed door. It opened in front of him. A striplight flashed a distress signal then shocked the kitchen with white brightness. A kettle was already crooning.

'Tea or coffee, boys?' Jack offered.

As they drove towards London a few hours later with warm clothes, full stomachs and Radio 2, towing a container of calves they'd picked up from Phil Scritt's yard, Jack, unused to passengers, found his attention drifting as usual.

He wondered where Miranda was. He couldn't get used to her not being at home. She used rarely to leave the house, except for the time she enrolled at that gym. He'd told her there was no need, and she didn't bother for months at a time until one day she'd be greeted by her own voice, not Jack's, welcoming her home, her weight on the mat confusing the keypad. And then she'd plunge into drastic rehabilitation. The trouble was that when Miranda went through one of her weight-watching phases Jack felt obliged to as well, as a means of offering moral support. Press-ups, push-ups in bed and breakfast bedrooms, in the old days; nowadays his belly rests on the ground and he exercises around it. He ordered salads in transport cafés and then felt faint at the wheel; drank those dietary milkshakes Miranda consumed so many of, Jack joked, she should have been losing pounds a day. She cursed him but he swore that he loved a large lady and so did most men, we want something we can get a good hold of, pet. She took no notice, bought him weights on his credit card that he lifted lackadaisically once a month. There's not enough time, not enough time. Jim Reeves on the radio is singing 'Distant Drums' and Jack wonders whether it's true that time bends: whether one day we'll pick up radio waves from the future. Or, for that matter, the past.

Jack turned off the radio. In today's programme in our series *Science Fiction, Science Fact*, he announced inside his head, Fritjof Capra, Stephen Jay Gould and Jack Knighton discuss some of the less obvious implications of travel across time.

'With the right instruments could we hear, for example,' he said, 'Scarlatti playing one of his own harpsichord sonatas?'

Assailed by the realization that he'd just expressed an inner thought aloud, within the hearing of witnesses, Jack blushed. But before he could scan backwards and verify that he'd not said anything embarrassing, Solo along the seat by the window snuffled in his sleep, while Ben behind him said, 'You've got a kitchen in here.' Ben was lying on the bunk above Jack's head.

'I've got everything,' Jack said, half turning his head, relieved. 'It's useful in emergencies, kipping in the cab, cooking up a meal.'

'I like it. You could live in it,' Ben opined.

'I wouldn't like to live on the road, myself; I need a base. But people do.'

'And books as well.'

'That's my science library,' Jack told Ben. 'Astronomy books. Physics. My wife didn't used to like me reading in the house. I'd come out and read in the cab. It's a habit now.'

Solo lurched awake a little later, and suffered a startling WhatWhereHowWhenWhy second before the infinite confusing fragments of reality jigsawed into sense.

'Jack says gypsy trailers are cleaner than most people's houses, Dad,' Ben groaned, 'n you don't have people all around you.'

'I just had a weird dream,' said Solo. 'We were trying

to make a recording of sounds that happened in history.'

'That's not weird,' Jack disagreed. 'What kind of music was it?'

'Wasn't music,' Solo said. 'It were speech. It were Charles Dickens giving one of his public readings.'

Jack nodded. 'Now that would be something.'

In sunshine, they descended the M40 at a decreasing speed: lanes were rerouted via coned contraflow systems, side to serpentine side, from Oxford to Uxbridge. *In Case Of Emergency, Stay With Vehicle. Spray Possible Ahead. Sorry For Any Delay.*

'So much traffic,' Solo observed.

'The motorways are going to grind to a halt before long,' Jack replied. 'Truckers are already taking alternative routes: loads of them go cross-country to avoid places like the M5/M6 interchange on a Friday night.'

There were lorries all around them, Solo realized, not having been in the south-east for years; they were surrounded by trucks thundering like heavy remorseless bull terriers across the quaking landscape.

'Too many cars, that's the trouble, slowing us lorries down,' Jack complained. 'They should be tolled.'

'Told what?'

'Using microwaves beamed from transmitters in roadside gantries to transponders in the cars. No-one'd need to stop. We have the technology.'

'You what?'

'Get all these people off the road, back onto the railways,' Jack affirmed. 'All non-essential journeys. We truckers have got perishable goods to deliver. They're clogging up the economy.'

Baulked by the obliquity of Jack's position, Solo struggled to formulate a polite reply, but Ben made a suggestion.

'If it was only buses could go in the fast lane, and cars couldn't overtake them,' he said, 'people would go on buses.'

To which both Solo and Jack nodded sagely.

On the M25 the thick traffic slowed down or speeded up for no discernible reason, in intermittent waves. Whenever the speed dropped below forty the vehicle noise lowered enough for them to hear the livestock behind.

'It's nice to tow animals, isn't it?' Ben said. His voice was not unlike those of the calves.

'They're going abroad to be reared in crates, Ben,' Solo told him.

'That's right,' Jack agreed. 'They have to, like. Can't here, it's outlawed.'

Behind the men Ben's head nodded clumsily from side to side.

'Should be everywhere, all over Europe, in my opinion.'

'Oh, no, you see, Solo,' Jack explained, 'a ban would be in breach of the Treaty of Rome.'

'Who gives a toss about that? We're talking about cruelty.'

'Don't talk to me about cruelty,' Jack replied. 'I could tell you a few things. At the risk of upsetting Ben, like.'

Ben focused on Jack expectantly, who took the silence as invitation.

'No, I mean not being racialist, like, but I've seen a Polish lorry so low, hardly high enough for donkeys, it was carrying horses to Italy. Three days with their heads bent.'

Ben imagined horses in the container behind them.

'I seen a sheep lorry once broke down near Hannover,' Jack continued. 'Driver telephoned for a tow and went to a hotel to get some sleep. They were bleating that much, that long, a passer-by alerted the police. Come and found them all squashed in. Out of a hundred and fifty sheep, half of them were dead from suffocation.

'Mind you, pigs are the worst in a way, being more intelligent, like, more sensitive. They get car sick like children, see, so farmers often fast them for twenty-four hours before departure so they don't vomit and die on the journey.'

'There's a simple answer,' said Solo. 'Don't move them. Not when they're alive.'

'You're probably right, son. I try not to think about it.'

'You can just drop us anywhere,' Solo told Jack as the lorry stop-started around the north circular. 'At a tube station, f'rinstance.'

'Nonsense. I'm not having you two struggling with that baggage.'

'It's out of your way, Jack.'

'Hardly. I'm dropping you at your sister's and that's it. Although why you should choose to have a holiday in London beats me.'

'Oh, you know, show Ben the sights.'

'The Tower and that, eh? Where blue ravens live, Ben. Make sure you don't leave your dad behind. They'll lock him up as soon as look at him if they've got any sense.'

With Solo map-reading the London *A-Z*, Jack took his rig right into the road whose name Robbie had written on the scrap of paper Solo held in his hand. The lorry came to a halt with an extravagance of squeaks and sighs, as if it were the robotic magnification of its driver.

'Give me that piece of paper a minute,' Jack demanded, leaning across Ben.

Solo stalled: did Jack wish to inspect it? Would he identify the handwriting as a man's? Ha, his brother-in-law, that's who it was. Or was he going to invite himself in for tea? Instead Jack plucked a pen from the dashboard. Solo relinquished his slip.

'If you need anything, if you're coming back through Birmingham, here's my address and phone number,' Jack spoke as he wrote. 'Just to keep in touch, like. And now I'll leave you lads to meet your relatives.'

Solo climbed down, lifted Ben and bags to the ground.

'Thanks very much, Jack. We'll see you.'

'See you, Solo. Take care, Ben.'

Solo closed the door, squinting in the London sun, and they waved as the lorry, its cargo lowing sporadically, inched unerringly away between parked cars.

19

CARTOONS

In Brixton police station one month earlier Rebecca Menotti had filled out a Missing Persons form in a crowded vestibule, distracted by bedlam around her and wondering what this wretched person could possibly possess worth stealing, or how that one could be allowed to be behind the wheel of the motor vehicle that had been rammed by someone else's. This woman wanted protection from the borough council, that man from his brother. The world is full of victims, she saw, queueing to hand the form back in. Was she one?

The desk sergeant promised to circulate the details along with the colour photocopy Rebecca gave him of Fuyuki's Polaroid, Sam Caine a dead-eyed mystic, but said they could do no more than that. Sam was no minor, not even a relative of hers; he'd disappeared seemingly of his own free will.

'He's the father of my unborn child,' Rebecca protested angrily, knowing even as the words emerged that they served only to reinforce the policeman's assumptions. 'He has no free will,' she remonstrated furiously, to be met with no response. 'Something terrible has happened to him,' she seethed, the desk sergeant's bland attention turning Rebecca's anger back to her; on to Sam. She left, made an appointment with a solicitor on Acre Lane, who suggested she attempt to engage the media. Maybe write an article about it? A book, even? Get on daytime TV, those shows would love her story, pregnant woman abandoned by boyfriend. Where's the father of my unborn love child? Why, she'd have the whole nation of housewives looking out for him.

A notice outside the Universal Pentecostal Church informed Rebecca: *A sound heart is the life of the flesh: But Envy the Rottenness of the Bones*. She gazed at a window display of *Sits Vac*: for beauticians and others in the hospitality industry. Whatever that was. Juice meanwhile used a desktop publishing program on the computer where she worked to scan the photo of Sam and make a floridly decorated leaflet with the word MISSING above his image, and beneath it HAVE YOU SEEN THIS MAN? with Rebecca's name and phone number.

'Why all the graphics, Juice?'

'You don't like it? It took me hours.'

'It looks like a party flyer.'

'You know, next time I can play around with the face, Becca. You can do all sorts. Add a moustache, a beard. Give him a nose job.'

Rebecca tried to ignore her. Maybe she should hand it out to club queues; to people coming out in the mornings.

'I could make him look older, younger, Becca. Different coloured eyes. Shorter hair. Give him a wig.'

'Juice. Why?'

'Try to see through his disguise, of course.'

'Disguise? Why would Sam be in disguise? We're

searching for a sick man, not hunting a criminal.'

'Just trying to help.'

Juice went ahead and manipulated Sam's image as Rebecca asked her not to and the results were upsetting, odd, seductive. Rebecca made hundreds of copies of the original flyer and distributed them round Brixton in cafés, shops, record stores; pinned more on noticeboards in surgeries, libraries, health clubs, the Lido; pasted poster-size versions to walls. She sent a photo to the *Big Issue* for their weekly gallery of the lost. And she did get up early and hand flyers to people coming out of the Fridge, Substation South, the Academy. Watched them stumble off into the morning, dropping her leaflet on the pavement. Back at her flat she sneaked a peek at Juice's altered images of Sam in his various computer-imagined guises: a series of fake portraits, portraits of possibilities of her lover, of what he might have become. Of what he could be made into by whoever had found him or, if she should recover him, herself. They should have been pictures of Sam growing away from her; should have helped Rebecca get used to the fact that he wasn't coming back. What was unsettling was that they suggested rather fantasies of what she might have done. Other versions of her one man; transformations of him into all the men she could need.

Not that Rebecca could imagine pulling any man now: she felt blotchy and lumpy and couldn't stop herself bingeing on junky snacks. In one day she gorged herself on two jars of peanut butter. Her back ached, and when she slumped into a chair she lifted sore feet and rested her legs on a bin in front of her.

One bright September Wednesday Rebecca took the number 3 bus into town with a handful of leaflets, and spent a couple of hours in Trafalgar Square. She opened an exercise book but sat there without making any notes for the diary: found herself visited by vague recollections of her parents in Devon, in a state in which memories seemed like autonomous images with their own whim, indifferent to her will.

The sun was fierce but couldn't entirely expel an underlying autumnal briskness from the air. Rebecca watched the pigeons with vertigo never climbing higher than the first plinth of Nelson's column. Time slowed on a lazy day. She watched a Japanese TV crew take longer than they seemed to need to film nothing in particular; children crawling on the lions; sketch artists with their flimsy stools.

A shaven-headed young man in dirty yellow dungarees with the eyes of an alcoholic shambled slowly by. Rebecca gave him 50p and a flyer, too. 'The kingdom of heaven is within you,' he slurred by way of thanks, and looked at the flyer. His eyes seemed to clear as he did so. He said, 'You'll find him,' closed his eyes, turned, and stumbled away.

The pigeons on the ground, alternately spooked by dashing infant or enticed by a woman scattering bread-crumbs, wheeled round the square in wing-beating waves. Rebecca's resentment at Sam Caine's disappear-ance evaporated in the late summer sun. She felt content to sit and watch, her brain mushy; to forget herself. Maybe he's left me two things to remember him by, she thought: a baby, and amnesia.

A multitude of people strolled through the metro-politan space, haunted its edges, drove around it, swarmed in and out of the National Gallery, Charing Cross Station, St Martin-in-the-Fields. There was something both experimental and archaic about the shifting process of individuals of every age, size, colour, origin. But the sheer volume was loosening. Rebecca's own sense of self dissipated, never mind her hopes of seeing Sam Caine again. Her attention gathered around a group of four pubescent girls cavorting at the edge of one of the fountains. They leaned over, tested the numbing water, splashed back at each other, chased one another with negligible scooped handfuls dribbling away across the flagstones. At first they stifled their enjoyment, giggles looking and sounding like painful hiccups. Then one removed her shoes and dipped her toes in. The others followed. Another rolled up her jeans and paddled a few steps. There was no apparent leader: the girls took it in almost systematic turns to push another boundary.

Rebecca observed them. In this public place in the heart of London there was no-one to stop them, they ceased looking over their shoulders, and abandoned their own restraint. From the look of them – clean casual clothes, lunch-box-bearing shoulder bags – they were no street urchins, had come into town on some expedition: they clearly had no spare clothes with them so it would be lunacy to get wet on a day like this, sun unconvincing, chill in the shadows. Rebecca watched them wade further, splash more, get first trousers wet, then shirts, shrieking, in progressively euphoric stages until all four of the girls were soaked through, laughing uproariously, ignoring the world while calling its attention to them. Liberated, from something, into something. Watching them, Rebecca realized that she the observer was also perfectly poised: that like them she too was on the cusp of two phases of her life, of her womanhood. Half of her identified with their caper, wanted cold water tingling her skin; and half sat back and indulged them, borrowed pleasure second-hand.

Back in Brixton, that evening Rebecca observed the vapour trails of successive aeroplanes on the flight path from Heathrow. A child lay on the sofa bed where Sam had slept, staring up through the skylight at the cream and turquoise sky. Somehow Rebecca had allowed herself to agree to babysit this boy and now she was telling him stories to help him sleep.

'Dat one?' Ben O'Brien asked her.

'From the shape of the wings it looks like . . . Malian Airlines, flying to Timbuktu. It's carrying a circus and the last of London Zoo. There are no children left there, see? Maybe you knew that. They all grew up and went to live in other countries, and the old people left behind wrote to the Queen of England and said, Send us a circus. We want to see the clowns.'

Parallel white trails frayed outwards, dissipated, then another plane pierced the edge of the frame.

'An dat one?'

Solo had arrived that afternoon. He and Ben sat on the steps until Rebecca came home and let them in. She spent an awkward hour with them, the man guarded and shifty, the disabled boy staring intently at her.

'So you know Davey of old?' she asked.

'No. He's a friend of a friend.'

'Oh,' she said. 'Who?'

'Another friend. That is, some other friend's friend. You wouldn't know him.'

'I wouldn't?'

'I don't.'

'Ah.'

Solo fingered the MISSING flyers. 'This a friend of yours?' he asked, and pocketed a couple, furtively, like beer mats.

Eventually Davey came home, took Solo to his and

Juice's room, leaving Ben upstairs. Rebecca put the TV on for him while she cooked a meal, but whenever she glanced across he was gazing at her rather than the screen. Gemma purred on his contented lap. When Solo came back up, Ben said something, it sounded unlike words, 'Uh a uh a uh ah?'

'Excuse me?' Rebecca asked.

'He said, "How do I get this cat off?"' Solo told her, smiling.

Later, when Davey said he and Solo had to meet someone – who? oh, a friend of the friend – and would she mind babysitting the kid who Solo reckoned would be asleep any minute, she looked at the boy and he had a beatific smile on his face. She could hardly refuse.

A vapour trail turned to cotton wool, and a rhyme came into Rebecca's mind from childhood. She recited it unfaltering for Ben, both of them looking up into the indigo frame.

> There was an old woman tossed up in a basket
> Ninety-nine times as high as the moon;
> And what she did there, I couldn't but ask it
> For in her hand she carried a broom.
> 'Old woman, old woman, old woman,' said I,
> 'What are you doing up there so high?'
> 'I'm sweeping the cobwebs out of the sky
> And you can come with me, by and by.'

'Build a spliff, mate.' Driving with one hand, Davey handed over papers, lighter, plastic bag of dark green herb. Solo opened it and sniffed. Rich and sweet.

'Sensimilla, is it?'

''Fraid not,' Davey shrugged.

Solo skinned up and passed the joint to Davey, who

lit up, took a grimacing drag, passed it back. Solo inhaled gratefully. He was so wired, the effect was immediate. He visualized the smoke roiling along transparent capillaries and pipelines of his nervous system; he drew and held another acrid inhalation in his lungs and felt the calm virus surge soothingly through his limbs. He spluttered when he exhaled an attenuated pall of smoke.

'From the island of Vis,' Davey informed him. 'Off of Croatia, yeah? Used to be a military island. Closed to outsiders. The army kept the best grass in Yugoslavia to themselves.'

The car had slipped into slow motion at some moment in the last few seconds, Solo noted. Although it was covering the ground as if still travelling at normal speed. Like those special effect shots where they take out alternate frames and stretch the ones in between. Quite a trick done live. Solo leaned back.

'Islands are good places for weed,' Davey continued. 'Dunno why. In the Caribbean, fishermen reckon ganja improves their sight.' He passed the spliff back to Solo. 'For night fishing.'

'Is that right?' Solo asked.

'Maybe it dulls their cones or somefing.'

Cones? Solo looked out of the window. He couldn't see any cones, but the streets seemed to have lost their usual scale. Roadsigns, Belisha beacons, bollards, looked like toys, like the models from railway sets. Pedestrians stood out as distinct individuals for tantalizing microseconds. 'Once we were scallywags,' Solo murmured.

'We were ragamuffins,' Davey said.

'Always rumming around,'

'. . . trying to find . . .'

'. . . certainty,' Solo sighed.

417

'What?'

'Nothing,' said Solo.

'You know, years back I used to go up your way. Liverpool, Leeds, Man City. I was a little hooligan.'

'You look a bit different from the razzers round us,' Solo told him.

'I was in the Firm, West Ham, honorary Paki.'

'Yeah?'

'An Asian hoolie, not a lot of us about. Remember that Harry Enfield fing? We went up to Elland Road and waved wads of dosh at the Leeds fans. "Loadsamoney!"'

Davey chortled and coughed. Aye, thought Solo, that was the trouble with satire, as Robbie – whose favourite reading it was – used to point out: it could be turned inside out like a rubber band.

'Anything I should know in advance?' he asked.

'All right. This is the thing, right? The place we're going is called The Club. It's just someone's place, but it's called The Club. The man we're going to see is the Man. He's the gaffer. People call him Boss. I call him Boss.'

'What's his name?'

'Fuck knows. Are you listening, mate? You call him Boss. His Club's called United.'

Solo leaned back his heavy heavy brain on the head-rest and smiled. It all made sense, even this bonkers Asian Cockney. He had the videos in his bag good as money in his pocket, money minted and printed already, he could feel it in his dexterous fingers.

Standing on the pavement, a camera stared down at them impassively. Davey waved at it; again; pouted. A car disappeared round the corner of the empty street, red brake lights blinking goodbye, goodbye. 'Maybe there's no-one home,' Solo ventured.

'There's always someone home.' Davey rang the bell again.

'Maybe we should come back another time,' Solo suggested. 'Maybe—'

A bolt was thrown and the door opened. A black man so huge his sheer bulk did something to the air and knocked Solo's breath back down his throat.

'All right, Chief?' Davey greeted him. 'Chief Steward,' he informed Solo over his shoulder as they entered a rubbly vestibule. 'He's the doorman,' Davey explained as he adopted the crucified stance, submitting himself to a frisk. Solo followed suit. The doorman, dressed in a blue tracksuit, looked in Solo's carrier bag then patted down either side of his torso. It'd only take the slightest underestimation for this hulk to crush a couple of ribs, Solo figured, holding his breath. Each pat shook him up.

The doorman ushered them without a word through a turnstile that clicked with a self-satisfied finality, and followed them down steps.

The basement, Solo thought; I'm sure I don't like basements. But the stairs gave on to a wide concrete tunnel, brightly illuminated by strip lighting that ran ahead along the middle of the ceiling at close intervals. Odd ones flickeringly malfunctioned. The tunnel curved like an indoor running track. A green tennis ball lay on the ground up ahead, except when they reached where it should have been it was still further on, and turned out to be a light, fluffy football. Davey half stepped over and with his sole rolled it back to the doorman behind, who coaxed it from one foot to the other and then punted it forward between Davey and Solo. It disappeared round the bend ahead.

'Chief was on Chelsea's books when he was a kid. Weren't you, Chief? Could have been a black Micky

Droy. When he got to fifteen they said they had to let him go, he was too big to ever make a footballer. Ain't that right, Chief?'

Solo turned as they walked for Chief's confirmation but he gave none either verbal or gestural, only stared straight ahead between Solo and Davey, as if readying himself to kick another football. Which indeed he did as, presumably, they caught up with the one projected earlier. As the ball once more disappeared Solo noted that the bend was now curving in the opposite direction from the way it had earlier, their serpentine path describing the letter S. When did that happen?

Their footsteps echoed. The air in the tunnel had a mildewy mustiness augmented by the tang of a changing room. The artificial light was beginning to become oppressive to Solo: he was going to develop a migraine if they had to carry on much further, he could sense the buzzy flicker at the periphery of his vision. They were going to come out somewhere in Kent at this rate; in a wood miles outside of London.

All of a sudden up ahead was the other end of the tunnel: it terminated at a lift. Chief pressed a panel, the doors opened, he ushered Davey and Solo inside, leaned forward and touched a button on the control pad, leaned back out, turned. The doors eased shut on a narrowing vision of the vast doorman walking off back down the tunnel the way they'd come, a silent hero.

Solo gazed up at the digital indicator above the doors: it rose as they rose soundlessly, except for a slight hum. 'What happens if someone rings the door bell when the doorman's at this end of the tunnel?'

'They'll just have to be patient, won't they?'

There was a hiss at the eighteenth floor. The doors sighed open and there before them stood another guy even bigger than the doorman. It struck Solo instantly how insignificant Chief had actually been. He wanted to rush back after him – to purloin him in the tunnel – and explain how unintimidated he now was.

'Hi, Lloyd,' Davey said. 'How ya doing, mate?'

Lloyd led them along a wood-panelled corridor and opened a door to a startlingly bright warehouse loft apartment, lit by banks of floodlights in two corners: this half of the floor was carpeted in radioactive green AstroTurf, the penalty area of a full-size football pitch. The penalty spot and lines were marked in white lime, the chalky smell evident under the hot lights. Fan heaters behind the goal billowed the orange nylon net. Solo felt a prod in the ribs from Davey's elbow, following whose example he took off his shoes and left them in the corridor.

At the far end of the loft was a more domestic sunken area towards which Solo limped with self-consciousness after Lloyd and Davey, owing to the holes in his smelly socks. They stepped down from the AstroTurf into a lounge of leather armchairs and sofas, a deep white carpet, and half a dozen lurid-tracksuited black men sitting, lounging around: they observed Solo and Davey with dulled eyes, as if already disappointed by these new arrivals. Solo felt his white skin an affront to them, not to mention the faded colours of his clothes, of too many mixed-wash incidents in cheap launderettes, to say nothing of his smelly feet; undoing himself by such interior derision.

Davey greeted the men with nods and odd words and sat down, indicating that Solo do likewise beside him. The leather sofa creaked. No-one said anything more; though a human voice gave utterance some-where: through a doorway straight ahead of him Solo saw a woman, middle-aged, vast as Chief or Lloyd but with fat, not muscle. She was drying dishes in a kitchen. The sound issued from her. She was taking plates from a drainer, wiping them dry and stacking them; moving in and out of view. And talking to someone. Solo strained unobtrusively to make out words; could not do so.

The men, Lloyd, Davey, now himself, he understood, were waiting for someone. They were becalmed, a group of leaderless men, awaiting animation. Sitting, standing around. One man was off to one side at a bay window, looking through a telescope at the night sky. Then the floodlights flicked off, they were plunged into what seemed like darkness until Solo's eyes became accustomed to the low level of lighting that now prevailed.

The guy in the bay window gazed through the telescope. One of the tracksuits was browsing among videotapes, another leafing through a *Hello!* magazine. They were waiting for the dentist! No. On a window sill lay yesterday's newspaper; dried by the sun, or jaundiced by the news it carried. Solo fingered the three video boxes in his bag. Why had he brought them all? Now he had no bargaining power. Idiotic. He felt a gelatinous gob of phlegm come rising up his throat: it slid into his mouth. What was he to do with it? To spit it out seemed disrespectful. Trying not to grimace, Solo swallowed it back down.

Who was the woman in the kitchen talking to? Her words were incomprehensible, but there was a singing quality to her voice, a bell-like tinkling that resonated sweetly from the kitchen.

The bald man at the telescope was slighter than the rest. Solo gazed back at his folded hands. Scared to look anyone in the eye, he snatched shifty glimpses of the scene around him. If it's true we store all the images we see, he reasoned, then if he were to rewind the memory of that evening it would consist of clothes, floors, walls, feet — plus odd dazzling frames of people's eyes, looking at him. Solo realized there was no-one else in the kitchen. The monumental woman was talking to herself. Sing-song. Or to someone imaginary; hypothetical. There she existed, and functioned, within her own reality. Listeners were co-incidental, tangential, to her.

Attention in the room meanwhile was shifting: without display it was being subtly refocused in some paraliptic manner, some deep rhetoric of cool. Solo's own attention was redirected, he found himself watching the guy watching the stars: whose arm left the telescope and beckoned. Solo started. He checked round the room, received a nod from Lloyd, got up and walked over to the bay window. The astronomer stood up. He was barely taller than Solo, about the same age, not much bulkier than the wiry Mancunian, with brown skin and caucasian nose, lips.

'Have a look,' he said quietly. The telescope was pointed at the moon. The man spoke slowly. 'That thin halo you see, it like the Babylonian king's crown. Make me feel good to see it. It be an indication that the ruler will have him a successful reign.' The man's accent was a mix of assorted elements: Queen's English, Jamaican patois, Cockney, an American twang.

Solo came away from the telescope. He looked out of the penthouse window, saw St Paul's close by, Big Ben not far away. The river was down below, beyond it south London. Wait a minute. When did they cross the river? The man had put his arm round Solo's shoulders; they walked back towards the sitting area.

'Astrology didn't used to be about individual, little people's horoscopes,' the man explained. 'Originally it was about public events: war, famine, plenty. And about the welfare of the king. Because upon his favour with the gods did the fortunes of the whole country depend.' He sighed. 'Then it become all trivialized. Probably by the Assyrians,' he conjectured. 'Sit down.'

Solo resumed his seat beside Davey, who said, 'Hi, Boss.' The Boss ignored Davey, addressed Solo.

'I share a birthday with Vincent Price, Christopher Lee and Peter Cushing. What does that tell you?'

Solo tried to formulate an adequate reply, but the Boss seemed to realize it was too difficult for a first question and raised a finger as if for a waiter. 'Lloyd, ask Evangelina for a pot of tea for our guests.' To Solo he said, 'I believe you bring something for me?'

Solo could feel all potential attention in the room focus upon him. He wanted to say something, even if it was only a yes, but all he could do was nod, smile wanly, as if he'd brought a gift, a regal offering.

'He's got the Liverpool E's,' Davey said.

I've got the Manchester Unease. I've got a Northern Disease. There was an awful overpowering smell. It came, though, not from his feet or his armpits but from the Boss. A musky aroma. Was it a black smell? No, Wick didn't have it, nor Syreeta. A London smell? Was it the reek of power? Was—?

'I've heard about them,' the Boss said. 'The purest MDMA to be found outside Switzerland. Perhaps they should only be given away, to brethren with marital problems.' He chuckled at this. No-one else did. Solo's smile merely weakened. 'It seem wrong to make money out of married couples' misfortune.'

Words sprang suddenly from Solo's mouth. 'Bad sex. It's one failure on top of another, Boss.' Words unbidden, where did they come from? Dummy. He'd been taken over by the ghost of Luke Savage. Its effect was that of a conductor silencing musicians: a silence doubled.

To Solo's relief the Boss chose to ignore it. 'Is you ever been to the Far East?' he asked instead. 'No? You should. Manchester Airport, indeed. Me see all these hippies on the plane, on the beaches. Thailand, Bali, Goa. These people dem reject the crass values of our consumer culture and cross the world in search of an ancient, noble way a living. You having any idea of the contribution to global warming made by aircraft fuel emissions?'

Solo shook his head. One of the big men said, 'A hole in the ozone layer is a bullet in the head of the planet,' and those around him nodded.

'What do they do when they get there?' the Boss resumed. 'They foul it up with their white trash hippy shit. You ever been to Ko Samui, Ko Pan Ngan? No? All over the islands are these pyramids of plastic water bottles. Everywhere. Periodically they burn a pile. Foul. It vex me, man. I hate the smell of burning plastic in the morning. You should go. You look like a Second Hand Man and proud of it. An Oxfam dresser. Cancer Research couture. Sue Ryder cool. Go to Khao San Road in Bangkok, Solo, you can buy Calvin Kleins and Giorgio Armani real cheap, real cheap. You should go just before the monsoon season.'

He knows my name. How does he know my name?

'The air's so sultry, thick, it be like halitosis. It's faecal, repellent, but it's enveloping. Draw you in 'cos you can't escape it. You know? It like the earth's bad breath. Air like soup.' He arched forward. 'The horror, the horror.' Leaned back, chuckling to himself, wiping his skull. Solo didn't know whether he was in a movie or turning real life into one. The Boss was compact, economical, he moved and spoke deliberately, he was like a slow, heavy-lidded reptile that might yet strike without warning. Solo was spellbound by the man's authority, his charisma; scrutinized his every gesture. He was like an idol, Solo was idolizing him, as if his behaviour held a secret, a solution to some as yet unknown riddle; a key that might give Solo life; might keep him alive.

'Now, what you think? Would you like to show me the Liverpool E's?'

Solo took a video box out of his plastic carrier bag and handed it to the Boss. The Boss took but didn't look at it. 'Do they still call us southern softies up there?' he asked.

'No,' Solo said. The box cover promised Tom and Jerry.

'Do they still say black players go missing when it get cold and muddy in the winter?' The Boss began to unpick the cellophane with his fingernails.

'No.'

The cellophane was obstinate. 'No, they do not. Lloyd?' Lloyd stepped forward, produced a blade, accepted the box from the Boss and slipped the blade into the edge, sliced it open, tore the transparent skin smoothly off.

The Boss stage-whispered to Solo, 'We call him Bungaloid. You know why? No? Because there's not a lot upstairs.'

Solo tried to fix the noncommittal smile on his face.

'Not because he'll take a bribe. Lloyd the most honest brethren you'll ever meet. You don't recognize him, Solo? No? Strange. He famous. His face is on Unwanted Posters all over the country.'

Was he daring Solo to laugh? And how the hell did he know his name? Lloyd handed back the box and the Boss opened it. He took out the video cassette and looked at it for a few moments. Solo hadn't seen the contents: had no idea what was physically inside the boxes; pills, powder, what? The Boss turned the cassette round in his hand, read the label. Handed it to Lloyd. 'Put it on.'

Solo had to say something – if only 'Stop'; mightn't the video player's inner workings crush the chemical contents of the cassette? – but he found himself fixed, immutable, on the sofa, his body turning to jelly and heavier than Lloyd or any of the other men. Lloyd inserted the cassette in the player. The Boss pressed remote buttons. Onto a black screen came nothing. Solo had to explain. That's it, this is them, they're in there, it's not a fucking video. But he couldn't. Wait. A drawn image. Titles. Hectic music.

A big bulldog lay sleeping in his kennel. The piano became a gentle and soothing lullaby – interrupted by ironic arpeggio: Jerry the mouse leaned over the top of the kennel with a fishing rod and line. He hooked a juicy bone and pulled it up out of the dog's dish. Tom the cat, meanwhile, lay sleeping also elsewhere, beside his dish which had a fish in it.

A desperate whisper from Davey in Solo's ear: 'Are you taking the piss?' The Boss and his men watched the screen impassively. Jerry hooked the fish from Tom's bowl. Solo didn't so much sweat as exude viscous fear. They were in no hurry. Jerry lowered the dog's bone into Tom's bowl. Solo only hoped that it would be painless. Maybe being thrown straight out of the window, or taken out and shot. He fully inhabited his own puniness, felt his vulnerable limbs, his brittle chicken bones, his fragile skull. He didn't want to be tortured. Or cut: had always had a terror of being slashed. Stanley knives and razors. Jerry lowered the fish into the bulldog's dish. Davey whispered, 'You brought a fucking cartoon?' He was sorry to have implicated Davey in this; maybe they wouldn't blame him. The mouse lowered a note which settled beside the fish: *Fair swap, sucker*. What about Ben? He'd be looked after somehow. By someone. Better than me. Just don't slice me up with that blade, 'cos I don't know anything, Solo whimpered to himself.

So that he didn't realize at first what was happening around him: the Boss began chuckling, and some of his men did too. Solo registered it only when the bulldog woke up and saw the note and growled. Now everyone laughed. And the dog went for the poor duped cat.

The Boss laughed like someone being tickled, assailed by something midway between a blow and a caress. It was impossible to tell whether his soldiers were simply following his lead, but it certainly looked as if they all found it equally, painfully, uproariously funny. Almost as funny as Solo did, relief flooding through his body, flushing the adrenalin away.

When the cartoon was over the Boss turned off video and TV with the remote control and wiped his eyes with tissues Lloyd offered him. Then he turned to Solo. In the second or two that he turned, Solo realized how illusory was the relief he'd felt, what deep trouble he was still in.

But the Boss smiled. 'We can do business,' he said. 'We love the cartoons, star. Don't know how you knew, but you done your research. Maximum respect.' He made a fist and Solo did likewise and they touched. Lloyd brought over a small silver package to the coffee table. The Boss unwrapped it.

'I've been sent this by our Macedonian friends,' he said. 'Would you like a try some with me, Solo?'

'How?'

'How? Snort it, I'm guess.'

'What with?'

'What?'

'I don't have any money.'

'You don't have any money?' The Boss and then his men found this hilarious. 'He don't have any money. Give him some money, Lloyd.'

Lloyd handed Solo two fifty-pound notes. Solo, the Boss and Davey snorted coke. There was a smell of fried food. The fat lady carried in a half-time tray of tea, while one of the men brought white plastic carrier bags of fish and chips.

'Fish,' said the Boss. 'You like fish? I like fish.' He bit a huge lump out of battered flesh and chomped on it. 'I make sure my boys have plenty,' he said through a white mushy mash. 'We pay a lot more attention to diet than we used to. It's good for the brain. Protein.' Specks of which he spat at Solo.

'Sounds like a bit of cod philosophy to me,' Solo said.

'What did you say?'

All around, people stopped eating. Solo winked at the Boss. 'What do you call a Scouse in a semi-detached house, Boss?' he asked.

'I don't know. What?'

'A burglar.' Shut it, Solo, a voice inside his head scolded him. Fuck this coke.

'Hey, that's funny. You hear that, boys? That's good.'

'What do you call a Scouse in a Mercedes?'

'What?'

'A drug dealer.'

'Solo. I like it.' The Boss screwed up the remains of his fish and chips into a wrapped ball and tossed it onto the floor, from where one of the men bent down and picked it up. He wiped his hands on a kitchen towel. 'Trouble is you always feel greasy and bloated before you've finished, don't you?'

'Yeah, I always thought sex were overrated, too,' Solo said. He was saved by the telephone. One of the men over at the periphery had been fielding calls, whispering into a mobile phone. Now he held it to his chest and for the first time interrupted the Boss.

'It's the Italian.'

The Boss considered for a moment. 'Take care of it. Lean on him if you have to.'

'If you say so.'

'It'll be a piece of cake.'

'A pizza cake?'

'No, man,' said one of the others. 'The Boss say a Pisa cake.'

'What?' the Boss asked bemusedly.

'Nothing, Boss,' said the man with the phone, turning away. 'I'll lean on him if I have to.'

'Ah, Solo. Solo,' the Boss resumed. 'You know, I want get out a this here business. Move into new technology, there's the future. Virtual stimulants, cyber hallucinogens. The brain is our pleasure garden. Computerized enlightenment. Save me having to deal with the Afghans. You know what I mean. A guy I was at school with. He was another naughty chap, as it happen. I once bit a piece of his ear off, man, I loved that kid. He got a microchip company, it was so successful he had to move to smaller premises.'

There was a pause. The Boss shrugged. 'So, Mr O'Brien. How much you want for the Liverpool E's?'

Solo was stumped. How much had Robbie said they were worth? Five thousand? No, that's how many items there were. Wasn't it? 'Twenty thousand pounds,' he blurted out, and held his breath.

This time the laughter erupted from everyone all around him. Including Davey. Even Lloyd was snorting this time. Evangelina in the kitchen, for God's sake,

430

giggled in a musical way. It ain't over till the fat lady laughs.

'He wants twenty K for the Liverpool E's,' the Boss spluttered.

Eventually the laughter abated. The Boss collected himself and addressed Solo. 'Do people up in the north there call me a scumbag? Does your associate by the name of Mr Robert Stiles think I'm a scumbag, Mr Bagman O'Brien? If we do business, I a honest man. I'll give you a hundred gees for the Liverpool E's, not a cent more nor less. When can you bring them?'

'Soon.'

'Of course you can bring them soon, Solo. You can bring them tomorrow. Same time. Same place.'

'Right.'

'Lloyd, would you see our guests out?'

The Chief Steward met Davey and Solo when the lift stopped and accompanied them back along the tunnel. How does he know my name? Solo fretted. And Robbie's? 'When did we cross the river?' he asked Davey.

'Hey, Chief,' Davey said, stopping and turning. 'Solo here just asked when we crossed the river.'

Chief pointed to a small puddle a few yards away from them. He indicated a drop of moisture clinging to the ceiling, from which gravity and possibly pressure from above managed to extract a droplet as they watched.

'That the river,' said the Chief, and all three of them looked at the ceiling.

In Davey's car Solo prised open the remaining pair of cassettes. Black featureless video tape spooled out, trailed from the car window.

'What are you doing?' Davey asked.

'Bad films,' Solo explained. 'Guns. Knives.'

They passed Brixton Underground station.

'You can drop me here,' Solo requested. 'I need a walk, Davey. I need to clear my head.'

'Sure.' Davey pulled over. Solo got out.

'I'll be there soon.'

'See you later.'

Hands in pockets, fingering the reassuringly tough texture of two fifty-pound notes, Solo strolled till the car had curled out of sight, then turned and ran to the tube station.

20

LINES OF INTERSECTION

For weeks, months now, Roderick Pastille had lain low licking his wounds, considering TV presenting offers and memoir publishing deals, in the cottage in Herefordshire where he surprised himself by spending much of the summer, pottering around the barn, old stables, garden sheds. He gave a relaxed television interview on the lawn, in which he made clear that he harboured no ambition for the leadership and never had done, only hoped in due course to be able to serve his party and his country once more, and for the moment was content to concentrate on his business interests. He rather hoped to jog people's memories in the City – to be *offered* some business interests – not to mention the panjandrums in the party for when a safe seat became vacant at the next old codger's demise. Russell, watching the programme with him back in London when it was transmitted, assured Roderick the winking problem seemed to have been overcome.

It had been pure coincidence that he was back in Manchester clearing out the flat he wouldn't need any more when he heard the news of the riot coming in from Crapton; Roderick still wasn't sure whether his instant response was due to intuitively spotting an opportunity for a return from the wilderness, or more likely simply forgetting he was no longer the bloody MP. But it was a start. Subsequently, the important thing was to come back with a splash and the best place for that was the seaside. Party conference time was approaching: Roderick was still a senior figure in the party, who'd be welcomed back on the podium at Brighton, where a rousing speech and ovation should secure him a forthcoming candidature as well as restoring his public profile for Ben Ali Al-Shalir and his silent brother. The gratuity they slipped him used to be no more than a perk of the job, a cash bonus in a brown envelope, but had become his staple income. How demeaning it was to have to justify oneself to a pair of camel-humping immigrants. One of the final acts of his government in office was the use of a ship anchored offshore for an overspill from Dartmoor Prison; it joined others already floating in the English Channel full of illegal aliens. Should have used decommissioned ro-ro ferries, he'd argued at the time. And set them adrift on tides pointing towards Australia.

Martha Polkinghorne, meanwhile, was also applying herself to a distasteful task. Also, as it happened, on the orders of an immigrant. Guru Loop told Martha it would be good for her to look after Penny Witton, and when Martha asked him how, he said, sternly, 'Why not start at the bottom, the way your Jesus did? Or rather,' Guru added, giggling, 'I mean to say: at the feet.'

Here she was in a hotel in the spa town of Buxton with massage oil from the Body Shop and Penny was leaning back in a chintz-covered armchair, her hands on the rests – she'd shut up, now, at least – with Martha kneeling on the floor before her. Penelope had a face wrinkled by age and pain and rectitude. She grimaced as she removed with tubular arms, crooked fingers, her flesh-coloured tights, to reveal one bony leg and the other swollen, oedemic. Her skin white with red blotches, prominent with purple veins and myriad bumps like goose pimples; plucked chicken skin. Her legs tapered down to appendages that could hardly be more wrecked had Martha unbound the broken feet of an old Chinese grandmother.

She knelt at Penelope's feet; practically genuflected before her. What indignity. Martha recalled a newspaper column she'd read in some other hotel, years before, about a gang of psychotic hoodlums in New York. They'd stormed into a crowded restaurant waving guns around and yelled for every motherfucker to hit the floor. They were after cash and jewellery. All the terrified diners and waiters threw themselves to the ground. Except for one man. An undistinguished, late-middle-aged family man, a paunchy, besuited kind of guy. One of the crack-head robbers shouted at him to get on his knees or he'd blow his fucking brains out. The old chap shook his head and said in a calm, quiet voice, 'No. I don't kneel for anyone.' That was it. That was what he said. As if everything was fine and he didn't want to make a fuss, it was just that, you see, he didn't kneel for anyone.

So the psycho pulled his trigger and blew the man's brains out.

The columnist, Martha recalled, inveighed against the misplaced male pride that robbed a family of their husband, father, good people of their friend. Women wouldn't make so foolish a gesture, the female writer opined: they had things in perspective.

The article had haunted Martha, as odd things do that challenge us to define ourselves. Was she not a woman? For she hoped that given the same awful circumstances she'd do as that quiet man had done. He knew himself, it seemed to her, which was surely the point of it all. He'd decided how to carry himself through life and was able to do so even under the most intense pressure; in the screaming face of death. Throughout his life – whatever its length – he'd kept his dignity.

And now here was Martha losing hers, kneeling at an old woman's horrific feet. Beneath one nody, and one bloated, ankle each misshapen foot was covered with gristly bumps and boils, with corns and bunions. Had she worn bad shoes all her life, obeying what? Some religious imperative? Penitential footwear? Did she stand for hours at a time in a tray of slush and snow? The knuckles of her twisted toes were swollen, arthritic, and her heels were scabbed with hard dead skin. Penelope's feet were knotty, sclerotic, as if the blood supply rarely reached them; as if the heart made irregular deliveries. Martha could feel a pulse throb reluctantly, complaining through leathery veins, and Penelope winced and moaned. So Martha slowed down, loosened her grip, soothed her slippery fingers gently, repetitiously, over Penny's tender instep, around her heel. Across her arches, in between her toes. Until the old woman's groaning ceased and she sat back in the armchair, eyes closed.

It dawned on Martha that this might take longer than she'd bargained for. She tucked her feet into her thighs, held her back straight and subdued her thoughts to the patient rhythm of massaging Penny's foot in her lap.

Penny Witton for her part was sinking. Wave after

wave of gratitude swam through her. That Indian healer had told them a story about a herd of sixty elephants, how one of the calves was stranded on the far side of a fast-flowing river. The elephants wouldn't leave this one behind: holding on to tails with their trunks they managed to weave a daisy chain of rescuers ('Like supermarket trolleys with trunks!' Guru Loop rather weakened the image by adding). They reached the young calf on the far side and brought it safely across. But three bull elephants were lost, swept away in the deluge.

By the end of the story, listeners were misty-eyed. During that afternoon rest period a number of them scuttled into Sheffield and bought mementoes to give to Mr Loop, who clearly had a particular affinity and love for those animals. One woman bought a cuddly toy, another a framed print of a David Shepherd painting with an African elephant advancing, ears flapping; a third purchased a small figurine, a fourth a copy of the first Babar book; while Penelope herself discovered a video shop in which she found a David Attenborough classic for sale.

She thought then how hostile this girl, Martha, was, how surly and unbecoming: Penny had shown the video to her, and she was sure Martha sneered at these gifts placed that night outside Mr Loop's door.

Penny slept badly, had to clamber down from her bunk to visit the toilet: the noise she made there in the silence of the night surely disturbed the others. This illness meant the progressive loss of dignity; a ruthless equation. Penny had been given differing combinations of drugs. It was difficult to keep up with which doses were for the disease and which alleviating side effects brought on by others. Cisplatin caused unbearable nausea and vomiting, and stunted her hearing.

Doxorubicin brought on mouth ulcers and made her heart shudder. Bleomycin seemed to give Penny difficulty in breathing. Others induced pins and needles, muscle spasms. Anti-emetics had little effect; most gave her a flu-like fever. The doctors juggled type and dose of drug. For constipation, nurses administered enemas, suppositories, further pills, till the balance swung the other way.

And what can she expect next? Incontinence, of course. Humiliation. Degradation. But even that horror will come and be bearable. What's worst is simply the pain. Penny decided that cancer is not a strong enough word, the hard C's not hard enough. How about a hard G? Gancer. Look, that's already more accurate, she decided. Gangrene, gutrot, gonorrhoea, this letter better conveys a sense of the disgusting nature of such diseases.

The morning following gifts outside his door, after the sloppy porridge of breakfast and after the healing meditation, Mr Loop gave a short talk without notes or indeed punctuation in which it was hard to tell whether he was spluttering with rage or with laughter.

'Stories are bloody stories!' he spat at the score of ladies sat not quite cross-legged before him. 'I don't tell cuddly tales about bloody animals! I talk about human beings, good God. We're here because of us! This is not a zoo. It only seems like that, ha ha. Parables!' he exclaimed. 'Metaphors, for pity's sake. Have any of you ever seen an elephant up close? No? They're very big and clumsy beasts and they smell. And what's more they have a very strange bloody sense of humour, actually.

'I'm not a wise man,' he said exasperatedly. 'I'm a quack man. I'm a duck. And you're geese, for God's sake.'

The young woman said nothing. She didn't rub it in, Penny had to give her that. She felt stupid partly because pain itself should have taught her the necessity of metaphor. It was impossible to describe directly, she could only say something like, It feels as if someone's stabbing me in the guts with barbecue skewers. Or, My stomach's on fire. The irony, Penny realized, was that she'd never been stabbed or roasted, and that people who had experience quite different sensations from those we imagine. A man who'd been knifed she once heard describe how it felt not like a sharp, violent penetration but more like a blow that lands and doesn't let up.

At the last minute, as they were leaving Guru Loop's retreat, Martha asked for Penny's telephone number. A fortnight later she called and they met in Oxford, where Penny was receiving a further bout of experimental treatment in The Laboratory's basement. The scientists there advised her not to drive away. Just as well: whatever they gave her made her both bilious and frothy, buoyant in the chemical liquid with which she was fed.

Martha picked Penny up from the B&B on Polstead Road she'd checked in to. 'Mr Bone, the administrator,' she told Martha in the latter's grey van, 'claimed that it's our ability to register and understand pain that gives us our sense of self. He said that animals whose pain centre has been deadened in one leg will, if they get hungry, eat it. They simply don't recognize it as part of themselves any more.'

'They experiment on animals there?'

'No, you don't get it, dear,' Penny smiled. 'On us. Except. Well. I hadn't thought.' She stared out of the window. 'Do you think . . . Oh, my. What have I done?'

Penny remained pensive as they drove into the

439

Cotswolds. After treating each other to tea in Chipping Camden, they went for a warm, woozy stroll. Martha had parked her car tight to a fence and when they returned to it, its hot chassis had been slobbered over by cows.

Martha was a farm girl but she'd not known what the cows were hoping for from the shiny metal. 'They're curious animals, though,' she told Penny. 'If you're talking and there are cows on the other side of a wall they'll come right up to it. They're attracted to the sound of the human voice.'

Though Martha was naturally taciturn they must have talked more but that was about all Penny could remember of their conversation, for some reason. Maybe it was the drugs. Soon, though, even this memory was submerged by the deep, grateful waves overcoming her body. She couldn't tell where Martha's strong hands were, only knew her spinster shop-keeper's ruined feet had waited sixty-nine years to be so pampered. It was impossible to feel where the younger woman's powerful fingers were soothing, stroking, kneading, because the sensation they generated was not specific but rather a flowing current of pleasure through her feet, up her legs, around her body.

Martha was no masseuse but she guessed that few people had their feet caressed so long and tenderly, even if she was doing it less for Penelope than for Guru. She remembered him telling her once how he'd been here a year or two before he understood that he'd have to adjust his stories for a different culture. How he slowly realized, for example, that fables in which a mother's love, or child's love for her, were paradigmatic, could here be resisted by his pupils. As he came to see the damage between generations. Guru was a good teacher, Martha figured, because he denied that he was one. He told her to take this old woman out when she'd rather by far have looked after him, but here they were, the woman's knobbly, throbbing feet not quite so stark and ugly now, as Martha infused them with rich sensation.

Oh morning bliss: to leave the cab and sit alone in an unpleasant place and listen to the strains of oneself. In a motorway service station, perhaps; on an overnight ferry. But oh the welcome ache of peristalsis in the rectum. And a fond farewell to an intimate friend. Bombs away! Was it the truck driver's complaint or Jack's especially? He'd rarely suffered constipation with the first rig he owned, that old boneshaker. Maybe this one's too smooth. He knows he ought to consume more roughage and greens but he only eats in transport cafés and packs in bacon egg'n'sausage, it sits there in his fat gut like the mortar of a collapsing wall, turning in reverse to shit, falling no further, stalling in his stomach, his colon; a gridlock of food congealing; a bottleneck towards which he hurled more food as he drove – crisps, choc bars, sweets – like cars towards an already stifled city.

Jack Knighton drove back from abroad towards Birmingham, towing a container of French mugs, cups, saucers, plates, a huge packed tight container of pottery, heading back to the Black Country, and he was thinking that there are different ways of going back to the beginning. Every journey is distinct. You just have to see your way clear to it.

In one of his encyclopedias in the cab, the entry on the history of astronomy began something like, *A practical acquaintance with the elements of astronomy is indispensable to the conduct of human life.* And

Jack thought how true that was, at least for him, it was his hobby after all, driving along the motorway here he was like some supercharged molecule, really, a maverick atom. Most people didn't know much about anything nowadays, it was all too dauntingly complicated. Perhaps it was true that there was a time, an epoch that ended around the turn of the century – a hundred years ago – when an educated Victorian could master the elements of the major arts and sciences. But no longer. Not now. Knowledge mushrooms outward in proliferating detail and so the more ignorant we become, necessarily, and thus estranged from one another. In an expanding universe? The atmosphere becoming thin?

Take astronomy itself, though. Think of the patience the first stargazers had: night after night their persistent observation of the heavens. The unrelated generations of them, centuries of data compiled, millennia of painstaking record. And even then, how long it was before astronomy was separated from astrology. Throughout the Middle Ages astronomers cheerfully contributed periodical predictions of a date for the end of the world. Johannes Stöffler, professor of mathematics at Tübingen University, designer of a clock for the town hall with an astronomical dial, foretold that in 1524 three planets would meet in the sign of Pisces and thus that year would see a universal deluge. Many responded, across the whole of Europe, wassailing then heading for the hills. A certain President Aurial in Toulouse went so far as to build a huge, landlocked Ark. Only for the year to be distinguished for a drought – leaving him and others with egg if not flour on their faces.

Many serious men believed that the planets they scrutinized were animated, that comets were messengers of divine justice, that stars were moved around the heavens by hardworking angels. Tycho Brahe, the master of pre-telescopic observation, divined, from the appearance of the comet of 1577, the birth in Finland of a prince, who would lay waste Germany and vanish in 1632. And Brahe's innovative pupil, Johann Kepler, spoke of astrology as the foolish daughter whose existence was necessary for the wise mother, astronomy.

Even now, five hundred years after Copernicus's system proving that the earth itself is one of the heavenly bodies, innumerably more people consult their daily horoscope than ever study actual stars in the sky.

People make mistakes. You go back to the beginning and what do you find? Ignorance. You look at some midway point along the journey, and you see the gradual separation of ignorance and knowledge. And Jack tries to find the time it began to go wrong because it was such a gradual process. That his body settled, resculpted by gravity and indolence into the womanish figure of a lorry driver. That in the bathroom he brushed his teeth while she peed, and he swore the sound of the stream of her piss was louder than his own, lately, his youthful stallion's cataract guttering to a prostatic dribble, and Jack began to sit down too. Jack with his moist eyes; his dampness; his corporeal dreaminess. That she left the toothbrush in her mouth as she reached to pull toilet paper off the roll with which to wipe herself.

Was there a moment, then? Was it that one and only time he hit her – Jack flinched at the memory of the blow – slapping her hard with his open palm? Miranda yelped, staggered back across the kitchen. Her cheek red, a swift blush. It resolved nothing: Miranda stared at him a moment in abject fear and fascination. She couldn't quite believe what he'd just done. 'Do that again,' she said. While he was dying inside. 'Do that again,' she dared, coming towards him, and he turned and stumbled from the room.

Or was it earlier, long before, with the first problems they had had? When Jack first worked the long clock-changing journeys, came home and was helplessly unresponsive to Miranda's meaty body, was dead to her. She frogmarched him to Marriage Guidance like an item of evidence in his own prosecution, and the therapist advised them to talk, relax, look, for one week, but don't touch.

Common advice: it sounded ludicrous, but they agreed to put it into practice and it began to work before they'd even got home: as soon as he wasn't allowed to touch Miranda it was all Jack wanted to do, with a hard ache, while she breathed effortless pro-fanities into his ear, let slip items of clothing in the corridors of their new centrally heated house, and danced for him: Miranda forced Jack to watch her perform a dance of the seven veils that reduced him to a slavering wreck.

The memory overtook Jack as he drove; he wandered all over Miranda's body, a barely audible chinking of china pinking from the trailer behind him.

The second week they were allowed to touch each other so long as they avoided the genital areas, and their bed became a priapic torture chamber, Jack a helpless squirming prisoner. Day after night, night after day Miranda lavished attention on his naked body, biting sucking stroking every inch of him except for his unbearable hard-on. He must he swore have come this close to where the male and female merge in a myth of perpetual orgasm, two rivers in a tantric valley, he was almost there so close, throbbing for friction, any, her vadge, her mouth, her breast, her hot breath would be enough to bring him off.

And when they were finally allowed congress Jack didn't – as he feared – come and go in a catastrophic rush but found his body patient. He made love like a craftsman, it was his turn now to please Miranda and he did so, taking his time, doing to her what she'd done to him, feeling more powerful a man than he ever had, an artisan, measured, turning her towards a finely tuned satisfaction.

Was it too good in those weeks that followed? Was that the problem? Of course they couldn't sustain it.

People make mistakes. A journey comes to its end, and then we start again. Thales, the great Hellenic astronomer, gained his fame by successfully predicting the solar eclipse of 585 BC: by that act more than any other was a love of science inspired among the Greeks. And yet the same Thales conceived of the earth as like a great flat disc floating upon an elemental sea. He also reckoned that the attractive property of a magnet was probably due to its possessing a soul.

It wasn't too good to go too far back. You could dwell on the wrong things. On what did Jack dwell? Miranda's lavish bosom; the bounty of her slap-up buttocks; the mound of her lubricious loveliness. As he drove up the motorway towing a trailer full of minutely jiggling pottery.

While a long way away . . . as far away as you can get, really, on an island; let us go there, with only a brief backward glance north across the Peak District at two women in a hotel room. Let us leave Jack's jiggling container full of china, not far short of his delivery point at Phil Scritt's depot off the M6, and swoop into the

445

Potteries. Turn and glide, south, over the industrial debris, the black brickworks and brown canals, the plastic shopping malls and the undulating suburbs, of England's second city. Flit over swelling Shakespeare country. Soar across the Cotswold escarpment, sandstone villages and rolling pastures, corrugated with the strips of medieval fields. Sweep on over the Ridgeway, above the chalk Downs, into Sussex air space. Do we feel now that opening out, that sense of unrestriction – a tilting of the landscape or of the heart upon it – before we actually see the sea? And let us zoom along the front, the wide promenade, to a hotel and conference centre. The air is full of bluster. Rollerbladers are blown off course, a pensioner's hat flies off as if shot from his head. TV news crews shiver. Flags in front of the hotel are infuriated by the wind.

Inside, conference delegates partook of lunch and there was in the restaurant and bars, in huddles in vestibules, in odd congregations on the wide stairs, a tickly and prickly atmosphere; one of huffy animosity, from people who had taken umbrage. From a tribe who felt doubly hard done by: they'd lost an election and just been insulted for it.

Russell Crowe had led the infantry for his friend, bless him, in a one-man sortie deep into enemy lines that morning with a speech in which he argued that far from failing to get the message across to the electorate, they'd succeeded all too well. It was the wrong message. 'We were seen as a mean, uncaring party,' he berated. 'The people didn't like us.' A suicide mission that appealed to Russell's sense of fun.

To many it was an act of provocation to have this blackamoor on the platform at all. The odd Asian entrepreneur was all very well but this Negro telling us what we were about? Russell went on to say that today, under this new government, too many people were excluded and it was up to us to include them. Russell then listed those minorities exiled in the margins over the last twenty years – single parents, inner city kids, rural children miles from a school, villagers without a local shop, the elderly subsisting on state pensions, jobless young blacks and browns and yellows. He made it sound as if their exclusion were a fresh phenomenon and claimed that the party ought to address them specifically.

It was no wonder the farming, golfing, investing fraternities collected peevishly and sulked back for the afternoon session, at which the first speaker, Roderick Pastille, strode to the podium and after lengthy applause – this favourite son of the party faithful had only increased his standing with his magnanimity in defeat, not to mention his courage in the Crapton riot a month ago – he began: 'I should like to talk today about animals. We are the party of animals. We are the natural party of the countryside, of farmers, of pet owners. We understand, because we live it, the relationship between animal and man. The reasons for hunting, shooting, fishing. The tender relationship of husbandry. The difficult, caring decisions necessitated by our stewardship of the land. In short, we understand the love of man for animal.

'Which is why I say three words to you good friends today: *ban animal experiments*. It is time to put a stop to practices that have undoubtedly yielded us much valuable information in the past but whose usefulness has diminished to the point where to continue is to carry us into the realms of cruelty; of barbarity, indeed.

'Let me explain. We all distrust statistics, I hope, but some are necessary. Here's one. During the Victorian era, with the rise in vivisection, the Cruelty to Animals

447

Act was passed in 1876. Since that time – little more than a hundred years – one hundred and seventy million animals have been experimented on and killed. Last year alone, some three million cats, dogs, pigs, goats were sacrificed in this way.'

A moving image blinked onto the vast screen behind the speaker: an out-take from a certain video shot some months earlier, it showed Roderick playing with a floppy-eared beagle puppy on his lap, tickling it behind its ears. 'It would be the easiest thing in the world', Roderick continued, 'to show you horrific footage of inhuman acts, but let us leave that to others. Do you know why beagles are used in experiments?' he asked, as behind him his magnified self hugged the moist-eyed puppy. 'Because beagles are friendly, trusting, intelligent, their confidence easily won. And do you know how many dogs alone are used each year in experiments in Britain? I'll tell you. Fifteen thousand. Every year.'

The unease in the audience was palpable. This wasn't the subject for a conference speech. Was it?

'The entire cruel edifice of vivisection rests upon a single deceit: animals do not feel as we do; their suffering cannot compare. They are different from us.' Roderick paused to let this concept sink in. 'And yet it is of course only their similarity to us that can justify doing experiments on them at all. Let us not lose sight of the fundamental point that, as the eighteenth-century philosopher Jeremy Bentham put it: the question is not can they reason, nor can they talk, but can they suffer?

'How very different we humans in fact are can be seen from some of the bizarre mistakes that have been made in medicine in recent times. Penicillin, the great breakthrough of this century that has protected us from infection, was deemed too risky for years because it kept killing the cats and the guinea pigs upon whom it was tested. Arsenic, on the other hand, had no effect on rats, mice, sheep even. While aspirin kills cats. Thalidomide? Didn't seem to bother pregnant animals, did it? Or morphine? A valuable sedative for us, but give it to horses or goats, as foolish scientists did, and it excites them: they'll be skittering around the field – or the laboratory, indeed, smashing up test tubes and beakers.

'Insulin, the great boon for sufferers of diabetes, is a quite harmless substance. But it was tested for years and produced terrible deformities in chickens, rabbits, mice.'

There was stirring in the auditorium, a shuffling, though less of feet than of thoughts. Had poor fruit Pastille lost his marbles? There was always something a little unhinged about his more flamboyant performances, wasn't there? And was that stricken smile of defeat on election night not, in retrospect, both the first sign and precipitating axefall of catastrophe? Did the insult strike home infinitesimally deep inside him: a premonitory if not actual cardiac occlusion; a critical surge of schizophrenic adrenalin; subtle encephalitic rearrangement? Mice? Rabbits? And yet, and yet. No-one was leaving, could quite tear themselves away. They may be witnesses to the ruin of a man, but on the other hand: animals. Mad Cow Disease. Calves bunched together in cruel transit. The countryside. Perhaps he had a point.

'Eighty per cent of people who visit a British doctor, ladies and gentlemen, need no treatment.' Roderick waved a hand dismissively. 'A little reassurance, perhaps, a listening ear. I can't vouch for Irish doctors,' he added suddenly, looking aside from his autocue, and the entire audience's attention focused. 'You know what they say: there's no such thing as a good listener in Ireland. Only tired talkers.'

It was as if his speech by its heterodoxy were creating a vacuum, which the conference delegates now filled with laughter. And of course unbounded relief, since they all knew that madness and humour are mutually exclusive. Roderick returned to the speech as Mr Bone had scripted it.

'And yet eighty per cent of people who visit a doctor will be prescribed drugs. Which they will quite possibly become dependent upon, since it's in the drug companies' interest to get patients addicted to their benzodiazepine tranquillizers – which those companies deny, of course. They're addicted to making money, and they're in denial of that addiction. New types of which tranquillizers are all tested on animals yet, let us remind ourselves, are no more than slight modifications of old ones.

'Ten to fifteen per cent of patients in hospital are there with drug-related problems. And did you know, ladies and gentlemen,' he said, again looking past his autocue, addressing the hall directly, 'that whenever the doctors and the surgeons have gone on strike, our mortality rate has fallen?'

The delegates laughed again, and cheered this time too, back on solid ground. Doctors, we don't trust them. Drugs are evil.

'Naturally, we want to be healthier than all our ancestors. But when were the British people healthiest? You know, don't you? During the Second World War. Our medical establishment is obsessed with high technology medicine. We've got specialist coronary care units for heart attack victims in every hospital, we've got more highly trained cardiologists. And what've we got? More people than ever before dying of heart disease.'

By now Roderick Pastille was in full grandisonant flow. His voice gained resonance; he seemed to grow larger on the stage, his gestures were declarative, generous, commanding. He knew how to appeal to the old codgers and the young galoots of the party too, green and eager as he once was, whose numbers would swell in Opposition. He knew you had to get them in the head – flattering them with a quote or two – but also to get them in the heart, not bleeding, no, we're not like that, but pumping. Inflame that Union Jack striping like a stick of rock the aorta of an Englishman. And get them in the guts, hot and steaming, primed for action.

'We say, No more animal experiments to test cosmetics. What wealthy women's pampered nonsense. What vanity. We say, No more animal experiments to test weapons. What cowardice. Is it British to fire guns into the strapped down bodies of pigs? Is it a part of our martial tradition to kill monkeys with chemical weapons? Is Porton Down truly part of England? I leave the answer to you. And you. And you.'

Roderick had the rare charismatic gift of being able to energize the large gathering, while at the same time convincing individuals they were being specifically addressed. He continued, his voice tattooing the speech, maximizing it, gesticulating and punctuating sentences into epigraphic groups of words, drumming his message home. 'What we should be doing – what this party should be doing – is persuading people to stop smoking, eat less fat, take more exercise, lose weight, eat minerals, vitamins, iron, and to deal with the stress in their lives. To learn, in short, a few things from our parents and grandparents.'

Roderick paused for breath, swept back his hair, as

the audience applauded, especially strident the pensioners; the older they were, it seemed, the keener they were we should learn from our parents and grandparents.

'The scientific establishment would do well to follow the lead of the Department of Organology in Oxford, with which I'm proud to have been associated in recent years, and which as you may have heard has become the first experimental laboratory in this country to categorically repudiate, and announce the phasing out of, all experiments on animals.'

Roderick waited for the approving applause that greeted this information to die down before continuing.

'We and the scientists there have together said: "Enough is enough." Alternatives are widely available and more credible today than subjecting animals to cruelty. Cells taken from diagnostic biopsies, for example, tissue removed during surgical procedure, fragments of organs, even, can be grown on culture dishes, and more has been learned from them about viruses, how anaesthetics work, the impact of chemicals on human tissue, than in a century of vivisection. And computer technology promises even greater possibilities, with programs already devised that duplicate the complex physiological systems of the human body.'

Roderick took a deep breath, puffed out his chest, and launched into his concluding rhetoric. 'There is a turning of the tide in this country, fellow delegates,' he said, clearly taking leave of the autocue once more, winding up his speech. 'On the one hand more and more people are seeking natural health alternatives to invasive surgery. On the other we are reassessing our ancient relationship with animals and realizing that some in this technological age of ours have taken terrible advantage, inflicting cruelty upon our sentient friends in the animal kingdom, and for ever-diminishing benefits. Labour in Opposition promised a Royal Commission on this subject but read my lips: they will not deliver. Labour has no idea of the depth of feeling on this issue: the Socialists as usual know nothing of animals or the people who steward them. This government cares not a jot for those people. Those people's voices must be heard, and the place for them to be heard, ladies and gentlemen, is in our party. Because they are us.

'I repeat: *ban animal experiments.*'

In Oxford in Mr Bone's small office he and Joe Snow watched the speech on a small black and white TV monitor they'd unplugged from a research student's video edit suite. An aerial made from a coat-hanger obtained a fuzzy reception. As Roderick collected his papers – conveying the impression he'd made the speech from notes – and left the platform with applause ringing in his ears, Joe said, 'You're not going to take my hooded rats away, are you?'

'We've got people now,' Mr Bone reminded him. But he registered the lad's obvious distress. 'Don't worry, Mr Snow. No-one said anything about stopping the work. He said we're going to phase it out. Quite a different thing altogether. Take about, oh, a hundred years, I should think.'

'That is a relief.'

'He's a fine speechifier, though, isn't he? Even if we can claim a portion of credit for ourselves.'

'Did you write it?'

'Oh, just a few facts and figures,' Mr Bone admitted modestly. 'I was thinking more of the energy with which he delivered it. The attack, as it's called.'

453

'You mean Mr Pastille's enthusiasm? His energy?'

'Let's just say Winston Churchill enjoyed a similar prescription,' Mr Bone divulged. 'And so did Anthony Eden. It's a Tory tradition, Joseph.'

21

JOGGING

Solo O'Brien joined the legion of the homeless, in the centre of the capital. To buy time while he worked out what to do. Begging scraps from the back doors of cafés, sleeping in shop doorways, the posture of submission came easily to him. Hiding; his body in a permanent crouch. Through October Solo shunned the company of others, but older men drew him in to their reeling camaraderie. Reeking, flesh soaked in alcohol. Younger ones collared him, agitated or spacy: between a rock and a hard place, Solo thought. He knew he had to leave Ben where he was, somewhere, anywhere, safer than with him, until he sorted it out. He just couldn't figure how he might begin to do that.

Had Robbie put the drugs somewhere else? Solo had to go back to Manchester; but if he went back they'd kill him too. Whoever they were. His friend, Robbie, helped him in his life; but not only was Robbie dead, he was the very one who'd got them into this trouble in the first place. Liverpool gangsters knew about him and so did these London ones. Until Solo convinced them he was an innocent party, they'd be after him; but if he went to them, they'd surely do away with him anyway. Why would they believe him?

Some conundrums are impossible to resolve. Solo knew no-one here would help him. They were all hiding too. Some dawdled, slurred by dereliction; others strode from one place to another with dirty blankets slung over their shoulders. Cloaks of the homeless worn proudly. Self-appointed nightwatchmen, guarding the conscience of the city.

'Hey, Kojak!' a kid yelled. 'Where's your lollipop?'

Joggling along a tarmac footpath behind the backs of houses, fat Jack Knighton came to a juddering halt. He was drowning in air, needed to gulp more breath than his lungs could give him. His heart jack-hammered against his ribs, his chest was inflamed, each knee throbbed, his face was on fire.

'That's the way, Jacko,' he gasped to himself, doubled over, hands on knees. 'Sprint a little, walk a little, mate. Like we used to in footie training.'

Eventually, after a few more such rasping false starts (and all too authentic stops) Jack got his second wind and flew. Sleek and hairless. He was getting the hang of this exercise malarkey and no mistake, and he understood with his frisking step, as his light-headed vision found its prospect glow, that oxygen was being carried like an elixir in the blood that gushed through greedy caverns and hungry tunnels, and that endorphins were being released in his intoxicated brain. The marathon runner's grim euphoria. It was good to know how this universe within operated. And that it would be soon unrestrained, aerobically unyoked of its flabby straitjacket.

Jack took the same route daily, passing young mothers by triangular playparks and pensioners exercising ungrateful old dogs, through his own and the two poorer, adjacent estates: the first of these, pre-fabricated rows of pre-cast concrete and glass, broken toys littering, washing hung in the communal gardens; the second, fragile semi-detached houses, thin-walled, with small scuffed lawns and desultory shrubs. Each type of housing had sprouted its own recent addition. Satellite dishes on the square concrete prefabs. Porches before the doors of council houses bought by their tenants (whether these signified WELCOME or KEEP OUT Jack wasn't sure). And, jogging back to his own network of fragrant avenues and culs-de-sac, identical conservatories had bubbled and blistered from the skins of the houses, like a strain of some bourgeois virus.

Jack could in this way retrace by his plodding foot-steps each day the trajectory of his own material progress through life, from his labourer father and flighty mother's humble tenement in Walsall through the council maisonette he and Miranda had moved into when wed, then bought and soon sold, to his present desolate abode. He thereby traced too the reverse route he would surely take alone: work was drying up from Phil Scritt and Jack had no impetus to seek new employers. Even without Miranda's expenses he had to earn a monthly fortune to pay the mortgage plus the interest on the credit on all their fixtures and fittings. No sooner had his spendthrift wife departed than bankruptcy appeared in her place, though more constant a companion: the prospect of imminent ruin accompanied Jack everywhere, in-ducing anxiety, panic and a strange sense of elation.

His mouth filled with viscous gob. He spat, weakly, felt it splat against his ear, knew a slug's trail of phlegm clung to his cheek. Wiped it off. At least he didn't smoke; then heaven knows what he'd be hawking up. Miranda had that habit of never quite stubbing her cigarette right out, so that smoke plumed from dog-ends in the ashtray, all the more bilious as their filters burned.

Don't think about Miranda, my darling.

The way she used to leave a tap running. What did such profligacy indicate? Leave it, man. You'll upset yourself again.

The number of times I must have grabbed a saucepan off the stove before, like a white loaf rising in panic, milk boiled over.

Stop it. Dash. Sprint. Yes: running. This is OK, this is good. Got the hang of it I have, some people never do, like that bird there she is again with the ponytail, bobs up and down with every step, it's got more bounce than she has. Whoosh: overtook her no problem, mate. I'll say hello pet next time, she'll hear a voice from this flash, this blur past her, the Woodgate Roadrunner, like. I'll have to slow down and reverse back to her. *Attention: this pentathlete is . . . reversing.* Oh, I'm flying, mate.

Solo sat on the front step of Jack's house, careful not to lean back against the door and set off alarms. The last thing he wanted was police attention: the sure consequence of their involvement would be Ben's removal from Rebecca's custody as he was taken into theirs. First appearances could be deceptive, but even that virtual stranger was better than an orphanage; irretrievable fostering.

It was possible that Jack'd be away for days, hauling across Europe, in which case Solo would have to be patient; find some place to flop and keep coming back till Jack returned. It was a shame he had such a chintzy address, Solo would surely attract attention to himself here, an ageing scruffy guttersnipe loitering.

Solo watched a pudgy bald man crawl along the pavement beside the main road; he ponderously crossed it and entered the close. The thing that was more amazing than the fact that the bright green shell suit the man wore was ten years out of date was the idea that it had ever been anywhere in. It had to rank, Solo figured, alongside tank tops, flared patchwork jeans and those leggings with hanging gussets that women brought back from holidays in Turkey, and which made it look as if they had udders, as notable fiascos of fashion. This poor bloke looked in addition as if he was half blind, maybe, groping his way through a medium thicker than air; an invisible fog, resistant to his progress. It dawned on Solo that the old crock was jogging, or trying to, a few moments before he recognized the one person he'd come all this way in search of, the fat trucker, good Samaritan Jack Knighton himself. His skull now bravely shaven.

Once reunited and inside the house, Jack juggled oranges, carrots and ginger from a cupboard. 'Out of tea and coffee, old son,' he said, sweatily, as he proceeded to peel, cut, segment. 'I thought you was a bailiff when I sees you there. Still, I think the juicer's paid for.' Jack stuffed portions of carrot into the cup of the machine. 'I'd really value your opinion on something, Solo, being a Mancunian. Do you think Villa'll win the league next season?'

Solo opened his mouth but before he could express an answer Jack switched the juicer on, which whined like a dentist's drill and drowned out the possibility of hearing anything – other than the laughter directed cheerfully at him.

Jack poured two glasses. Solo sipped his, under polite obligation, and found himself forced to then swallow the rest in one long uninterrupted gulp. 'That is serious,' he gasped through orange lips. Then the ginger hit his brain. 'Jack, I'm beginning to see the point of this health trip.'

'I try and do a cycle or a run. But this time of year a bicycle's too quick, like. With the dozy wildlife. You get nutted by butterflies; flies in your eyes. Solo, you go in the lounge, take it easy now while I shower and change and I'll be down in a tick.'

The deep white leather sofa accepted Solo's relatively negligible weight with a modest sigh, and he found himself beached against its back, unflexed legs stuck straight out, feet feet from the ground. Two or three photograph albums rested on the glass coffee table. To reach them Solo had to clamber right off the sofa again.

Solo soon deduced that, besides Jack's wedding album, there were collections of photos from his childhood and youth and it seemed least prying to leaf through those. The same young and only child was in every photo in a tight maternal embrace; then from the age of seven or eight the boy's large mother vanished, and now the photos were either of the child or taken by him of his gaunt father, each recording the other's particular solitude.

The child is the father to the man, it's said, yet the one in these pictures looked utterly unrelated to Jack Knighton. Now fat, genial, balding – correction: bald – Jack had emerged from a thin, wiry-haired, suspicious-looking child. Solo couldn't recognize him in any single image: could only identify Jack through a series of photos, by tracing him backwards through the albums' narrative flow. He was a child, moreover, who kept hiding his face from the photographer; until it dawned on Solo that Jack's entire generation was one

460

of squinting children: their parents had snapped their Kodak Instamatic portraits with the sun behind the camera. Descendants, he speculated, will look back on these weak-eyed ancestors and marvel at their own optical evolution; wonder whether at some point eye drops had been put in the water like fluoride.

Solo, perched forward on the sofa, was surprised by Jack's voice behind him. 'I've been sorting through them lately.' Jack collapsed beside Solo: the leather cushion complained with a brief disgruntled fart. 'When I was a kid,' he continued, picking up one of the albums, 'I used to study the family pictures because I couldn't quite believe it; like I wanted to verify this miraculous but, I don't know, uncanny proposition: that I came out of my parents. And they came from my grandparents. And so on. You know: they were begat by so and so, who were begat by such and such. That biblical procession, like. You know what I mean?'

Solo nodded his head tentatively. 'No,' he smiled, shaking it. 'I lost touch with all my folks way back.'

Jack opened a page of holiday snaps, the small surly boy and his well-endowed, swimsuited ma on beaches; in front of caravans. 'North Wales every year,' Jack indicated. 'You know, Solo, captivated one whole summer I was by people standing in the sea. I used to watch them waddle down to the water and wade in up to their waists. They'd inspect the view, gaze out like they were expecting some particular ship to appear on the horizon. Eventually I asked me dad about it and he said, "Ya thick little sod, they're having a piss." After that I watched them even more keenly, of course. I wanted to run down and shout it out, tell everyone else. Never did, mind.'

Jack sighed at the memory. Solo watched his soft regretful face. All of a sudden Jack turned his watery eyes on Solo and said, 'So, are you in trouble, old son, or what?'

'How do you know?' Solo started.

'I guess you wouldn't leave Ben nowhere for no reason.'

'Well, sort of, Jack. I need somewhere to stay. Somewhere to hide.'

'Who from?'

'It's better that you don't know.'

'Oh, I see.'

'For your own good. The less you know the better.'

'Yes. It makes sense.'

'Sometimes having information can get a person hurt.'

'That's true.'

'These are dangerous people we're talking about, Jack.'

'Or not talking about.'

'And the less number of people involved the better.'

'I understand, Solo. You don't have to tell me anything.'

Over the following hours Solo proceeded to tell Jack everything. Jack in turn told Solo of his beloved's departure and Solo comforted him with the story of his own abandonment by Syreeta, his Black Queen. Somewhere along the way Solo broke off to bathe in a luxurious bathroom and dress in one of Jack's spare voluminous shell suits, while Jack rustled up a lo-cal chicken risotto and some bottles of the lager and hock he no longer imbibed but made an exception of tonight, until the two of them collapsed into drunken unconsciousness in the early hours; Solo on the sofa, Jack on the thick-piled floor, though it made no difference to either of them which it was.

In the morning Solo woke with his cheek irritated by

the carpet, lifted his head and banged it on the under-side of the glass coffee table so hard he sank back into sleep. Woke an hour later back on the sofa, sweaty in his shell suit, rose gingerly, saw no sign of Jack. A grating sound drilled into his ears but then it ceased and Jack breezed in with a jug and two glasses.

'Hangover cure,' he explained. 'Detox. Tangerines and guava, mate. Vitamins B1 and C.' He set them down and poured. 'I've been considering it like, Solo, and you can stay here, of course, for as long as I've got the place before they repossess it. Relax. Think it through. And we can fetch Ben as soon as you say.'

Autumn had come, with no news of Sam Caine. Rebecca's helplessness like that of one whose lover had gone missing in war. Hope, thought, even sorrow, spiralled in on themselves. She reached for the delusion that he had left her, so that she might be able to purge his loss.

In the seventh month of her pregnancy Rebecca took to falling over. Her swollen uterus pushed against the femoral artery, constricting the blood flow. A leg went numb, Rebecca buckled. So far it had happened in the flat, and once, twice travelling on the bus, after getting up from sitting down. Not when she kept on the move; not, so far at least, while shopping.

Rebecca tended to follow exercise regimes in phases of enthusiasm: would swim, work out, take another dance class, yoga at the Brix, aikido in the Unitarian Church Hall. Every spring she used to get the taste for jogging, ran up Effra Road and into Brockwell Park, around the park and home. She'd time herself, her prowess, each day completed the circuit a shade quicker, self-absorbed, mind preoccupied by body. Till all of a sudden – with the hot days of summer, the Lido open – the activity would seem pointless, tedious, and she swam lengths instead, with a waterproof stopwatch. That old irresolution.

Shopping expeditions now involved the exact opposite process: each day Rebecca was slower to labour down Railton Road. But each day she saw a little more outside herself, saw more than she'd seen for the six, seven years she'd lived in Brixton, and thus reminded herself why she'd moved here in the first place. There was a secret appreciation she possessed and held close to her, beneath the obligatory veneer of metropolitan cool: that of a West Country girl brought up in a semi-rural culture far from the mainstream – notwithstanding her own father's immigrant status, which didn't count to a child, was particular to him. Her background meant there was a fascination for her, an exotic flavour to her existence in the midst of a mix of peoples, which she imagined she'd never entirely lose. London was a melting pot but Brixton had been so long an immigrant area that it embodied both London's recent history and its heterogeneous future.

So that however accustomed to city streetlife Rebecca became it took only the slightest adjustment or reminder to see again through a recent arrival's eyes the young Italians and Spanish squatting in out-of-sync estates, the Afro-Caribbean raves after midnight, the Portuguese enclave at the bottom of Stockwell Road, the Chinese in Lambeth, the Maltese and Cypriots.

By her eighth month Rebecca walked at about the same speed as Ben, the boy who had been left with her, at a pace comfortable for both of them, she now and then holding the weight in front of her splayed dancer's feet on the pavement in time with Ben's slapping footsteps. Each one the culmination of the rigid robotic performance of his limbs. They dawdled down Railton Road on foggy November mornings, people's racial differences merged in PC pea-soupers, ambled back in clear afternoons, wispy striated clouds in the blue above like the loosened white hairs of some old mad-woman of the sky.

At first Rebecca hadn't been able to understand Ben's speech, only saw his delight at the mirrored shops in Atlantic Road, the Indo-Caribbean fish-mongers with their red- and yellow-belly snappers, mackerel, bream, salmon; with dried fish whose reek made him laugh. And the butchers with their goats', pigs', chickens' feet Ben was intrigued, appalled by, kept stumping back to, as if to make sure they hadn't got up and trotted off all on their own. And the Cockney greengrocers with the cheap fruit stalls in Electric Avenue squawking their prices, raucously flirtatious with ribald Jamaican matrons. Ben stared silently at the barrow boys, their strangulated vowels as alien to him as his would have been to them; TV phantasms made flesh. Until they clocked him there, staring, this moony eyebrowless boy, and carving an interval from their hawking they'd say, "Ere ya go, son, 'ave a plum, lovely'n'ripe, there ya go, treat yerself, an' 'ere's a mandarin.' Ben'd jerk his white head wild-eyed to Rebecca, clock her consent, beam at the fruitseller.

'Ya wanna feed 'im up, darlin', and yerself wiv anover one on the way, two by the looks of it, lovely broccoli, plenty of iron, to you love two pound a pound.'

Indeed she had another one. A postcard arrived, postmarked France, saying, *Sorry, I'll come back for him when I can. Solo.* Davey denied all knowledge of everything, said he'd never met or heard of Solo before he showed up that day, had no idea how Solo's friend

465

had got their address, or Davey's name. Davey washed his hands of the affair, said he had enough trouble convincing his employer that he wasn't implicated in a seriously disrespectful scam.

Rebecca couldn't see what had been so wrong with her inconstant life to have been so duped. One man had come along, messed up her head, planted his seed inside her and disappeared. Another dropped by for an hour and left his son behind. She was a modern woman: what was she supposed to do? Abort, abandon, and she couldn't. The effrontery of it was so enormous that, Rebecca realized, she was taking it in her increasingly crab-like stride, had stepped off a path of exciting, lonely, selfish, brave and difficult self-determination to a parallel one that had been there all along, occupied by a procession of pregnant women, lonely, brave, self-absorbed, in whose wake she now walked; with others already following on behind.

Brixton wasn't a bad place to bring up a child, Rebecca reckoned, nor for another to move to. She told Ben his father would come back but she didn't know when. He sobbed at night, and wet the sofa bed; Rebecca bought a plastic cover but Gemma purred in his ear as he slept and Ben didn't leak again. Rebecca sometimes watched him. A frown would occupy and depart from his face: it looked as if his unconscious was concentrating on the difficult art of sleeping.

Ben was both vulnerable and indecipherable. Rebecca found it impossible to tell whether when he spoke, moved, ate, it was with reluctance or customary impediment. He may have been falling apart or he might have come to a decision to put his eight-year-old trust in Rebecca. That was possible, she thought: a survival mechanism, understanding that she wouldn't have the patience to take on both responsibility for the boy and the job of coaxing him into a relationship. Maybe he was like Sam, in fact: finding himself reliant on someone, able to just let go.

On their shopping expeditions, Ben liked to handle the West Indian fruit and vegetables Rebecca bought – plantains, yams, okra, sweet potatoes, ugli fruit – and to hand out Rebecca's leaflets – HAVE YOU SEEN THIS MAN? with the photo of Sam Caine – that she'd pretty well stopped distributing herself. At Kwik Save, while Rebecca leaned against her trolley in the most inefficient supermarket queues in Britain, in the area beyond the checkouts people would take the flyer from Ben (did they see his albino African skin?) sometimes look at it and ask, 'Is dat your pa, dear?' And Ben would grunt at them with a sound they opted to take for an affirmative, and moved on. 'Tek it easy, buoy.'

Rebecca relished the way the older generation of West Indians spoke, bending and curling words just as her Devonian grandfather did, letting words linger in their mouths, to taste them, to lend them a flavour. Creamy accents, both homely and sensual. The old ones talked as they walked, languidly. The younger generation – hers – didn't have the leisure for such a pace, it was a rural rhythm of speech and they were an urban generation, who only when they smoked good weed and played loud drum'n'bass recapitulated the old, slow, funky drawl.

Maybe conversing with them helped Rebecca decipher Ben's speech. It may have taught her to listen; to listen with faith that the sounds would fall into place, sentences construct themselves from his chaotic-sounding utterances, an unfamiliar music making sense. Juice was briefly intrigued, she taped Ben's voice, sampled it in her studio, then ignored him as she had Sam.

Rebecca realized Ben spoke like a two-year-old, or a deaf person, his consonants swallowed by his disability, vowels flattened. She had to listen hard and with maternal patience, had to scan possible meanings using the number of syllables she heard, bearing in mind the topic under discussion and clues like gesture and expression.

'Uh uh a aah uh a ur?' he asked unintelligibly, with meaningless bovine utterances. But she saw his lips pressed together from the beginning of the fourth syllable, which meant it could have been a B, M or P; on the last his lips had half-pouted and she heard less the sound than the effort, the attempt, at a consonant at the back of his mouth, a hard C, G or K. She could guess it had been a question from his raised brow and reply-expectant manner. And in addition he was indicating her belly. Her pregnancy. Or the foetus within.

'Uh uh a b— uh a g—?' Ben had asked.

'I don't know,' Rebecca replied. 'I could have found out when they did a scan, the last time I saw anyone, months ago, but I didn't want to know. And they didn't figure I needed an amnio.'

'Uh?'

'An amniocentesis is when they put a needle into a pregnant woman's tummy, into the amniotic fluid. That's the liquid the baby's floating in. They take a bit to test it for any abnormalities. See if the baby's going to be ill.'

'Ill?' Ben frowned.

'Not ill, but, you know, if they've got something wrong with them. Not little things. They wouldn't have been able to see my cross-eyes.'

'You, lovely eyes.'

'You're a little charmer, are you? One for the girls,

eh, Ben? No, the amnio's looking for things that, well, the baby could die from.'

'Laa muh.'

'Not like you, no. What? Why are you going to die?'

'I muuh.'

'You might, might you? Well, you ain't yet.' What if she had had an amnio, and – if such is possible – they'd identified cerebral palsy? 'What about you,' she asked, 'what do you think it's going to be? Boy or girl? Do you know?'

Ben nodded his head, all out of control on his shoulders.

'Well? Tell then.'

'Buuuu,' Ben said, laughing. 'I huua.'

'You hope, indeed,' Rebecca whacked his arm. 'Getoutahere.'

Ben watched Rebecca rubbing wheatgerm oil into her belly, asked if it was for the baby, imagining she was feeding it in this way. When she explained it was to soften her stretching skin he offered to help, with body language that was the keenest possible request to be allowed to, so she let him. And when she squeaked with surprise, she then guided his hand to the minuscule feet that had kicked her.

'Buuu,' Ben pronounced for sure, serious and teasing both, as if only a boy could kick like that. When there he was, his withered left leg in a calliper; with the conformity of the enforced outsider subscribing already to a shared myth of masculinity from which he himself had been excluded.

Rebecca found it hard to believe she could carry on expanding for a month or more. She had to pee every five minutes, and got bouts of acid heartburn. When she ate, all blood drained to belly and baby, she slumped, dazed, brainless. At night she could only sleep on her side. And yet she felt wonderful too, ripe with health and a simple self-sufficiency. Rebecca spoke more with Ben than anyone. She'd registered with no midwife, attended one antenatal class, changed the subject if Juice or Fuyuki brought it up.

'There are tribes in the Amazon, Ben, with a child-birth practice called couvade.'

'Whah?' he grimaced.

'How it works is, the mother doesn't suffer pain. She'll quit working for a couple of hours, give birth, and return to her field. It's the husband who bears the pain. He goes to bed during the delivery and stays there for days, groaning and thrashing about. No, don't look like that, it's true. If he's unconvincing, the other villagers don't believe he's the father.'

'Acting,' Ben said.

'Yes and no, I guess. They're fooling themselves, too. The new mother comes and waits on the poor suffering husband. She entertains relatives who drop by to offer him their congratulations.'

Rebecca bought a book of photographs of an embryo, foetus, baby, growing in the womb. A tiny alien asleep inside her.

'Can you believe I was like that once?' she asked Ben. 'You too.'

Ben frowned. 'I'll do it for you,' he said.

'Do what?' she asked.

'That thing. The father. Acting.'

'Thanks, buddy,' Rebecca said, and hugged the boy beside her, the book across their laps. The other book, the diary, she still worked on every day. At first she'd convinced herself she kept it up for when Sam Caine reappeared, and then it was a consolation for her. By now, though, she understood she was writing it, too, for her child.

Rebecca still hadn't told her father. He phoned most Sunday evenings, and their conversations that she'd always looked forward to became increasingly mendacious, fake, filled with what she didn't say. She had arranged to take Sam down a fortnight after the rave in the forest. That would have been difficult enough – to present that simple man to her father – but it'd be even harder pregnant and alone. She would soon. She'd have to. Brixton wasn't a bad place to bring up a child, though. Someone was shot at the end of the road three or four years back; such things happened: a drugs killing, turf wars. Her father used to telephone whenever Brixton was in the news to make sure she was all right but after a couple of years she'd placated him; or maybe it was more a case of such incidents going unreported. The casualties were criminals and the police suspected that publicity only fanned the flames. A line or two in the *South London Press* the meagre obituary for a junior yardie. Wider coverage when the Atlantic pub was finally raided, and closed down. A couple of times Rebecca had been frightened: once a gang of boys demanded money from her bag; but they lacked conviction and she'd pushed through. A man had once stalked her all the way home from the tube. By the time she locked the door behind her Rebecca's heart was pounding in her chest from the effort of not running. But that was all and she knew statistics showed men were far more likely to attack other men than women.

'It's nice . . . here,' Ben said. She could decipher his speech now. The grunting, mooing utterances made amazing sense. They just came slower than other people's.

'Is it better than where you come from?'

'I'm not saying . . . Crapton was rough . . . but the pit bulls . . . went round in . . . pairs.' Ben's laughter,

Rebecca had to admit, still sounded pretty wild.

No, it wouldn't be a bad place to grow up, Brixton, it was only a shame they'd not be able to. Rebecca had started to let the mortgage payments slip in May, made none since July. Her building society had enquired whether there was a problem, then began to send letters of decreasing politeness, increasing menace. Not that Rebecca blamed them; she didn't, after all, reply. If it had been the other way round she might have been belligerent herself; if everyone behaved the way she was doing the entire property system would collapse. Now there was an idea.

The fact was, Rebecca felt bad and kept burying it. She knew she should have told Davey and Juice. They were still paying her their rent, after all, and she was converting it to cash, figured she'd need a nest egg, however small, for when whatever happened. What was going to happen was, Rebecca estimated, that the building society would foreclose, tell her she had to leave, and a number of unreplied letters later bailiffs would evict her – and Davey and Juice too, she accepted, without wishing to dwell on it.

When that process reached its expropriating conclusion – which was already overdue by Rebecca's estimation; almost six months without payment showed remarkable patience on the building society's part, unless of course there was a long queue of repossessions ahead of her; or there were just not enough bailiffs to go round – then, Rebecca assumed, she would go back down to Devon. Back home to Daddy. Kind of pathetic, she granted, at the end of her riproaring twenties. And not to plan, not even to warn him, just to await the crisis and know he'd hold his arms open. While as for the flat, she valued it more than ever, scrubbed it scrupulously clean, hid wires, covered plugs, in preparation; made a nest. There was no doubt, though, that she'd have to run: she had made one call to the building society, back in June after, infatuated with her lover, she'd simply failed to earn the monthly amount required.

'I'm afraid you didn't negotiate a partial payment scheme,' the broker's voice informed her.

'That's all I've got, I'm afraid,' Rebecca had cheerfully admitted then, in love, immune.

'If you'd like to come in and discuss it, we can make an appointment.'

'No, that's OK. I'll try and make it up next month. Don't worry.'

'That's not the way it works, Ms Menotti, as you'll see if you check your contract.'

'Well, stuff the contract.'

'You may find, Miss Menotti, by failing to make even a single payment in full you'll be dangerously close to ceding ownership of the property to us.'

'Look, mister, if you want it that badly you can have the flat.'

'I'm afraid it's not that simple, Miss Menotti.' Rebecca rather knew it wouldn't be. She could hear the broker's nasal glee slipping down the phone line. 'With the size of your mortgage and the price of property there.'

'Go away,' she'd dismissed him all those months ago, and replaced the receiver gently in its cradle.

22

CHRISTMAS

Like Rebecca Menotti, Jack Knighton too had property problems: he was also – along with his guest – being threatened with eviction. Like the filling in a thick, mayonnaise-rich butty, he was being squeezed out of his house. On the one hand the building society, on the other a solicitor's letter delivered from a firm representing his estranged wife, who was suing him for divorce on the grounds of mental cruelty and demanding a settlement in respect of half of what they jointly owned, plus all the unacknowledged work she had put into their life together as unpaid housewife, secretary, accountant, skivvy, plus a portion of Jack's estimated salary over the forthcoming years in gradually decreasing percentages. Although, now that he and the plaintiff were no longer living together, it seemed reasonable to suppose that he might work more hours than before: hence the generous starting figure.

The letter continued chock-full of jargon, increasingly opaque but seeming to intimate that if Jack paid off the outstanding mortgage and credit instalments then their client might accept the house and possessions and leave it at that.

'We'll both be homeless,' Solo told him.

'I'll have to live in my cab.'

'Couldn't you kit out one of those containers? Live in a yard some place and if you want a change of scene just hitch it to your rig and cruise.'

'Whenever I've passed them travellers parked up in some lay-by,' Jack mused, 'I always thought, "You poor buggers, I've got a home to go to with all mod cons. I couldn't live like that."'

Solo had been lying low these weeks past, calculating the possibilities, engineering schemes, hatching plans for the future, without getting anywhere at all; repeatedly postponing that future. Anxiety soured his stomach. He tried to figure it through: Robbie had made a terrible mistake, that was obvious enough; he'd never got hold of anything but children's cartoons in those video cassettes. Yet he'd been brutally punished, in the riot. The Boss in London knew all about the Liverpool E's (he knew who Robbie was; and Solo's name) so they *had* gone missing. Unless some other little guy had set Robbie up and made off with the swag. In which case it should have come onto the market by now and Solo might be out of danger.

Solo assured himself the heat would soon be off, pretending he was anything but paralysed with fear. Jack went to work some days on short distance assignments, twice overnight to France (from where he mailed Solo's postcard to Brixton). Solo submitted himself to the hectoring tone of Jack's wide-screen TV, hopped between all the channels Robbie had dreamed of being able not to watch. He never turned it off, let it often play to an empty room.

'It'll work out, mate,' Jack said. 'Somehow.'

'Sure, Jack.'

'Do you believe in God?' Jack asked apropos of nothing obvious.

'No. Yes. I believe in the mother of God; I believe in her son. Brainwashed as I was,' Solo smiled, and then, seeing Jack's frown: 'Catholic upbringing. It sticks. Why? You?'

Jack seemed hypnotized by the question. 'Maybe', he said eventually, 'God was a child. A child made the world.'

'That makes a kind of sense.'

'God made the world in six days and on the seventh day he said, "Oh, what the hell, I'll finish it some other time."'

Solo smiled. 'You never had children?' he asked Jack.

'Miranda said I'd make a useless father.'

'Why?'

'I'm too much of a kid myself, she said. Besides, we couldn't afford it.'

'Did you not fancy it yourself?'

'Me? I'd love to have a nipper like yours. You're a lucky man, Solo.'

Every evening Solo circled the telephone with his guts turned to liquid; each day the pregnant woman he'd spent an awkward hour with became imbued with qualities Solo ascribed to her. He came close to dialling the number on the flyer he put by the phone in the sitting-room – HAVE YOU SEEN THIS MAN? – but couldn't push the buttons. Solo dwindled in captivity (as the MISSING man had), his self-confidence leaching away, the idea that his son was better off without a rumdum dad like him clarifying itself daily.

Jack was more assertive. The solicitor's Solihull letterhead gave credence to his assumption as to where Miranda had gone: he called his mother-in-law, who refused to admit she even knew where Miranda was, and under her breath she called him a monster her long-suffering daughter was better off without. With no alternative Jack engaged a solicitor of his own, a suave Scotsman with the gift of simultaneous interpretation, able to translate Miranda's solicitor's missives into the English language and Jack's replies or counterclaims back into legal jargon. To Jack's surprise, the process was dispiriting but painless, really, the jargon a barrier that barricaded the heart. Although it didn't appear likely he'd be able to keep the house, there'd be no other debts once it had been sold.

Jack didn't need to discuss his legal dealings at home with Solo, his lodger and his friend, or indeed very much else. Their first night of drunken confessions had flowed to a glut of woozy recollection and boozy disclosure, of mutual mawkish amazement at the hands that life had dealt them: through it each unburdened himself to the other. They woke to find themselves survivors after all, who'd forged in a single evening the unremarkable, binding love of men. Each knew as well as you could know anything in this world that he could trust the other with his life; it was the knot that Solo had tied with Robbie, and that Jack had never known existed outside wartime in the buddy movies he and Solo watched with TV dinners on Ikea trays. Or Jack fetched some French beer from the garage, in tiny two-swig bottles, empties accumulating on the glass coffee table, when a game was on Sky. Solo spoke to the players as if he knew them, 'Nice ball, mate; good save.' Or admonished them like hopeless cousins, 'You are flaming useless, son,' shaking his head, 'you're a joke.' While Jack watched silent, spellbound, enclosed. Until at a moment of drama – a bad foul, missed open goal – he erupted, startling Solo on the white sofa beside him.

As far as Penny Witton could see, there was a fundamental difference between orthodox and
complementary medicine, neither of which she had
ever paid much attention to before: if doctors had the
nous to diagnose a tumour early enough then a surgeon
had a reasonable chance of cutting and scooping it out;
of radio- or chemotherapy killing off any cancerous
cells remaining. Once the disease was widespread,
however – as with her – surgeons were like snipers
against an advancing army. Holistic practitioners, on
the other hand, may be charlatans or misguided fools,
yet if they did effect a cure it could sweep through
the matrix of flesh, a virus in reverse. It was out in the
realms of magic that miracle cures were found.

Penny had lived her life as correctly as she could;
kept her sense of humour keener than most. It was less
a mistrust of medicine than pride, she acknowledged,
which delayed the diagnosis that might have given
hope of successful surgery (had God let her down or
she him? she wondered). She used to regard faith
healers, rebirthers, hypnotherapists, gaining popularity with the credulous and weak, as criminals.

It was certainly humbling how quickly your mind
could be changed for you. A brain tumour seemed
sufficient; all it took was a death sentence, and Miss
Penelope Witton was driving all round the country
looking for a cure, throwing her scepticism out of the
car window on the way. After withdrawing from
the experimental laboratory in Oxford she resolved to
try anything that didn't involve the use of animals, and
once she'd gone to a gestalt psychotherapist a friend of
Mavis recommended, a whole world opened up:
Penny visited a psychic engineer and a past life healer;
attempted electro-crystal therapy and zero balancing;

had her ayurvedic horoscope read, her Arthurian tarot; tried cranio-sacral therapy, neuro-linguistic programming, travelling ever further into the wilder realms of healing even as she grew weaker, on a whistle-stop tour in search of salvation. She swapped stories with other women who'd been rolfing or re-programmed their DNA with Ascended Masters. She visited a shaman with a native American name and a regional English accent in the front room of a suburban semi. It seemed to Penny in her enfeebled state that while she herself only continued a remorseless decline, straitlaced England had been transformed behind her back, had become a nation of healers, of crackpots and cranks reaching out to each other. While she was abandoning her own fairy tales: the virgin birth, the resurrection, and other legends of her own powerless faith.

After Martha had massaged her feet in a Buxton hotel Penny handed over her wretched body for reflexology, reiki, shiatsu, kinesiology; to soothing witches, witch-doctors, voluptuous enemies of science. Who soothed but couldn't cure her. She imbibed healing herbs, ancient remedies rediscovered. If she could just stay active and discover the hidden wizard who could save her, or alive long enough for science to come up with the cure. The one thing she wanted to avoid was hospitalization: she had to put that off as long as possible. For one thing, once they got you in there you were prone to come out in a box; for another, Penny had served as a hospital visitor for years. Had looked in on parish widows in geriatric wards, slumped in stupefied rows in front of a ubiquitous television, confused by the brash present it threw at them; on distressed old bachelors alone with the masturbatory tremor of Parkinson's. She'd sat beside them, offering

anodyne gossip from the church, till turgid awkward-
ness, always, impelled her to leave. Only the heart
wards offered relief: as Guru Loop had told her group,
the heart is connected to fire. To joy — its lack or
abundance. And it was true, heart wards were often
full of humour, of old men flirting with the nurses,
cracking grim jokes from one bed to another, decrepit,
incorrigible comedians. Who'd dry up periodically
into deeply depressed silence.

Anything but incarceration. Penny drove herself on
around the country until, in November, she accepted
that, afflicted by migraines and double-vision, she
couldn't trust herself to drive. She took taxis and trains
but found herself struggling for breath along the platform, confused over directions, stumbling with
addresses; caught out by pain that slid a sudden
stealthy knife in through her ear or her navel,
surgically probing for malignant growth then twisting.
Penny squirmed, fumbled for pills and swallowed
them dry, retching. Prayed they'd take effect before she
cried out, fell, threw up.

There was no reason why Martha Polkinghorne
should, but without being asked she less offered her
services than simply assumed the role of chauffeur.
She dropped Penny off, picked her up again at an
appointed hour, checked her in to hotels. Despite the
intimacy of a van interior, however, the companion-
ableness of winter afternoons on the road, Martha gave
little away. Penny tried to make herself comfortable
and then initiated conversation, but enquiries were
answered tersely. 'I'm freelance,' Martha said about her
work. 'Travel a lot.' Where? 'Here and there. Different
places. All over.' And she had a way of closing her
lips when she'd given the brief statement that was all
she intended to, with finality; stoppering sentences.

No, she'd got no family. Gone. Lost contact. Dead.

As they glided in her anonymous van Martha put on tapes to deter talk, dreadful music of the kind that plays in shops, soothing muzak, easy listening; Ambient Music of the Rain Forest; awful drivel, it was like driving down the road in a lift, Penny thought. Then, the noise endurable only by ignoring it, when a side of the tape was over Martha broke her hostile silence to say, 'That's beautiful, isn't it, Penny? I listen to a lot of music driving.'

Martha helped Penny from the van; lifted, almost carried her, more like a nurse. And the truth was Penny was losing interest in conversation; cared little of Martha's life. Till all she really wanted was something stronger for the pain.

Davey finally figured out he had to drag the Christmas tree in backwards, so that it could hug itself through the doorway, and scattering needles across varnished wood he heaved it up the four flights of stairs to the loft room.

'Well,' he said modestly, 'it's a special occasion, innit?' and Rebecca assumed that since it was the first such gesture she could ever remember him making, it must be for the boy. Ben helped her and Juice to buy decorations and to hang them. Baubles, self-balancing candles, fairy lights, foil-wrapped chocolates. Rebecca made a stable out of a cardboard box, and Ben peopled the nativity scene with figures Rebecca found in Woolworths. Animals were easy – a hippo stood in the byre, a giraffe kept watch like a periscope through a hole in the roof, and the lion did lie down with the lamb in Brixton – humans less so: three Spice Girls took the place of Wise Men, while Wallace and Gromit seemed to have consummated their relationship to the

481

extent of providing a Virgin birth together. Rebecca justified this with the story her belly dance teacher had told her, of a subsect of Allaoui Muslims who believe that the Messiah will be born to a man, since woman is unworthy of such a high honour; the men in this sect practise the Oriental dancing of birthing ritual in preparation for the time when one of them will give birth to their Deliverer. The offspring in this case, however, was less divine: in Ben O'Brien's Brixton stable, Bart Simpson lay serenely in the crib, his shock of straw-coloured hair blending in.

Standing back to admire their arrangement, Rebecca felt Ben's small hand slip unconsciously into hers. She looked down but he was staring at the stable.

Juice stretched from the precarious platform of Rebecca's rickety stepladder to pin streamers from the high ceiling.

'You've got to make an effort,' she shrugged, breathlessly, when she staggered upstairs with a heavyweight turkey minus organs, Byzantine entrails removed.

'We've got all the trimmings,' Juice said, gesturing over her shoulder at the slow thump, thump, of Davey labouring up the stairs one at a time, lugging Tesco carrier bags so full that the plastic stretched over consumable shapes looked fetishistic, his smoker's heartbeat complaining wildly.

Rebecca customarily spent Christmas in Devon, but since the building society seemed kindly to be allowing her to stay on, and each extra day made the flat more precious to her, she had postponed seeing her father. His first Christmas without her; he'd taken the news well. Juice said she'd be here for the festive season – no family jamboree in Sussex, no Swiss skiing this year – and Davey would be around for sure: he'd escaped his family through a journey east to west of the capital, north to south of the river, the switch of allegiance West Ham to Chelsea a symbolic change of heart. He usually spent Christmas alone in the flat, apart from a few friends who came in and got pinned on a cosy yuletide bender. This year, however, they'd all be together for once, with the addition of Ben and a bump inside Rebecca who was due to emerge no more than a week later; and she'd tell them it was all almost over; she really would.

The story, she typed in the diary on her laptop, *is surely moving towards its conclusion. Is it pregnancy or the act of writing itself, and staring at the screen, that is giving me a kind of mild delirium? I imagine the story is being eaten up behind me by a virus, is fading from the computer like ink from a page. The virus works its way forward methodically, from the beginning. A computer universe, contracting. A microchip amnesia.*

The answerphone on Phil Scritt's personal line, whose ex-directory number few people knew, gave the instant message, 'I'm afraid I'm not free,' followed by a pause, after which: 'but then again, who is?' accompanied by a self-congratulatory chuckle cut mercifully short by the pips.

Martha didn't give a message – it was her custom to leave no trace – but she knew Phil was in the habit of screening calls: and that they were thus in their mercenary relationship locked in stand-off positions, Martha in some hotel booth or roadside call box enduring that dumb message, Phil at home hovering by the phone, waiting to see whether whoever was bugging him now was worth talking to. Eventually Martha hung up for the umpteenth infuriating time, gathered up her pen, paper, coins, was walking back to the van

483

from the old-fashioned Dr Who box at the side of a quiet road in Cheshire when the phone spookily rang behind her. She trotted back and grabbed the receiver, put on a terrible yow-yow accent.

'I'm afraid I'm too important to come to the phone right now.'

'Is that Martha?' enquired the familiar voice. 'It's Phil here.'

'Of course it's you, you prat.'

'I felt like speaking to someone. I dialled 1471,' said a Brummie voice pleased with itself. 'Then I dialled 3. Reconnected automatic.'

'You're a technological genius,' Martha agreed.

'I didn't get where I am today by not understanding office equipment.'

'Will you shut up, Phil? I've got a problem. I need your help. What are you doing for Christmas?'

'Be with the kids. My turn this year. Got my folks round. The brother and his lot too.'

'Damn that.'

'Why?'

'I don't want to spend Christmas with just me and this woman I've promised to.'

'Here, Martha, I didn't take you for a gusset nuzzler. What woman?'

'An old biddy, Phil. I've become her nurse, taking her all over the place, and she's dying on me.'

'I don't get it, Martha. Drop her. Abandon her somewhere.'

'I can't.'

'So what's the old girl need? A chauffeur? That's easy enough. Has she got money?'

'She needs a bit more than just driving around.'

'I get the picture, Martha. Leave it to me.'

* * *

484

There were certain people to whom Christmas came early. Entertainers whose TV Specials were recorded in October. The Queen making her speech weeks in advance. Nurses taking time off in lieu because on the day itself they'll be tending the sick in jollified wards. And VIPs posing for official photographs, like Roderick Pastille, who had the brainwave of gathering his family around him one Thursday in November in their brightly lit, festively decorated Highgate house for an exhaustive day-long shoot for an 'At Home' feature in *Hi!* magazine, to appear in the Christmas edition. It was a piece spread over several glossy pages of plastic smiles, unimaginative furniture and family unity. A skilled stylist remade Heather in a parade of only slightly unbecoming outfits, the photographer moved her and Roderick around the house and photographed them with identical expressions, and the same waxwork complexion, in every room, so that it looked as if they'd remained in one place while a backdrop was changed behind them. Between the adults sat three children who, being the offspring of a famous parent, drew the viewer's attention to that feature – nose, eyes, sensual lips – that recalled their politician father, thus making them look like poorly fashioned dolls. In front of them sat two dogs with unfeasibly long, lolling tongues, owing to the heat of the lights, who looked drugged or possibly stuffed, stultified as they were by the tedium of photography.

Having in this way fulfilled his Yuletide familial obligations, Roderick joined Russell on Christmas Eve for a week-long gambling binge in the Mayfair den: a fantastic card school with poker, bridge, brag. Lashings of whisky, cocaine, cigars; not to mention boys, girls and their partying friends. Festivities indeed: gone the yule days of metropolitan loneliness, sad orphans of the city shuddering in isolated bedsits a million miles from nearest and dearest, if such existed anywhere. No, now they came out and caroused in the best booze-ups, chill-outs, raves and parties of the London year, for people stripped bare of all other allegiance beyond their Bacchanalian revels.

Juice cut the turkey on the sideboard while Davey heated carrots and sprouts in the microwave and brought them to the counter.

'Legs or breast, Ben?' Juice offered. She loaded roast potatoes, bacon, chipolata sausages on the plate.

'Chestnut or sage stuffing, sir?' Rebecca asked. She dolloped bread sauce, poured gravy. Davey opened red Rioja, aqua libra, mineral water. Ben helped light candles. 'Kaakuuh,' he demanded, and they crossed hands: Christmas crackers snapped apart with a bang, spilling folded paper hats, toys worth less than the minuscule space they took up in the world, and rolled-up jokes.

'What d'you call a murderer who leaves cornflakes and Weetabix at the scene of the crime?' Davey read.

The girls played dumb.

'A cereal killer,' Davey revealed. Ben groaned.

'What's round and bad-tempered?' asked Juice. 'A vicious circle.'

Rebecca placed a red paper crown on Ben's white head, a yellow one on her own. They read out their jokes, discarded their toys.

'I'd like to propose a toast,' Rebecca said, raising her wine glass. 'To our guest here. And to Juice and Davey for doing all this, and for being such great flatmates.'

'Yeah, to flatmates everywhere,' Davey responded.

'And you for buying this place, landlady,' said Juice.

'It was you who quote took on the responsibility unquote.'

Rebecca took a sip of oaky wine. 'And I have an announcement to make,' she said.

'So do I,' said Juice.

'Me too,' added Davey, none of them hearing each other too clearly. Ben's eyes darted; perhaps he harboured the hope that announcements came in the form of jokes.

'I'm afraid you, we, all of us are going to have to leave this flat,' Rebecca began.

'No, no,' said Davey. '*I've* got to leave. That's my announcement.'

'Hang on,' said Juice. 'How do you know? I haven't told you yet. I was waiting till today.'

'I hate to have to break the news like this,' Rebecca regretted.

'I'm telling you now, 'cos it's Christmas,' said Juice.

'It's not that I want to leave,' Davey admitted. 'Thing is I've been given a hint. The word, know what I mean? A nod's as good as a wink to a blind horse, as my old man used to say.'

'The simple fact is, the building society's foreclosed on the mortgage. I'm being evicted,' Rebecca revealed.

'Pop's bought me a pied-à-terre in Putney,' said Juice. 'On condition I don't bring him.' She turned to Davey. 'That is: you.'

'It's too hot for me south of the river, owing to the shenanigans of our friend from the north, so . . .' Davey dried up, then flowed again: 'Me? Me? You think? I want?' He shook his head as if a dog had hold of the scruff of it. 'Yeah, but you don't get it, I'm moving up to Harlesden. Off of the Boss's turf.'

'Wait a minute,' said Juice. 'Rebecca, what? You're

487

chucking us out? You're letting your best friends be thrown on the street? Just like that?'

'How long have you known this, you two?' Rebecca demanded.

'Well, actually, you know, you'll want to just be with the baby now,' Juice told her.

'Hey, girl,' said Davey, 'I'm talking to you. I always knew something like this was going to happen. Daddy's trust fund bears fruit and it's bye-bye boyfriend, take a hike your bit of rough from the East End. How do you like that, Ben? Take note, kid. Look and listen, and learn a lot about women here.'

Ben gawked at Davey, Juice, Rebecca.

'Just a moment,' Juice rejoined. 'I thought you just said you were going to leave me.'

'Yeah, for your own good, girl,' Davey responded indignantly. 'For your own ungrateful, undeserving protection.'

In Jack's house, Solo followed the host to the kitchen. 'You ladies stay right there. We'll clear this away.'

'Got the brandy ready?' Jack asked.

'I'm not sure this is such a good idea,' Solo told him.

'Got the matches ready, mate?'

'Jack, the old girl's eaten less than a fly in Lent, the bird's a health freak, you can tell by her skin, you're on your diets and I can't eat currants.'

'There's no currants in this.'

'Or raisins or sultanas.'

'Bring the brandy butter, Solo.'

'Fruit. Christmas pud. I can't eat it. Never could.'

'Let's just make the fireworks display, eh? It's Christmas.'

In the lounge Penny Witton sat uncomfortably hemmed in to an upright chair with pillows behind beneath her and either side against the arm rests. Haggard, bent, she looked as if were the pillows to be taken away she'd flop in all directions, spineless and de-muscled, palsied as Ben ever was.

Opposite her, Martha steeled herself to accept a small portion of whatever muck Little and Large served up next and eat a mouthful. She could manage that, and it would be polite. She'd give a lot to be alone right now in a hotel room with a book or remote control. Loneliness could eat away at you, could hollow you right out; but at least you didn't have to put up with other people.

Uh-oh. 'Here they come, Penny.' Of course this ordeal would be worth it to get Penny off her hands. Poor jaundiced woman. Flesh loose over her bones.

The filmy alcohol flame danced purple-blue on the pudding. Martha forced a smile onto her face: she could feel the lines it etched in her skin.

'Another beer, anyone?' Solo asked, though he was the only one drinking it. Martha watched him open a can at arm's length: a man used to upsetting himself. Sure enough froth spumed out, bubbles flew, the smell of beer gagged the room. At the same moment Jack spooned into the Christmas pudding, and the rich, soused aromas of once dried fruit long marinaded in liquor met that of beer in the centrally-heated double-glazed air-conditioned room. Penny threw up like a baby: her body didn't make a fuss about it; a gloopy milky mess just rose from her stomach and out of her mouth and down her front.

As, some minutes later, Martha helped her back from the bathroom, Penny, her apologetic face turned aside, registered the leaflet by the telephone. Once she was on the sofa, breathless, she uttered, 'I know that man.' Martha ignored her, helped Jack clear dishes and accompanied him to the kitchen, where she discussed the terms of his employment as Miss Witton's chauffeur.

'You can see you'll need to do more than just drive.'

'I did a First Aid course. St John's Ambulance.'

'I'm squeamish, I don't mind admitting. Not about blood, or pain, but the intimacy of it. It's revolting.'

'No, love, it's natural. Doesn't bother me. But without wishing to upset you: it won't be a long contract, will it?'

'I know that man,' Penelope repeated, and Solo joined her on the sofa with the flyer.

'This man?'

'I've seen him.'

'You sure?'

'At The Laboratory. I've never told anyone about it. What I saw. Because I wasn't sure, I thought it might have been a dream. But the man I saw was this one. I'm certain.'

'Tell me about it,' Solo asked, and she did: Penny described the laboratory where she'd been a guinea pig, spoke of her hallucinatory levitation, and of the man trapped up on the top floor.

'But this place is real?' Solo asked.

'Oh, yes,' she affirmed. 'It's real.'

Later, Martha and Solo took a stroll through the estate to let Jack and Penny see how they got on. It was a damp, mild afternoon.

'You want to leave her here now, today?' Solo asked. Martha nodded. 'Where are you headed next?' he asked.

Martha shrugged. 'South,' she said.

'Yeah?' Solo asked. 'Can you do me a favour? You see, someone's looking after my son, and I might be able to do something for them. I won't tell you what it is, it's sort of dangerous. The thing is, I could do with a lookout.'

'A lookout?'

'Maybe. Maybe not. I could tell this someone to meet us there. It's possible she could be the lookout.'

Martha stopped walking and scrutinized Solo fiercely. Her look induced in Solo an instinctive lurch of fear. The look of someone you didn't mess with.

'Oh, no, don't worry, it won't be dangerous for you; for the lookout; the driver. Just for me.'

'You want me to drive you south?'

'To Oxford. We just need to make one phone call.'

'You're going to break in somewhere?'

'Sort of.'

'You're going to steal something?'

'Not exactly.'

'And you want me to stand outside like a lemon?'

'In a nutshell.'

'Are you kidding me?'

'What?'

'Has Phil been yapping?' she muttered to herself. And then to Solo, 'Do you know anything about me?'

'No.'

'Listen, friend: I don't mind helping out if it'll get you lot off my back. But let's get one thing clear. You can be the bloody lookout.'

Squiffy, drowsy with food and alcohol, Rebecca, Davey and Juice slumped amidst the desolate excess of the Christmas table, paper hats skew-whiff on their heads. Ben dropped off on the sofa. Rebecca sat immobile, hands on either side of her enormous belly, food stuffed into her restricted stomach, convinced she was going to burst.

As Davey raised a cigarette he paused and held it there, studied it a moment, from different angles, as if it could be different from the thousands he'd smoked before. 'I don't know why,' he admitted, 'the Boss won't let it go. He's got this idea that Ben's dad was taking the piss. That he was a bag boy for a northern mob. One of the lads was good enough to warn me, reckons the Boss may snap. Keeps muttering about me, like I was responsible.' Davey scowled at this injustice with the conviction of an innocent man. 'It'll just be best to get off his patch, and let the whole thing blow over.'

'That's the story,' said Rebecca.

'Is how it goes.'

'So we're going our separate ways,' said Juice. 'What about Ben here, Becca?'

'He's coming with me.'

The doorbell rang and reverberated through each of their insides as if it were the dead of night. Davey's brown skin paled.

'Maybe it's Fuyuki,' said Juice brightly. 'I'll go,' and she clumped down the stairs.

Davey swallowed an Adam's apple of fear. 'Fuyuki's in Tokyo.' Rebecca nodded.

Juice opened the front door to two large white men in sheeny double-breasted suits, one with short gelled hair, the other with a neat ponytail. The latter handed her an envelope. 'Magistrate's eviction order to tenant,' he said. 'We're the bailiffs. Time to go.'

He took a step towards Juice, assuming with his bulk to usher her in before him; to lead him into the flat.

'Wait a minute,' she quavered. 'It's addressed to Rebecca Menotti. I'm not her.'

'I don't care if you're Baby Spice's big sister, darlin'.'

'You can't come in if I'm not Rebecca,' Juice shrilled.

'Don't make this difficult, girl. I've got a turkey to get back to.' The man laid a hand on Juice's shoulder: its limp weight alone was frightening; if he'd wanted to he could have palmed her aside as lightly as a curtain. Juice had never felt less solid. She relinquished all thoughts of resistance, let her shoulder be turned, led the way upstairs.

The man with the ponytail gazed around the loft room. He had the constricted bulk of a weightlifter. Ben woke up. The man explained to Rebecca and Davey: 'We'll make it simple for you. You've got an hour to pack what you need and be out of here while we're changing the locks. You can come back with a van and pick up the rest of your junk the day after tomorra.'

'But that doesn't give us—' Rebecca began.

'No buts, darlin'. You heard the rules. Fifty-nine minutes left.'

'That's hardly in the Christmas spirit, is it now, chaps?' queried a quiet, treacly voice behind them. Everyone turned. 'Signs of unwelcome, Scroogeish behaviour,' said the Boss, coming up the stairs.

The two bailiffs looked at each other and back at the slender figure as he reached the floor. 'Do you live here?' asked the one who hadn't done any talking yet.

'What that to do with you, I'm wondering, coming down here in a Brixton, asking about my living circumstances?'

''Cos if you don't live here, mate,' the ponytail told him, 'you can mind your own sodding business and clear off.'

'Well, there a proposal worth considering,' the Boss said. 'Guess what, gentlemen. I reject it already.'

'Now listen, son,' said the man with short hair, slighter, older than the other. 'We've got a job to do here, so why don't you just toddle off?'

The Boss took a step forward. 'What's your business?' he asked.

'Our business is none of your . . .' The older man's voice trailed away as he picked up at the periphery of his vision, reflected in the window halfway up the last flight of stairs, two figures skulking on the landing below. Each, he discerned, at least as large as his partner. They hovered far enough away not to cramp the Boss's style; to allow him to do whatever he wished to do alone. Close enough to ensure his safety.

'What my colleague's saying, coon,' the ponytail took up obliviously, 'is if you don't walk down those stairs on your own two feet—'

'No, John,' his partner interjected, 'I wasn't saying that.'

'Yes, you was, you was gonna say we'd be glad to help this tosser over the banisters.'

The shorter man's eyes darted between window reflection, the Boss and his colleague. 'No, John, I wasn't suggesting that.'

'What?'

'He say, John,' said the Boss, 'that he weren't suggesting that at all.'

'You shut your fucking mouth, nigger.' The ponytail approached the Boss and his colleague together, coming close as he could before he'd have to make a decision, fork towards one of them. With a look of irate puzzlement he said, 'Listen, mate, don't contradict me when we're working together. I got you this fucking job.'

Rebecca, Davey, Juice and Ben watched enthralled, aghast.

The shorter man ignored his furious colleague, addressed the Boss: 'We're just here to do a job, see, serve this eviction order, get rid of these people, lock

494

this place up and leave. Why do you want to get involved?'

'Angary,' said the Boss.

'I'm fucking angry now, you nig-nog ponce,' said the ponytail. His colleague stepped forward to block his way as Lloyd and Chief began lazily to ascend the last flight of stairs. The ponytail had time to shake his mate's restraining hands off before he saw them, and stopped dead.

'Angary', explained the Boss, 'is the right of a belligerent to use or destroy neutral property when pushed to necessity. You two is a pair of office boys who should have been kept in the office. Especially on a Christmas Day.' Lloyd and Chief had by now loped up the stairs, and flanked the Boss. 'I believe, myself, in the cautioning system. So I give you boys a yellow card; I give you one warning. If I come across you again make sure you not there, because you don't want me to see red. Understand? Capisce?'

The two bailiffs nodded wanly. 'Lloyd will see you out. Lloyd, see these chaps out, please. Oh, and give them a tip.'

Lloyd took a roll of bills out of his pocket, snuck the rubber band over his wrist, and peeled off two twenty-pound notes, which he handed over, then made way for the men to proceed down the stairs before him.

The Boss came across to the kitchen counter and pulled himself up a high chair. 'Ladies, gentlemen, forgive the intrusion,' he said. 'Kick a Mary out the stable, indeed,' he tutted. He leaned forward to Rebecca. 'My name is Cornelius, but people call me Boss,' he said, proffering a gold-braceleted, gold-ringed hand. 'Even my mother,' he added mock-apologetically. 'A shame it necessary to disturb this family Christmas,' he said.

'But something wrong, you see. Which have to be put right. That's all.'

Rebecca couldn't take her eyes off this man. She didn't think she'd ever seen anyone so preternaturally self-assured in all her life.

Jack brought tea to his guests. 'It's settled,' he said. 'Penny's seen the guest suite, and you're happy with it, aren't you, for now? We can move to your place in Bradford in the new year. Solo can vouch for how comfortable my cab is. I'll ferry you wherever you want to go.'

'Jack, mate,' Solo said. 'I'll be off. Martha's offered to give me a lift.'

'Where are you headed, son? You planning to fetch Ben?'

'I hope so. We're going to a laboratory that Penny told me about.'

'You're hoping to rescue that man?' Penny asked.

'Man? What man?' Martha demanded.

'It's the man in that picture, Jack, I hope. You know, Rebecca's lost friend.'

'Come on, then,' Martha said, shaking her head. 'Let's get moving.'

'Wait,' said Penny. 'Stop. I have a favour to ask. If you're going to The Laboratory. That we all go.'

'All of us?' Martha asked.

'Please,' Penny said. 'Let's free the animals.'

Floating (4)

Martha and Jack helped me out of the bath and once more we negotiated the awkward stairs. I felt like a dead weight, tired limbs around a great lump, but Jack was still a lot heavier than me, and Martha was the strongest woman I ever met. The living-room was warm. Jack rubbed olive oil on my back, soothing relief into muscle.

I was exhausted, but I couldn't rest because whatever position I attempted between contractions, standing or sitting, squatting or kneeling or lying down, pain spread from my back through my body.

So I walked, round and round the living-room of the cottage. Naked, sweating and oblivious. Grabbing and leaning against Jack with every contraction.

Then at some point the contractions changed: no longer heartless waves pounding me, they seemed to focus, began squeezing down, more powerful than before. Yet, in some way that didn't make sense, less painful.

'They're pushing,' I gasped, grabbing hold of Jack on one side and Martha coming over to hold me on the other.

'That's good, you push,' Jack encouraged me.

'She doesn't need to push,' Martha said. 'Contractions are the body pushing on its own.'

By now I was half standing, half squatting. Jack supported me from behind. Out of utter empty weariness, from some place I hadn't known existed inside me, a new strength surged through my body, and I yelled out with delight, and power, and terror. And carried on yelling into the darkness around us.

'Don't squeal like a pig,' Martha told me.

'There's no need to talk to her like that,' Jack rebuked her.

'But she's right,' I gasped.

'Moo like a cow if you want,' Martha advised. It was the first time I'd heard her laugh. 'Whatever note that comes out, bring your voice down from there. Don't let it go up, or the power that's in your voice will rise and be lost in the ceiling.'

I felt myself disintegrating, my self disappearing. Being or about to be discarded. I was a husk ripped apart by the force of birth to let another new being come through me. I screamed with every push at the force that was killing me; at the people useless beside me; at the unborn murdering baby.

'Does it sting?' Martha asked. 'That means the baby's crowning.'

'One last push,' Jack encouraged me.

'Shut up!' I yelled at him. 'Don't say that. You don't know.'

Sweat poured from me. I gasped for sips of water.

'Slowly, slowly,' Martha said. 'You're doing fine.' What crap; I wasn't doing anything, except surviving, so far, by the skin of my teeth. And was it panic in Martha's voice?

'Maybe there's a lip in the cervix.'

'What?'

'You're doing great,' said Jack.

'What did she say?'

'I said you're doing fine.'

I could feel the baby's head; its round solid mass, cramming against my pelvis. The baby came down with each contraction then slid back up between them. Descended. Returned into the uterus. Tossed to and fro by muscular force. I could feel the child, too ridiculously big to come out of me. My only, desperate, ambition had been to survive, but suddenly I felt a sadness; couldn't bear to contemplate the trauma the baby must be suffering. As it was rammed against me, retreated, rammed again.

23

FREE THE ANIMALS

Nineteen across, eight letters: *down under study of English fruit growing?* Too easy. *Pomology.*

Last one, eleven letters: *Sounds like coach makes a mistake with this old firearm.* Obvious. *Blunderbuss.*

Francis Montagu completed the last of his crosswords, swapped biro for torch and stepped out of the receptionist's glazed cubicle in the darkened foyer of the Department of Organology like a museum exhibit come mysteriously to life. Monty didn't mind working through Christmas, was relieved to be able to make his periodic security patrols in peace, without having to check the credentials of the increasing numbers of young academics beavering through the night nowadays, each anxious that a dozen others were qualified to take their jobs.

'It'd be sad to be on the dole,' Monty said to himself in the security lift. He inserted his metal card in the clock on the top floor and headed towards the far end of the long corridor. A light glowed through glass partitions from one of the rooms away to his left, and he veered off down a minor passage towards it. Monty knocked on the door, which rattled, and opened it.

'Everything OK-K-K in here?' he asked.

'Fine, Monty,' Joe Snow, hunched over a workbench, said without turning round.

'I must be insane,' Martha decided. 'I need my head examined,' she said aloud. She drove her van down the M40 at a steady seventy, dipped headlights of the lorry behind fixed in her wing mirrors.

'Where are you from?' Solo asked.

'I always work alone. Rule number one.'

'There's no need to speak to me. Our exit's Junction 9.'

'How did I get into this? It's your fault. Confusing that poor woman.'

'I didn't do anything. She saw the picture.'

'Junction 9 coming up. Where next?'

'We're meeting them at the services by a roundabout under the A34. Just north of Oxford, Jack said.'

'Did Guru have any idea what he was letting me in for? I wouldn't be surprised if he foresaw the whole thing. Planned it, probably.'

'Look, I'm sorry if you've got into something you don't want to.'

Martha drove with an intent concentration on the depopulated motorway.

'It probably is my fault,' Solo admitted. 'I get most things wrong. You're right.'

Martha leaned across, selected a tape from the glove compartment in front of Solo's lap, inserted it – clack – and *Theme From Harry's Game* mellifluated from tinny speakers.

With Penny safely asleep in the bunk back above his head, Jack in his cab behind them clicked a tape in too – a nice transition in this fragment of road movie, a sound cut from her music to his tape inserted, an aural before the picture cut. *Soundtracks of the Sixties*: it seemed to Jack, however, as if he were hearing Elmer Bernstein's theme from *The Magnificent Seven* for the first time because it was no longer the accompaniment to fantasy; no, Jack experienced the surging fear and confidence of a member of the chorus stepping into a starring role – albeit an ambiguous one. On the one hand he and his companions constituted the first two-thirds of a convoy setting out on a do or die mission into occupied territory, to rescue an innocent from enemy hands, in the spirit of John Wayne, or coming down from the hills, out of maize plantations, to join Brando as Zapata, or indeed recruiting other righteous mercenaries – he, bald, the natural for Yul Brynner's role – to protect a poor Cotswold village (Jack couldn't resist upping the volume, risk waking Penny; the majestic chords swirled around the cab, swelled his body). On the other hand he was simply ferrying this sick old woman in what he (and she and the others) knew was a first and last glorious gesture, to free the animals from this laboratory. To which end Jack had borrowed an appropriate trailer from a corner of Phil Scritt's yard. So he was Ryan O'Neal as the Driver and Morgan Freeman as the Chauffeur too.

Hurtling north up the M40 from London to meet them, meanwhile, came Davey and Rebecca.

'Tell me again,' Rebecca demanded. 'Solo said he knows where Sam is?'

'He thinks he does. He's with someone who says she saw Sam.'

'They'll take us to him.'

'We're going to look for him, Solo said.'

'You think he's been searching for him? I'd given Sam up, Davey. I really had. I'd come to terms with never seeing him again.'

'Don't get your hopes up now, girl.'

'It's the time of year for miracles, isn't it?'

'But how are we going to tell Solo', Davey asked, 'that we ain't got the kid?'

For back in the capital Ben O'Brien was the Boss's house guest, baby sat by Evangelina, the singing maid of operatic stature, and half a dozen of the United squad who amused themselves by stopwatch-timed piggybacking him across the AstroTurf and tossing him increasing distances to each other, this strange, neither-quite-white-nor-black child, giggling, terrified.

Roderick Pastille, meanwhile, was playing his favourite game in Russell Crowe's apartment, with a dozen companions: Russell dealt to each player a card, two of which were knaves. The holder of the Jack of Clubs announced him or herself, and was blindfolded, and hands tied behind their back. They were then snogged by the holder of the Jack of Hearts, for the duration of an old-fashioned egg-timer's fall, and had to guess the identity of their amorous assailant.

'The lips have it,' Rod pronounced, as he shuffled the cards.

On the top floor of The Lab, Joe Snow patiently shaved wafer-thin slices of a human brain, filed the slides in ordered packs. Like a painfully slow sous-chef he reduced this jellyish cauliflower to nouvelle cuisine portions, as if for some exquisite epicurean cannibal. What delicacy nature's jewel, the human brain, Joe thought. The very yolk of a man, cracked from his skull. And each mind a galaxy all of its own inside its cranium.

The human brain was a universe that had taken eternity to reach this point, a universe it fell to a chosen few to explore. With an eternity ahead in which to do so. As far as he was concerned, Joe was the humble technician at his bench, dismantling God's work: this brain in whose axons, dendrites, synapses, Sam Caine once resided.

Rebecca waddled into the Pear Tree Services with Davey. Arcade games fizzled and burbled at them, through the foyer and into the virtually deserted cafeteria. Solo, as she approached him – surrounded only by an odd entourage: a fierce looking blonde with a split eyebrow; a bald, shell-suited fat man supporting a frail old woman – was equally crestfallen.

'Where's Ben?' he demanded.

'Where's Sam?' Rebecca asked.

Jack was already at her side. 'Sit down, love,' he tendered, ushering Rebecca to a chair he slid out from the table so she could manoeuvre her belly in.

'Let's all sit down,' Davey suggested. 'We've got some talking to do.'

'You're right,' Solo agreed. He introduced Martha and Penny, then wasted no more time. 'Sam isn't here,' he said. 'We hope he's just down the road. We've got to collect him,' he explained.

Jack contributed little. Seated a few silent feet from Rebecca, with her brown cross-eyes, her crooked nose, her wild hair. He understood at once that he'd never seen anyone he found as beautiful as this hugely pregnant woman. Jack tried, shyly, not to look at her. But it was too difficult to do. And then, when he gave in, he couldn't stop.

A word came into Jack's mind. Luminosity: the intrinsic brightness of a star.

Monty, the night porter, descended to the basement.

There was no-one studying there tonight, and its south side was the one area of the department he did like people to be around, for it spooked him, this underground zoo. Upstairs he enjoyed being alone, but down here he wished he wasn't the only security on duty. Performing the opposite of scrutiny Monty kept his eyes on the floor of the corridor, aimed for the clock at the far end and back to the lift with a scurrying shuffle. But even so the passage was a gauntlet of tormented sounds and glimpses through frosted glass of infernal beasts he wanted not to think about. Joe had once flippantly suggested that Mr Bone might have designed the building as an analogue of an advanced mind. In which case here in the basement lurked the primitive brain: where fear of death and urge to kill mingled and persisted. Monty didn't trust the doors, locks, bars that restrained the animals down here. He imagined a circus of mammalian freaks of hidden intelligence and concealed ferocity, slavering for the opportunity to break free and wreak revenge on humankind. Starting with an innocent night porter.

Martha pulled cotton-polyester-elastane leggings up over her calves, knees, thighs, crotch, bottom; slithered top down over head, shoulders, breasts, torso. Second skin of a thief in the night. Toolbelt around her waist, then pumps, balaclava, gloves. She climbed out of the van.

'You wait by those bushes,' she told Solo and Davey. 'Give me that photo. I'll open a door for you. Be patient.'

Jack had parked his rig in Mansfield Road. 'I just worked in the shop, mind,' Penny, buoyed up by the adventure, told Rebecca. 'Out at the sanctuary they have all sorts brought. They're open three hundred and sixty-five days a year, never refused a single animal in thirty years. Rabbits, ponies, sheep. Goats, oh, the rank tang of them, you know, as if their species has been affronted. Thousands of cats; dogs, all sorts.'

A rap on the misted-up window startled them from Penny's recollections: it was Davey, who relayed progress. 'She's going in.'

Solo crouched amongst the shrubs between football pitch fence and the Department of Organology, and watched Martha survey the building. The concrete cube sat in the corner of the playing fields, round the outside of which ran South Parks Road. Martha was grateful for a window left open on the third floor of this side of the building. She prowled silent, furious. Every aspect of this escapade seemed designed to maximize risk. Given time how differently she'd have done this: wandered along the road in daylight, a tourist in the city; looking askance at this rude anomaly, this building from a brutal future thrust into the medieval university at the end of the twentieth century – although of course it had appeared futuristic only for a brief period, was already coming to look precisely of its time, ageing all the more rapidly for the flourish of its modernity, like those details of science fiction films – haircuts, music – that date them fatally. Or she'd have jogged around the perimeter of the pitches, an unfit academic pausing often for breath in the shadow of these walls she had now to master blindly.

Walls, fortunately, with more striation close up than had appeared in the residual city light from a distance. Between slabs of pre-cast concrete were fillets, bands, into which Martha could squeeze toes and fingers. She stood and assessed the ascent to the open window up above, would have to rely upon assumptions of uniformity in the concrete; could rest on window ledges on the first and second floors. At least the night was mild. The worst thing was to have to stretch tight, cold muscle.

To Solo watching her it looked as if Martha was absorbed in meditation upon her imminent endeavour, a ritual of preparation – calming herself; visualizing her body some seconds hence – or else rapt in wonder at some stark beauty of the prospect above her. Even from many yards away he could hear the sound of her deep yogic breathing. At one point he thought she'd gone, had slipped away, and he scanned the area; but then when he looked back there she still was. And then abruptly the spell was broken: as if bumped from behind Martha moved forward, in a few steps gained the ledge of a ground floor window. She climbed without haste, felt for a ridge above or tested a toehold then eased herself up, emitting to Solo's observing eye a sense of power appropriately issued. He watched her call gravity's bluff, as climbers do, until she attained the sill of the open window and was swallowed by the huge building like Jonah in the whale's mouth.

'Irma Vep in is she?' Davey's voice whispered as he kneeled beside Solo.

'Yeah. Now we wait.'

Martha placed her hands on a wooden work surface below the window in a small laboratory, brought her feet down behind her, inched on all fours with her bum in the air through a debris of phials, boxes, papers, then leaning her weight forward through her arms to her palms – fingers splayed over the edge of the bench – she sprang her feet up, and her body arced through the air, gathering momentum but then flexing so that she landed softly on the floor.

Martha's plan was to find the missing man herself

and take him outside; let those chumps shiver in the bushes like a pair of voyeurs. This burglar worked alone, the last thing she needed was a couple of clumsy assistants. She'd never stolen a human being before, it was true, but the principles of theft surely remained the same. And so she prowled through the old Musical Studies section on the third floor of the Department of Organology, where soft strains of the muzak she liked were piped into the deserted corridors, the partitioned offices, for its soothing effect, presumably, on the animals within. If so, though, then incongruous too because why indulge creatures that were being otherwise tortured?

Looking for a lost man Martha went from room to room, from one experiment to the next. From blind kittens, their conjunctivae and eyelids sewn together, to cats with wires protruding from their eyes connected to measuring devices screwed into their skulls, strapped tight bodies rotated and tilted in gyroscopic machines.

Security as such seemed lax here but Martha had to be careful to avoid her slinking presence being captured by tape recorders, video cameras, machines monitoring animals' heartbeat, pulse, metabolic rate: with the use of computer technology experiments could be continued without human presence, twenty-four hours a day. Perhaps too such clinical technique was a means of removing the notorious variable of the observer from the equation of testing procedure. An intruder, Martha presumed, might influence results even more than a scientific observer (not to mention incriminating herself, her passage through the laboratories traceable in a trail of audio-visual clues) except that the animals she witnessed could hardly be expected to register more than the trauma to which they were already subject. Beagles with stomach ulcers, Labradors with balloons made from condoms pushed into their guts through metal tubes and filled with liquids.

Carrying on through Plant Sciences, Anthropology, Human Behaviour, departmental names kept on even while The Lab had spread its intent through the building, Martha by her witness revived those titles: she was a wandering spirit through extraordinary landscapes of human behaviour. In the centre of one room was a large ants' nest: night and day were simulated through the use of lights, and Martha watched as ants were beckoned into an artificial morning and a variety of instruments producing gas, liquid, noise, distressed them, while cameras recorded the particularities of their panic. In another, three badgers were forced to swim through a tank filled with crude oil and water, and furiously licked off the oil coating their fur. She watched from outside the door on which was pinned a sign reading, *Renal Failure: The Effect of Oil Ingestion on Kidneys.*

In the lorry cab Rebecca bit her nails, Jack waited with the dumb patience of a stargazing daydreamer used to traffic jams and Channel crossings, and Penny worried away at the memory of what she'd seen those months ago: maybe there'd been no animals at all; she'd never seen the man before in either reality or imagination, the sight of that leaflet by Jack's telephone had produced an instantaneous yet retroactive delusion. Why had she dragged these people here? Were there no limits to a sick woman's humiliation?

Hiding in the bushes, meanwhile, Davey had withstood the temptation to light a cigarette, had fought the narcotic urge for nicotine, the need to calm his anxiety.

As time elapsed, however, apprehension gave way to boredom, and that overcame him. Solo took one too and their cigarette ends when they inhaled glowed like a big cat's eyes in the dark.

'They reckon we can be observed from up there,' Solo whispered, pointing vertically. 'Even at night, what with infrared: they could be watching us right now. CCTV cameras in space, man. And once we've got identity cards, with electronic chips, they'll be able to track our every movement. Inside or outside, same thing.'

'You're paranoid, mate,' Davey told him.

'EU fraud watchdogs use satellites to check on farmers who've claimed subsidies for olive groves. So you know what the growers are doing now? Planting plastic trees.'

'Give over.'

'Jack there's something of an amateur astronomer, he's one of the last of them. 'Cos instead of looking up at the stars, people are sticking, like, mirrors up there to look down at us. You think I'm paranoid?'

'Listen: we were really worried about our mate John, right? He thought people were out to get him. Caning it every weekend he was and if you tried to say anything he'd jump down your throat. The more he took the worse it got, he was convinced they were following him, talking about him.'

'Who?'

'Just *them*. Too many pills. You know how it is. It was sad to see.' Davey broke off, took a drag on the remains of his cigarette, stubbed it out in the soil.

'So what happened? How is he now?'

'Oh, he was busted a few weeks back. Bill from the Hill had had him under surveillance for months.'

'He were earning?'

510

'Had to pay for it, didn't he? Funny thing is, when the bizzies paid their visit all he had was a few trips in the fridge. Pure chance.'

'Lucky bloke.'

'Not really. They planted charlie, speed, dollars, the lot. He's looking down a long dark tunnel, John is.'

'Bastards.'

'They had the right man. Wrong day. It wasn't their fault. You can't really blame them. Hey, we ought to whisper.'

'You're right.'

'Paranoia's just a form of clairvoyance: what you fear will come to pass, that's what I reckon. If you fear being watched from space, madly enough Solo, then someone will start to observe you for sure. So, yes, I think you're paranoid.'

Maybe Solo wasn't the only sentient being in the vicinity suffering some kind of persecution complex, either. It was quite possible the blindfolded monkeys whom Martha now watched were too. They were shot in sequence by a radio controlled firing squad, each in the digitally precise same spot above the eye, and filmed to see how long each took to die. Or those she observed helplessly being observed by video cameras as they stumbled and blundered around a room of randomly shifting obstacles, blind, their visual cortices having been removed.

Martha may or may not have been invisible. But the effect upon this observer was odd, rare: she found herself defenceless, reduced, a child again; a girl from her father's farm aghast at such cruelty. The way he treated his animals, his embrace of them and of the world, of life itself – of her – she had long since forgotten in the amnesia she'd opted for, and now images of him came flooding back, along with sensations of her buried childhood self long before he ever touched her.

The autumn morning Paul burst into the kitchen at breakfast blurting: 'Bess is in the dyke.' They all knew where he meant. Panicked from the table, dashed across the yard grabbing ropes, and she swears her father never even slowed down when he reached the irrigation trench: there ahead of them he jumped and disappeared. A faint splash. By the time Martha got there he'd already looped a rope around Bess's neck – the terror in her eyes – and was hauling himself out. 'Hold it, all of 'e,' he ordered curtly. 'Keep her head up.' While he ran, clumsy and blubbing with the weight of muddy water in his clothes, for a tractor, with which they eventually towed her undignifiedly out; delivered her from slippery death.

Or the cold spring night he let her, alone, stay up with him in the barn as one ewe after another lay down in labour. The buttery light, their whispered voices, the smell of soiled straw and wool and her father's bloody sweat-stained clothing; ewes' back legs slowly buckling as if their groins were paralysed, lying on their sides, a lamb emerging sheathed in yellow membrane. 'Come on, little feller,' her father welcoming a new arrival to existence. 'There you goes.' And the first time he had her help one, her own tiny hand compared to his reaching into the ewe's swollen vagina, stretching cervix, finding the lamb's head, easing it out. Deliverance.

She had forgotten the man she was supposed to be searching for, the job at hand. Martha walked the first steps on her own via dolorosa through a doom painting sprung to life, a bestiary made flesh, an animated Bosch cartoon. Martha was transfixed by cages of rats bouncing, jumping up and down they were, licking their feet frantically, till she twigged that the floors of their cages were being heated up, cooled down; by a room of ferrets (Charles had a pet one, tawny like these, it was only the sharp musk emanating from him told her he'd smuggled it indoors again; he'd wink at his younger sister as it purred under his shirt). This score of ferrets were being simultaneously fed and drugged by intravenous tubes, so that they vomited periodically, their sick collecting in a trough below the raised cages, and sluiced away.

Martha stopped, leaned her head, her hands, against the glass door because she had to, her knees were slack, her chest was porous, spongy. That such things were done floored her. About to sink, a sound, a voice, snapped her to her senses. She spun round, adrenalin surging, alert. Time stopped for her. Along the corridor a young man in yellowish overalls, leaning on the long handle of a wide dry-mop broom. A cleaner.

'Not yet,' the young man said. He stood beside the lift, lazy, unhurried. Shaven-headed, clear-eyed. They looked at each other, twenty yards apart.

'What?'

He gazed at her. Then he leaned the mop against the wall. 'Not yet,' he said, turned and walked into the lift.

It took Martha a few seconds to compute that she had to catch him. By the time she'd dashed to the lift the indicator above signalled it was ascending. Martha pushed through swing doors and leapt onto the stairs, pumped up the zig-zag flights, burst through to an identical corridor above. The man was there, three-quarters of the way along the corridor, strolling nonchalantly away. He paused and turned, pointed to the side, then resumed his slow pace away.

Martha sprinted. She'd reached the spot where the man had turned when he disappeared through the swing doors up ahead. As she approached them she saw there was no lift here, and when she passed through the doors found only ascending stairs. Towards a door, with an emergency exit bar across it that Martha shoved down to release, giving on to the roof: a flat grey rectangle on which there appeared to be no sign of the cleaner. Martha patrolled the space, avoiding old puddles of dirty water, breathing with relief the moist night air. There seemed no place he could have descended to from the edge of the roof – other than the ground six floors below, and she could make out no spreadeagled body. She decided to relinquish pursuit of the man and forget him, and was soon back in the corridor below. She paused and saw what the cleaner had presumably been pointing out to her: in a small glass-partitioned room a man at a bench worked methodically, repetitively, at some machine, shaving slivers of something, collecting them on glass slides. A clock on the wall above him showed three o'clock in the morning. Martha entered.

'All right, Monty?' Joe murmured.

'I'm not Monty,' Martha said. Joe turned slowly from the bench. The dazed eyes of a man lost in detail came slowly alive.

'Do you just work in this one cubicle, or do you know what goes on elsewhere?' Martha demanded. Joe made no reply, only gaped at her. 'I asked a question and I need an answer,' she said, taking a step towards him.

Joe Snow swallowed. 'Industrial espionage,' he quailed. 'Mr Bone warned me about it.'

Martha reached into a pocket of her belt. Joe flinched backwards. 'I only work here,' he assured her.

She pulled the flyer out, unfolded and showed it to Joe. 'Where is he?'

Joe glanced at the flyer. 'I never heard of Sam

Caine,' he said quickly. 'We don't use subjects' names.'

'Look at it,' Martha ordered.

Joe's eyes flicked between the photo and his interrogator. Then he seemed to come to a decision and blundered forward from his stool. Whether or not he was attacking Martha or simply trying to get past her and escape, she wasn't taking any chances. Grasping his forward, right arm with her left hand, and putting her right arm round his neck, she pivoted and at the same time crouched into him. Then, pulling both her arms, and using what was left of Joe's own momentum, Martha fetched him over her lower back. Dropping onto her right knee, she brought him down on his back, to complete what she considered to be a perfect crossbuttock throw.

Joe, whose unbalanced body always lagged somewhat behind his brain, felt the entire Department of Organology spin an incredible cartwheel around him, ending with him stuck upside down to the floor, gravity having done one complete turnabout too. It was only as he gradually got his winded breath back that he began to understand what had happened. An assessment quickened by the stranger standing over him.

'We didn't do anything wrong,' he pleaded.

'Get up,' Martha said impatiently, extending an arm and helping pull Joe to his feet. 'Where is he?' she demanded.

Joe tried to think. 'Everywhere,' he shrugged.

'What do you mean?'

'Different places. How can I explain? In areas . . . like here!' Joe said, startled by what had occurred to him. He turned on his stool, gestured to the residual lump of tissue in the autoclave. 'There.'

'What is it?' Martha enquired.

Joe Snow looked at her peevishly, as if disappointed

that he should be intimidated by someone so stupid. 'His brain, of course.'

Offering no further resistance, Joe accompanied Martha to a door by which Solo and Davey were granted admittance to the building, so that they too could witness the fragmentary identification of their quarry that the white-coated man promised. He led them to and through the basement, showing off the sights along the way. Past a hundred rats sewn into pairs, fifty sets of fake Siamese twins. Past half a dozen Guernsey calves with different organs – liver, kidneys, lungs – damaged systematically to see how this affected their response to various drugs. Past the brains of animals kept alive outside, though still attached to, their bodies. Past the heads of monkeys transplanted onto the cancer-ridden bodies of other creatures. 'Your man's kidney is in there, I believe,' Joe indicated.

He took them into a large chamber in which three drums rotated like tumble-driers: inside a baboon, an orangutan, a chimpanzee. They fell from side to side. The chimpanzee's hands were taped together so that it couldn't break its own bi-circular fall. Blood and broken teeth. 'Baboon's got your man's liver, if I remember right,' Joe explained with furrowed brow. 'Orangutans,' he said. 'Lovely apes. You know they make love on average for three times longer than a human couple?' He shook his head admiringly.

Davey was the first of the three to say something. 'What is going on here?' he asked.

'Why, this', Joe declared brightly, 'is the centre of the whole organology department. Through there's where all the drugs research goes on, and here's where we subject the organs to stress. Our biotech work is really just beginning—'

'Wait, wait. Hold on.' Solo shook his head. 'Take it slow, mate.'

And so Joe strolled, explained to Solo O'Brien the nature of this enterprise at whose heart they were; taking on his mentor's mantle, he forgot they were intruders, spoke as if to prospective investors, visiting academics from other disciplines.

'Science is the new art, of course – the brothers are Medicis, if you will, Mr Bone our Botticelli – but what of religion? I mean, what is it all about?' Joe turned with a rhetorical flourish.

'I don't know. What all?' Solo wondered.

'Religion. Medicine. Art. What is it everyone fears?' Joe asked, echoing Mr Bone in his ear. 'We fear obliteration. Annihilation. In a word: death. It makes us nauseous. We crave above everything to beat it. At the end of the day, we'd give up all fame and wealth for an extra hour, a minute of life. Immortality: here, we're pursuing that elusive dream. Systematically extending lifespan through organ transplant, genetic manipulation, chemical enhancement. With, to be frank,' Joe winked, leaning closer to Solo, his breath smelling of pear drops, 'the help of plastic surgery, because our clients don't tend to be wealthy enough to make donations to The Laboratory until they're, shall we say, getting on in years.'

'Keep the brain active?'

'Let the body change around it if need be.'

'Is that what we are?' Solo asked. 'Brains?'

'Mr Bone says so, yes. Otherwise we're just cells. Which degenerate. Did you know that at the tip of each chromosome is a tail of DNA called a telemere? It's a sort of protective sheath, but it shortens as each cell divides. Until eventually it sort of frays, and the chromosome dies. Our geneticists reckon that by extending the length of telemeres, they can trick the body into staying young.'

'That's what you're doing here?'

Joe laughed out loud. 'It's the least interesting part of our work. No. When you're young, you think you'll live for ever, right? You don't believe you're going to die. Then what happens?'

'You realize that actually you are,' Solo said. 'Reality sinks in.'

'That's one way of looking at it,' Joe agreed. 'But what is reality? Whose reality is more valid, the teenager's or the middle-aged man's? Whose is preferable?'

'Sure,' said Solo. 'I see what you're saying.'

'We believe we may have discovered the site in the brain from where our intimation of imminent extinction leaks into consciousness.'

'You've isolated', Solo questioned, 'the fear of death?'

'No, not fear. Fear is not primary. We're talking about people's realization of their mortality. The search has taken us a long time, because it's undeveloped in other mammals.'

Joe Snow, carried away by his advocacy and Solo's curiosity, hadn't noticed that they were now alone.

Solo nodded. 'I guess animals don't have it.'

Joe shrugged. 'Possibly they do, lying dormant. But unlikely. It's the human design flaw, as Mr Bone puts it. A detrimental side effect of evolution. Let me show you something.' Joe led the way down a side corridor and opened a door to a cubicle. 'One of Willem and Magenta's experiments,' he announced. Cages lined one wall. 'These rats', Joe enthusiastically explained, 'have had electrodes implanted in the hypothalamuses, wired into their pleasure centres. In each cage are three levers. If a rat pushes lever number one, food is delivered. Number two: drink. Number three activates the electrodes, which give them an immediate, but transient sensation of pleasure. These hybrid albinos are clever: they work out how to press levers and what they'll get.'

'Albinos?'

'Hooded rats, yes. And they choose to press only the pleasure lever, even though they starve to death.'

'Not too bright.'

'The question is, would humans do the same? That's what Magenta wants to test. She's certain they will.'

'I come from a crack-addled estate,' Solo reflected. 'I saw it. And she's right. She doesn't need to do the experiment. Just tell her to look around.'

'You'll understand, then. Either way you look at it, it all comes down to the brain.'

'What about our identity, though?' Solo wondered. 'Like cloning: does Dolly have the same memories, sentiments, personality, as the sheep she came from?'

Joe stuck his finger in the air. 'Good question,' he said excitedly.

They carried on through dim rooms devoted to interbreeding between various primates, rendering offspring with a monkey's body and a tarsier's eyes, a chimpanzee with the spectral face of a lemur, dozy, drugged, in rows, attached to life-support machines and a battery of monitors. On dissecting tables impossible to distinguish bodies gutted, hollowed out, organless, entrails spilling out.

What better place than Oxford, Joe explained, for such an enterprise as this? Money was all it took to encourage the cross-fertilization of ideas. Take drugs, for example: they had organic chemists on hand on one side and anthropologists at the Pitt-Rivers Museum on the other, receiving contributions towards their field trips in the Amazon, perhaps, in exchange for handing over specimens of ololiuqui and ayahuasca. Not to mention philosophers at All Souls who could justify such practice. Had he heard of the old subterranean railway tunnels of the Bodleian Library? They were now used for a new underground network of academics from many disciplines feeding this furnace of research from which a phoenix would rise.

Davey, meanwhile, had dropped back some time earlier: he'd entered the drugs research department and found himself inside a fantastic pharmacopoeia. Armed with feeble rudiments of school chemistry he read the names, symbols, numbers of samples like a tourist stumbling upon hieroglyphics in an Egyptian tomb; but the descriptions of their effects upon human guinea pigs, like a Miss P. Witton, were more accessible.

'The subject reported a blossoming of flowers like lotuses of many different colours, opening their petals in front of her, accompanied by a sensation of weight-lessness and the conviction that she and her whole body were levitating some yards above the bed. This delusion was compounded by the belief that when she looked down from this position the bed in which she had been lying was quite definitely empty.'

Davey gathered boxes together. Martha, too, had broken off from the others, drawn to a door through which she passed into an unlit vestibule. The door closed lazily behind her, further bedimming the area, and she progressed through another door into a darker chamber whose murky extent she only glimpsed before the second door closed too.

Martha felt her pulse rate slow, mind clarify like settled liquid, sinews loosen. Why did this building exert the influence it did? Of course, she was back once more in her childhood, in the pitch-black chamber, their palaestra, the Polkinghornes' pit; she felt no fear of the darkness, attuned her senses for information, began to move about. She soon became aware of someone else in the room: an abrupt, intermittently discontented breathing. Listening intently, she ascertained there was only this one other; and that it was no human, from the rich sour smell of it. Martha approached it stealthily through the inky darkness, till she could feel through the air its flanks quivering before her: she reached out and touched it gently and firmly so as not to startle it. It seemed unflustered by her. Roaming around it, patting its broad rump and swollen hams, Martha deduced that this was a massive bull. She circled it and found no shackles: it stood of its own accord, untroubled, enjoying her attention; accepting its due, perhaps; a god among cattle, a great bovine idol.

Martha ran her hands over the bull's head, which seemed to be of normal size, and thus out of proportion to the monumental body. She made her way back towards where her sense of direction suggested was the door by which she'd entered, groped around for a light switch, eventually found one and pressed it: in the centre of the bare stable-like oval chamber stood a creamy brown, enormous, musclebound freak of genetically mutated nature. Apart from its head only the shanks and hooves were of normal size, but they were forced to support three, four times, she estimated, the customary weight of obscenely swollen muscle. The animal looked as if it had been blown overfull of air, was a cartoon character, only illusorily three-dimensional; or it had been pumping iron in a bovine gym, not to mention a liberal intake of steroids, till it had worked itself out to a standstill; the power of a bull was not contained in this huge specimen, as she'd sensed, but rather diminished. It reminded Martha oddly of a dwarf despite its size, of too much matter packed into too little skin, too small a frame. A beast of burden whose burden was itself; it could barely move.

She flicked the light switch and returned the bull to the darkness.

Monty sat in his porter's snug absorbed in sage rumination upon the *Oxford Times* crossword, when he became aware of senior technician Joe Snow walking across the vestibule towards him flanked by two fellows he didn't recognize through his pebble specs, probably foreign graduates, and another one behind, a female academic but all covered up: must be working in quarantine conditions.

'There's no need to worry, Monty,' Joe assured him, 'but these people need to tie us up. Don't panic. And they want the keys to the basement outside door.'

'Keys.' Monty peered intently at Joe as if deciphering this information he'd been given.

'Keys to the bathroom,' he said, finally. 'Mixed up shoe securers. Of unknown weight? No, better: means of weighing fish skin? Five letters. Or should it be six?'

'God, I wish I could smoke,' Rebecca regretted. 'Fuck it, I can. Give me one, Davey.' The acridity in her mouth was harshly blissful. Smoking tasted better with tears than anything; coffee, wine, anything. Whatever crying does to the mouth. The nicotine surged through her blood, tingled her fingers, seethed along the umbilical cord to her womb. From her to the other within her. After three, four drags its beauty palled, became

522

unpleasant. She dropped the cigarette to the pavement, stubbed it out.

'Now I know, that's all. It's best to know,' she said.

Solo said nothing. He was uneasy at the way Davey had told Rebecca everything they'd seen, in no way protective of her. It shocked him, made him aware of his outdated northern gallantry.

'I'm sorry, girl,' was Davey's only succour. An arm round a shoulder.

Rebecca broke away, walked off along the dimly lit pavement. This is not the way Sam Caine was supposed to go, she thought. For as well as abandonment, she had envisaged his death, too, in different forms.

She had imagined him in an accident, then expiring in A&E, with a heartbeat flickering to a beep on the screen and nurses' shoes running, doctors' coats flapping, slapping paddles on his chest. Gag to his mouth. Electric shock administered, the indignity of such resuscitation. The exhausted peace when it fails.

She imagined Sam had committed suicide, gone when he chose, he alone. Swimming out to sea, maybe, further, further, until all strength was gone. His tombstone a cairn of clothes on the beach, crashing waves his muffled drum, their whispering on the sand the only exequies he, or she, desired.

She had imagined it, but not here. He should have been read his last rites, a priest beside his bed to pray for him, commend his soul to a merciful saviour. Who might wash it in the blood of that immaculate lamb, which was slain to take away the sins of the world. Sam Caine's sins purged and done away with, that he may be presented pure and without spot before thee.

Rebecca returned to Davey's car. 'Experiments,' she said, slowly, the syllables sounding disordered on her tongue. 'The altar of science. It's funny, I feel little sadness, and I know it's because I'm so pregnant: the hormones make you selfish, to protect this.' She stroked her bloated stomach. 'There are different versions of posterity,' she said.

Jack, meanwhile, had reversed the lorry down to the underground loading bay, and he and Martha led animals in pairs out of The Laboratory, up a ramp into the back of the lorry. Rain began falling. They put each of a dozen couples of animals into a different stall. Two sheep, dogs, cats, rhesus monkeys, rabbits. Species one or other could identify. A pair of donkeys, ferrets, pigs, mice, rats, hamsters. In the truck the animals were becalmed, as if in a vet's waiting room.

'Where to?' Jack wondered. 'We can't just let them loose in the countryside. Penny's animal sanctuary? It's a hell of a way away, and we may just get it into trouble.'

Martha was unable to help, until it dawned on her to scan through the places she'd made mental note of on her walks in the country; her nominal refuges.

'Yes, Jack,' she said, surprising herself. 'I know somewhere,' she told him. 'In Herefordshire. A cottage with outbuildings and a barn. I'll give you directions.'

24

RAIN

Despite an extensive police search, it was not until late in the morning that a postgrad student came by chance across the disappeared security porter, Francis Montagu. Tied up in a corner of one of the dog kennels, wittering away to himself, licked by an eager young beagle left behind. At about the same time Mr Bone discovered Joe Snow up on the top floor strapped into a car seat in which a baboon had recently been travelling – hurtled forwards at regular intervals into thirty miles per hour fake car crashes – with a significant difference being that Joe's skull was met not by an automated hammer but by thin air.

The police could hardly be blamed for failing to immediately detect either these two missing persons or indeed the culprits who made good their getaway – Jack, Penny and Rebecca in the lorry towards a secluded residence in Herefordshire complete with (Martha hoped) vacant stables and kennels; Martha herself in convoy with Solo and Davey, her van and the latter's car stuffed full of heavenly, hellishly enticing substances heading for a greedy world.

The fact was, the police had their hands full that night and so did the rest of the posse they rounded up of RSPCA volunteers, of animal trainers co-opted from Chipperfield's Circus's winter quarters up the road at Chipping Norton, of old bird-minders with their catapults and rat-catchers too brought out of retirement, of police grooms and dog-handlers dragooned from neighbouring forces, rounding up the animals that escaped from the Department of Organology that Boxing Day night.

The police and their deputies rounded up disorientated chimpanzees, pulled furry lizards off walls and commandeered a punt from Cherwell Boathouse to chase an escaped mock turtle, but their success did not extend much beyond that. Half a dozen armed Special Forces officers from Kidlington were mightily pleased with themselves when they surrounded a muscular man posing like a triton in a fountain at the front of the Radcliffe Infirmary, until the night porter there emerged and pointed out that this attendant of Neptune was made of terracotta and had been there a hundred years.

The police were hampered by the weather: it began raining shortly before dawn. Theirs was a mopping-up operation, of radioactive rats who were shunned by their multitudinous natural counterparts and of a luminous owl roosting on the Martyrs' Memorial. In University Parks, sleeping birds exploded from trees as rhesus monkeys who'd forgotten how to climb tried to scrabble up into the branches. Escaped dogs coalesced into a pack of fire-breathing, livid-eyed hounds: they found and followed the scent of the literate fox who overturns dustbins in Jericho in search of food and books. The police persuaded some hunt saboteurs they knew in Cowley to help capture the dogs with their trouble-seeking noses and their hunting horns. As they cornered the last one they heard a yelping overhead and at that moment the first fork of lightning illuminated both a hound hunting high in the stormy air above and their own misbegotten alliance.

It would be possible only gradually to ascertain with any degree of accuracy what or who escaped from the infernal laboratories of Mr Bone, because at the time Ben Ali Al-Shalir, chairman of The Laboratory, honorary vice-head of the Department of Organology, arrived at the scene by helicopter and claimed that those caught accounted for every single escapee, and he thanked their captors effusively. But one could subsequently put together the record of Mr Bone's trial on kidnapping charges; the newspaper articles detailing the HASH FOR HOSPITALITY scandal that ruined Roderick Pastille's political career; the Home Office's explanation of the reasons for its refusal to grant British citizenship to the brothers Al-Shalir; and the minutes of the hebdomadal meeting of Oxford University at which it voted by a reluctant majority to close the Department of Organology and its coffers; not to mention sightings and rumours from around the city.

It would then be possible to discover that a sea hare made it across the river and over the fields to Marston; that chapalu cats still haunt the gardens of Wadham College; that bagwyns – half horse, half goat – grazed on Angel Meadow; a pony with antlers infiltrated Magdalen College Deer Park; while a shaggy-haired wild man like a wodewose – surely a crustie, another captive from Sam's rave – stumbled through the rain to Wytham Wood, from where shrikers have also been heard. A great dog as large as a bullock, with a dark green coat, was hit by a skidding car on Longwall Street, while during that morning's rush hour blind rabbits were squashed on the wet tarmac by post-Christmas commuters driving down Banbury Road.

Later, teenage girls seeing to their ponies on Port Meadow on foggy winter mornings would validate and encourage each other's sightings of a centaur frisking with the herd towards Wolvercote, its handsome face bearded, with piercing blue eyes, a muddy but finely muscled torso merging into the body and hind legs of a horse – like which creature rather than man, they insinuated from behind their hands, he was hung. Similarly, escaped wizard's shackle eels and leeches in the waterworks would come to be blamed by residents of Linacre College for the epidemic of slimy creatures squirming into the orifices of their nightmares.

Such were the shape-shifting creatures of mythology released from The Laboratory. The nightwatchman checking CCTV screens of the cameras hidden in fake Victorian streetlamps around Radcliffe Camera Square would keep secret for weeks his bewilderment at the sight of what looked like a baboon rising onto its back legs and making off with a student's bicycle, pedalling a little uncertainly. While the grotesque bull that Martha had found had stumped clumsily out of the basement on his overloaded shanks like some cheap clay model in a low budget animation: the last to leave was the last to be found, having limped only as far as the undergrowth in which Davey and Solo had earlier skulked, where he stood utterly immobile in the steady rain, blinded by the dim light of day. Four lion tamers from the circus surrounded the bull fearfully, not sure what to do, until Mr Bone appeared and bad-temperedly led him by the nose back to his darkened pen.

Loaded down with the bottled ingredients from the

results of Mr Bone's experiments, Davey and Solo, followed by Martha in her van, drove to London. It was as they left the M40 and joined the shortest motorway in the world down to Shepherd's Bush that lightning threw the capital into relief – Solo knew this time was his last chance, a lifeline he mustn't throw away – and as they crossed Vauxhall Bridge that the heavens opened, a cloudburst hurling needles of rain at the earth, pelting car roofs, stinging the tarmac, tormenting the river on either side. Solo stared out. The Thames frothed and churned.

Jack too neared his destination, trawling through the rain into the west. As the route grew more rural so it became harder to decipher the map and, though he was used to navigating alone, it would have helped this time to have assistance. None was forthcoming. Having released the animals, and set off with two dozen of them in the back of the lorry, Penny had dozed off. She seemed to have lapsed into a mild delirium. Almost asleep, she muttered under her breath. Rebecca soothed her.

'The creatures, that creep and swarm on the earth,' Penny murmured.

'There, there.' Rebecca stroked her arm. 'It's all right.'

'Every living thing I made, I will blot out from the face of the earth, said the Lord.'

What's this? Jack wondered, peering through the turbid windscreen. A T-junction or a crossroads? I should have got that damn wiper fixed.

'I think she's waking up,' said Rebecca. 'How are you feeling, Penny? We're almost there.'

'We are,' Jack agreed.

Penny looked at Rebecca wildly.

'Just relax now, it's OK.'

'Be fruitful and multiply upon the earth.'

'What's she say?' Jack asked, as Penny closed her eyes once more.

'She's gone again.'

Chief Steward opened the door. He rummaged through the cardboard boxes each of them carried, shook plastic canisters of pills, sniffed a vial of purple liquid, appraising Davey suspiciously, heavy-lidded, dead-eyed.

'Sorry, mate,' Davey shrugged. 'I can't tell you nothing, it's for the Boss alone.'

Chief frisked them. As he patted Martha down she realized that the force she was able to exert against normal people would be ineffectual here. They were led through the turnstile and down the stairs, where Chief stood aside to let them go ahead, and he followed them along the winding tunnel.

Jack found the cottage, isolated at the end of a rising track. It was dark and empty. Mildewy smell of winter abandonment; old sheets draped over sofas; a dining-room table with chairs stacked on top. The window Martha had told Jack to enter by opened easily: he found keys on a hook in the porch where she said they'd be, and unlocked the front door. He carried Penny in, light as a young child, and laid her on a sofa until he'd made a bed upstairs. Rebecca found candles, lit a fire in a woodburning stove, connected Calor gas in the kitchen.

Roderick Pastille's country abode amounted to a homestead, a walled enclosure the hill-border farmers who built it had once used to keep animals in, marauders out. With Rebecca and Penny tucked up inside, Jack backed the lorry into the yard behind the cottage. He proceeded to house the twelve pairs of animals they'd brought in sheds, old stables and barn, in which he found some musty bales of hay and straw. He tugged sheep, goats, who gave little resistance, and deposited the smallest hamsters and mice in cages or wooden boxes. It was raining solidly; water ran into his eyes and he could hardly see what he was doing between the lorry and the shelters. It took hours. He filled buckets and troughs with water. Finally, exhausted, soaked through, Jack stumbled back to the house. He peeled off his sodden clothes and draped them over a clothes horse in the kitchen, and towelled himself dry. He climbed to a room between the sleeping women, crawled under scratchy blankets, put his head on a mildewy pillow and sank into deep sleep.

The Boss welcomed Davey and Solo like a double dose of prodigal sons, like homecoming twins, addressing them on the pitch and ushering them into the den while performing a series of handshakes and high-fives of forbidding complexity which Solo, aping Davey, muddled through.

'It real good to see you boys. I'm wondering where you is and then here you are all a sudden. And who this blonde in tow? Got a new moll already, Davey? Sit down, all a you. Make yourselves comfortable. Tea, Lloyd.'

Solo caught sight of Ben's callipered leg in the kitchen. Was he restrained there? Around the den were three or four men lounging; a couple wore pyjamas, and yawned. Martha felt their eyes glow; a woman uncomfortably vulnerable, wished she could be invisible now.

'And what is this you carry?' The Boss affected surprise. 'You bring tribute?'

'Boss,' said Davey, 'I've got a story to tell which you may be more than a little interested in.'

Davey proceeded to explain – with occasional nervous contributions from Solo – what they had encountered at The Lab: animal experiments and human trials, chemicals bottled like genies, descriptions of human guinea pigs' experiences.

The Boss listened without expression, with concentrated stillness, as if he were meditating on teachings Davey recited; except that it seemed that he gave off something which began to remind Davey of Gemma, Rebecca's cat: the Boss was purring.

'We've got twenty more boxes of this stuff, all with chemical formulae attached, ingredients, equations. Forget the Liverpool E's or whatever they were, Boss, this is serious shit.'

When Davey had finished, the Boss remained silent for a while. 'Garth,' he said finally, addressing one of his men, who'd been quietly perusing the paperwork Davey handed over. 'You listen?'

The man nodded. 'I heard about this place,' he said, an incongruous cut-glass accent emerging from a body-builder's frame. 'There've been rumours for a while. It was only just getting started when I was up at Oxford. Undergrads went there who couldn't get in anywhere else. In Clinical Pharmacology we rather looked down on Organology.'

'Another thing,' Davey interrupted. 'There were animals not only cut open and played around with, but consumed. Substances obtained from the bodies of animals, Boss. Delicacies extracted from the Colorado River toad.'

'A hidden tradition,' Garth concurred. 'The salamander of alchemical repute. DMT dream fish in the Pacific. Hallucinatory mullet poisoning.'

532

'A disgusting liquid derived from the liver and bone marrow of giraffes,' Davey added. 'Yes, I had a sip, I admit. Hit the ceiling. It was juicy, Boss, I'm telling you.'

'If this is all true,' Garth said, 'it's tremendously exciting. It's California on our doorstep. The Philosopher's Stone. Wealth beyond your wildest dreams, Boss. Let me take the material back to the yard, and I'll make a full analysis.'

'It's yours, Boss,' Solo told him.

The Boss smiled lizard-like at Solo. 'Some of the lads will accompany you to your vehicles,' he said. 'We don't want no more disappearing act. What your plans?' he asked Davey.

'Me, Boss? I don't have none apart from the usual. A bit of this and that, you know. Duckin' and divin'.'

'Small fries sadden me. You want to come on the payroll?'

'Serious?'

'I been thinking on enlarging the squad, with Europe in mind; these chemicals may be just the ticket.' He got up, put his arm round Davey's shoulder, began walking out of the den towards the door; his men followed, as did Solo and Martha. Solo looked back over his shoulder at what he could see of Ben, that leg, immobile, in the kitchen. He had to say something but his mouth was too dry, his heart too high in his throat.

They herded across the glaring AstroTurf. At the far door the Boss squeezed Davey's shoulder and said, 'You can be our token Anglo-Asian. Lloyd'll sort out your contract, digs, so on.' Relinquishing his grip, the Boss stopped and let the others file past him. Solo, summoning purpose to his vacant limbs, paused beside him.

'Ah, Solo O'Brien,' the Boss pre-empted him with a

sly grin. 'I almost forget. You'll be wanting to take your boy.' Solo followed his gaze to the kitchen where, as if she had supernatural hearing, Evangelina appeared in the doorway. She leaned over and pulled Ben gently to his feet, and removed a blindfold from his eyes and plugs from his ears.

'No need to distress him, I thought,' the Boss explained. 'A special young man. Make sure he taken care of in future, no?'

'Yes,' Solo agreed. Carrying a cat box, Ben made his awkward way over. His father bent to pick him up. Ben shook his head, only handed over the box. Solo took it and walked slowly out behind him.

By the time they got to the street, the United men had almost finished unloading Davey's car and Martha's van beneath vast umbrellas in the deafening rain.

'You take it easy,' Davey yelled to Solo. 'Don't let Gemma out of her box: cats hate travelling. Tell Rebecca I'll put the rest of her stuff in storage. She's got my mobile number.'

'Thanks, mate,' Solo said.

'Yeah. I'll see you.'

Martha drove her van out of London in low gear. The tyres made a swishing sound as they ploughed through the water, as if through an endless ford. The black clouds threw hail-size pellets of rain at the wind-screen: it was like driving through a carwash. Blaring horns sounded, lights and shapes floated perilously by on either side. The three passengers could hear the fourth behind them, Gemma miaowing disconsolately as she patrolled the confines of a taped-shut cardboard box.

Solo hugged Ben tight, absorbing the feel of his son's

body, inhaling the smell of his hair. Ben kept crouched into himself.

'This is no good,' Martha decided. 'We'll stop at one of the Heathrow hotels. I'm knackered, anyway.'

Solo nodded. Ben, wedged between him and the window, had been silent. Now he made a noise for the first time. 'Uh Err Uh.'

'Is he in pain?' Martha asked, startled.

'No,' Solo told her.

'Uh Err Uh?' Ben repeated.

'You sure? What's he say?'

'He said "Rebecca",' Solo told her. 'Yeah, we're gonna see her, mate. We're on our way.'

25

UNDULATION (DANCING PELVIC CIRCLES)

The following day dawned feebly. Rain fell from the sky and kept falling; a self-renewing wall of rain. Martha ploughed her VW van through it, stopping at a supermarket on the outskirts of Monmouth. 'We can buy whatever we want,' she said. 'Enough for all of us for a week. I'm paying.'

Ben perched on the back rim of Solo's supersize trolley like a helmsman, a navigator of the shopping lanes, Martha pushed another, and they sailed up one aisle and down the next.

It was an unreal excursion. One of Solo's fantasies in the dog days was to rescue from death by take-your-pick drowning/ train/rabid animal the offspring of Mr Sainsbury, Mrs Asda. Who'd utter gratefully, Help yourself, friend. Whatever you want, please, it's the least we can do. A reverie in contrast to the reality of a lone parent's bargain-hunting trawl: of making straight for the counter of items REDUCED – crushed, defrozen, seals broken, Best By The Day Before Yesterday. Fork-lift pallets of dented half-price tins. Plain-wrapped own-brand everything. Broken biscuits, mass-produced bread, processed cheese, bruised fruit, powdered coffee like sand; rough Dutch tobacco off the guys outside, straight from a Channel port. Coupons cut from free magazines, money-off vouchers, eagle-eyed for special offers. The penny-pinching, scraping by, making do dreariness of it.

And now a fantasy come true, skewed only slightly. This woman helped rescue *his* son, then cash sponsors a ride around the supermarket funfair: money's no object, each item comes gift-wrapped with rarity. Fruit juice with shreds of orange in it; Colombian coffee he knows will be bitter, feminine, rich, dark, smooth; organic vegetables, Greek yoghurt, parmesan cheese . . .

'We're on a day-trip to the middle class,' Solo told Ben. He felt himself becoming hysterical, almost. Ben joined in, shared his father's glee. 'Stop. Go back. Get that, Dad.' 'What?' Pause. 'I don't know.' Falling on each other. Though the absurd truth was that it all made little difference to Ben. He had eccentric child's tastebuds, was content with Marmite sandwiches, fish fingers and baked beans for a change, the odd glass of milk.

By the time they'd traversed the entire supermarket both trolleys were piled high with bounty.

They stopped again at an animal feeds supplier and loaded Martha's van with sacks of grain, nuts, pellets. The lanes became successively narrower, windier. No Through Road. A lane flourishing a Mohican haircut wound up around a hill.

'If every road was like this,' Solo said, 'you'd save a third of the costs of tarmacking. And the cities would be greener.'

'We're almost there,' said Martha.

'Imagine all the motorways with grass strips down the middle of each lane. No swapping lanes, obviously: you'd have to choose yours at the outset, each one a different speed. Fifty, sixty, seventy. Safe or what?'

Solo whistled at the elevating view of the valley below, through the passenger window. 'Trees,' said Ben, looking above.

The first sign of the cottage was a red placard on a stake at the verge: FOR SALE. 'Perfect,' Martha said.

They arrived to find Jack heaving and breaking up bales of hay, distributing messy armfuls around the stables and sheds. 'Am I glad to see you,' he greeted them; to Ben, 'Seems like a while since I give you a lift in my cab. You remember?' Ben nodded. 'Might have been the last time it rained. It's making up for it now.'

Inside they encountered Rebecca, a huge-bellied slow relentless washerwoman: she'd amassed a tray of cleaning utensils and was brushing, dusting, scouring and wiping every surface. Jack, having been outside an hour, was amazed by the sudden banishment of cobwebs and grime, by the hoovered floors, by the replacement of damp mildewy odours of a holiday home in winter with those of Lemon, Pine, Aqua Fresh. It was clearly a wrench for Rebecca to stop but when she saw Ben she managed it, and squatted to hug him. He lurched into her embrace with perilous alacrity.

'We got you a surprise,' he said. 'In the box.'

On cue a slow, reproachful miaow emerged from the cardboard container. Jack opened it and Rebecca was reunited with Gemma.

'It'll drop in the next day or two, Jack,' Solo confided sagely. 'Syreeta went mad like this before Ben came. Nest building.'

Martha found Penny in a small bedroom at the top of creaking stairs. She was sleeping, her face wasted, drawn, on the white pillow, haggard but peaceful. Unruffled blankets described a sparrow's body. Martha pulled up a chair, waited, watched Penny wake, eyes opening with a frightened look and then expressing recognition.

'You've come back.'

'Looks like I couldn't leave you.'

Penny tried to smile but it reached the surface as a wincing, sickened realization that the pain was no nightmare left behind but here, still, awaiting her in unwelcome consciousness. She groaned.

'Where's your medicine?' Martha asked, but Penny didn't hear. Martha bent towards her. 'Where's your medication, Penny?'

Penny had closed her eyes again, dying to retreat inside the cave of sleep in which her body had briefly sheltered from the pain. Martha rummaged through an opened suitcase on the floor, found the box of alkylating agents and cytotoxic antibiotics, antimetabolites and vinca alkaloids. Analgesics and opiates. She administered a cocktail. The water with which she washed it down dribbled from Penny's lips, off her chin. She was scarcely aware of Martha's presence, or of Jack, who'd slipped in.

'The drugs don't work,' he whispered to Martha. 'Or they work too well.'

The cancer was a rude presumptuous intruder, uninvited yet calling all its host's attention to itself; it was spreading, but to Jack the cancer seemed more as if it were pulling Penny into itself, a black hole inside her, sucking her in to its hollow promise of extinction. 'Shout if you need anything,' he whispered, and left. His footsteps squeaked on the stairs.

Penny grimaced, and groaned to herself. She looked as if she were being told a terrible story she didn't want to hear. If only. She should be in a hospice, Martha understood: needed expert nursing care, more powerful pain relief. What drugs they did have here were running out. Martha noticed that Penny's lips were moving; she was muttering something. Raving to herself again.

'What's that?' Martha asked, and leaned closer.

Penny lay with her eyes closed, with a disgusted expression on her worn face – you promised all that, Lord, and give me this? Her grey eyes opened, too wide. Then they reclosed a little, to a normal aperture. Her grey eyes delved into Martha's.

'Please,' Penny managed. 'Help me die.'

The rain fell and kept falling. Days of rain. Rain is waiting, waiting for the rain to cease, teaching patience – its hypnotic power being its own study aid; slowing the pace of life, the pulse, metabolism, mind. Waiting for the sun, the lament of English film-makers, deckchair attendants, ice-cream sellers; the long moan of English childhood.

Rain is memory, a screen before, a glaze over, the eyes, turning the gaze inward. Rain falling too itself mnemonic, synaesthetic: sight, sound, smell, evocative taste of rain.

Having cleaned the house, Rebecca slumped. Beached on the sofa, reluctant to move. Ben leaned against her; she told him stories of her Italian grandparents, her father, a Devon childhood, and dozed off herself in the middle of them. Then Ben clumped outside with Jack and Solo to feed the animals. Jack hauled the boy over his shoulder, stumbled across the yard through heavy rain to the small barn where feed and hay were stored.

'Now this is what we've got,' Jack explained: 'donkeys, sheep, dogs, cats, rhesus monkeys, rabbits. They all need names. Ferrets, pigs, mice, rats. And hamsters.'

'Why's that monkey with a finger missing shaking and chattering his teeth?' Ben asked.

'Withdrawal, I reckon. She's been addicted to some poison.'

Solo stood back, watched them talk.

'And what's he doing?'

One of the cats was slouching around the extent of its cage and darting periodic, anxious glances off into empty space, as if seeing ghosts. 'I suppose something was done to it, and it's still expecting that thing to be inflicted.'

Jack soaked dried meal; poured grain into a metal bowl. Ben watched the cats crouch to eat, sneakily.

'Have they all got something wrong?' he asked.

'Most of them,' Jack told him. 'Damaged. Flawed in some way.'

'I thought so,' Ben nodded, grave and content. 'Jack. Noah was an albino, you know.'

'Was he? We'll set them free, Ben, the wild ones, as soon as they look like they can survive.'

Solo wandered off, away from the cottage, through the wood. The hillside had deep gashes in which swollen streams flooded towards the river below. The rain let up a little, seemed to back off: was like smoke down in the valley. Solo realized it was still here, too, fresh droplets less falling than materializing on his clothes and hair.

Brown leaves and black soil rendered a mulchy mud

underfoot into which Solo's holey trainers sank with every step. The path, made by rabbits or deer, he assumed, threaded level through the wood, through a carpet of green stalks Solo took to be bluebells; with some coniferous shrubs and rhododendron bushes which gave the feeling that some manor house or castle stood just around the corner. A flock of birds were roosting in the branches of winter trees overhead – fieldfares or redwings he thought, unsure whether forgotten school lesson or TV programme were responsible for the supposition; they emitted soughing waves of sound.

Among the trees, Solo could identify the corrugated barks of oaks and odd sycamores, that had allowed their trunks and branches to be home for bright green moss which made Solo think of wood sprites, dryads. He himself was a creature whose natural habitat was concrete, tarmac, glass, a street urchin, but the dank decaying smells of the wood recalled childhood visits to Wicklow, lone trudges in the woods there, escaping from relatives – an aunt kissed him avariciously, sucking his cheeks; a tough uncle scared him – to hide in the branches. Other than when tree-climbing he'd always been bored there, his grandparents' lives slow and tedious, and ached to return to Manchester; yet now, here, this seemed almost too obviously a better place for Ben, away from pollution and danger. A trick of the mind played by nature.

There were hazel coppices here, thickets of other shrubs, but most impressively, majestically, towering beech trees: spaced courteously, chivalrously apart, leaving clearings untrespassed by other trees but carpeted obligingly by plants and flowers.

The beeches were clearly mature trees, as old as the century perhaps, huge, with smooth, sensuously curving grey trunks and arterial branches. Now – in winter, leafless – their glory evident. Vertical leviathans. Solo studied them as he strolled, pausing before one and then another, enraptured by their forms, enthralled. He'd never looked at any trees like this; his gaze drank in each trunk's singular formation, the liquid folds of wood; followed their branches' patient exploration of the air. Every tree, scrutinized in this way, appeared as one attempting to become the archetype of its species, an exemplar Solo acknowledged, until he moved on to the next.

Solo hadn't looked at trees intently as this before, but he had the sense that he had experienced them this acutely, and it dawned on him that his keen contemplative gaze was like his body as a child climbing. Once a boy wrapping limbs, entwining himself around branches; now a man's rapturous attention. What tremendous power, he marvelled, to propel them upward, against gravity. Or, inversely, perhaps it was a dream that impelled them towards it, inspiring them into the air, into their medium, the dream of becoming a perfect tree. It struck him that their branches and twigs related to the brain, to dendrites and axions – whether literally or symbolically, to textbook drawings – to Ben, indeed. How these trees, some with stunted limbs, torn bark, were yet each a kind of paragon of a beech tree.

The path curved up and out of the wood to open, bleak pasture that tonsured the hill, dotted with stunted hawthorn trees; espaliered by the wind. Solo climbed to the convex summit and strolled around it until he figured from the perspective of the view that the cottage lay below him. By now drenched, he dropped down and through the wood again till he hit the track they'd arrived by, a hundred yards south of the cottage, the FOR SALE sign nearby. Below the lane a pipe jutting straight out of the steep field spurted water, as if the hill was taking a leak, an endless piss in the rain.

Jack kept a fire going in the sitting-room. Rebecca gazed at the flames. Jack put another log on and stared at it in a mildly challenging way.

'I could watch this for ever,' Rebecca said dreamily.

Jack contemplated the flames. 'Driving across Midlothian's odd,' he remarked. 'The landscape's sub-dued by pylons, they're like insects crouched over the earth. All these overhead cables, telegraph poles, I always wonder where all that electricity's coming from and going to.'

'I've never been to Scotland,' Rebecca admitted.

'Now Edinburgh's a funny place,' Jack told her. 'The big fashion there's tracksuits. On a Saturday the crowds out shopping are like a massive training session.'

Rebecca chuckled, Jack continued, 'Their nightclubs open on a Friday at four in the afternoon. So after work at the end of the week people don't go home to get ready to go out, they just run straight to the clubs and get slaughtered right away. You ever heard of that in England?'

Rebecca responded by standing up and undulating her hips in swirling, voluptuous patterns.

'You all right, love?' Jack asked.

'Backache,' Rebecca told him. 'Pelvic circles relieve it.' Jack watched her.

'In our belly dance class,' Rebecca said, 'our teacher taught us these by telling us to imagine we had a pencil in our pussies and were drawing a figure of eight with it.'

Which she clearly continued to do. Jack knew

he blushed, and tried hard not to look at her. Knew that she looked at him, from the sound of her hungry laugh.

Rebecca sat down. 'You're a beautiful dancer,' Jack told her.

'No.' She shook her head, smiling. 'Oh, maybe I could have been not bad. I love it.' Rebecca resumed gazing at the fire. 'You know, I was thinking, just now, how growing up is a journey, through tunnels, towards a beckoning light of maturity. Sophistication. Whenever I got to what I thought was a light the tunnel narrowed, there were bottlenecks, only some people squeezed through. I'd be one of them. So I'd get used to the next, narrower tunnel, it was fine, towards the light again, and another, tighter, bottleneck. It was the progress of an above average child, you know? Primary, secondary school; into sixth form; on to university; graduating to the job world. With years of dreaming of basking in the light behind you. But in the real world . . .'

Rebecca gazed at the fire.

Jack looked at her. Received an intimation of a deep need he didn't have inside himself and couldn't know. Some unfulfilled and unfulfillable desire, a prodigality, a hunger in her very genes. That was perhaps what made her – more than the bloom of her youth and pregnant beauty – so attractive.

'No,' he said. 'You're a wonderful dancer.'

Ben fed the animals. Solo opened tins of dog food, packets of seed. They mixed bran mash in buckets, scattered handfuls of pellets. Ben held carrots on his open palm for the two donkeys: when he saw their rocky brown teeth he feared he'd lose half his arm. He forced himself to keep his nerve, hold his trembling hand steady, as they used their thick lips, comically delicate, to mouth the carrots off him.

Each fresh dose of morphine alleviated Penny's distress only for minutes at a time. She struggled to speak, mostly incoherent, with moments of lucidity. 'I thought you'd escaped me,' she told Martha. Her speech inebriate, slack-mouthed; as Jack and Rebecca had come to decipher Ben's utterances, Martha found Penny increasingly difficult to comprehend. 'Don't', she implored, 'move me.' There was a window at the foot of the bed through which Penny could see the misty valley. 'I want to die here,' she insisted.

'The drugs are nearly gone,' Martha told her.

Penny groaned, but it was impossible to tell whether in response to Martha or to her own discomfort. 'Release me,' she begged, and Martha turned away.

The anaesthetic thawed: pain reappeared as if it too were being administered, injected intravenously and spreading haphazardly, wantonly, through her ravaged viscera, seizing her organs. She was being squeezed from inside and had no resistance left, a rudderless boat tossed about and buffeted by drowning waves of pain, its power holding her under for breathless nauseating periods.

Martha sat beside her, impotent. It was one thing to walk away from someone else's suffering, and deal with that. Now she could only witness it helpless, resentful. This old woman reduced to a tormented scrap of diseased tissue and bone. A pathetic wreck. And the longer it went on so surely her life before receded, Penelope's experience focused all on this hideous period.

There was little Martha could do: moisten Penny's lips, hold her bony, reptilian hand. It'd been so long now since Penny had imbibed more than sips of water that even her incontinence had just about stopped. The remaining fluid in her desiccating body seeped out now and then into the sheet, beneath which Martha slid plastic bin bags.

Rain thrummed and spattered against the window. Martha distracted herself; though she didn't have to try. Memories came to her. She returned to her mother's kitchen on wet winter days when she couldn't go where she'd rather, outside with her father and twin brothers in the cold wet fields. The kitchen warm and moist, condensation on the windows, steam rising from pans on the Aga, aromas scenting the humid air. Her mother, Ruth, a weak stranger who had no time for her daughter nor Martha for her. Never allies in the male household; not enemies either, just uninterested, separate. Martha desired only to escape from her mother's environment, was grateful that Jacob stayed behind. Her mother taught her nothing, Martha realized. Had she anything to teach? An inert, passive woman, seeing out her uneventful life within limited confines. Martha had learned everything from her father.

The rain drummed on the roof, poured into the earth. Penny's face twisted into a grotesque caricature of itself; she moaned weakly. Beyond tears, beyond endurance. Why did her body not give up and let go? Martha took her hand, uttered soothing words, sounds, as if to a baby, that she was sure Penny couldn't hear. What kept her going? It was disgusting. Martha had never seen anyone in such a state, so far from human. She felt bubbling within her an emotion that felt less like pity than anger.

Jack woke at night with a full bladder and, stumbling

through darkness, was flummoxed as to what time it was. In the city, he realized, you can always judge what stage of the night has been reached by sounds: the rhythms of human activity, the levels of background noise, traffic and machinery. He understood, too, that although he had no idea whether it was now eleven thirty p.m. or five thirty a.m., in time one would learn to recognize different rhythms here: more subtle gradations of light, changing smells through the open window augmenting the sounds and absence of sounds of animals.

The earth was sodden and swollen with rain until it could absorb no more. Rain fell, and coursed in streams through the wood, gushed and gurgled over the fields around the cottage. Down in the valley below, the brown river broke its banks and slowed with relief from a desperate torrent to a sliding inexorable surge, the valley basin become a wide Ganges, a Nile, in the Welsh Marches. The lower slopes of the far side of the valley were subsumed by the river: small fields surrounded by hedges and banks became ponds, lakes, or, inversely, square green islands in a muddy brown sea. In the gloom, dusk fell surreptitiously.

Rebecca, slumped on the sofa, felt as if she was running out of air. She had no compulsion to move except to deal with bodily needs, was able to sit for hours at a time staring at nothing. Sam's death, confirmed, was some kind of relief; she knew she would grieve for him, but not yet. Later; for ever. Instead, her mind was vaguely occupied by scrappy thoughts, partial snatches of conversation repeating in her skull without consequence, fuzzy colourless images. She scribbled notes in her exercise book and found her fingers flying across the page: she watched herself write, her mind detached. I'm suffering from *cacoethes scribendi*, she told herself, the irresistible urge to write. I'm Scheherazade in reverse: it's birth, not death, I want to postpone; of course I don't want to finish.

Jack sat on the arm of the sofa. 'This friend of mine's just getting going as a freelance photographer,' she told him. 'Went home to Tokyo for Christmas. She was planning to buy herself a digital camera. An image, flashed through the lens, isn't imprinted on film emulsion, but encoded on disc. Fuyuki said this disc can then be attached to a mobile phone and the information transmitted through the air: a photographic image reconstitutes itself at the other end, ready for immediate publication.'

This Scheherazade isn't telling stories to an emperor holding a death sentence over her, Rebecca thought. Apart from the obvious one: some think of God as a narratophile – a narcissistic one for sure – who needs to be told stories of the world he once created. They say that God was a priapic infant (our universe composed of onanistic seed) and he's now a sterile old man. His reluctant sperm ejaculates into the cold, endless atmosphere, to freeze as dead planets.

'I never heard of that one,' Jack said. 'I don't mean to interfere, but shouldn't you do more exercises, love? Prepare yourself, get ready? I don't know.'

Rebecca smiled breezily. 'Oh, I'll be fine,' she said. 'Don't worry. Everything's OK.'

A voice in her head told her she needed shaking up, but there was nothing she could do to answer it. She seemed capable of two modes of being, an inert depression or bright vacuity, neither helping her face the event coming closer every minute that passed, inevitable, inescapable, too momentous to admit to.

*   *   *

Martha shivered in front of the full-length mirror in the bathroom. She stood quite still, dismay countered by the virtue of so unflinching a gaze. At least her breasts were still firm, she reckoned, setting herself and barely clearing the pencil test. It was strange: time's exaction was not quite as she'd expected. Not so much gravity's pull, more like she'd been pushed in, compacted, from both ends, squidging her strong body towards the middle. She was surely, she thought, an inch or two shorter than at twenty. A stone heavier, anyway.

Downstairs at supper she told the others of an ancestor buried in the graveyard of the parish she'd grown up in. According to the dates, John Polkinghorne had accomplished the feat of living from 1683 to 1527. He presumably owed this paradoxical lifespan to a drunken stonemason, a slip of the chisel, but the posthumous error had earned him something close to immortality.

'The source of great pride,' Martha explained. 'Not just in our family, but the whole village would drag visitors to the church and show it off.'

When she was a child, she said, at that stage when you're intoxicated by the impossible logic of infinity and eternity, she and her friends would try to wrap their brains around the riddle of the dates and be pleasantly defeated.

Ben stared at her with incomprehension, as if at the gravestone itself. Solo said, 'Yeah, like was he really born many years after his own children?'

'Now, I just think the problem was caused by having a gravestone.'

'How do you mean?' Jack asked.

'Memorials should be made of wood,' Martha said. 'And last as long as those alive who can remember.'

*　*　*

Ben walked outside on his own to visit the animals in the sheds. He called in on all of them and spoke to them. One or two he summoned up the courage to stroke, but most appeared to possess forbidding teeth or claws. One of the dogs, however, a young beagle, greeted Ben's arrival with such enthusiasm he felt it would have been churlish not to let him out. Ben sat on the ground and the hound smothered him in licks and playful nips and pushes, knocking the boy off-balance so that Ben kept falling to the ground and having to haul himself back up to the sitting position. A clumsy bouncing toy.

Once the beagle nipped Ben a little too smartly and drew blood. Ben couldn't say it hurt, it felt more like an insult than pain. He crossly shoved the dog back in its kennel. The dog appeared impervious to the cut it had inflicted; rather, grabbed its chance to be insulted, and beseeched Ben to give it more attention. It was difficult to refuse. Ben headed off towards the rabbits.

Martha stayed with Penny virtually all the time. The others visited the room, took turns to relieve Martha, read aloud, whether Penny appeared awake or asleep. Ben sat across in a corner and watched. Each abided a while, till they were repulsed by the woman's agony.

On the evening of the fourth day Jack called Martha downstairs to supper, and she told them, 'I'm about out of Penny's medication. One more dose.'

Solo grimaced. 'It's not doing a lot anyway, is it?'

'She needs more and stronger painkillers.'

'How much worse can it get?'

'A lot.'

'We've got to take her to a hospital, haven't we?' Jack ventured.

'She doesn't want to go,' Martha said. 'She's adamant. At least in her moments of clarity. She does not want to be moved.' Martha bit her lip. 'It'd be wrong to move her. Penny wants to die here.'

Rebecca had been listening to the others as she ate. 'We don't know how long that might take, do we?' she asked. 'It'd be more cruel to let her suffer the pain unadulterated.'

Martha took a deep breath, sighed; her shoulders slumped. 'She wants me to kill her.'

The others were perplexed. As if Martha had just issued a conundrum it might take a while to solve. And while they concentrated their minds, they could barely move or breathe, let alone speak. Ben didn't try to solve it, but watched the adults in their petrified condition, waiting for one to stir. Jack was the first.

'You shouldn't have to do it on your own,' he decided.

'No,' Rebecca agreed. 'We'll all help.'

'Take equal responsibility.'

'Thanks,' Martha said, though her tone suggested it wasn't clear whether they'd said what she wanted to hear or merely complicated matters further.

'Wait a minute,' said Solo. 'I can't.'

'You can't?' Jack asked.

Solo was hunched over his food, as if even though he'd lost his appetite he was ready to defend it from others. 'To end someone's life?' he said. 'It's not a decision for us to make.'

'Don't you think this has to be done, mate, if that's what the woman wants?'

'No, I don't. It's not for us to play God.' The others looked at him. 'I'm sorry.'

'You think we should take her to hospital?' Rebecca asked him.

'I don't know what I think. I'm not being tyrannical about it. I'll accept a majority decision; if you three want to go ahead. I won't grass.'

'That's not the point,' Rebecca rebuked him.

'It's one of the points,' Martha nodded.

The silence returned, but different now: the conundrum had not been solved, exactly, but Solo's resistance clarified what the others needed to do. Rebecca bent awkwardly forward and took one of her shoes off; she unclipped the heel and tugged from it a plastic sealed bag. Inside were two white pills. 'Give her one of these, Martha. And have the other yourself.'

'What are they?'

'MDMA,' Rebecca said. 'Ecstasy. This afternoon I remembered they were here. Months old. I'd forgotten all about them.'

'Are you joking?' Martha asked.

'No. Really. Try it. It'll help.'

Martha frowned. 'I'll think about it.'

'What can I do?' Jack asked her.

'I'll call if I need you,' Martha told him. 'Thanks.' She went upstairs.

'This midwife I knew,' Solo said. 'A Hebden Bridge hippy. She'd taken acid one time, when she got called out for an emergency. She helped the woman give birth while she were tripping. Off her head completely.'

'That could have been awful,' Rebecca frowned.

'Yeah. She said it were fine. Guess she had some Valium to come down with, maybe.'

'Most people I know', Rebecca considered, 'hardly ever take legal drugs, antibiotics, whatever. Avoid them as far as they can, they don't trust the pharmaceutical companies, the overworked doctors, the chainstore chemists. They trust acupuncture, homoeopathy, much more. Plus of course at weekends

553

they guzzle illegal drugs made by criminals, un-researched, entirely uncontrolled. Are we nuts or what?'

'Bonkers,' Solo agreed.

'Mad,' Ben nodded.

'I never took LSD or any of them things,' Jack said. 'What's it like?'

Rebecca groaned.

'Bad as that?' Jack wondered. 'I thought as much.'

'Oh, shit,' Rebecca moaned, squeezing the side of the table.

Martha crushed one tablet to fine powder and when Penny was lucid stirred it into a couple of fingers of warm water. Penny sipped it in painstaking stages, while Martha swallowed hers and waited for them to have an effect.

Rebecca staggered towards the sofa, clutching at the backs of chairs, at Jack's hands, her own stomach.

Solo took Ben upstairs, to the furthest bedroom. 'Why's all this happening to us?' Ben asked, as Solo helped undress him.

'What do you mean, why?'

'Is there a reason?'

'Of course there is, Ben,' Solo told his son emphatically, as he tucked him in.

'What is it?'

Solo shrugged. 'I don't know.'

Not a flicker of a smile passed over Ben's face, only a faint disappointment.

'Not funny, huh?' Solo shook his head. 'You're getting too old for my sense of humour.' Ben's pupils had the glaze, eyes the faint bruise, of a child's fatigue. It was true, too much had happened and was happening

554

around him; ironic, it was, that Solo wanted his son to escape a hazardous life and these last months had been madness.

'Dad,' Ben interrupted his thoughts. 'Why can't we choose our families?'

'Maybe we can,' Solo shrugged.

Ben brightened. 'Yeah?'

Solo felt anxiety clutch at his guts. 'Why, who would you choose?'

'Rebecca,' without hesitation.

'Good choice. Who else?'

Ben laughed. 'Jack.' This was a more enjoyable verbal game than the one the adults had just played downstairs.

Solo calmed his son's forehead and temples. 'You must be tired by now, Ben. It could be a long night. And day.'

Ben closed his eyes, still smiling. Solo stroked his arm. Eventually the boy drifted off. Downstairs, Rebecca too had fallen asleep in the small bedroom there.

Solo found Jack, looking shaken, in the kitchen. 'I thought she was going to have it and none of you were going to help me,' he whispered.

'They must have been rehearsal contractions,' Solo guessed. 'A false labour.'

'Thank Christ it stopped,' Jack said.

'Don't worry,' Solo grinned. 'It'll start again.'

'Hold me,' Penny whispered. Martha cradled the old woman's perished body in the candlelight, a mother and infant, an all-female *pietà*. She felt a warmth spread through her body, her limbs soft and pliable, the room pulsate.

'I'm scared,' said Penny, and Martha's heart ballooned in her chest. She held the wretched woman, she held her mother. 'It hurts so much.' Martha held her weeping; squeezed Penny tight. The warmth kept welling up from underneath.

Penny's body barely breathed as Martha squeezed her close to herself. It felt so good, that maybe everything was released. Was it possible to forgive a mother who let what happened happen? Why not? It felt so good, weeping, cradling her mother in her arms, at last; cradling Penny, for whom empathy flushed through her, for whom she wept.

Penny's bodily fluids slowed, her mouth became dry. Circulation thickened and stopped. Blood settled into sediment.

She grew cold, and pale. Her body became lighter, heat rising. She was dissolving. Her breathing became shallow and distant; her pulse faded; her last exhalation evaporated into space.

'It's over,' Martha gasped, letting go her grip.

Darkness surrounded Penny. She felt herself rising. She entered a tunnel but the darkness remained thick, impenetrable. She was being pulled along, could no longer hear, or sense at all, anything, except her movement. She wanted to tell someone what was happening to her, but there was no-one to tell. She felt lonely, for a long time.

Weeping, Martha laid Penny's body out, bound the jaw, laid coins over the eyes, blocked the orifices with cotton wool. The look of pain on Penny's face had been wiped away by death, replaced by an expression of confusion at what lay beyond.

Penny became aware of a light ahead: she was moving towards it. Her loneliness and anxiety fell away, replaced by a sensation of warmth. She was being led but couldn't see by whom, glimpsed only their brown hand leading hers, a blur of yellow trousers. As she came closer to the light it occurred to her that the light was in fact some sort of being. The light that radiated from this being both originated from itself and was more than light, she understood as she approached it. It was light and it was love, so strong, so intense, that she thought it would melt her.

Lamb of God, have mercy upon us.

What a fool she'd been. Dancing with the charlatans. Indulging the cranks and crackpots; or were they indulging her?

Penny had been convinced that she was being cured months earlier, when Guru Loop had stroked her prone body with a peacock feather, reciting a mantra, and her heart became full of heat; waves of heat had issued from her heart and spread through her body, surely healing her.

Other memories came, fleeting, tumbling one after another, from a half-lived life, without love, in a house of secrets. Penny felt ashamed. But the being of light, who she understood had called forth these memories, gave her no impression of judgement. Instead she felt herself drawn closer towards it, into it, until she became suffused with light, surrendering to a sense of vast expanding airiness, and Penny knew herself to be dissolving; her nervous system returning to the source of its being.

Jack tiptoed around the house, checking on its occupants. Rebecca breathed a shallow sleep. Under a blanket curled up in a chair in the living-room Solo kipped like a visitor. Upstairs, Ben snored to himself. Penny lay on her bed, her still body already a fading copy, an effigy of who she'd been. Martha kept a vigil on cushions on the carpet beside the bed, radiant as she slept.

Jack went outside to pee, not wishing to wake anyone, only realizing as he stood there, pissing noisily on the ground, that it had stopped raining; that he'd been drawn outside by the very silence. The sky above, overcast for days, was startlingly bejewelled with clusters of stars. The moon was a sliver short of ripeness. Jack pocketed himself and looked up with folded arms. The most striking constellation was Orion the Hunter. Jack followed the line of Orion's Belt down to Sirius, the brightest star in the sky, and up to the constellation of Taurus: at its far edge lay the compact cluster of faint stars known as the Seven Sisters, the Pleiades. He could make out half a dozen with the naked eye, but knew that with a decent pair of binoculars could discern many more. They were young stars, unseen by the dinosaurs; barely forty, fifty million years old.

In Orion itself Jack could discern the Nebula, our most prominent local stellar nursery, a faint, misty patch of light: a huge cloud of gas twenty light years across, lit up by four fierce young stars, the Trapezium. It was a breathtaking sight. Jack seldom got to study the sky like this; the light pollution of Birmingham made it impossible from home. What would it be like to observe from here every night? He'd get a decent telescope, set it up below a skylight in the loft of the barn across the yard.

The sun, gone now, waited in the wings: the Egyptians' god Ra being ferried beneath the earth to be born anew the next morning; Apollo of the Greeks, who rides across the sky in a chariot. The sun was born five billion years ago and is now in the prime of life, in the pomp of its powerful middle age; the nuclear reactions deep in its central core turning six hundred million tonnes of hydrogen into helium, and four million tonnes of matter to energy – light, heat – every second.

Nothing, however, lasts for ever, which is the great lesson of astronomy, Jack reckoned, this study of the slowest changing processes and longest lasting elements of life. Eventually – in another five billion years – the sun will have consumed all the hydrogen at its core. The core will shrink and become hotter, while its outer parts will expand to form a red gigantic globe, engulfing Mercury, possibly Venus. The Earth's oceans will boil and our atmosphere be driven off, into space. Life on this planet will cease.

Then, over time, the atrophying sun will lose its outer gas. The remains will turn in, towards an incredibly dense, compact white dwarf star, which will slowly cool down and fade from view.

Whose view, Jack wasn't sure of. Such particular human perspective seemed trivial, though whether this was in comparison with the brevity of his own life span or the eternity of time itself he couldn't say. Certainly the final fading of the sun would happen long after Earth's extinction; Jack imagined, though, the sight of the dying sun, five billion years hence. It's said that there are atoms inside every one of us, of which we are composed, that were formed by the explosion of supernovae long before the sun and the Earth were born. We came from stardust and will surely return, will indeed bear witness, in some unimaginably subtle way, to the death of the sun; and, even, to the birth of other solar systems.

In the meantime there could be worse ways to spend this life than in contemplation of the stars. A lot can happen, after all, in just a single year; in one revolution of the sun. Except, Jack realized, that not only was his neck aching, but also he was toe-numbing, nose-biting, brass monkey, bollock-freezing cold. He returned indoors, poured himself a hot water bottle, and crept upstairs to bed, in the midst of a household, a cluster, of strangers he felt both responsible for and protected by; one of a group of stars in some remote constellation. Solo, his mate; Martha, brave, intimidating, dauntless; Ben, a child he wished he'd had; beautiful, hugely pregnant Rebecca.

They awoke to a silent, frozen world, the sky an endless blue, the air with a crystalline clarity. Ben and the two men met in the kitchen: when one of them spoke he whispered, as if the words would become brittle, would crack and crackle, disturb the stillness. It looked like a new world outside; they felt like the last people on earth.

'We should have some birds to release,' Solo said. 'A raven.'

'A dove,' Ben contradicted his father.

'Ben's right,' Jack recalled. 'A dove came back with a twig in its beak.'

Solo nodded in corrected agreement. 'Breed abundantly, said the Lord,' he quoted from memory, 'and be fruitful and multiply upon the earth. How is our pregnant woman?'

'In the night she had a show, she said. "A discharge of mucus,"' Jack recounted with a shudder. 'I made her a mug of hot milk and she went back to sleep. She's not awake yet. I thought', he added, 'that's why we was whispering.'

'I suppose I were whispering so as not to disturb the dead,' Solo whispered.

At that moment they were silenced by a scream from the bathroom above. Jack paled; Ben looked convinced that the dead had awoken. 'It's Rebecca,' Solo twigged.

'Oh, my word,' Jack moaned, and launched himself towards the stairs.

Rebecca had just entered the bathroom when she wet herself; as a result she relaxed and did so again, the contents of her bladder following the bag of waters from her uterus. She sat on the toilet bowl to compose herself, and set to having a shit, a task that had become increasingly arduous with each constipated day of the later stages of her pregnancy. She waited for a hint of movement in her bowel, and was just about to squeeze her muscles to help it along when they began to do so on their own: a long slow roll of muscular action began and built in her abdomen and lower back, massing in a straining crescendo which she found she was involuntarily forced to accompany and assist with the power of her lungs, letting forth an animalistic roar.

Ben's calliper clacked across the yard, and round to the front of the house. Grown-ups weren't meant to suffer like that. He crunched slowly across grass, distrustful enough of uneven ground, extra wary of slipping. Everything liquid was turning to ice. The flooded fields down in the valley were thickening into ice rinks: from the dry triangle of the corner of one meadow a group of cows gazed lugubriously at the encroaching ice, as if thinking, We were put here to graze and before we knew it we had to learn to swim. And now you want us to skate?! I'd like to skate, thought Ben. Maybe skating would be easier than walking, I never tried. Maybe Rebecca will give birth to a daughter and I'll teach her to skate. We'll stay here and the river will freeze over and it'll always be frozen here. We'll learn to skate together, down in that valley. We're entering another Ice Age, that's what it is. A glacier will form and rise up the valley until we can step out of the cottage with our skates on, we can just glide down to the valley and back again. Except that it won't stop there. Still the ice will swell and rise and swallow the cottage, the sheds, the animals, us. Like mammoths frozen into the ice we'll be found in a million years, the white-haired boy skater and his junior partner, our bodies frozen in beautiful poses, in a perfect *pas de deux*.

A voice said, 'If you think it, then it's done.' Crisp in the dry silence.

Ben turned. A man stood a few yards away, gazing in the direction Ben had just been doing. He had on a woolly hat, a thick padded jacket, yellow trousers. His nose was red and running in the cold, steam rose from his clothing. A walker.

'Who are you?' Ben asked.

The man returned Ben's look. 'There is no difference,' he said. Ben stared at him. 'You think', the man continued, indicating with a sweep of his hand the valley below and around them, 'that, say, hills are hills, and trees are trees. But you look at them long enough, and one day you see that really there is no difference. That hills are trees, and trees are hills.'

The frozen words iced in Ben's brain. He couldn't tell whether the man was telling him, Ben, something especially, or simply sharing his thoughts. 'Really?' Ben asked, wanting him to continue, even though he didn't understand what the man was saying. When they spoke their breath condensed in the cold air, the words transformed into another medium; as if a transmitter might pick them up in the future and convert them back into speech. Memory as clouds.

The man had turned his gaze back to the valley. 'Yes,' he nodded. 'Until, perhaps, one day you may attain enlightenment. And then, once again, you may find that mountains are mountains, and trees are trees.' He smiled at Ben. 'See ya,' he said, and began to walk away down the track.

'Who are you?' Ben called after him.

The man stopped and turned. He shrugged. 'I'm a walker.' He turned back and strolled off down the track; raising an arm, he waved without looking back.

Martha had slept undisturbed. She woke up, and stretched. Her limbs, despite the cold, felt malleable, rubbery; mind both relaxed and wide awake. Penny's lifeless body seemed hard to equate with the human being who'd inhabited it so recently. Martha went to the bathroom, peed, drank a glass of rural water, brushed her teeth. Aiming for the kitchen, she was distracted by shouts from the bedroom downstairs. Martha knew what she'd find, and decided that although she was ravenous she'd better look in before grabbing some breakfast. There was more than just shouting coming from the room, it occurred to her as she approached. But it was only as she entered that it made sense: music. The door swinging open combining with the clarification in her mind, however, only served to make the spectacle she met more dramatic. It was an audio-visual snapshot of bedlam. A tape of Arabic music played on a ghetto blaster. Snaky clarinet, an inebriated accordion. Hollow hiccuping drums, and a wailing male voice. In the middle of the room Rebecca stood swaying, hands on her huge belly, hips describing both circles and forward and backward undulations in the same repetitive movement. She was dancing, but her face told an ambiguous story: Rebecca too was wailing, some way out of tune with the singer on the tape; her eyes were half hidden under drooping lids and her face was slack, trance-like, pained and happy at once.

Also singing, and even less in tune, was Jack. As well as copying the Arabic wailer, he was aping Rebecca, swaying his womanly hips, encouraging her. To their side Ben, too, was doing his best, his calliper jerking like a piston, moaning loudly, sounding to Martha more than ever like an enthusiastic calf.

Jack saw Martha standing there. 'Come in,' he shouted, and held a hand out. As she tried to make up her mind whether or not she was ready for such commitment, Solo, whom she'd not noticed in the corner, slipped past her and out of the room.

Solo went outside. This feeling of superfluity was becoming too common. He scouted around the property, decided on a spot at the edge of the wood, a small clearing, within sight of the house. He looked through the sheds and found a spade and a heavy iron bar.

The ground was frozen solid: raising the iron bar and spearing the ground with all his might did no more than break chips off like concrete. But Solo persisted, chipping at the earth like a deranged sculptor, a man possessed: lifting, bringing the bar down; lift, drop; up, thud, grunting like a man in a chain gang, allowing himself no respite until he could feel his cold muscles warm up, elasticate. Sweat exuded from his skin, steam rose from his clothing. He drove on through the punishment of the task to its exhilaration. A few inches below the surface the solid icy earth gave way to mud, and Solo swapped bar for spade without slacking in his effort.

'Do you want to push?' Martha asked.

'I don't know,' Rebecca gasped. 'I don't think so.'

'Good. Wait then. You're not ready,' Martha said with confidence.

Rebecca hardly heard her. The contractions came one upon another with only sporadic pauses between, no rhythm with which to predict and soothe their arrival. Waves that lifted her to ever higher, sharper peaks. She had no troughs in which to relax, to breathe slow, instead had to grab quick light gasps of breath.

'You're doing brilliantly, pet,' Jack said at her shoulder.

Rebecca felt too hot, moved away from the fire, then too cold. Burped; hiccuped. Wanted to empty her bowels again and was sure something came out.

'That's it. Don't push yet,' Martha ordered.

Rebecca felt sick, thought she was going to vomit for a minute and then she did, a throatful of sickly gloop erupting.

'Don't hold your breath.'

It was never going to happen. There was no baby. It was never going to end, this pain.

'That's it, love,' Jack said. 'You're doing wonderfully.'

'Will you shut up and get away from me?' Rebecca yelled.

Jack paled. 'She must be almost in transition,' Martha said. 'You're nearly in transition, Rebecca. You're almost ready. Hold on. Jack, why don't you make a cup of tea?'

Jack caught glimpses of Solo when he passed the

kitchen window, freeze-frames of a masochistic performance. Solo stripped in the freezing afternoon, peeling layers of clothing – jacket, pullover, shirt, T-shirt – and also disappeared by degrees, lowering himself into the ground.

Jack came out and joined him as Solo finished, and was pulling his clothes back on again.

'Good job,' Jack said.

'It's deep.'

'We can bury her tomorrow.'

'She's not going anywhere. How's Rebecca?' Solo asked.

'Exhausted, I think. I've never seen anything like it, mate. But she's strong. I don't know. I'm surely glad Martha's here.'

'Yeah?'

'She says she reckons it's looking like a gentle birth. You could have fooled me.'

'I think she means gentle for the baby, not the mother,' Solo told him.

Sounds rose from the valley through the crisp atmosphere: cars, tractors; a mother calling to children; children calling dogs.

'Look at that sky.' Solo pointed to the west. The clear blue azure gave way to a thick cloud-filled, salmon-coloured expanse, strident purple edging. 'It's going to snow.'

'You must be joking, Solo. It's too cold to snow. Come on: let's get back inside.'

Snow began falling at the onset of dusk, and settled instantly on the bone-hard earth, creating the unsettling illusion that the afternoon was becoming lighter at the same time as it grew darker.

* * *

Inside, the cottage dimmed and Rebecca lost all sense of time. The contractions were agonizing assaults from within: what had germinated inside was the thing that would squeeze her to slow but certain death. 'How much do you think I'm dilated?' she managed to demand.

'You're probably nearly there,' Martha assured her. 'You've only been going about ten hours. That's not long. Don't push yet.'

But how could Rebecca resist the urge to do so? What else was her body begging her to do than expel this burden from her? But more hours slowly passed. She grew weaker; surely she must do the job before she lost all her strength.

'Please,' Rebecca pleaded. 'I'm so tired.'

'Can't you give her something for the pain?' Jack asked Martha. 'For Christ's sake, was there nothing left over?'

'Relax,' Martha told him. 'You look more distressed than she does. It's natural, Jack. She can do it.'

'Martha says there's a danger her cervix could be getting smaller,' Jack whispered to Solo. 'Swollen. Said she saw that sometimes. On the farm. Rebecca mustn't push yet.'

Solo put Ben to bed.

'I don't want to, Dad,' Ben said. 'I want to help Rebecca.'

'You'll be more helpful being wide awake tomorrow,' Solo told him. He stroked Ben's arm till his son fell asleep. Then he slipped out of the cottage and walked up through the trees and onto the hill above. He made his way easily, could plan each crunching footstep, see every footprint in the snow behind him in the light of the full moon. The patchwork of fields in the valley below slid up into his rising perspective. The only sounds Solo's quickening breath and his tread on the snow.

Ben waited till his father had gone. He got dressed again and stumped downstairs. 'How long is it now?' he asked Jack.

Jack looked at his watch. 'Sixteen, seventeen hours, Ben. A long time.'

'Something's changing,' Rebecca said.

'What?' Martha asked.

'It's a different feeling. It doesn't feel like gas inside me. Mother of God. This is it.'

'You're ready,' Martha said.

'Sure?' Jack asked.

'Yes, Rebecca, you're ready. Push.'

'I can't.'

'Yes, you can. Now you can.'

Too tired even to shake her head, Rebecca closed her eyes.

'You're strong, love,' Jack told her. 'You're super-strong. You can do it.'

'Let it come,' Martha said. 'Can you feel it? Just let it happen.'

Rebecca nodded. 'Yes. I can feel it.' She summoned up all her strength, and she surrendered to what her body needed to do: a wave of energy surged through her. An overwhelming urge to bear down and muscle the baby into and through her vagina. The conviction that she could do it.

Solo stood on the summit of the hill above the cottage, from which he had a three hundred and sixty degrees panoramic view. It was almost midnight now, yet he could see clearly lunar fields, snow-covered hills, settlements whose electric light flickered orange through the atmosphere. The ripe moon shining on the white landscape gave an unearthly clarity to Solo's vision.

I'm just not good enough, he thought. There's people better than me.

The temperature was low but the air calm, windless. Solo turned slowly where he stood, gazing at the country around, below him. The first church bells he heard came from a long way away, hallucinatory, but others followed: pealing towards him from different directions and distances, as if from other times; half a dozen, more, from village churches all around him, ringing out the old year.

Whether they were out of sync with each other, or had to traverse varying distances and so reached Solo at different times, the bells began tolling for midnight one after another. Solo dithered, as if hoping the bells might continue for ever until they got it right. He held his arms out to the sides, and turned in slow circles.

Then something trembled inside him, a shiver of purpose in the cold night, and he stopped: facing away from the cottage and the valley and the walled homestead, Solo walked off down the other side of the hill, into the new year; into the solitude of a future alone.

Ben stood behind Jack. Jack sat on a low, hard chair: Rebecca knelt on the floor in front of and facing him, her head and shoulders across his lap. He stroked her back. 'That's it,' he said. 'That's it.' She raised herself up to a squatting position and strained again.

Rebecca gave herself to surges of desire to press the baby further out. Martha knelt behind Rebecca, her hands held ready. 'We're almost there,' Martha said.

'Heave, girl.' She knew that spaces between the baby's skullbones were closing up as it jammed inch by inch into Rebecca's pelvic girdle and down through the birth canal. It would come out damp and sticky with mucus, she knew; purple, with an elongated head, a flat nose. Martha made ready to grasp the head, to push it to one side so that one of the baby's shoulders could slide out first.

Sam Caine is a dead man, sinking six feet under. May your eyes be his periscopes.

Without a father, you have a more complex paternity. But this is also a Polaroid, a portrait of the world you enter; your country. A world that is always changing: the one you grow up in will be different from that you were born into. Its every detail shifted; one a shadow of the other.

I offer you no more than a snapshot of your pre-history, Alex. It's not simply a gift. By the time you read this, you'll know I did it for myself. It's fiction, of course. When it came down to it, history wasn't for me. That's why I never stuck to anything: I hadn't found what I wanted to do yet, that was all. It takes some of us time to find ourselves.

Rebecca grunted as she pushed. She couldn't see but she knew she was nearly there; that the baby was emerging. Jack supported her. Ben kept his eyes on Rebecca, on her face that registered too many things to make any sense.

Rebecca groaned once more and shuddered. Jack leaned over and saw a moist, bloodied, slithering figure flop into Martha's hands, covered in vernix, limbs splaying out in surprise. Its eyes tight shut. Rebecca turned and collapsed back against Jack.

Martha lifted the baby and placed it on her belly. Its umbilical cord pulsated.

The baby opened wide his eyes: astonished, piercing blue eyes. For the briefest moment, Rebecca thought, he looked directly at her. Then his eyes slowly clouded over, and it seemed to Rebecca that, as they did so, she witnessed her son forget everything that had gone before; all the secrets he could have told her. Whatever he'd seen and known was wiped for ever from his memory, as Alexander Samuel Menotti took the first breath of his new life, sucked a great intake of air that oxygenated his blood, and wailed.

THE END

IN A LAND OF PLENTY
Tim Pears

'IMPOSSIBLE TO RESIST . . . A GENEROSITY OF SPIRIT THAT
IS GENUINELY UPLIFTING. I COULD GO ON AND ON ABOUT
HOW WONDERFUL IT IS, BUT READ IT FOR YOURSELF'
Time Out

In a small town somewhere in the heart of England, the
aftermath of the Second World War brings change. For ambitious
and expansive industrialist Charles Freeman, it brings new
opportunities and marriage to Mary. He buys the big house on the
hill to cement their union and to nail his aspirations to the future.

In a quick succession, three sons and a daughter bring life to the
big house and with it, the seeds of joy and tragedy. As his children
grow up, Charles' business expands in direct proportion to his girth
as Britain claws its way from the grey austerity of the war years.

As times change, so do the family's fortunes for better and for worse,
ebbing and flowing with the years. Their stories create a powerful
and resonant epic, nothing less than the story of our lives.

'ASTONISHING AND AMBITIOUS . . . EACH DETAIL IS RESONANT,
AND THE AUTHOR'S REALISM AND COMPASSION IRRADIATES
THE WRITING. A STORY ABOUT PEOPLE – US – AND THEIR
CONTEXT, WRITTEN WITH AUTHORITY AND UNSHOWY GRACE.
EARLY NINETEENTH-CENTURY FRANCE HAD BALZAC, WE
HAVE PEARS TO TRACE OUR FORTUNES AND FOLLIES'
The Times

'A BIG BOOK WITH A BIG HEART. PEARS IS AN
UNASHAMEDLY MOVING WRITER AND THIS MARVELLOUS
BOOK WILL REDUCE MANY TO TEARS'
Punch

'HIS GENIUS LIES IN TELLING A STORY ... AN OPERATIC
NOVEL FULL OF DEATH, SEX, BROTHERS, SISTERS, COUSINS
AND THROBBING HEARTS'
Daily Telegraph

0 552 99718 8

BLACK SWAN

IN THE PLACE OF FALLEN LEAVES
Tim Pears

'CONSTANTLY DELIGHTFUL AND CONSTANTLY SURPRISING
. . . THIS NOVEL IS SOMETHING COMPLETELY NEW AND
EXCITING . . . COMIC AND WRY AND ELEGIAC AND SHREWD
AND THOUGHTFUL ALL AT ONCE. PLEASE READ IT'
A.S. Byatt, *Daily Telegraph*

The summer of 1984, one of the longest and hottest of the twentieth
century: police and miners fight running battles; unemployment
reaches record levels; the nation's teachers are on strike.

In a faraway Devon village hidden in a valley, however, the world
has stopped turning and time is slipping backward. 'This idn't
nothing', Alison's grandmother tells her, recalling the electric
summer after the war when the earth swallowed lambs. But
Alison knows her memory is lying: this is far worse. She and her
friend, Johnathan, awkward son of the last of the Viscounts, think
time has stopped altogether, when all they want is to enter the
real world of adulthood. In fact, in the cruel heat of that summer,
time is creeping towards them, closing in around the valley.

Like the crooked landscape in which it is set, this poetic novel is
a tapestry: of past and present, memory and discovery, elegy and
hope. By turns moving and funny, *In The Place of Fallen Leaves*
is one of the most memorable and widely acclaimed first novels
of recent years.

'HIGHLY ATMOSPHERIC . . . IT HAD AN INTOXICATING,
MAGICAL QUALITY WHICH COMPLETELY BEGUILED ME'
Jeremy Paxman, *Independent*

'A REMARKABLE FIRST NOVEL, WHICH RENDERS DOMESTIC
DETAIL FASCINATING AND MAKES IT QUITE POSSIBLE TO
BELIEVE IN MAGIC'
Sunday Times

0 552 99536 3

BLACK SWAN

EDDIE'S BASTARD
William Kowalski

'A REMARKABLE DEBUT'
Time Out

Billy was deposited as an infant on the doorstep of Thomas
Mann's home in a simple wicker basket with a plain two-word
message pinned to his shawl reading 'Eddie's Bastard'. Eddie,
Thomas's son, had been killed in Vietnam three months earlier,
and his father had given up on life, having lost his only son. But
now, suddenly, Thomas has a grandson and an heir – if not to the
once-vast Mann fortune (for Thomas recklessly squandered that
in a foolhardy enterprise involving ostriches just after his
heroic return from the Second World War), then at least to
the long legacy of the Mann family stories, stretching back to
the Civil War.

In this rich, deeply resonant literary début, William Kowalski
explores the power of family, the meaning of history, and the
bonds of individuals united and divided by love. By turns
hilarious, thrilling and heart-breaking, *Eddie's Bastard* is a novel
that stays in the mind long after the reading is over.

'CLEVER, EMOTIONAL STORYTELLING WITH LAUGHS,
TEARS, AND LOVE'
The Times

'A BOOK WRITTEN WITH SUCH ELEGANCE, MATURITY AND
HUMOUR IT IS DIFFICULT TO BELIEVE THAT THE AUTHOR IS
ONLY 28 YEARS OLD'
Good Book Guide

'WICKEDLY FUNNY AND GENUINELY MOVING'
Attitude

0 552 99859 1

BLACK SWAN

KNOWLEDGE OF ANGELS
Jill Paton Walsh

SHORTLISTED FOR THE BOOKER PRIZE 1994

'AN IRRESISTIBLE BLEND OF INTELLECT AND PASSION . . .
NOVELS OF IDEAS COME NO BETTER THAN THIS SENSUAL
EXAMPLE'
Mail on Sunday

It is, perhaps, the fifteenth century and the ordered tranquillity
of a Mediterranean island is about to be shattered by the
appearance of two outsiders: one, a castaway, plucked from the
sea by fishermen, whose beliefs represent a challenge to the
established order; the other, a child abandoned by her mother
and suckled by wolves, who knows nothing of the precarious
relationship between church and state but whose innocence will
become the subject of a dangerous experiment.

But the arrival of the Inquisition on the island creates a darker,
more threatening force which will transform what has been a
philosophical game of chess into a matter of life and death. . .

'A COMPELLING MEDIEVAL FABLE, WRITTEN FROM THE
HEART AND MELDED TO A DRIVING NARRATIVE WHICH
NEVER ONCE LOSES ITS TREMENDOUS PACE'
Guardian

'THIS REMARKABLE NOVEL RESEMBLES AN ILLUMINATED
MANUSCRIPT MAPPED WITH ANGELS AND MOUNTAINS
AND SIGNPOSTS, AN ALLEGORY FOR TODAY AND
YESTERDAY TOO. A BEAUTIFUL, UNSETTLING MORAL
FICTION ABOUT VIRTUE AND INTOLERANCE'
Observer

'REMARKABLE . . . UTTERLY ABSORBING . . . A RICHLY
DETAILED AND FINELY IMAGINED FICTIONAL NARRATIVE'
Sunday Telegraph

0 552 99780 3

BLACK SWAN

A SELECTED LIST OF FINE WRITING
AVAILABLE FROM BLACK SWAN

99313 1	OF LOVE AND SHADOWS	*Isabel Allende*	£6.99
99820 6	FLANDERS	*Patricia Anthony*	£6.99
99734 X	EMOTIONALLY WEIRD	*Kate Atkinson*	£6.99
99860 6	IDIOGLOSSIA	*Eleanor Bailey*	£6.99
99824 9	THE DANDELION CLOCK	*Guy Burt*	£6.99
00686 6	BEACH MUSIC	*Pat Conroy*	£7.99
99767 6	SISTER OF MY HEART	*Chitra Banerjee Divakaruni*	£6.99
99836 2	A HEART OF STONE	*Renate Dorrestein*	£6.99
99587 8	LIKE WATER FOR CHOCOLATE	*Laura Esquivel*	£6.99
99770 6	TELLING LIDDY	*Anne Fine*	£6.99
99759 5	DOG DAYS, GLENN MILLER NIGHTS	*Laurie Graham*	£6.99
99801 X	THE SHORT HISTORY OF A PRINCE	*Jane Hamilton*	£6.99
99848 6	CHOCOLAT	*Joanne Harris*	£6.99
99796 X	A WIDOW FOR ONE YEAR	*John Irving*	£7.99
99758 7	FRIEDA AND MIN	*Pamela Jooste*	£6.99
99859 1	EDDIE'S BASTARD	*William Kowalski*	£6.99
99737 4	GOLDEN LADS AND GIRLS	*Angela Lambert*	£6.99
99807 9	MONTENEGRO	*Starling Lawrence*	£6.99
99874 5	PAPER	*John McCabe*	£6.99
99536 3	IN THE PLACE OF FALLEN LEAVES	*Tim Pears*	£5.99
99718 8	IN A LAND OF PLENTY	*Tim Pears*	£6.99
99817 6	INK	*John Preston*	£6.99
99810 9	THE JUKEBOX QUEEN OF MALTA	*Nicholas Rinaldi*	£6.99
99777 3	THE SPARROW	*Mary Doria Russell*	£6.99
99780 3	KNOWLEDGE OF ANGELS	*Jill Paton Walsh*	£6.99
99673 4	DINA'S BOOK	*Herbjørg Wassmo*	£6.99